ALTER ROAD

~

MARK JAMES

Alter Road

First Edition: 2020

Printed in the United States of America

10 9 8 7 6 5 4 3 2 1

ISBN-13: 978-1-948035-41-5 (Paperback)
ISBN-13: 978-1-948035-42-2 (Ebook)

Edited by Janet Musick
Cover designed by Spomenka Bojanic
Interior designed by Debbi Stocco

Published by Defiance Press and Publishing, LLC

Bulk orders of this book may be obtained by contacting Defiance Press and Publishing, LLC.
www.defiancepress.com.

Public Relations Dept. – Defiance Press & Publishing, LLC
281-581-9300
pr@defiancepress.com

Defiance Press & Publishing, LLC
281-581-9300
info@defiancepress.com

PART ONE: NO POWER, NO PEACE

CHAPTER 1
DAY 0

Tension always accompanied a dispatch regarding a structural fire, and a certain quietness settled over members of a fire company as they approached the reported address. Oftentimes, they could see flames from several blocks away, or an orange glow against the sky at night. The more experienced the company, the quieter it was. And, with an average of two calls per day every day of the year, all of Detroit's fire companies that comprised the city's thirty operating fire stations were, if anything, experienced.

During winter, like now, that tension was even higher. It was bitterly cold with temperatures below freezing, and most of the back streets remained unplowed from the previous day's snow storm, which still lingered with flurries and a bone-chilling, blustery wind that sapped the warmth right out of the old, poorly insulated wood-frame houses that made up the majority of the homes of Detroit and its surrounding inner-ring suburbs—homes with utilities like gas, heat, water and electricity. Among Detroit's poor and jobless, however, which arguably accounted for more than seventy-five percent of the city's labor force, such utilities were a luxury. Unable to pay a monthly electricity bill, many people relied on dangerous fire-causing devices like portable gas and kerosene heaters to stay warm during the winter months.

This winter had proved to be more brutal than normal. With the latest cold snap lasting almost sixty consecutive days, and with the jet stream remaining far to the south for the foreseeable future, there was no end in sight. With the greatest economic crisis affecting the nation since the Great Depression deepening still further following recent financial crises in China and the European Union that sabotaged the still-fragile U.S. recovery from its own recent financial crisis, the ranks of the unemployed swelled—and, consequently, so did the number of house fires in Detroit and its surrounding suburbs. In previous years, the average number of deaths by fire in Detroit was forty-five to fifty, an already tragically high number. This year, however, the number of fire-related deaths had surpassed four hundred, and it was only mid-February.

* * *

Engine 54 of the Detroit Fire Department was the first to arrive at the address on Alter Road on the east side in the Jefferson/Mack neighborhood adjacent to the town of Grosse Pointe Park.

Alter Road is perhaps the most startling boundary between neighboring communities anywhere in America. Not only is it a political boundary, it is also an economic and social boundary between the mostly poor and black City of Detroit, and the mostly white and largely affluent townships of Grosse Pointe, Grosse Pointe Park, Grosse Pointe Farms, and Grosse Pointe Shores. The median household income in Detroit was just twenty-six thousand dollars. One block over from Alter Road, in Grosse Pointe Park, the median household income was more than four times higher, at one hundred ten thousand dollars.

Alter Road was where Detroit ended. The next street over, one block to the east, was Wayburn Street in Grosse Pointe Park. The well-kept, cozy homes along leafy Wayburn Street were snuggled close together, creating a vibrant and family-friendly neighborhood.

On Alter Road, though, the homes were sporadic and spaced out. Overgrown unkempt lots filled in the spaces where dense housing once stood, making the Detroit side of the Alter Road divide seem more like the country than a city. Only a few of the homes that remained were actually lived in, and most of them were in disrepair. The rest were abandoned years ago and were crumbling where they stood. Alter Road and the Jefferson/Mack neighborhood were not an anomaly for the City of Detroit. They were representative of nearly *all* of Detroit's neighborhoods.

It took Captain Nelson Carter and his fire crew less than five minutes from the time of the call to arrival at the scene. It was snowing heavily, keeping visibility to less than a mile, as they pulled out of the station. It wasn't until they turned onto Alter Road itself that they saw dark gray smoke drifting up ahead and blending in with the snow. A crowd was gathered on the street in front of the burning structure.

Captain Carter parked the firetruck in front of the burning house, which appeared to be a small Starlight Bungalow Sears Catalog home, probably close to a hundred years old, common to Detroit's working class neighborhoods. He spotted a fire hydrant jutting out of the ground in front of an adjacent overgrown empty lot. The fire crew wordlessly laid out the fire hoses across the street and connected them with the truck and nearby hydrants. The crowd was quiet as well, and the only sounds came from the fire truck pumps as the crowd watched the firemen work.

* * *

Detroit Mayor André Murray sat behind a large oak desk, poring over the latest data and a write-up on Detroit's economy from the Federal Reserve Bank of Chicago. Jazz music played softly from a small radio at the edge of André's desk. It was tuned to a local station at a low enough volume to not be distracting.

André flipped a page and continued reading while keeping time with the music by tapping his fingers on the desk. Despite the herculean efforts of a generation of civic work aimed at revitalizing Detroit's economy and improving the city's finances, including tens of billions of dollars in investments in downtown and New Center, "official" unemployment had now surpassed fifty percent following the latest global financial crisis that plunged Detroit right back to the depths of the 2008-09 Great Recession, and then some. People were calling it the Second Depression or, more colloquially, the Great Depression 2.0. People were leaving, and the bleeding of population was projected to continue largely unabated.

The 60-year-old mayor grunted. It wasn't anything he didn't already know. A veteran and author of so many economic development projects and proposals over the years, André had learned long ago to temper his expectations of success, and to look for silver linings wherever he could find them.

It wasn't all doom and gloom. The automobile industry was making measurable progress incorporating Silicon Valley-led "autonomous car" technologies in which cars drove themselves and talked to each other, exchanging information such as location, speed, destinations, and other data. While the mass production and sale of self-driving cars was probably still some years away, the benefits appeared to be enormous, including fewer traffic accidents, reduced insurance costs, reduced congestion, higher speed limits, and more.

There were some drawbacks as well, but Detroit was now firmly behind the technology. Many of the jobs emerging from the new and associated technologies, particularly in engineering, had started to converge on Detroit because of its agglomeration of multiple automobile manufacturers and their suppliers—at least, what remained of them. Those jobs required higher education and skills, and therefore paid wages at least as high as those of the bygone era of assembly line production. Certainly the low cost of living in Detroit made the city more inviting for young engineers and computer scientists.

This was the silver lining Mayor Murray seized on. He shoved his chair back from his desk and swiveled around to look out on the city. He stared out his window, lost in thought as he watched snow flurries tumble lazily from the leaden sky.

The jazz song ended and the radio host chimed in with the early morning's headlines to lead off the news program beginning at the top of the hour. André swiveled back to his desk and reached across it to turn the volume up when the radio host mentioned Great Lakes Energy Enterprises, or GLEE, a global utility company and one of Detroit's largest employers. He leaned back in his chair and listened.

The first part of the news segment was dedicated to an interview with Mrs. Louise Jackson, a 55-year-old woman who had lost her granddaughter to a house fire a few months earlier. Mrs. Jackson held a daily vigil outside the corporate headquarters of GLEE to call attention to their policy of shutoffs due to late payments. The vigil had started solo but had grown to more than fifty people on any given day, and sometimes up to as many as two hundred people or more on weekends.

André stared off into space as he listened intently. He was well aware of Mrs. Jackson and her vigil. GLEE's globetrotting CEO, Charles Desmond, had personally called André and asked him to do something about the vigil and the growing crowds. Desmond said he was concerned for the safety of his employees, but André suspected that he was more worried about embarrassing publicity if the protests persisted or grew any larger. André promised a larger police presence; at the same time, he pressed the CEO to do more about the shutoffs.

After some testy back and forth over several phone calls, André secured an agreement whereby GLEE would implement a relief program for low income households. GLEE instituted a telephone hotline for customers in shutoff status that was, naturally, entirely automated and gave callers the run-around. It was nearly impossible to reach an actual human customer service representative, and there was no internet website that consumers could go to. The so-called relief program was, by design, a colossal blow-off of the mayor and citizens of Detroit.

But you pick your battles, André mused. Jobs and attracting businesses and people to the city and the downtown was the most pressing priority, and had been for decades. But now…

André swiveled around to look out on the city again and thought about the potential ramifications of Mrs. Jackson's vigil.

* * *

The scene on Alter Road in Jefferson/Mack was ugly. Captain Carter and his company were busy battling the blaze as flames licked out of the second-floor windows and leapt skyward from the roof. One crew had cut its way into the home with a Halligan bar and did a sweep as fast as it could before retreating. The team could not climb the stairway to the second floor; it was fully engulfed in flames and the first floor ceiling had disintegrated in multiple places.

"It's bad, Chief," said a young firefighter, removing his mask as a ladder crew sprayed water down on the house from above. "Maybe the worst so far. We couldn't get upstairs. But, from the look of things," he added, nodding to four battered cars parked in the driveway and along the curb in front of the house, "I'd say the house was pretty crowded."

Nelson nodded solemnly and turned as loud crackling sounds, followed by a deafening swoosh, marked the complete collapse of the house into itself. Angry flames leapt high into the sky. Swarms of glowing embers danced across the night sky like angry fireflies amid still-falling light snow.

CHAPTER 2
DAY 1

Jason Reid printed out his schedule for the day and hopped into his work van. He had two energy-efficient thermostat installations to do, two apartment units and a house to be hooked up for power, and three scheduled shutoffs.

It was company policy to work through the shutoffs first and work your way down to the efficient thermostats. It was all about the money, Jason suspected. Shut off those who aren't paying to stop even one more penny of energy outflow, add new clients to get that income inflow (which included the initial connection fee) and, lastly, delay any savings on the part of environmentally-conscious consumers by installing energy-saving thermostats last. Surely it must add up.

It was a temporary job, although it paid okay. He just needed enough money, about a thousand dollars, which he'd have saved in another month or two, maybe three, to get to California. His mom—fifty, obese (it was her thyroid, she insisted), bad knees, diabetic, and his pop, 55 going on 80, bad back, overweight, ruddy face, calloused hands—were so very proud of him getting the job with GLEE. "Now there's a company that's growing," his pop liked to say.

Jason drove east on Jefferson Avenue. Reaching over, he turned up the radio. "How high's the water, Mama?…Four feet high and risin'," sang Johnny Cash.

People milled about alongside the road after he passed the sprawling—and now closed—Jefferson North Assembly Plant where the vaunted Jeep Grand Cherokee was once built. Jason glanced at the time display on the dashboard. It was 8:25 a.m.

An eerie feeling settled over him as he stopped at a traffic light. He'd drawn a lot of angry stares, and the tiny hairs on the back of his neck stood up. There wasn't much traffic, but an unusual amount of people were just standing around. The light turned green and Jason drove on. Heads turned in his direction. People pointed at his van, their faces hard with anger.

Jason slowed as he neared a large group standing on both sides of the road; he was careful to give them a wide berth. A teenager sprinted forward and hurled a bottle at his van. Jason swerved. He felt two *thunks* against his van and stole a look into his side mirrors. The teenager had landed a direct hit, as did a second one, and they both gave chase behind his van for a full block before giving up.

Fifty people or more walked about in the middle of the street ahead of him, and Jason slowed to a crawl. As he came upon them, the group parted without looking to let him pass, but their faces and demeanor turned hostile when they did look.

The crowd swarmed around Jason's van, forcing him to stop as they pounded on its front and sides. Pieces of the windshield smashed inward, leaving a large spider-web configuration of cracks. His driver side window smashed inward, and arms reached in to grab him.

"Get the fuck off me!" he yelled, fending off the arms groping for him. The driver side door was yanked open and he was pulled out onto the street, scraping his hands and knees on the ground. He covered his head as the crowd pummeled him with kicks and punches.

The van, now driverless, surged to the right and bounced against the curb. Forced back left onto the street, it careened along until it rammed into a light pole.

"Kill that muthafucka!" someone hollered. Jason, realizing *he* was "that muthafucka," scrambled to his feet and dashed away. He absorbed more punches as others took swings at him as he ran by. A rock whizzed past his head as he made his escape.

The crowd turned its attention to the van and pounded it with rocks and whatever debris they could find. Jason slowed and stole a look back. The crowd swarmed the van, yanking at the doors and breaking the windows. He turned and walked east at a fast pace, still the focus of a lot of attention.

"Yo, man, get the fuck out of here!" yelled an older black man, who appeared to be somewhere in his fifties. About the same time, a boy about ten ran up to Jason and hurled a pebble at him. Jason instinctively threw his arms up in defense, but he was too late, and the pebble skipped off the top of his head. He stumbled and fell.

"Get outta here, boy!" the same man snarled at the kid. The boy fled down the street to join the others now setting fire to the van.

"Come on, white boy," the man said, offering a hand to help Jason stand. "Let's get your crazy ass outta here before you get yourself killed."

* * *

Ian Nguyen was up at 5:30 a.m. He did his morning wake-up routine of brushing his teeth, getting dressed, and downing a bottle of Red Bull before meeting up with some of his long distance track and cross country teammates for a 6:00 a.m., fifteen-minute shuttle to Belle Isle, located in the middle of the Detroit River. Once there, the team ran twice around the roughly five-mile circumference of the island and were back on campus in time for Ian to take a quick shower, down a muffin, surf social media, and check his emails before his first class at 9:00 a.m.

Social media was abuzz about a fire in the Jefferson/Mack district of Detroit, accompanied by hashtags like #EndtheShutoffs and #NoPowerNoPeace. Ian skimmed a breaking news article about the fire tweeted by the Detroit Free Press in which an entire extended family had tragically perished. His breath caught in his throat when he saw the name of one of the victims presumed killed in the fire: Mrs. Bernadette Price. That was the name of his 9th grade social science teacher, who had taken an interest in him and made him think about college. As he read the article, it was pretty apparent that his former teacher and the Mrs. Price in the article were one and the same.

In class, Ian's mind wandered as the professor lectured about endoskeletons. He nodded as though he was paying attention, but memories from high school and Mrs. Price wouldn't wait. It was Mrs. Price that got him into cross country running, an offhand suggestion for him to find both a place of inner solitude and something to focus his hyperactivity and simmering anger on.

He had had a tendency to resort to fists at the first sign of anti-Vietnamese or anti-Asian sentiment, real or perceived, among his mostly black and Latino classmates. Running calmed him. His teams, both in high school and now in college, were a diverse group, and he learned he had a lot in common with his fellow runners and students.

His cell phone vibrated repeatedly in his hoodie pocket, and he glanced at it whenever he could while the professor lectured.

Text messages and emails rolled in, most of them about Mrs. Price, but he couldn't read any of them without getting noticed. He fidgeted; the class seemed to drag on longer than the scheduled fifty minutes, but glimpses at the clock confirmed that time was simply moving at an excruciatingly slow pace.

When class finally let out, Ian headed for the Student Center. He navigated through unusually busy pedestrian traffic to get into the Center and tried to find a place to sit. At last, he found a spot and sat with his second Red Bull of the day to read his emails and texts, trying to learn more about what had happened to Mrs. Price. When he finished, he texted Sarah. In addition to being a runner on the women's cross country and track teams, Sarah was active in the campus Amnesty International group, serving as the group's vice president. It was another reason he liked her. She was passionate about social justice and human rights. And she was a fellow runner.

Ian: Did you hear the news about Mrs. Price?

Sarah: Yeah, I've been texting you. We're protesting outside SC right now.

Ian: Ha ha, I am inside SC. Price was my 9th grade teacher!

Sarah: No way!

Ian: I'm on my way out. See you in a few.

* * *

Out in front of the Student Center, roughly three hundred students were gathered at Fountain Court. Many students were between classes, but the majority seemed to just be hanging around.

"Yo, Ian!" someone called to him.

It was Walter Clay. A few years older than Ian, Walter was dreadlocked, well-dressed and bespectacled. He looked like a hipster intellectual—but he was genuine. He was a first-year Ph.D. student in Physics, and was the president of the campus African American Society.

With Walter were several other AAS members and two athlete friends of Ian's, both of them football players. Each of them met Ian with a brief embrace and a "What's up, brother?"

After bumping shoulders with Trevor, a cross-country teammate, he turned around to find Sarah and three of her friends, women's cross country teammates Tina, Dakota, and Michelle, coming toward him.

"Hey, there, big guy," Sarah said, punching him in the shoulder.

"What's all this? Is this for Mrs. Price?" Ian asked, gazing at the fast-growing crowd as more students were apparently ditching their classes to be there.

"Yeah, man," said Sarah.

"Hey, bro!" Roland, a grungy skinny kid from Wisconsin, bumped shoulders with Ian. Roland was a friend and another cross country teammate. "Thought you might be here, man," he told Ian.

Ian, jostled by the group around him, noticed that the crowd had rapidly increased in size and was still growing.

The dense crowd faced the small rock fountain at the center of Fountain Court, where a group of activist students representing the campus Black Lives Matter and African American Society student groups led various chants, including shouts of "No Power, No Peace!" and "Stop the killing, end the shutoffs!" Different students took turns with a single bullhorn passed among them to rally the crowd and voice their thoughts, but it was hard to hear over the din of the growing crowd.

After more inaudible rallying words from another activist, the throng surged forward along Gullen Mall southeast toward downtown, and Ian and his friends were swept along.

"Let's stick together," Roland yelled. "This is wild!"

Roland was getting into it. He held Tina's hand and tried to get her pumped up as well.

"No power, no peace!" the crowd shouted as it strode from Gullen Mall down the middle of Second Avenue, halting traffic and swarming around stopped cars. Roland pumped his fist in the air to emphasize each chant. Others slapped their hands on the hoods of stopped cars. A young couple in one car—probably fellow university students—were clearly frightened as the crowd enveloped them. In another car, an elderly woman seemed to take it in stride, just watching and waiting for the large crowd to pass by.

As they marched down Second Avenue, Ian recognized a few members of the university faculty marching right along with them, including the dean of the College of Liberal Arts, though he couldn't imagine any of them slapping cars or threatening drivers. He chuckled at the thought.

Residents, too, streamed in from side streets and joined the march. Their numbers continued to swell as they walked, and the growing crowds also filled in along the parallel-running Cass Avenue, a commercial corridor, all the way to downtown. Ian and Roland emulated other marchers by jumping up and down to try to see how big the crowd was, but the march stretched as far as they could see, both forward and backward.

"Wow, this is *massive!*" shouted Roland.

A helicopter with 'POLICE' clearly marked on the tail boom made a low, loud pass, rose up and hovered high over the expanding march.

The noise was overwhelming. There was the helicopter above, sirens at various distances, protestors chanting, hands clapping, car horns honking, music playing, and people yelling to talk with each other over the racket. People all along the march had whistles—Ian wondered where they got them—and blew them spasmodically, adding to the incessant uproar.

Some kind of commotion seemed to be happening up ahead and, as Ian and his friends marched on, they came upon a police car abandoned in the middle of the road with its siren still blaring and its headlights and emergency lights flashing. Its four doors were flung wide open. Its windshield was cracked and splintered, and two of the door windows were smashed.

Some of the marchers jumped on top of the police car. Two young guys stood on the hood and another on the car's roof as they kicked at and stomped on the emergency lights, trying to break them and strip them off.

The three protestors were forced to jump down as another, larger group of young men began rocking the police car; more people joined them, including Roland—against Tina's protestations—and the car was eventually tilted over onto its side, eliciting a raucous cheer from the crowd. And still the siren blared.

CHAPTER 3

Tony "JD" Wiggins, a 29-year veteran of the Detroit Police Department, had only recently become the city's chief of police. He had joined the force (or 'the Farce,' as the rank and file called it) after graduating from Cass Technical High School and, after three years on the job, took night classes at Wayne County Community College. Some fifteen years later, he even earned a law degree from Wayne State and passed the bar exam, and his fellow officers began calling him "JD" for his Juris Doctor. Soon thereafter, JD was promoted to major and assigned his own precinct.

That was fourteen years ago. And now he had just one year to go for a full thirty years of service and retirement with a full pension at the young age of forty-eight. But first things first; into the breach once again.

A firm believer in community policing—posting officers to districts in which they lived and encouraging them to be active members of their neighborhoods—Wiggins found it difficult to enact. The police department was too short-staffed and getting smaller each year, and the city too geographically dispersed to fully enact community policing. So he had to rely more on "strategic policing" and long-term, real-time crime data analyses in which police assets were deployed from across the city to where they were needed most, which often changed from month to month, sometimes even day to day.

It was a game of Whac-a-Mole. Wiggins took a page out of the

U.S. Army's playbook and "swarmed" crime hotspots with hundreds of police, sometimes nearly the entire on-duty police force from across the city. Car and foot patrols, even cops on horseback, would saturate the area for days on end until, naturally, they would be needed elsewhere in other parts of the city—often two, three or four areas at the same time—where crime spiked as a result of the relative absence of police. Then police would redeploy and swarm to the new hot spots, and on it went.

When reports of crowds gathering along Alter Road and Mack Avenue in the Jefferson/Mack neighborhood in the early morning following the Price fire and the attack on the GLEE van started coming in, Wiggins issued a "Code Blue" for the Fifth Precinct—the signal for an emergency "swarm." The Jefferson/Mack neighborhood was not a high-crime area, at least by Detroit's standards, but the calls were mounting fast and the precinct was swiftly overwhelmed.

The first patrol cars to respond came under a barrage of rocks and bottles at Mack Avenue and Alter Road, and they withdrew to safety. They called out a 10-34, the police code for "riot," for all of Jefferson/Mack and tried a mini-swarm of their own with all the patrol cars in the precinct they could muster. But people were gathering all along Mack Avenue from Alter Road in the east to Gratiot Avenue four miles to the west, and that was simply too much geography for the precinct to effectively swarm.

Chief Wiggins reluctantly issued the "Code Blue" for the rest of the precinct. For the next thirty minutes, police units from across the sprawling city sped, lights flashing and sirens blaring, to the Jefferson/Mack neighborhood. Mack Avenue in particular was of most concern; this was where the crowds first formed and where the GLEE van was attacked. A police helicopter took flight above.

A confrontation between crowds of angry protesters on Mack Avenue and the fast-growing numbers of police, dressed in helmets and wielding batons and shields, flared as the police methodically moved in. They would cordon off a particularly rowdy segment of a crowd in a pinching move, then swarm in and subdue a number of protestors and haul them to a waiting police van. This was repeated multiple times, and the initial flashpoint appeared to be coming under control even as more crowds amassed at various intersections well beyond the Fifth Precinct.

The Detroit Police Department's use of strategic deployment could arguably handle unrest confined to a particular geography. Even multiple hot spots spread out over several miles might be effectively managed with good communication and coordination, the mobility of police units, use of helicopters, etc. But given the gutting of the department over the last few decades due to budget shortfalls year after year, anything beyond an isolated incident would be more than the department could handle. It was overstretched as it was just handling day-to-day crime and patrols, and the various small scale Code Blues.

When reports of crowds gathering at other places came in, like along Grand River Avenue, Chief Wiggins grew anxious. He knew he didn't have the resources to cover much beyond Mack Avenue and the Jefferson/Mack neighborhood. If this turned into anything like the Black Lives Matter protests in Ferguson, Baltimore, and other cities in the 2010s, or the national Trump protests in 2020, as unlikely as that could be, Detroit PD would be in serious trouble. He sighed as he picked up his phone and dialed. He would have to cancel all leave and call in the night shifts. "I need to speak with the mayor," he said.

* * *

Ian, Sarah, Tina, Roland, Dakota, and Trevor didn't know where the march was going, except that it was headed for downtown. Ian imagined they were marching to City Hall. However, as they passed Cass Technical High School to their right, the twenty-five-story Great Lakes Energy Enterprises corporate tower, with the word 'GLEE' emblazoned on the top of the tower astride its logo of a powerfully built man wielding a lightning bolt in one hand and the sun in the other, emerged directly in front of them, marking the entrance to Detroit's downtown. It was then clear to all where they were heading.

It took a little more than an hour for the head of the march to trek the just under two miles from Fountain Court to cross over Interstate 75 and enter downtown. As they crossed the interstate, the congruity of the march melded into an even larger sea of protesters and pedestrians occupying the streets and sidewalks all around the four-block long and two-block wide corporate complex.

As Ian and his friends crossed the interstate and entered downtown, they were blown away by the sheer size of the crowds in the city. There was an excitement in the air as well, and Ian was struck by the kinds of people they encountered. There were people of all ages and all walks of life and, while the majority of people were black, the crowds were ethnically diverse.

Overhead, the police helicopter Ian and his friends had spotted earlier remained overhead. Two other helicopters circled the downtown; Ian spotted 'WHWK Skyhawk' displayed on the tail boom of one helicopter with a cartoonish eye and beak painted on its front nose. He watched yet two more helicopters, one hovering far to the west and the other hovering off to the south. Pointing to them, Ian shouted to his friends, "There must be more marches coming!" but no one could hear him.

* * *

Approximately three miles to the west of downtown in Detroit's West Side, Michelle wrapped her arms around Aaron's narrow waist and rested her chin on his shoulder, causing Aaron to stutter-step as she clung snugly to him. AJ smiled and threw his arm over her shoulders, put his lips to her forehead and made a sucking sound. "Mmmm…brains," he said in a zombie voice, "mo' brains." Michelle giggled and pulled away from him.

Now Aaron 'AJ' Jones and Michelle Gibbs walked with a crowd of nearly twenty others, mostly high school students who, like DJ and Michelle, had just gotten out of school for the day. Social media had buzzed all day about the fire the night before and about scores of people marching on downtown in protest. Some teachers were visibly upset by the news of the fire, and some had even abandoned their planned lectures for the day and instead talked about the GLEE shutoffs and Mrs. Price. And, as the school day wore on, social media reported large protests and sporadic rioting. The kids all knew something big was happening and they couldn't wait for school to let out.

After returning home from school, AJ and his friends met up and strolled south along North Campbell Street amid sparsely spaced single-family homes—most of which were abandoned long ago and crumbling into ruins—to Michigan Avenue, which they found packed with crowds on the sidewalks and in the boulevard. A large crowd milled around a few blocks to the south at the intersection of Michigan and Livernois, and Aaron and his friends made their way to the large and gathering crowd.

A parked car several blocks ahead burned with flames dancing out of all of the broken windows. Thick black smoke billowed into the sky. More columns of smoke rose in the distance toward downtown. It seemed that the land itself—broken and burned houses, abandoned buildings, and the brown roots of overgrown vines and weeds that teemed untamed during the summer months—had shifted beneath their feet and somehow set aflame random cars and buildings that had thus far escaped the rotten touch of neglect.

Car traffic was light; the few cars that did pass blew their horns and were packed with young people, some hanging out of the windows and giving the "V" sign. Two GLEE vans heading south on Livernois came upon the intersection and found themselves under a barrage of rocks and bottles. They zigzagged through the intersection, ignoring a red light, passing through the gauntlet of flying projectiles.

There was anger among the crowd, especially among the older

adults. But, for the teenagers and young men and women in their twenties and thirties, the atmosphere was electric. They fed off of each other's excitement around a feeling that they hadn't really known before, a feeling of being part of something important.

A police car speeding west down Michigan Avenue toward the intersection with its siren blaring and lights flashing absorbed a barrage of assorted missiles before the driver slammed on the brakes. The car skidded to a halt. The crowd fearlessly swarmed in front of it and unleashed another, even more withering barrage of rocks and debris.

The police car reversed and peeled backward, its tires smoking. A Molotov cocktail hurled against the vehicle exploded in a burst of flames on its hood. The driver threw the car into a 180-degree turn and fishtailed east, leaving a trail of smoke as it headed back in the direction it had come.

The restive crowd, including DJ and his friends, raised their fists and cheered in approval.

* * *

"Shit," muttered Assistant Chief (Field Operations) Elliott Wilson, standing outside the Detroit PD's Mobile Command Center (known as "the beast" among the officers), which was parked in an empty lot behind the intersection of Gratiot and Mack Avenue. He had just ended a call with the chief of police on his cell phone and now it chimed with new text messages. "Isolated unrest," he said, shaking his head and chuckling. "There goes *that* theory."

"What's that?" asked Commander Ronald Rawlings.

"Nothing," Wilson answered. "Downtown's erupting," he added cryptically.

* * *

For Ian and his friends, the atmosphere downtown was like a big party. Many protesters had homemade signs reading "End the Shutoffs!" and "No Power, No Peace!" and more. Like at Fountain Court on the Wayne State campus, multiple young people held bull-horns and led marchers and protestors in chants. Most participants had come with friends and family, and they chatted loudly to be heard over the clamor surrounding them.

The demonstrations appeared largely spontaneous, but organized quickly through social media and word of mouth. For most, it was a welcomed disruption of work and school, like a snowstorm, but it was also meaningful. They were doing something and hopefully making a difference.

Things were decidedly different, however, as the close friends navigated the crowds and got closer to GLEE headquarters. They could see police personnel lining up all along the eastern perimeter of the corporate headquarters along Grand River Avenue and First Street. The officers were decked out in full riot gear with shields, helmets, and batons. The northern perimeter, Plum Street, was free of police and packed shoulder to shoulder with protestors, with more streaming in. The other side of Plum Street seemed to be the main event, and Roland and Tina led the way, purposefully plotting a course through the thick crowds to the end of Plum at Third Street.

"Roland," pleaded Tina, begging him to slow down. As they entered Third Street, the crowd grew more dense and was packed in between the GLEE complex of four buildings to their left, including the company's main tower, and the sprawling Grand Arnault Casino and Hotel complex to their right. Somehow it seemed befitting to Ian that the power company would be co-located alongside a massive casino.

The crowd blocked the main entrance to the casino and hotel, where a group of burly men stood abreast of each other in front of the entrance to prevent protesters from entering the lobby. But the protesters were focused on the GLEE building, not the casino. With the large complexes on either side of the road, and Interstate 75 be-

hind them, Ian and his friends felt hemmed in. While the march felt righteous and just, even celebratory with all kinds of people coming together rather spontaneously, the crowd along Third Avenue seemed more on edge, more militant.

They appeared to have arrived at the center of it all. It was a small, nondescript street corner, the corner of Third Street and GLEE Plaza Drive, right across from the main entrance to the Grand Arnault Casino and Hotel. GLEE Plaza Drive was gated and ran between the main tower of GLEE headquarters and the GLEE parking garage, the bottom two levels of which comprised the executive parking lot. The Third Street entrance to GLEE Plaza Drive was the exclusively reserved executive entrance to the complex; company employees entered the parking garage from Bagley Avenue via a ramp that took them to the third level and higher. Bagley Avenue marked the southern perimeter of the GLEE corporate complex.

Multiple television cameras were trained on various reporters in sports jackets, all of them with their backs to the corner of Third Street and GLEE Plaza Drive, the epicenter of the demonstrations. It occurred to Sarah that the corner was where Mrs. Louise Jackson led her daily morning vigils in memory of her granddaughter and to protest GLEE's policy of shutting off electricity to households behind in their payments.

And there, amid a small tightly-knit group of people of various ages huddled together, an older woman looking distinguished and somber was standing behind a young man with a bullhorn. Sarah pointed out who she thought had to be Mrs. Jackson to Ian.

"Pretty cool," responded Ian.

"Who's that?" asked Roland, not hearing Sarah over the din of the crowd. "Who?" he asked again.

"Never mind!" Sarah shouted and returned to watching the small group and the young man with the bullhorn.

The bullhorn was tinny and nearly inaudible amid the cacophony of whistles, voices, and competing chants. Nevertheless, the young man's voice carried over the racket.

"How many more needless deaths?" he shouted.

"No more!" the crowd responded in a single thunderous voice.

"How much longer do we wait?" the young man asked.

"No longer!" the crowd roared.

Roland and Tina pumped their fists as they shouted with the crowd, and Ian and Sarah joined in as well.

A block south of the epicenter of the protests on Third Street, and across the wide fork intersection of Bagley and Michigan Avenues from the GLEE headquarters and Grand Arnault Casino, sat a third sprawling complex of concrete and glass. This was the former temporary Grand Arnault Casino, which had operated there from 1999 to 2007 while its new location was being built across the street.

The IRS had been originally located in the building before the casino moved in, and then it stood empty—like so many buildings in Detroit—for several years until it was fully refurbished and upgraded to serve as the joint headquarters for the Detroit Police and Fire Departments. Now the Detroit Public Safety Headquarters, or DPSH, the 600,000 sq. ft. facility housed nearly one-third of the city's 2,500-strong police force, the upper echelons of the city's fire department, and a number of other city departments and state offices.

In other words, Detroit's center for police and emergency response was located in the heart of the fastest-growing protest anyone could remember, with tens of thousands of protesters and demonstrators converging on a six-block radius surrounding the GLEE corporate headquarters.

* * *

About three quarters of a mile to the east as the crow flies of DPSH and the GLEE Corporate Headquarters, Mayor André Murray was holding a press conference. A podium was set up in front of the Woodward Avenue entrance of the Coleman A. Young Municipal

Center, out near the sidewalk so that the towering Spirit of Detroit statue of a seated man, powerful and muscular, holding the sun in one hand and a family standing in the palm of the other, served as a backdrop. That forced the closure of Woodward Avenue to accommodate the press and a growing number of others who gathered to hear the mayor's words.

The mayor reported that isolated pockets of unrest existed, mostly in the city's East Side, in the Jefferson/Mack neighborhood near Grosse Pointe Park, and that the disturbances were largely sporadic. A GLEE van had been set on fire and its driver beaten, and multiple cars had been hit with rocks and bottles, mostly on Jefferson Avenue. Police, he said, were on the scene and managing the situation, and he asked that citizens remain calm and respect the law.

The mayor eulogized Mrs. Bernadette Price and her family. He was familiar with the name, and after a brief inquiry by his staff, he learned that she was a popular school teacher with more than thirty years of service in Detroit City. She was a two-time Michigan Teacher of the Year recipient, and she had been awarded the prestigious NEA Foundation Award for Teaching Excellence, presented to her by President Barak Obama himself near the end of his term in 2016.

The fire had claimed Mrs. Price; her husband Tommy, a retired forklift operator on disability and a veteran of the First Gulf War; her daughter Angelika; five grandkids; her daughter's boyfriend; and another young woman, a childhood friend of Angelika, and her child. The children's ages ranged from one to twelve years old.

Angelika had been foreclosed on in the previous year despite working two part-time jobs, including one as a nursing assistant at the Detroit Medical Center. And, despite their own financial woes, mostly due to the cost of medications and other health care bills related to Bernadette's diabetes and Tommy's bad back, the parents took in their daughter and her three children. They had fallen two months behind in their electricity payments and, with the addition of late fees on top of what they already owed, they fell even further behind.

GLEE had cut their power off six weeks ago.

"Poverty is no crime," the mayor said, concluding his remarks about Mrs. Price and her family. "Enough of the shutoffs!" he exclaimed. "We must put lives before profit.

"Tomorrow morning," the mayor continued, trying to get ahead of the unrest in Jefferson/Mack before it spread (the massive crowds attending the Mrs. Jackson vigil notwithstanding), "my administration is filing papers in court for an injunction against the GLEE Corporation to immediately halt all shutoffs in Detroit and to restore power to those without it during this cold weather emergency. Further," he added, "I am requesting the state and federal governments to declare the City of Detroit a disaster zone in order to implement emergency procedures like this injunction and to free up emergency funds to aid us in these extremely difficult times."

CHAPTER 4

The girls huddled together, which had the effect of bringing the boys in closer as well. They had been standing, taking part in the vigil and protest for more than three hours as many different speakers took their turns with the Mrs. Jackson group bullhorn. The speakers were largely people who, like Mrs. Jackson, had lost family members or friends to recent fires after GLEE had shut off their power, and many had also known Mrs. Bernadette Price.

It was nearing 4:00, and the crowds had reached incredible sizes. To Ian, it seemed as if the whole world had come out. He had never seen such large crowds in Detroit's downtown, not even during Lions games on Sunday afternoons during football season.

It began to flurry again.

"I'm hungry," announced Dakota. It was clear that she wasn't really into it so much, at least not now, all of a sudden, perhaps because of the snow shower.

"This is history in the making and you're hungry?" asked Trevor as he wrapped his arms around her.

"It's getting colder," Tina piped up.

And it *was* becoming colder, with the blast of snow and a lot of standing around in the frigid weather.

"Yeah, let's go," said Ian, "I'm hungry, too." Truth be told, Ian was getting bored with the protest.

The group looked to navigate their way back the way they had

come, but the crowd had thickened to the point that people were standing shoulder to shoulder and were not able to part for them, so the friends headed for Bagley Street at the southern periphery of the GLEE complex instead. The going in that direction was much easier, and they soon discovered why.

When they reached the corner of Third Street and Bagley Avenue, the crowd was much thinner and stretched out along Bagley Avenue and the wedge-shaped Michigan Third Street Park that separated Bagley and Michigan Avenues. Throngs of police in full riot gear were lined up in the street on Michigan Avenue. Behind the police line were even more police, countless more, standing around informally, some in riot gear or partially so, talking with each other and watching the protests. Television and media trucks were parked amid the multitude of police, and people entered and exited the large concrete complex behind them that nearly rivaled the casino in size.

"What is that, police headquarters?" asked Roland. His question went unanswered because, though it took them a moment to register, it was obviously so. The headquarters was a fortress, a beehive, and countless police seemed to ooze out of its pores.

* * *

Chief Wiggins stood on the steps of DPSH, gazing out over the masses of police methodically falling into muster and putting on shields and helmets. Beyond the police encamped on the lawn of DPSH, protesters continued their chants and noise-making as they maintained their still-growing siege on GLEE corporate headquarters. A young and militant few attempted to provoke a line of Detroit's finest who, by training, looked disinterested.

Wiggins imagined that the scene was not unlike watching opposing Civil War army camps gearing up for battle as they warily sized each other up across a wide bucolic field that both sides knew would

soon be despoiled with the blood of wretched young soldiers.

He shook his head and dismissed the analogy; this was a protest in a free society, not combat. Not yet, anyway. But he had his orders. It was already after 4:00, and hundreds of GLEE employees were trapped in their building and unable to leave. The casino, meanwhile, had been on lockdown since mid-morning, stranding guests, and new arrivals were unable to even get near the building because of the siege.

After strategizing with his assistant chiefs and directors, and the mayor, Wiggins decided that Third Street was the obvious target for a spear-like thrust to clear out protesters and end the siege on the GLEE executive entranceway and the casino across the street.

Wiggins didn't want to make any move at all. The police force was already stretched thin dealing with the unrest out on Mack Avenue and now Grand River. It seemed to him that they should let the downtown protest run its course. Come 5:00, most people would be heading home for dinner before it got dark. Mrs. Price was a god-damn legend, for Christ's sake, and the protesters were mostly families and working folk. And they were right to be angry; anyone could see that.

The mayor, however, was in full damage control mode. André Murray had been fielding calls all day long from panicked CEOs. Understandably, the casino's CEO (or "boss," as he was known) Angelo Diodato, and Charles Desmond, the CEO of GLEE had called, but also the CEOs of the Cash-in-a-Flash payday check-cashing company, Pleasant Peninsula Bank, Detroit Machines & Tools International, and others, even the owners of the Detroit Tigers and the Detroit Lions. One particularly unpleasant call came from as far away as Baltimore, from the CEO of the prestigious S&K Investment House that had stakes in some of the downtown development projects, including the recently completed Pistons Arena complex housing the Detroit Pistons professional basketball club.

The mayor and members of his staff came out of DPSH, and the mayor stepped up next to Wiggins.

"I know you want to give them space, JD," Mayor Murray told Wiggins as they looked out on the mass of police gearing up. "But not *this* space." He swept his hand across Bagley and Michigan Avenues and, turning in a near circle, he enlarged the scope of his arm to encompass the whole of the downtown. "Understand?" he asked. Wiggins nodded reluctantly. "Don't go bleeding heart on me, Chief," added André calmly. "I know you understand. And now is the time for absolute clarity. So tell me, why not this space?"

Wiggins quietly bristled and glared at the mayor.

Murray continued looking at him impassively, waiting for the right response. "Tell me, why not this space?" he asked again, not relenting.

The chief removed his police cap and ran his hand over his bald head as he tried to keep his temper in check. "Investments," he said finally, with a sigh. Then, with more force and looking defiantly into the mayor's eyes, "Investments. Billions of dollars are invested here," he said, nodding to the downtown. "And it's got to be protected."

"You're goddamn right," Murray responded. He turned and walked away briskly, his staff falling in behind him.

Members of the police chief's executive team, including his assistant chief of administration, Harold Washington, stood a few steps away as the police chief spoke with the mayor. When the mayor left, Wiggins nodded to them.

"Clear them out," he said, nodding in the direction of the protesters, "and issue a Code Blue for the downtown."

"But Mack and Grand River are still…" protested Washington, but he was interrupted by the chief.

"Just do it, man," he ordered brusquely. He pulled his police hat snugly back onto his head and walked down the steps to join the rank and file gearing up. He worked his way through the police officers, shaking hands and smiling as Assistant Chief Washington watched.

Puzzled and a little angry, Washington turned and walked back inside DPSH to issue the orders.

* * *

The runners walked eastward on Bagley Avenue among the thinner but still sizeable crowds along the southern periphery of GLEE headquarters. They could see that the hectic activity of the police on the other side of Michigan Avenue was actually becoming somewhat organized; the police appeared to be coming together in purposeful groups, mobilizing.

"Wait," said Roland, stopping dead in his tracks. A block ahead of them, cops on horseback, backed by ranks of police in full riot gear behind them, filled in across First Street, cutting off their path.

"Oh, man, we have to go back," said Sarah, her voice marked by a sudden nervousness. The group looked around for a way to leave the area, but the only way out was back up Third Street between the GLEE headquarters and the Grand Arnault Casino.

As they looked on, however, the masses of police slowly lined up on Michigan Avenue across from the intersection of Third and Bagley, and crossed the street, forcing protesters to retreat. Demonstrators ran back up Third Street into the packed crowds, or east along Bagley toward the runners. But police had already closed off that route behind them and were now walking westward on Bagley, tapping their shields in sync.

"We have to go!" exclaimed Trevor.

The group jogged back toward Third Street. Police methodically walked in synchronized steps. They tapped their batons against their riot shields with each step. It produced a menacing sound. After about five steps, they stopped walking, but still they tapped their shields with their batons, counting to five beats, then took five more steps. It was a well-practiced, graceful choreography. And it was terrifying. The runners' only way out was closed off.

Barely audible over the crowds and the police tapping their shields, a recording played out over multiple police vehicle-mounted loud speakers: "CLEAR THE AREA...THIS IS AN UNLAWFUL

ASSEMBLY...CLEAR THE AREA IMMEDIATELY OR YOU WILL BE ARRESTED."

The north end of the crowd on Third Street, already packed shoulder to shoulder, pushed back against the protesters at the south end running from the police. The whole crowd surged southward, pouring out from Third Street onto Bagley.

The police lines did not move and many protesters were pressed up against them by the surging crowd. Multiple rocket-like projectiles launched from behind the police lines flew high in the air before falling to the ground right in the middle of the massive crowds on Third Street, leaving contrails behind them as they flew. White smoke billowed out of the projectiles after they landed, forming multiple clouds that hugged the ground and spread out, sending protesters scattering.

"Tear gas!" shouted Roland.

"Oh, man," exclaimed Trevor as a surge of protesters ran straight at them. Police lines slowly and methodically walked east on Bagley and tapped their shields in sync behind the scattering protesters, while another line of police slowly and methodically walked westward from First Street, also tapping their shields.

Ian's group and the other fleeing protesters were trapped. They had nowhere left to run. The police were closing in from both directions, menacingly as they tapped their shields. They moved slowly, shuffling forward like zombies (police zombies, thought Ian), but still they came.

"CLEAR THE AREA...THIS IS AN UNLAWFUL ASSEMBLY...CLEAR THE AREA IMMEDIATELY OR YOU WILL BE ARRESTED."

"We're trying, dude!" shouted Roland in futile defiance at the approaching police, his voice lost in the angry clamor of the crowd.

"Come on!" shouted Ian. He gripped the wrought iron fence surrounding the GLEE complex and agilely climbed up and hoisted himself over, carefully avoiding the spear-like tips that topped the fence. The other runners followed suit, as did many fleeing protest-

ers, at least those who could. They darted for the GLEE building itself. There was nowhere else to go.

To the runners' left, on Third Street, scores—hundreds, it seemed—of protesters scaled the fence to flee the tear gas and a stampede of panicked protesters.

And now they were *angry*. They poured into the executive parking lot on the ground floor of the GLEE corporate parking garage and began kicking and jumping on cars and smashing windows. Tear gas wafted in, further fueling their rage. Others threw rocks and whatever they could find at the windows and locked doors of the executive entranceway where security guards were seen hanging back inside, fear on their faces.

The runners were at the ground floor executive entranceway where protesters were trying to smash their way in; the tear gas was thickening and the runners started gagging. mucus streamed from their noses and their eyes burned; covering their faces with their arms and rubbing their eyes made them burn even more.

It was excruciating. Ian slumped to his knees. Trevor and Roland grabbed him under his armpits and dragged him with them, themselves gagging. Tina vomited.

Roland let go of Ian and ran straight for the entranceway and drop-kicked the locked glass door. Others came with tire irons and car jacks lifted from the parked cars. The glass cracked and splintered into spider webs before a protester was finally able to kick through the glass at the center of the spider web after multiple assaults.

An unknown protester, his face hidden behind a bandana, poured bottled water over Ian's face, then forcefully removed Ian's coat and then his t-shirt, despite the freezing cold. He soaked Ian's t-shirt with water and tied it around his face like a kerchief to protect against the tear gas, then wrapped the coat around Ian's shoulders.

Ian staggered to his feet with the help of Trevor, Sarah, and the protester, trying to regain his composure. He threw a brief hug of thanks around the protester, who then joined the crowd now swarming through the entrance to the GLEE building. Ian, Trevor, and Sarah followed, half-carrying Tina with them.

Inside, the runners and protesters found a brief respite from the tear gas but not the chaos. Protesters attended to each other, using bottled water to wash away the tear gas and mucus from their faces. Others began destroying the security counter, kicking and smashing it, ramming cylinder trash cans into the lobby walls, breaking through dry wall.

Protesters tried using the elevator, but it had been turned off. The stairway doors were locked. An authoritative voice boomed over an intercom. "THIS IS GLEE SECURITY. REMAIN AT YOUR DESKS. A POLICE OPERATION IS UNDER WAY TO CLEAR THE BUILDING AND PROPERTY OF PROTESTERS."

Roland crouched down to look at Ian, Sarah, and Tina. Ian had removed his t-shirt from around his face and was covering Tina's face with it, rubbing it as she hyperventilated. mucus streamed out of her nose.

"We can't stay here," Roland said, breathing heavily, his eyes red and inflamed, his face and hair caked with mucus.

"Where are we going to go?" pleaded Sarah.

"We have to run," answered Roland. "Just run; they can't catch us all."

"Can you run, Tina?" asked Ian as he removed his t-shirt from her face. Her eyes were both inflamed, her right eye swollen shut.

"Holy shit!" exclaimed Roland, seeing Tina's face. "Motherfuckers!" he yelled as he jumped up and began pacing furiously. Other protesters volunteered bottled water to pour over Tina's face and eyes to help wash away the tear gas.

Outside the lobby's south entrance, three cars—a silver Lexus LS, a black G-class Mercedes-Benz SUV, and a gunmetal gray Audi S8—were on fire, and thick black smoke filled the parking garage's executive parking lot. Soon the pervasive smoke drifted into the lobby. Protesters continued swarming through, emerging from the smoke, mostly running but some slowing to jump on cars, pound on their hoods, or kick at them. Outside the north entrance, protesters jogged and walked at a less frenzied pace along GLEE Plaza Drive North.

The runners gathered themselves and prepared to go out into the fray again, the boys dousing their t-shirts in water and wrapping them around their faces, the girls using their sweaters or anything else they could to shield their faces.

"Let's go!" shouted Roland, and the runners stormed out of the north entrance.

They found the going a bit easier along GLEE Plaza Drive North, but as they emerged from the GLEE complex at Grand River Avenue, what they saw shocked and frightened them. They had fled one war zone and entered another.

The crowds were thick and a running battle of sorts ensued between crowds of protesters and riot police, including police on horseback who charged at protesters, forcing them to run, then pulled back to the relative safety of police lines.

Bricks, rocks, pebbles, glass bottles, cell phones, and practically every projectile imaginable flew through the air toward groups of police. In turn, police launched tear gas canisters and fired bean bag bullets, punctuating the cacophony of breaking glass, car horns and sirens, shouts and screams, and the pitter-patter of raining bricks and stones with the booms of police tear gas rifles and bean bag-armed shot guns going off.

The three-by-five block area across from Grand River Avenue between I-75 and Bagley Avenue was comprised mostly of parking lots where buildings had once stood. The lots were unusually full of vehicles, the majority of which belonged to protesters, and there was a mad dash for the cars as protesters swarmed over the lots, running, opening doors, blowing horns, yelling, hundreds of minor and near accidents, but never mind. Keep going and let's get the hell out of here was the impetus to the crowd's flight.

Multiple cars along Grand River Avenue and side streets—several, in fact—were overturned and lay on their sides or completely upside down. They were police cars, a couple of GLEE work vans, a city car. A city bus was engulfed in flames. It was dusk now, and the flames burned brightly against the darkening sky.

While the lots were nearly completely empty of buildings, a few remained standing as lone islands. They stood mostly at corners and were all run down. They were either abandoned or they served as unmarked extra storage space for various downtown businesses.

And now they burned. Smoke poured from the ground floors of two, and gently floated out of the upper windows of two more, as they seemed to be just getting started. One building, a six-story storage facility for GLEE, stood on the corner of Cass and Montcalm. It was a raging inferno, with flames furiously surging out of every single window and merging as one large angry fire that danced above the building itself. The building was three blocks away, but the runners could feel the heat enough to want to shield themselves.

They jogged north up Second Street and passed the one building, a church, that stood alone and unmolested. They crossed over I-75 and found themselves heading back the way they had come.

Once they had crossed over I-75, the crowds thinned out just a little. Car traffic, however, was thick and slow-moving as they headed north out of the lots. In the crowds walking away from the downtown, many people appeared distraught and even traumatized. That was certainly true of the runners. But there were no police here, and the runners and other pedestrians could relax a little, having escaped the chaos behind them.

As the crowds streamed northward away from the chaos, others went in the opposite direction toward the downtown. These were young people in their teens and twenties, and nearly all male. A few menaced older people who stood in their way, some even throwing punches and then darting away. A woman was knocked to the ground and, when her husband dared to intervene, he was set upon by multiple teenagers at once. They pummeled him with punches and kicks before they continued toward the downtown as though nothing out of the ordinary had happened.

Dakota was punched in the face by a teenager running by. It was a glancing blow, and Dakota wasn't really harmed, but she was shaken by it nonetheless. The boy was long gone before the runners could give chase, and besides, what really could they do, honestly, thought Ian.

As Ian looked back toward the city and watched the teenagers jog zigzagging through the crowds, snagging purses and cell phones and sparking some fights along the way, Ian's eyes drifted to the city's skyline. He could see that several more fires had been set, casting dull orange hues amid and among the bases of the tall shadows that marked the buildings of the central business district. Several helicopters circled the downtown above with search lights shining downward, their boom and undercarriage lights blinking white and red as they moved.

It appeared that World War III had descended on Detroit.

* * *

Some two hundred seventy miles to the north, across the Straits of Mackinac between Lake Michigan and Lake Huron, on Michigan's heavily forested, scenic, and sparsely-populated Upper Peninsula, 45-year-old Floyd Barksdale was sitting in his recliner in front of the television set when the telephone rang.

"Who do you think it is?" his wife Gloria asked as she struggled out of the couch and waddled to the kitchen. Floyd only grunted.

"Oh, Rickey!" she exclaimed, as though it had been years since she had spoken with Floyd's young nephew. (It hadn't). So dramatic, every dang call. "How have you been, my dear?" She spoke with a high-pitched flourish. Just gimme the flippin' phone, dear.

"Rickey boy!" shouted Floyd into the receiver after more loud small talk and finally being handed the cordless phone. "I don't got cable," Floyd spoke loudly after a moment of listening. "What time is it? Maybe it's on regular TV. Hey, honey, turn the news on!" he shouted.

"I'm right here, for gosh sake!" answered Gloria. She moved to the small flat-screen TV with some difficulty and bent over with her hands on her knees and her eyeglasses on the tip of her nose. She studied the TV before reaching and pushing the volume button. The TV grew very loud, a laugh track filling the interior of the trailer. "Oh, geez," she said to herself before finding the channel button.

"We're gonna miss it, dear!" shouted Floyd just as the channels began to change. Gloria brought it to Channel 13, but it was a commercial, and it was even louder.

"Sure you got the right channel?" demanded Floyd loudly over the high volume, but Gloria nodded emphatically and shushed him with a wave of her free hand as she studied the TV to find the volume button again to turn the darn thing down.

"Well, I don't see nuthin' about no riot," said Floyd into the receiver, "but I'll keep it on."

Gloria moved back to the couch and sank back in it with a deep grunt.

"Well, let's not get worked up just yet, boy," said Floyd into the phone. "We got a meet next Saturday anyways, so let's talk about it there. All right?" Then, after a pause, "Good, all right, then. See you then, Rickey. Bye."

Floyd Barksdale, "Colonel" in the Superior Volunteers militia group, held the phone out and waited for Gloria to work her way off the couch, take the receiver, and place it back into its holder in the kitchen. It took a while, and he returned to the beer he had placed between his legs and waited for the news to come on.

* * *

In the WHWK Channel 13 news studio just north of the city, in Southfield, Wayne State University intern Josh Fink monitored relevant Twitter and other social media live. Two in particular that proved to be popular were the hashtag feeds #EndTheShutoffs and #LivesBeforeProfit, the latter slogan inspired by the mayor's afternoon press conference.

Before the reported fire on the east side that claimed Bernadette Price and her extended family, the #EndTheShutoffs hashtag feed typically had fifteen to twenty tweets daily, but it would spike to as many as a thousand following a reported house fire. Following the Price family home fire, however, the hashtag feed jumped to five hundred in the early morning hours, and soared to more than three hundred thousand before 11:00 a.m. and kept on climbing. Throughout the day, the number of tweets averaged more than one hundred every few seconds, with messages like "They're killing us!", "Shutoff GLEE!", "Shutoff Detroit!", and "March on GLEE!"

Facebook posts with the hashtags had also blossomed throughout the day, and cell phone videos of the protests—and, later, the police attack—at GLEE headquarters were posted on YouTube and other social media outlets.

News of the Price fire, including articles about the lives of Mrs. Bernadette Price and her family, and news about the protests, whipped around the city and region—soon, in fact, around the world—through a range of social media outlets, including Twitter, Facebook, Instagram, and a multitude of others. The explosion on social media was a story in its own right, and Josh was tasked with writing it—his first foray into professional journalism.

And, as the day drew to a close and the sun settled on the southwestern horizon amid a fiery orange, red, pink and purple sunset, a charged atmosphere descended over all of Metro Detroit and beyond.

CHAPTER 5
DAY 2

The overnight hours brought a semblance of relative peace to Detroit. Both in the downtown and across the city's neighborhoods, most of the protesters had returned home for the evening. Some teenagers and young adults had gone downtown in the early evening to partake in clashes with police (and anyone else, for that matter) as police maneuvered to clear protesters away from the GLEE corporate headquarters. The Code Blue, however, had brought Detroit PD's full complement of 2,500 officers descending on the downtown and, by late evening, police in riot gear nearly outnumbered roving bands of aggressive young protesters.

Ian and the runners, meanwhile, made it back to Midtown without any more drama. The runners accompanied roommates Tina and Dakota to their apartment two blocks from campus and crashed there. They did their best to treat each other's residual tear gas effects and the bruise on Dakota's face from the punch she took, and then stayed up for a while watching the news on television and videos of the protests on social media. They were wound up early in the evening, but they were exhausted by 10:00. The boys tried to stay up later, watching movies, but they dozed off with the television still on.

Conditioned after more than a semester of early morning training, Ian stirred and awakened almost precisely at five-thirty the next morning. For a moment, he had forgotten where he was, and even the previous day's monumental events, but the hushed sounds of Sarah and Dakota speaking brought it all back.

He groggily stumbled to the bathroom and, when he came out, Roland and Trevor were also stirring awake—Roland on the couch, and Trevor on the floor across from where Ian had slept.

Ian walked into the kitchen and peered into the fridge. He didn't see Sarah as she prepared to brew coffee in the kitchen and, still half-asleep, ignored her. He was intent on finding a can of Red Bull and, not seeing any, merely grunted. Closing the fridge door, he saw Sarah. She stood with a hand on her hip and a *well?* expression on her face.

"Hey," he muttered, and walked back into the living room to pull on his jeans and mucus-stained t-shirt from the previous day.

"Are we going to run today?" he asked out loud to anyone.

Within a few minutes, the guys were dressed and out the door. They had to return to their dorm rooms and change out of their clothes from the previous day and, once outside in the brisk cold air, they decided to go for a run after all. "Be kind of cool, don't you think?" Roland reasoned.

After swiftly making it back to campus and changing, the runners met up across from the university bookstore. Rather than take a university shuttle to Belle Isle for their usual morning run, the runners opted to head down Woodward Avenue, a gentrified showcase of the city just over two miles in length linking Wayne State University with midtown and downtown.

It was still dark and traffic was light at six a.m., and they ran right down the Q-line light rail track into downtown, jogging effortlessly and gracefully in a tight formation like sleek fighter jets. An abrasive, caustic smell of smoke and chemicals assaulted their nostrils as they passed the Detroit Pistons' and Red Wings' Arena and crossed over I-94 and entered the downtown.

The downtown seemed very busy despite the hour. A fire company stood watch over the rundown six-story GLEE storage facility that had burned overnight. Now it was just a charred shell, its interior gutted, and its roof and upper floors had collapsed into an ugly blackened pile of smoldering debris at the shell's center.

A couple of smaller buildings that the runners had last seen burning were now simply gone, leaving blackened piles of debris and smudges on the ground where they had stood.

Police, meanwhile, seemed to be everywhere.

The runners attempted to loop around the GLEE headquarters, but it was surrounded by all sorts of police and fire department vehicles and police officers hanging around and looking cold and menacing. Portable stadium lights were trained on the GLEE headquarters' executive entranceway, and they could see the corporate parking garage's outer shell was blackened on the lower floors, stained by the oily smoke of burned cars and tires.

DPSH, meanwhile, remained as busy as they had last seen it. Scores of police loitered about on the sprawling lawn in front of DPSH, and dozens of tents had been set up. A mobile command center bus and several trailers were parked in the parking lot. It appeared to Ian and the runners that the police were camped out at the DPSH, even sleeping there—an interesting if ominous development. Ian didn't know what to make of it.

"What, the cops are the Army now?" Roland quipped, giving voice to Ian's thoughts.

Third Street, the epicenter of the previous day's unrest, ran North-South for nearly a mile from Grand River to the Cobo Convention Center on the Detroit River, and passed in front of DPSH and between the GLEE corporate headquarters and the Arnault Grand Casino. It was as if DPSH had grown across the street to now encompass all of Third Avenue, sprouting throngs of bored and cold police. It was closed to traffic, including pedestrians, preventing the three runners from getting any closer. So the runners headed south parallel along First Street to the Cobo Convention Center, where they looped around the massive complex to the Riverwalk and continued their run northward for the almost three miles to their regular jaunt at Belle Isle.

As they trekked along the waterfront, they could see police on horseback and in riot gear, like the previous day, but now lining up in front of the gleaming seven-tower Renaissance Center, the city's crown jewel and global headquarters of General Motors.

* * *

Araminta Cole was up at 6:00 that morning, but she was still groggy from sleeplessness. The night before was harrowing. Police helicopters had buzzed over downtown all night long, often passing directly over her house. At one point, she heard what she assumed to be gunfire in the distance, and what sounded like a shotgun going off on her street startled her at around midnight.

She checked in on her son several times during the night, but Brandon had been sound asleep throughout. Turning on the television as she began her morning routine, she stopped periodically to check the television for news of school closings.

She worked at Wayne State University as part of the custodial staff. She was a little torn. On the one hand, she hoped that schools and universities were closed and that she would have the day off. Brandon, of course, would be ecstatic, but that was part of the problem. If, on the other hand, schools were open, which would be a good sign that the previous day's events weren't spreading, Brandon would be in school and not running around in the hood and getting mixed up with God knows what.

There were no reports of school closings, and Araminta woke Brandon at six-twenty. He had a 7:00 bus to catch.

* * *

At 5:00 that same morning, an hour before Araminta arose, and thirty minutes before the runners awoke, Catherine Bowling rode in the passenger seat of a Detroit City Police car. It was thrilling for her, and she was surprised at how nice the car was. It was a new Ford Mustang with an updated paint scheme depicting the city skyline. "Can you drive with the lights and siren on?" she asked the uniformed driver like a little school girl.

The officer chuckled. "Sure, if you want me to." He flipped on the police lights and produced a loud WHAH WHA from the siren. He turned off the lights, however, as he turned onto Fiske Drive, a quiet residential street with nicely kept English Tudor homes. In another moment he turned into the driveway of Manoogian Mansion, the official residence of the mayor.

"That was fun," Catherine said as she opened the door. "Thanks for the lift, Officer...Thomas," she said, squinting to read his name plate.

"Anytime, Mrs. Bowling, so long as you don't have to ride back there," he said, nodding to the back seat.

"Been there, done that," she said with a twinkle in her eye, and closed the door.

"Welcome to Manoogian Mansion, Mrs. Bowling," said a young man dressed in a suit.

Catherine was ushered into the mansion's Ford Conference Room where several city officials and various department heads stood about, drinking coffee and munching on an assortment of refreshments and a full breakfast buffet. Catherine spotted the line of coffee urns at a table along the wall, but had to pass through a gauntlet of suits to get there. She took a deep breath and stepped forward, greeting the chief of police and exchanging pleasantries with the head of the Health Department, the head of Water and Sanitation, the director of Jobs and Economic Growth, and others, before reaching the coffee. *Victory.*

The mayor and his entourage soon filed into the room, and everyone headed for the long conference table at the center of the room. Catherine marched right up and took a seat while others fumbled about and deferred to one another.

"Thank you, everyone, for coming on such short notice, and at such an ungodly hour," began Mayor Murray. It was five-thirty sharp, Catherine noted, and the mayor and his staff commenced with briefing the various department heads on the previous day's unrest. A police captain shared intelligence on what to expect later in the current day, noting that social media remained abuzz with highly elevated activity during the overnight hours. "#ShutoffDetroit" was a new social media hashtag that had gone viral as thousands of people promised to "shut down the city."

Chief Wiggins, laid out his strategy—the "Code Blue" for the downtown—for preventing a replay of protestors laying siege to the central business district. He also talked about coordinating with the State Police, who agreed to reposition assets to back up Detroit PD, and with the Governor's Office.

The Transportation director, himself a former career cop, identified the most important routes to be kept open and protected by police escorts, if possible. He shared his concerns for city buses and their drivers, and how the department might respond to reports of gathering crowds and unrest, which mostly entailed rerouting buses or shutting some routes down completely. Changes in routes and schedules would be announced via the department's website and through its mobile app.

The mayor turned his attention to Catherine, and along with him all heads turned in her direction. "I know it's getting late, Catherine," he said, nodding to a clock on the wall, "but…"

"I am of the mind to close the schools, sir," Catherine interjected.

Chief Wiggins whispered into the mayor's ear, and the two conferred in hushed tones. After a moment, Police Chief Wiggins spoke. "We wish that you wouldn't," he said. "If the schools close, we could have thousands of juveniles on the streets."

"You could have that anyway," responded Catherine.

"Yes, of course," said the mayor. "But, if we close the schools now, we would be broadcasting an expectation of unrest when, really, yesterday's events could very well be a one-off thing, despite the social media buzz. If our schools remain open, that would keep most kids off the streets and signal a continuation of normalcy."

"Lots of businesses stake their decision to close or not on whether the schools are open or not," contributed Dawn Lambert, the city's executive for Jobs and Economic Growth. "If the schools close, lots of businesses will close," she said.

"You see our dilemma," the mayor told Catherine. "As superintendent of the school district, I know you're concerned about the safety of students; we all are. But I'm afraid that we could be pouring fuel on the fire, so to speak, if we close the schools."

All heads remained turned to Catherine. They were waiting for her to respond, to give in to the mayor. He could, of course, just order her to keep the schools open. Why didn't he? This was one of those CYA, cover-your-ass, moments, the mayor not wanting to give an order that would come right back to him, thought Catherine. Catherine glanced over to one of the mayor's staff, a young man taking minutes.

Catherine cleared her throat before speaking. "If things were to deteriorate, how do you propose to ensure that our school children are returned to their homes safely and in an orderly manner?"

The mayor seemed somehow physically relieved with Catherine's question and turned his head to the police chief for him to respond. Chief Wiggins took his cue and launched into a description of how unrest, though often sporadic, tended to be centered at specific geographical points, and that police would coordinate with schools and buses to navigate around hotspots. He proposed a plan to use police escorts for school buses where necessary and to allow parents to pick their children up directly from the schools if possible.

The chief's plan wasn't at all convincing for Catherine, but the mayor turned his attention to the chief director of Operations, who laid out a plan to coordinate city departments, from identifying essential personnel to scheduling trash pick-ups.

After another twenty minutes or so of administrative planning, the mayor and his entourage stood up. "Thank you, everyone, for coming," he said. "We've got a long day ahead of us. Godspeed, everyone, and keep the lines of communication open." He and his entourage then filed out of the room.

And that was that.

Though Catherine never directly acquiesced, she tacitly gave the administration something to work with. And so the schools remained open. So that's why the mayor seemed relieved, she thought with a half-smile on her lips. *He's good, and I just got played.*

Outside, an assortment of cars and SUVs were lined up in the circular driveway. Catherine spotted the Ford Mustang police car where Officer Fred Thomas sat drinking a coffee and exploring his smart phone. He looked up and saw her, then raised his coffee cup to wave her in.

"How'd it go?" asked Fred, driving down Jefferson Avenue toward downtown in what was a haphazard motorcade.

"That mayor is a piece of work," Catherine noted.

Fred snorted. "Ain't that the truth."

Catherine looked out her window and saw the massive Renaissance Center up ahead. To their left, three young college runners in Wayne State University gear gracefully navigated through the leafless trees of MacArthur Bridge Park after crossing over from Belle Isle. Their presence somehow proffered a palpable sense of peace and calm. *Maybe things won't be so bad after all,* she thought.

* * *

Arturo Ayala broke out three neckties, one for himself and one for each of the boys. Jacqueline ushered them into the master bedroom, already donned in button-down collared shirts and blue jeans. Arturo handed them their ties and stood in front of the bathroom mirror. He began putting on his tie with slow and deliberate movements, the boys copying his steps.

"We're going in style," quipped Arturo.

"My boys are so handsome," said Jacqueline, wrapping her arms around Artie's waist and resting her chin on his shoulder.

"Why we gotta dress up?" asked sixteen-year-old Frederick as he fumbled with his tie. "We ain't going to church," he complained.

"It's we aren't, and why do we have to," chastised Arturo.

"¡Chale!" he said, making fourteen-year old Martín laugh, "No somos quinqui."

"Besides," Arturo added, "it *is* church. It's "applied" church. We're standing up for what's right, and we're standing up for people who can't stand up for themselves."

Jacqueline handed each of the boys a card and told them to put it in their pockets. She handed one to Arturo as well and he held it in his hand and looked it over, raising an eyebrow. It contained emergency contact and other information, like blood types and allergies.

"Just in case we get separated or anything bad happens," Jacqueline said.

"No, I get it," said Arturo, shaking his head. "It's smart. I'm just impressed that you thought ahead and printed these things up," he said, leaning forward to plant a kiss on her lips.

Jacqueline leaned back. "Impressed that I thought ahead?" she said, frowning.

"You know what I mean," said Arturo with a smile, pulling Jacqueline into a hug. Almost stepped in it again, you dummy, he thought as he successfully, this time, planted a reluctantly accepted kiss.

Within minutes, the young family was strapped into Jacqueline's Jeep Grand Cherokee and were headed west on Nine Mile in Grosse Pointe Farms toward the East Pointe Park & Ride for the forty-minute rush hour trek into the city.

CHAPTER 6

Alexander Cooley was in his office at 9:25 that morning, munching on a bagel and mindlessly scrolling through his emails. It was the usual barrage of memorandums, policies, and meeting times, ninety percent of which didn't even pertain to him. *Delete.* He scanned the next email. *Delete.* After another half-dozen, he was all caught up and headed for the daily executive staff meeting.

"What's going on?" Alex asked Bobby, the kid three years his junior and right out of college, whose office was two doors down from Alex's. The board room was abuzz with hushed but excited talk.

"You didn't hear about the riots yesterday?" Bobby asked. Alex shook his head. "Yeah, man, there was a riot last night over by the casino. They were protesting a shooting or something," he said, his eyes bright with excitement. Alex only half heard him as he checked his phone for the Piston's score quickly before the meeting began.

Donnie Tillman, the bank's regional president, sat down at the head of the table and everyone, including Alex, put away their phones.

"Hope no one had any trouble getting home last night," Donnie said with a chuckle. "I understand there was some excitement downtown."

"What was it about?" asked Jim, the real estate point man thirty years' Alex's senior and, according to Alex, a total prick who didn't know how to operate a smart phone and was utterly clueless about apps, social media, and even the internet. How he remained a senior

51

executive in good standing was beyond Alex. "Was it a police thing?" Jim asked.

"Something about a fire," Donnie said with a shrug.

And, with that, the meeting turned to status reports and updates on assets owned by the bank, the daily housing sales briefing, an update on commercial real estate sales and rents, and so on. The meeting was adjourned after an hour, and Donnie was back in his office, staring at a spreadsheet on his computer screen reviewing a mortgage broker's pitch to finance five more homes in the Warren area. It's just another day, another day on earth, he sang in his head, a song with a dance beat that he had heard somewhere.

* * *

By the time Ian, Roland, and Trevor were back on the Wayne State campus, traffic had thickened with morning commuters. The day was getting on as usual and, for Ian, the events of the previous day seemed almost as if they hadn't happened.

Ian had a light Tuesday-Thursday class schedule: a Physical Geography class from 9:30 to 10:45, and a second class, World Civilization II, from 11:00 to 12:15. And then, except for assignments and studying, he was free for the day. Ian was a morning person, a rare bird among college students. It had become a running joke among his roommates and friends who would be half-asleep and easily agitated by the always cheery Ian in the early morning, and the roles would gradually reverse as the day wore on. Once mentioned by a friend, Ian guessed that it was so, and so he deliberately scheduled his classes to start as early as possible, preferably right after a long morning run, and to have them run back to back.

Geography class was a drag. Ian's cell phone vibrated incessantly. He stole glances at it when he could. Various student groups were calling for another march on downtown. Roland had texted Ian as well; he was eager to march again.

As Ian scrolled his text messages, a new one came from Sarah. She, too, was back on Fountain Court where, apparently, even more people and students than the day before were gathering.

As his Geography class neared its end, Ian was fidgety. He would have fifteen minutes to get to his next class, but so many of his friends were joining what was turning out to be possibly an even bigger protest than the day before. He simply had to go.

I'll be there, he texted Sarah.

History could wait.

* * *

Five hours into her shift, Barbara Hinton navigated a fourth generation LF Series NovaBus, city bus line 34, from 9 Mile southbound for the approximately one-hour trip toward the Rosa Parks Transit Center in downtown Detroit. She'd already been back to the center twice since beginning her run there, and this would normally be her final run before lunch. It was the seventy-five or so bus stops in one direction along Gratiot Avenue that stretched what typically would be a twenty-five minute drive into an hour, and Barbara was just ten stops in after turning around at the 9 Mile Park & Ride, the outer end of the line, when her bus was already beginning to fill.

On the radio, the two buses ahead of her had already reported that they were full and were now heading non-stop into the city. Barbara made it a few more stops before she, too, was full, having squeezed the last passengers (after a bit of a tussle) that she could fit into the bus at 7 Mile and leaving half of the crowd at the bus stop to wait for other buses minutes behind her. She radioed in that she was also loaded, changed the sign on the top front panel of the bus to read "Full," and drove right past the next stop where a large crowd waited. Many at the crowded bus stop ogled her, apparently hoping she would stop.

It was nearly 10:00, an unusual time for city buses to be filling up, and the bus stops became more crowded as the morning wore on. Barbara's route went more quickly because she couldn't make any more stops, and she did a mental calculation. She concluded that she would have to make another run, maybe two. Shit. She passed several more stops where large crowds waited at each of them.

As she neared the downtown, increasing numbers of crowds and pedestrians snaked their way past bus stops and toward the city, with many carrying makeshift signs. Barbara had heard about the previous day's protests, but her shift had ended just as protesters had begun to descend on the downtown. Not so today. Today they were getting an early start.

On the bus, passengers were enthusiastic, even jubilant. Overlapping conversations produced such a din of voices that it was hard to pick out individual ones. Barbara tuned it out, humming an old Tina Turner song, What's Love Got to Do with It?

"Pretty crowded bus," said a soft voice audible just below the din. In her large rearview mirror, Barbara saw a nicely dressed and bespectacled young man in the first seat, nearly pressed into it by a standing crowd that towered over him. "This can't be normal," he said sheepishly.

"No," Barbara chuckled, "not even for a Pistons game. Are you all going to the protest?"

"Yes, ma'am," chimed in a tall, well-dressed bearded man with a nice trim standing a few feet back. "It's long past time for us to stand up. Our lives matter and we need to make our voices heard."

The bespectacled young man nodded.

"We have to stand up for those who can't stand up for themselves," said another well-dressed boy, and a fashionable, beautiful woman standing behind him patted him on the shoulder and smiled at Barbara—a young family, she guessed.

"Well, God bless you and you all be careful," she said, bringing the bus to a stop at the Rosa Parks Transit Center, just blocks from GLEE. "Final stop," she announced, gripping a microphone. "Follow the crowds for GLEE Headquarters," she said, opening the doors. "Give 'em hell," she added. Her voice over the intercom was barely audible with the clamor of multiple conversations, but many passengers laughed as they departed the bus.

"Right on, right on," said the bearded man, offering a raised fist and a smile as the family stepped off the bus.

* * *

Andrew Wilson navigated his NovaBus on Linwood Street south toward the city. His bus, too, was filling up, and traffic had thickened rapidly—both unusual happenings on this particular route, line 29—and it was well beyond the morning rush hour. Passengers were lively with conversations, and Andrew did his best to concentrate on driving.

Pedestrian traffic on Linwood was also unusually thick. The bus reached capacity at Davidson Avenue and could take no more passengers. Andy progressed along his route slowly but bypassed the crowded stops. The sidewalk was too narrow for the crowds of pedestrians, and many were walking along the side of the road. Andy was forced to slowly navigate into the left lane and, as he slowly passed the crowds, some people waiting for a bus at a stop he bypassed gave him a thumbs-down sign, and others waved their hands in dismissal. Their body language suggested it was mostly done in jest, and Andy offered a thumbs-up in return. It was a rough part of town, he knew, but the crowds outside in the cold seemed festive.

The bus passed Joy Avenue when things took on a more sinister look. Groups of young people stood along the sidewalks on either side of Linwood, and some just wandered out into the middle of the slow traffic to cross. One car was forced to stop as a teenager wandered out in front of it. The driver blew his horn and a gaggle of teenagers swarmed around it, slapping their hands on the hood and trunk and cursing the driver. The driver—a large, muscular black man—got out of the car and, as he stood and stretched out, the kids scattered. Traffic remained halted until the large man climbed back into his car after gesturing at the kids, before resuming again, slowly. Some passengers roared with laughter.

Thick black smoke billowed a short distance ahead where more crowds were gathered and more people walked about amid the traffic. A boarded-up building on the corner of Hazelwood was apparently on fire; thick acrid smoke poured out of every opening and drifted across Linwood. People stood nonchalantly around the smoking building, even in the roadway, talking. They parted to allow the bus to slowly pass.

"Yeah, boy, it's getting real now," said a passenger.

"Burn, baby, burn!" someone shouted as Andy carefully navigated the bus past the smoking building.

A tussle erupted at the back of bus. "Hey, hey, hey!" Andy yelled, stopping the bus and turning around. "What's going on back there?"

"They're throwing stuff at the bus," several passengers answered.

"Yeah, man, don't stop!" someone yelled from the back of the bus. Andy and the passengers felt a "thonk" against the side of the bus. He turned around and started driving again. He grabbed his radio microphone and spoke into it. "10-34 at Blaine Street," he said, using the police code for riot.

"Where's the po-po when you need 'em?" a passenger joked, eliciting laughter. But, come to think of it, Andy hadn't seen a single police car since starting his route.

A minute or so later, a voice came over the radio. "10-34 at Grand River and Livernois." Then, another voice: "10-34 at Michigan and Martin," followed by yet another, "10-34 at West Grand and Rosa Parks."

That last one was straight ahead on Andy's route. He approached West Grand Boulevard where he normally would turn left, then right onto Rosa Parks for the remaining two miles or so into the city. This time, however, he simply stopped halfway through the intersection to consider his options. Menacing crowds were all over West Grand to his left, some pelting passing cars with stones and debris. There were less people, however, to his right, between Linwood and the half-mile or so west to Interstate 96.

Andy put on his turn signal and slowly made a right turn from the left lane, carefully keeping an eye on his right side mirror for traffic that he might be cutting off. He made the turn and cautiously made his way toward the interstate on-ramp. Mercifully, his bus was spared from being targeted by the dozen or so young men walking back and forth across the road, intimidating drivers. And, as he merged into traffic on I-96, probably the fastest way into the city from West Grand, yet another voice came over the radio.

"All buses return to Transit Center immediately."

CHAPTER 7

Tony Wiggins' heart sank when he heard the first 10-34 from the bus driver on Linwood. He had the downtown area pretty much buttoned-up despite the gathering of more protestors, perhaps even more than the previous day's. Tens of thousands, potentially. With the exception of a few officers broken into teams to escort city and school buses outside of the CBD, if necessary, every single member of the Detroit Police Department was in the central business district, and Wiggins was confident that they could manage any unrest there. It was the sprawling outlying areas that worried him. Perhaps if they could swarm an area quickly, they could nip any unrest in the bud.

A team of 30 officers remained on station from the day before at Gratiot and Mack Avenue, along with a mobile command center. Those officers, patrolling the entire four-mile length of Mack Avenue from Gratiot to Alter Road, reported restive, growing crowds and several arrests.

Wiggins picked up his microphone to issue a Code Blue for Linwood Avenue when the second 10-34 came in, this one from Grand River. Shit. Then the third one came in.

He issued a Code Blue order to three separate teams, each assigned to one of the three areas called in by the bus drivers. He knew there would be more, and he would have to send officers out from the downtown, something he was sure the mayor wouldn't allow.

* * *

Alex, formatting a recommendation report on the twenty-five mortgages proposal to investors and working to get an amortization graph to center properly, heard people talking in hushed tones in the lobby. There, he thought, and leaned back in his chair with his hands behind his head as he surveyed the chart. It looked good.

He heard Bobby ask the two office administrators what was going on, and that brought Alex to lean in his doorway and pick up the scuttlebutt. Large crowds were gathering in the downtown again, according to the women, in addition to rumors about a terrorist attack or shooting. Alex scoffed.

"In Detroit? I mean, why? Have they seen this place?" Bobby snorted.

Bobby and the two young women followed Alex into his office to look out his tenth-floor window. Alex was astonished. He hadn't heard a thing as he worked, yet the street was full of people, many of them holding homemade signs, and they appeared to be heading toward the north side of downtown toward the stadiums as though there was a daytime Detroit Tigers or Lions game. But it was out of season for both, and the Pistons were out of town. Still, the sidewalks were packed full; there had to be hundreds of people, maybe a thousand.

Alex turned to the computer on his desk and surfed to the Detroit Free Press. "GLEE Protests Enter Second Day" read a breaking news headline, along with photos of crowds of people and police gathering at the corporation's headquarters again.

* * *

Aaron and Michelle, along with Xavier and Devin, his neighborhood friends since forever, caught the school bus at 7:10 as usual for the ten-minute ride to school. Reggie, another childhood friend, hadn't shown up this morning. Actually, Aaron was surprised that anyone at all had shown up. They had stayed out late the night before, throwing stones at passing traffic, which consisted of only a few cars here and there.

Mostly they had walked along Michigan Avenue, meeting friends, talking excitedly, and wondering what would come next. It was a revolution, one kid from the neighborhood said with bravado. It did seem like something, with a ground-level orange glow casting dancing shadows on tall buildings downtown that they could see from their part of the city. A couple of parked cars also burned brightly nearby, the air acrid with smoke. And it was exhilarating, the cold air, the crowds, his friends' animated bodies silhouetted against the glow of the flames of the burning cars.

But when he returned home a little after midnight, his mother apparently hadn't heard about any revolution, and didn't care. At 5:30 the next morning, she shook him awake, threatening to throw a glass of water on his face if he didn't get up and go to school.

"Schools ain't closed, so you get your ass up before I put my foot up in it!" she bellowed when he suggested there probably wouldn't be any school today.

And she was right. School was open, as usual. Some revolution.

Once at school, though, things were different. Half—no, more than half—of the teachers, it seemed, had called in sick, and so he had a substitute teacher for his very first class of the day. It seemed as if half the students hadn't shown up, either. The hallway was noticeably less crowded between classes. The buzz among students, and even teachers and administrators, was electric.

Aaron and his fellow students grew restless. At lunchtime, he met up with Michelle and his friends, like they always did, but this time, with scores of fellow students, they headed for the exits.

They walked excitedly south along Vinewood Street for the mile from their high school to Michigan Avenue, a steady stream of euphoric high school students triumphantly ditching school.

Revolution, Aaron thought. He turned the word over in his mind, even silently mouthed it, trying it out, seeing how it felt on his tongue, while his friends chatted enthusiastically about all sorts of things.

"What?" asked Xavier, catching Aaron's lips move but not hearing him.

"Revolution," answered Aaron, saying it out loud.

"Yeah, revolution!" exclaimed Devin, dropping his skateboard at his feet and hopping on effortlessly. He raised a fist as he spun around, all in one graceful motion. "It takes a revo-lu-tion to find a so-lu-tion," he sang in a nasal voice, and giggled as he coasted on his board.

* * *

The news, much of it rumor, had grown more alarming as the day progressed, and Donnie Tillman, president of the regional Apex Superior Bank, called an impromptu meeting of executives and announced that they were closing for the day. Other downtown businesses, even the behemoth General Motors, were said to be doing the same.

Alex met with Bobby and other young executives in the lobby to check things out. They stepped out onto Griswold Street and right into a crowd of police gathered out in front of their building and all along the street, dozens of them. They were in full riot gear with helmets, shields, and batons, and a half-dozen or so were on horseback, the horses lazily clopping along the road.

Alex and his colleagues strolled a block down to Jefferson Avenue and watched as even more police on horseback and in full riot gear lined up along the wide boulevard, which paralleled the Detroit River that linked Lake St. Clair and Lake Erie. They lined up in front of GM's five-tower, rosette-shaped glistening, futuristic glass-and-steel Renaissance Center headquarters (hard to believe it was built in the

1970s, mentioned Bobby, offhand), and all along the streets of the Financial District.

Alex and his friends picked their way through the police lines and some gathering protestors. Alex felt out of place in his suit; he and his colleagues stood out amid the uniformed police and casually dressed protesters, some stylishly urban, most others grungy. The stares of some of the protesters as they passed, particularly among the young and hard-looking, revealed pure disdain for anything resembling authority, like police or white men in suits.

Emboldened by the presence of his co-workers and throngs of police, Alex straightened and returned a hard look back to the protestors.

One co-worker, an alum of Michigan State, who started at Apex Superior just a month or two before Alex, suggested that lunch and beer at the Top Hat, the posh revolving restaurant and bar atop the Renaissance Center, would be a cool place to drink and watch the protests unfold in the city below.

It wasn't far and, when they neared the 'RenCen,' they could see that it was crowded with GM employees and executives, workers from other nearby firms, and plenty of Financial District workers, all standing around watching the police and protestors.

* * *

Bernice Hamandawana, a graduate student in journalism at Wayne State University and freelance reporter for Motown Mirror, an independent online and live-streaming news site, was speaking into a camera held by fellow WSU journalism student Daniel Rush, a 20-year old junior. Bernice was musing on the growing protests in the heart of downtown Detroit when a young man with dreadlocks approached.

"Look!" he said, sweeping his hand to encompass the throngs of police in riot gear, others on horseback, all gathered in front of the

Renaissance Center. Daniel followed the young man's hand with his smartphone, filming.

The mayor and an entourage of city officials emerged, accompanied by a mob of journalists and reporters who moved briskly among them, speaking emphatically with what appeared to be the police chief and a number of corporate executives. A few immaculate-looking young men in suits—young executives, to be sure—stood in pockets behind the protective police barrier, looking festive and curious as they hung together and spoke in hushed tones among themselves.

"Look," the young man said again. "They're lining up together: the police, the mayor, the CEOs. The city is naked and everything is laid bare."

Leaning forward, his bright eyes softening with resignation, he spoke ominously: "They are lining up against us."

A toothy grin flashed across his face. "They're lining up against us," he sang, this time in a childlike, sing-song voice, "the mayors and the players.

"Lined up against thee," he continued singing, "thee with no electricity, no power, no peace in the city." He erupted in a contagious, hearty laugh.

"Bee!" someone called, and Daniel swung his camera around to pick up another dreadlocked young man, this one a little older, spectacled and dressed in a tan sports coat and jeans. He embraced Bernice, then clasped hands and shoulder-bumped the smiling singer. "Lee-Ron, my man," he said.

"Yo, Walter," said the young singer, "how you been, man?"

"You know each other?" asked Bernice.

"Yeah, girl," answered Walter. "This is LeRon Gordon, artist extraordinaire, and 'The People's Mayor'." Then, to LeRon, "Doing good, my man. Whatchya working on these days?"

"Doing some writing, you know, got some projects going on," answered LeRon and, with a knowing laugh, tilted his head to the throngs of police, "sticking it to the man."

"Is that one of yours, out by the Kronk?" asked Walter.

"You know it, brother," answered LeRon. "That's the 'Hurricane of Love'," he said with a wide grin. It was an abandoned industrial warehouse near the famous Kronk Gymnasium, itself abandoned and crumbled like Roman ruins, that he was referring to, its remnants now covered with a dark but cartoonish mural depicting a harrowing storm whose rain was bullets, and whose puddles were blood, the streets below dotted with fallen, mostly black, denizens like debris. The storm clouds, upon close examination, were police cars with uniformed police officers crouching behind them and firing their pistols on the world below.

It was a not-so-subtle dig at Governor Clifford Krueger who, when turning the city away from the state's coffers amid Michigan's ongoing budget crisis after slashing taxes by billions of dollars, offered his justification: "It's not more money this city needs," he had thundered like a preacher from a pulpit. "It's love! *Tough* love that this city needs!"

* * *

Ian, Roland, Trevor, Sarah, Tina, and Dakota—the Wayne State cross country runners—had marched with an endless stream of students and faculty from Wayne State, and residents from surrounding neighborhoods, straight down Cass Avenue again toward the GLEE headquarters. Lines of police and physical barricades kept protestors far from the complex this time, however, and protesters instead filled in along the streets and side streets of downtown.

The protesters shouted as they marched, alternating between "No power, no peace!" and "Shut off Detroit!" The runners, along with Walter Clay and other WSU students and student leaders, followed crowds to the Coleman Young Municipal Center on Jefferson Avenue, now familiar with Ian, Roland, and Trevor after their early morning run. Police lined up on both sides of the wide boulevard.

They looked like an army camped out in Hart Plaza west of the Renaissance Center, the gleaming headquarters of General Motors, with tents on the grass and brick promenade and cops on horseback.

Ian watched as the protestors—unorganized and standing around haphazardly, shoulder to shoulder, packed in along the boulevard—milled about and chatted with relaxed deportment. On occasion, and with increasing frequency, a random young man or woman (usually a young man) would walk up to the line of cops and stand nose to nose with an impassive, stone-faced officer. They would either glare menacingly at the cop, or scream, "No power, no peace!" or some other slogan, right in the officer's face.

Some screamed obscenities and threats, their body language hostile and threatening. They even feigned attack, trying to get the police to flinch. Ian watched intently. He didn't understand the action. The cops had nothing to do with GLEE shutting off electricity, so why scream in the face of the officers? Clearly it was meant to intimidate, but it seemed to Ian that it was akin to poking at a hornet's nest.

"Yeah, man!" bellowed Roland, just to Ian's right, as a protester spit into the faces of a line of officers. "Spit on the pigs!" the kid yelled with apparent amusement.

Now Ian eyed Roland blankly, and with alarm. Roland caught Ian's expression, lowered his voice and spoke under the cacophony of sounds. "Hey," he said, "it's a protest, man, just getting into it."

"We don't want any of that, young man," said a bearded older gentleman, talking directly to Roland. "We don't want any violence."

Just as he said it, a shirtless teenager ran straight up to the line of police and leaped into a wall of shields, sending officers and himself sprawling to the ground. A half dozen or so young men and teenagers raced into the melee, throwing punches and kicking at the officers struggling to get back on their feet.

The lines of police lurched forward and lost their linearity. The lines melded into the crowd and formed several pockets of baton-swinging, helmeted cops raining bone-crushing blows onto any unlucky protesters they surrounded.

The crowd surged forward.

"It's on!" shouted Roland, his face alight with excitement as the crowd around them surged toward the RenCen. The crowd parted, revealing a group of four helmeted and shield-carrying police working in sync, swinging their batons at anyone close.

Ian froze as he saw a college-age girl take a blow across her face. An arc of blood momentarily suspended in mid-air traced her descent to the ground.

"Let's go!" Roland shouted, tugging at Ian, who had turned to sprint in the opposite direction with his cross-country teammates. As they took their first step, the initial jump, a second circle of baton-wielding police emerged just to their front and left. Roland was still focused on tugging at Ian and, as he turned, he ran straight into the circle of cops.

"Roland!" shouted Ian as, seeing the cops, grasped at Roland's shoulder.

Roland saw the cops at the last moment and agilely stepped to his right to bypass them. But he never saw the baton that came crashing down across his temple.

* * *

For Ian, the world seemed to enter a strange new dimension where time slowed and nearly stopped, and the cacophony of sounds all around him went silent in an instant except for the crack of the baton across Roland's temple that now echoed ceaselessly in Ian's ears.

He watched as Roland gracefully took two more steps (maybe he wasn't hit after all, but that sound...) before crumbling straight down, his slim build crumbling in a heap. He lay face up, his legs twisted beneath him, his face turned toward Ian, his eyes locking with Ian's.

Ian went to him but was slammed to the ground. He was forced into a fetal position to try to protect himself as he absorbed the striking batons on his ribs and back, even on the back of his hands that covered his head. Then the muffled pitter-patter of clubs on his body ended almost as quickly as it began as the circle of police moved on to the next protester.

Ian opened his eyes and for a moment was confused. All he saw were legs running this way and that. Mostly, they were the legs of uniformed police attacking and expanding into an ever-widening perimeter.

Ian!…Ian! The sound of his name being repeated was muffled and far away.

Ian! It was Trevor, crouching over him, tapping him lightly on the cheek. Trevor was saying something but it was too muted to make out.

Ian sat up slowly, helped by Trevor. The world sped up now. It took another moment for the sights and sounds to sort themselves out, but his ears and head were assaulted by a cacophony of sounds near and far, alternating between subdued and roaring.

Trevor turned away from Ian and moved out of sight. Ian remained sitting, and Sarah's face, looking dirty and panicked, now filled his. She was saying something—the sounds were deadened again—and looking frantically past Ian and back. She was trying to get him to his feet.

Ian acquiesced and stood. When he took a step—all sounds now roaring again, but crisper—he was unsteady, and Sarah gripped him tightly around his waist.

"Help him, for God's sake!" Ian heard as the sounds in his ears popped into a penetrating roar. It was an awful, anguished-filled feminine voice pitched to its limit, cracking. Ian looked over and saw that it was Tina. She was being dragged backward by her curly hair by a helmeted cop as she kicked out and twisted and scratched at the cop's arms. She looked like a feral cat gone completely wild, and then it all came back.

Roland…

There, behind a wall of shielded, helmeted cops, was Roland lying in the road, on his side, his arms and legs stiffened and extended straight out, hands bent inward at the wrists, his upper body whiplashing. He was having a seizure and no one was helping him.

"Oh, no," Ian heard, not realizing it was his own voice, as it dawned on him that the side of Roland's head was slamming repeatedly into the pavement as he convulsed. "Roland!" he yelled, now pulling out of Sarah's arms and running straight toward the wall of shields standing between him and Roland.

"Get back, you little fuck," a smug cop warned, swinging his baton to keep Ian at bay.

"That's my friend!" Ian shouted, pointing to Roland. "He's dying!"

"Good!" smirked the police officer.

Ian, filled with rage, dashed between two officers, very nearly breaking through the line. But he was quickly subdued and shoved to the ground facedown. Officers handcuffed him with plastic ties while driving their knees into his back and driving his chin into the pavement.

Ian had a hard time breathing with the officers on top of him. He lifted his head and saw that two officers knelt at Roland's side and were now preventing his head from further slamming into the asphalt. One officer held Roland's head in his hands as his shoulders continued to rock back and forth. Blood poured through the officer's fingers.

CHAPTER 8

Daniel Rush had his camera trained on Bernice Hamandawana, Walter Clay, and the charismatic, toothy LeRon Gordon, 'The People's Mayor,' when a roar emanated from the crowd just ahead of them on Jefferson Avenue in front of the Renaissance Center. Though the boulevard was wide, the crowd in which they were embedded was standing shoulder to shoulder and front to back, packed in between the Detroit River on their right and the forest of the tall buildings of downtown to their left. The streets and side streets of downtown were also filled in. The crowds along Jefferson Avenue and the streets of downtown were becoming more dense by the minute as throngs of protesters continued to stream into the downtown from sprawling neighborhoods across the city. They trekked in by bus and by foot from the Northwest Goldberg district to the west. Other groups walked or bused in from the south, from districts like Delray, Melvindale, River Rouge, and Ecorse. Still others drove in from the suburbs north and west of the city, like St. Claire Shores, Warren, Clawson, Southfield, and beyond, snarling city-bound traffic on Interstates 94 and 75 and the M-10 highway.

Daniel held his camera up as high as he could, but could not see over the crowd of people around him. He had no idea what was occurring outside two dozen or so people immediately around and adjacent to him. The same was true for Bernice and Walter.

LeRon, however, had an idea and sing-songed his conclusion.

"The match is lit," he rapped, "now we move to the groove or get hit."
It seemed to Daniel that LeRon couldn't help but speak in rhymes.

The crowd lurched backward and Daniel's heart leapt in his chest.
Don't fall down, he ordered himself. People up front screamed and
Daniel was doubtless that people were falling down. He couldn't see
anyone fall, but he sensed it with the swaying of the crowd along
with the screams, and people were turning around to run.

Away from something. The look of fear on their faces—including
Bernice's and Walter's—sent a cold shiver down Daniel's spine. He
also turned to run. And he knew that his face, too, wore a mask of
fear.

But still he held up his camera, determined to film. He watched
as the crowd behind him also began turning around, turning their
backs to him, a wave of turning heads and bodies passing through the
crowd like dominos.

He was pushed into a trot from behind, but he gingerly tried to set
his feet in a deliberate manner so as not to fall. A visible wave passed
from behind him to his front and away from him, a wave of people
trotting, then running, scattering toward the Cobo Convention Center
to his front and the downtown to his right.

Debris of dropped cell phones, plastic bottles, bags, purses,
sneakers, fast food wrappers, and squirming bodies of people who
had fallen down remained in their wake.

Still the wave reverberated outward, and there was a sonic wake
as well of glass breaking, metal clanging on metal, screams, shouts,
curses, and a loud sustained storm of sound like hail comprised of
falling rocks and all kinds of other debris falling and bouncing all
across the pavement, everywhere.

The dense, peaceful crowds of people of all ages and backgrounds,
entire families, broke apart as they fled the onslaught of baton-wielding, shielded, and helmeted police officers unleashed upon anyone in
range of their sticks. The crowds along Jefferson Avenue and nearby
streets had broken into total disarray, a wave of chaos spreading outward across the downtown, with people calling out in panic for their

loved ones as individuals became separated from their groups by the tumultuous currents of frightened people that swept them along.

Bands of angered and scared individuals somehow organically and swiftly organized into units that clicked together. Horrified and anguished by being separated from loved ones, seeing family members trampled and being unable to reach them or help them or even stay with them as they themselves were swept away in the panicked crowds, they blended together, broke apart, and blended together again, small cliques working in unison, a storm being born.

They descended on police cars and news vans, swarming them, smashing them, overturning them, the furious bands of protesters passing around Daniel in a visible wave that spread outward. Two vehicles flipped and rolled away from Daniel as the protestors tore through ahead of him, leaving behind smashed and overturned vehicles just coming to rest as Daniel followed close on their heels. If anyone present had been through a tornado, the sights and sounds of things breaking all at once were familiar.

As Daniel ran, now on Washington Boulevard and separated from Bernice, Walter, and LeRon, but still filming with his camera, a prominent building had its lobby-floor windows smashed, and along the street several parked cars were set ablaze. Others were rolled over into the middle of either side of the two-pronged boulevard. Broken glass and debris littered the entire canyon between buildings along the length of the boulevard as far as Daniel could see.

* * *

For Jacqueline Ayala, her worst fears were realized. Arturo never even considered the possibility, but now, as he scrambled to get back on his feet before he was trampled to death, he thanked God for Jacqueline's foresight to print out their emergency cards with even a rendezvous point on Brush Street across from the Renaissance

Center, which could be seen from nearly any point in Detroit.

Which was where they were when the crowds surged and turned into a panicked, running free for all.

Arturo got back on his feet and was nearly knocked right back to the ground by stopping and trying to go back against the crowd. Instead, he was shoved forward by the panicked crowd.

"Jackie!" he yelled, now running to keep pace with the crowd while looking all about. "Jackie! Martín! Frederick!" he yelled, his head swiveling all around as he desperately searched.

"Artie!" he heard, and he barely caught a glimpse of Jacqueline jumping with her hand high over her head, but then she was gone, the crowd pushing them apart.

"Jackie!" he yelled again and tried to fight his way to where he last saw her, but it was impossible. They were being pushed farther apart.

At last, Arturo went with the crowd and prayed that she and the kids would do the same. They could all double back through the side streets of downtown to the rendezvous point.

Arturo jogged up Woodward Avenue with the crowd and broke north at Cadillac Park to Randolph Street, just a block away from Brush Street, but his way to Brush Street and the Renaissance Center was blocked. Crowds streamed up Randolph Street as well, away from the Renaissance Center. Police in riot gear—and now donning gas masks—walked in unison tapping their shields with their batons as a vanguard of cops waged war out ahead of them, chasing protestors and violently lashing at them with their batons.

Arturo heard the distinctive sound of tear gas canisters being fired, and Randolph Street was soon engulfed in the white gas clinging low to the ground and drifting outward.

Though the bluish-white smoke was still a block ahead of him, Arturo's nose and eyes burned and he was forced to turn back toward Woodward. That, too, he saw, was also now enveloped in tear gas, forcing Arturo to run north. Each time he tried to double back, he was met with the stinging gas and throngs of people running away from the center of downtown.

Arturo eventually found himself between Comerica Park, home of the Detroit Tigers, and Ford Field, home of the Detroit Lions—Brush Street!—and he ducked into a gate overhang at Comerica Park, and waited. He couldn't head south into downtown to the Renaissance Center; the crowd was thick and still moving in the opposite direction, away from downtown. Still, he hoped that Jacqueline and the boys would have found their way to Brush Street as he had done and, if they were pushed along, he might find them.

He now had time to pull out his cell phone. He had five missed calls, four from Jackie, one from Frederick. He dialed each of Jacqueline and the boys' phones, but no one answered. He frantically texted his location to each.

His phone buzzed in his hand as he texted his youngest son. It was Jackie. "Baby!" he answered, but she was cut off. He called her back and the same thing happened.

He texted again and waited eagerly for her reply. Within minutes, Arturo, Jackie, and Frederick hugged tightly. They had seen his texts and found their way to Comerica Park. Jackie and Frederick looked awful; their eyes and noses were red and inflamed, and mucus coated their jackets.

"We can't find Martín!" Frederick said before Artie could ask. "He fell, and then he was gone!" said Frederick. "I tried to reach him but we got pushed!"

"I know, I know," said Arturo, hugging his wife and son. "We'll find him."

* * *

Just over a mile to the northwest of the city line, in Southfield, WHWK Channel 13 news reporter Ernie Brown climbed into the station's "SkyHawk 13" Robinson R44 news chopper. The helicopter's engine was already revved up, its rotor blades on full spin. It was a few minutes before 3:00 in the afternoon, right about the time for the regular traffic report. Typically, Peter Schmies, the SkyHawk 13 pilot, would fly over the city solo and give the report himself directly through his headset. The station's various police scanners picked up reports of unrest in the downtown and beyond, however, so this time Peter was accompanied by Ernie, who would give live reports from the helicopter, and a cameraman.

With Ernie and the cameraman safely buckled in and wearing their headsets, Peter lifted off. Within a minute or two, the scale of the protests below was apparent as they neared the downtown. Lines of black dots snaked their way from major arterial roadways and secondary streets into the downtown like tentacles, thickening to cover the entire breadth and width of the downtown streets between buildings. From a distance, Washington Boulevard to Jefferson Avenue appeared to be the spine of protests, with no discernible gaps among the protesters packed in along the length and width of the avenues.

As the SkyHawk helicopter approached closer overhead, however, the thick lines of protesters along the lengths of both Washington Boulevard and Jefferson Avenue dissolved into gaps like Swiss cheese that opened and closed, and the lines themselves pulsated as protesters moved in either direction and into side streets.

They were running.

Washington Boulevard in particular seemed to drain off protesters as they appeared to stream en masse onto each side street, leaving some groups behind, including individual protesters who had fallen amid the chaos. Some now moved as stragglers and joined the exits to the side streets.

Ernie recorded his report of the protests turning violent as the cameraman zoomed in on police wielding batons and swarming aggressive protesters. Peter steered the helicopter in a circle over the city, and the cameraman panned out and focused on various clusters of protesters away from the police lines. Various bands of protesters attacked parked cars and building lobbies, threw debris, and kicked at cars and windows.

It was a full-scale riot down there.

Peter circled to the west side of downtown over the GLEE head-quarters. It was once again under siege, but this time it was by police who swarmed out of DPSH and enveloped the entire combined com-plexes of DPSH, GLEE, and the Grand Arnault Casino.

However, it was Grand River Avenue across Interstate 75 from downtown and the DPSH-GLEE-Grand Arnault complexes, stretch-ing northwest into the distance, that caught Ernie's attention. The avenue was one of those tentacles full of protestors that appeared to be marching into downtown. However, as Peter steered the helicopter northwest over Grand River Avenue and out over the Woodbridge, North Corktown, and Core City residential districts, it was readily apparent that these were not people marching into the downtown. Instead, these were locals from the neighborhoods that had gathered along Grand River Avenue itself, with thick crowds gathered primar-ily at major intersections along its path.

Vehicle traffic was thick and slow along Grand River Avenue. The intersection of Grand River and Fourteenth Street was particu-larly thick with traffic as large groups of people meandered into and out of traffic, forcing cars to inch along at a snail's pace. One car crept forward as a group of young people walked in front of it, and that apparently had angered some of them. They turned on the car and swarmed over it. They slapped on its hood and roof and tried to break the windows. The driver nudged the car through the crowd more forcefully as it became a target and forced its way through an opening, then sped away. A gauntlet of rocks and bottles landed all around it as it headed southeast.

Multiple other cars were targeted by the marauding group of young people. Ernie spoke into his headset with the station manager in Southfield. "We have to go live," he said, "I am watching a crowd attack cars on Grand River."

CHAPTER 9

A t age fifty-five, Forrest Avery ("Fave" to family and associates) was not your typical gangster. No longer the crazy-eyed, fly-off-the-handle young psychopath—an image he cultivated in his twenties, but now looked back on as foolhardy and he counted himself lucky to have survived that period—he was now a sort of elder statesman. He was deemed "the Boss," but only because his 57-year-old brother William "Pops" Avery kept an extremely low profile. All business and communication was done through Fave. He also worked as a mentor and advisor to his 35-year-old nephew Jayson, who was cool-headed like "Pops," his father.

Today, however, Forrest felt it was necessary to act as boss in his brother's stead. With a late morning errand to Woodward Avenue near Wayne State University, just over a mile from his house, Forrest cursed under his breath at the unusual amount of traffic of both vehicles and pedestrians. The way home, usually maybe ten minutes at most, dragged into thirty.

As he sat in traffic, he asked a teenager walking past with his young crew what was happening.

"There's a riot going on, man," said the boy, and Forrest chuckled at the Sly and Family Stone reference. The boy looked confused. Fave dismissed the kid with a wave of the hand. He obviously had no clue who they were.

Forrest had heard about the previous day's unrest, but only snippets, and he didn't pay it much mind. But now things seemed to be getting real. He flipped the radio dial until a news station came on, but it was talk radio. Nothing about a riot.

As he snaked his way home through the thick traffic, horns honked and people held up the "V" for victory sign. When he crossed Grand River Avenue back to his side of the tracks, crowds of young, hard-looking kids were gathered at each intersection. A few nodded knowingly at him with respect when they made eye contact.

He made it home and saw his nephew Jayson's black Cadillac Escalade EXT parked next to the curb. Fave's wife Greta was on the front lawn talking with Viola, Jayson's elegant young wife, whose bright eyes brimmed with intelligence, as her two boys squealed and played in the front yard.

"Hi, Forrest, how are you?" asked Viola as Forrest stepped out of his own Cadillac, a black sedan.

"Viola," he said, and gave her a hug. "Boys inside?"

"Yes. They're watching the news. It's awful," she said, then nodded to a helicopter hovering high over the city a mile or so away.

Forrest looked quizzically at the two kids. "Jayson didn't want us at home by ourselves with all that's going on," she said, reading the concern etched on Forrest's face.

"Can't blame him," he said. "I'll see you in a few."

Jayson stood in the kitchen and helped himself to green tea in the cabinet while two of his boyhood friends—now bodyguards and enforcers—Elijah Freeman and Darrell Alonso sat at the kitchen table. Darrell browsed his smartphone and Elijah stared intently into the living room where the HD television set played live news of the unrest unfolding downtown and elsewhere across the city.

Elijah and Darrell stood as Forrest walked in the front door. The three greeted and hugged when he entered the kitchen. He took a seat at the tiny kitchen table and the rest followed, filling each of the four kitchen chairs.

"Glad you two are safe, Fave," said Jayson, nodding to the back door, "with all that's going on."

Fave grunted, and Jayson studied him. His uncle's head was low-ered in thought, his eyes squinted. Jayson remembered when his uncle was a gold-toothed beast with a big smile that was more crazy than genuine, and bouncy energy. Jayson feared his uncle when he was a little kid, and he was protective of his younger cousins Raymond and Charles. They seemed oblivious to their father's reputation as dangerously unpredictable. But when they were killed as teenagers, Raymond in a drive-by shooting, and Charles shot dead in a sepa-rate incident, each within a few months of each other, Jayson saw a total transformation in his uncle. He went from that larger-than-life, brooding-eyed and edgy hustler with a streak of paranoia to the quiet, slightly stooped, soulful man he was today.

Fave straightened. "I'd like us to keep a low profile," he said. The others listened intently as Fave paused and deliberated the words for his thoughts. "This," he said with a nod to the TV set in the other room, "will pass." He paused yet again, still thinking.

"In previous…unrest—Baltimore, Ferguson, Los Angeles—a lot of that stuff was picked up on camera. Shit," he scoffed, "idiots even filmed themselves, putting it on the internet. It's all fine and good in the moment, but when it passes—and it always does—the police, the feds, they've got all the time in the world to review all that shit. They rolled up a lot of that business consequently."

The younger men nodded and grunted.

"I want our boys off the street," Fave said with authority, "let the Gees do whatever the fuck they'll do, 'cause you know they'll cock up things epic, bring the muthafucking UN down on their shit."

Elijah and Darrell snickered.

"Catch my drift?" asked Fave. He stooped his head and squinted his eyes again, and Jayson felt a palpable and familiar sense of pri-mordial danger somehow emanate from his uncle. Elijah and Darrell even drew back a little. Jayson smiled. Uncle's still got it, he thought.

Elijah and Darrell nodded with severity etched on their faces. "Get the word out," ordered Fave. "Pronto."

Elijah and Darrell departed, giving Jayson a hug on their way out.

And then all hell broke loose.

* * *

The pop pop pop of gunfire was unmistakable. Jayson had just leaned on the kitchen counter and eyed his uncle, who leapt to his feet and pushed past him. Jayson was startled by Fave's sudden movement, and it was only when he was chasing after him that he registered the sound of gunfire.

They ran through the living room as bullets tore through the windows, shattering a lamp and destroying a picture on the wall, knocking it to the floor. Small bullet holes appeared in the front door as wood splintered inward, then a bullet came through the window on the left of the door, striking the wall and ricocheting.

Fave and Jayson dashed through the front door. Darrell lay in the middle of the walkway in front of the house, gurgling and gasping for air, his hands wrapped around his throat. Elijah was kneeling beside him, his hands also pressed against Darrell's throat in an effort to stop blood that spurted between his fingers.

A low-riding blue Honda squealed away, with a young man sitting up on the passenger door frame, still firing a pistol. The car was quickly gone, but Jayson had his pistol out and fired multiple shots in its general direction, and scanned the street for any other threats.

Then he heard the screaming.

Viola…

Greta and Viola were lying on the ground by the bushes in front of the house, Greta on top of Viola, who scrambled out from beneath her, screaming for her children.

JJ and Tino…

The toddlers, running on the front lawn, stopped wide-eyed. Both started crying at the sudden commotion.

Viola and Jayson whisked each into their arms and checked them anxiously for injuries. But the bullets had all gone high, aimed at the house, and the boys didn't have a scratch.

Viola squeezed Tino and burst into tears.

Fave was on his knees alongside Greta, an arm draped over her shoulders. "Baby, are you hurt?" he asked repeatedly, but Greta didn't answer right away. She was in shock and didn't know if she'd been hit.

"Viola and the babies!" she screamed after a moment, scrambling to get up.

"Baby, they're fine, they're fine!" soothed Fave, pressing his hands against Greta's body, looking for a wound. There were none.

"Are you okay, Baby?" Fave asked again.

"Oh, Fave!" exclaimed Greta, and buried her face in his chest.

"Shhh, it's okay," soothed Fave. "It's okay."

"We gotta get him to a hospital!" shouted Elijah. He hovered over Darrell, his hands pressed against the wounded man's neck.

* * *

Aaron Jones and his friends Xavier and Devin practiced skateboarding in an open parking lot behind a long-ago abandoned garage and storefront on Warren Avenue, and across McGraw Street from the once-famous and now itself long-abandoned Kronk Gymnasium where several world champion boxers had trained, including Milton McCrory, Thomas "The Hitman" Hearns, Mark Breland, and Oba Carr, among others. The boys did jumps and ollies on their skateboards but also kept an eye out as Nathan Brody and Dwayne Evans, both older teens at sixteen, worked in front of what remained of an abandoned garage and storefront a block from the intersection where McGraw crossed over Warren in an "X" intersection.

The garage was Nathan's normal spot while Dwayne stood between the twin stone columns at the entrance of an abandoned bank the next block over. Typically, a car would slow down in front of the bank and Dwayne would take the money; the car would proceed to the boarded-up garage and Nathan would hand off the tiny bags. The transactions were done so gracefully and nonchalantly that customers in their cars barely had to slow down. And, if one wasn't paying close attention, the whole thing was practically unseen.

Kids acted as lookouts for police or any other sign of trouble and would alert Nathan and Dwayne with whistles and hand signals.

Groups of people stood all along McGraw Street, especially at the 'X' intersection. Whenever a car came down the street, the crowds jeered and pummeled it with rocks and bottles. They left Nathan and Dwayne to their work—they were armed, after all, and you didn't want to mess with them. With the unrest, there was little business to be had by car, but there were no police around and the streets pulsated with hundreds of people. They could do business right in the open, and customers lined up on foot.

The boys had to be sharp, however, even sharper than normal. A skinny man tried to sneak up on Nathan and steal a bag, but Dwayne saw him. The skinny dude didn't see Dwayne, who sprinted up behind him and pistol-whipped him in the back of the head just as he tried to snag a bag from Nathan's hand.

The man went straight down, face first, stiffened, and rolled onto his back, his arms outstretched and his eyes rolling up in his head, blood pouring from the back of it. He was knocked out cold. No matter; Dwayne and Nathan punched and kicked the prone man, then turned on another guy who got too close, watching. He stumbled away after absorbing several lightning punches to the face and head, only to be set upon by a group of teenagers who knocked him to the ground and kicked him repeatedly while laughing maniacally. When their attention turned to an approaching car, the man staggered to his feet and stumbled away.

The approaching car came slowly, blowing its horn. Teenagers sat on the passenger door frames, holding handguns aloft in one hand, and flashing a "V" for victory with their other hand. Many in the crowd hooted and jumped up and down, also holding their hands up in "V" signs. A bunch of happy Nixons.

The boys gawked at the car as the crowd parted before it, some children running alongside giving high-fives to the teenagers.

Xavier recognized one of the young men and whistled, but Nathan and Dwayne couldn't hear him amid the crowds.

"Yo, Nathan!" Xavier yelled.

Then Aaron and Devin saw it, too. These were River Gees.

Nathan looked over and saw the three boys waving their arms frantically and pointing. Nathan looked back to the car and made eye contact with the driver. Recognition filled both their eyes, and the car leaped forward toward him, clipping two guys in the street, sending them flying end over end like bowling pins.

Nathan turned and ran. "Run, Dwayne, run!" he yelled as he ran.

But it was too late.

The car stopped and six River Gees scrambled out and took chase, firing their handguns.

The crowds scattered for cover.

Dwayne cartwheeled backward as several bullets slammed into him, knocking him to the ground, his momentum sending his body head over heels in an awkward roll, his body flopping face down in a clump of weeds.

"Dwa-!" shouted Nathan, but a bullet slammed him in the middle of his back, clipping him in full stride and sending him tumbling forward, his body limp before he hit the ground. He rolled limply like a ragdoll, landing face up.

The six River Gees caught up to him and started stomping and kicking him. But Nathan was dead. His eyes and mouth hung open, revealing silver braces on his teeth, his head lolling limply with each kick.

"This is our street now!" yelled the driver, shooting his pistol into the air.

His name was Dmitri Johnson. The other boys followed suit, shooting their pistols in the air.

Aaron, Xavier, and Devin fled when the gunfire started. They abandoned their boards and headed straight for the abandoned Kronk Gym. Each expected bullets to tear into their backs, but Aaron stole a look behind him and saw Nathan go down. He fell on the cracked concrete lot adjacent to the boarded-up garage and store, and the River Gees pummeled him with kicks.

Aaron stopped and began walking backward, his eyes glued on Nathan. He could see that Nathan didn't move anymore and that the Gees now shot their guns into the air.

That could only mean one thing, that Nathan and Dwayne were dead.

One of the Gees looked his way. Aaron turned and ran for his life.

CHAPTER 10

Much of the crowd on Warren Avenue that scattered when the River Gees opened fire on Nathan and Dwayne ran east a couple of blocks and descended on Interstate 94. Drivers slowed as dozens of people appeared on the side of the highway, and traffic very quickly came to a standstill. Someone shouted "Stop the Traffic," and an impromptu protest began. Pedestrians marched through the stopped traffic and repeated the chant, "Stop the Traffic." The Channel 13 news helicopter, SkyHawk 13, passed overhead and broadcast the unrest below live.

"Protestors have entered Interstate 94," said reporter Ernie Brown. "By golly, that's dangerous," he said as oncoming cars braked hard to avoid crashing into stopped traffic and to avoid hitting the groups of pedestrians gathering along the side of highway. One car swerved into another lane to avoid crashing into the back of a stopped car and nearly ran over a protester.

Traffic soon came to a complete standstill all along I-94. Young people walked and ran between the lanes, slapping their hands on the hoods and roofs of the cars and menacing their occupants.

One driver panicked and tried to maneuver through the crowd, nudging several protesters and knocking three of them to the ground. Someone smashed a brick or rock through the car's driver side window and the car lurched forward. The three protesters were upended, their bodies tossed into the air like rag dolls, before the car stopped.

The driver and a passenger were pulled from the car, which then drifted driverless into more protesters.

"Oh, no," said Ernie as the cameraman continued to film live, "Oh, geez; I think we just witnessed some people getting killed…oh, no, several… protesters are down, run over. Oh, man, the crowd is beating someone, a couple of people…"

More cars tried to pass but there was nowhere for them to go; movement of cars drew the ire of angry protesters. Rocks, bottles, and debris rained down from scores of people lined up on an overpass onto the stopped traffic below.

Ernie was silent now as several drivers got of their cars and fought with protesters. Others abandoned their cars outright and ran back along the backed-up traffic.

One driver pulled out a pistol and opened fire on the violent crowd as they surrounded him. People scattered and dove to the ground.

"My God," said Ernie, "there are no words." He was silent again as the helicopter continued to circle above the catastrophic situation, still broadcasting live.

Protesters on the Livernois Avenue overpass also rained rocks and bottles down on the halted vehicles below, and many descended onto the highway to join the melee. Cars left abandoned were attacked, their windows and windshields smashed, their doors ripped off their frames. Multiple cars and a tractor trailer were set ablaze. Other news helicopters joined SkyHawk 13 to film the chaos from above.

Across town, mobs descended on the M-10 freeway as well, near Calvert Avenue, and traffic was forced to stop there, too, as protestors ran out onto the highway. Like on I-94, several drivers and passengers were dragged from their cars and beaten. Likewise, others abandoned their vehicles and fled on foot as mobs preyed upon the stopped traffic.

WLKE TV Channel 45's helicopter, Copter Lake 45, was covering a large and often violent crowd gathered in the streets at the intersection of Grand River Avenue and Oakman Boulevard when they learned of the M-10 freeway violence from their police scanner. They circled over the intersection one last time, then banked east toward the M-10. A sound of metallic *tings* filled the cockpit. News reporter Darrell Williams and the pilot exchanged looks but, before either of them could react, the copter's engine sputtered and the controls stiffened in the pilot's hands. Various alarms on the pilot's console went off at once.

"Hang on, buddy," said the pilot. The helicopter jerked hard to the right and dropped more than one hundred feet. "Mayday, we're going in," the pilot reported in an impossibly calm voice. The helicopter spiraled sharply to the right and lost more altitude, leaving a looping trail of smoke in its wake. The engine shut down with an ear-piercing whine.

Copter Lake 45 landed hard in the residential intersection of Webb and Holmur Streets, a usually quiet street where hardly any occupied homes remained, and overgrown vegetation had reclaimed empty lots in what was once a thriving and centrally located neighborhood. The helicopter slammed hard into an open lot at the corner of the intersection, breaking its pilot-side landing skid and tipping over. Its blades smashed into the grass and dirt and exploded into shrapnel. The tail snapped in half and the tail rotor churned up more dirt and grass before it, too, broke into pieces.

The helicopter body came to rest on its side.

* * *

The pilot of Detroit News Channel 10's helicopter "City 10" heard the calm "mayday" of Copter Lake 45's pilot and emphatically pointed out the disabled helicopter in the distance to his camera man, who trained his lens on the chopper. The videographer captured the chopper as it spun out of control and crash-landed in the residential neighborhood.

"Oh, dear God," shouted City 10 reporter Luis Sanchez, "Copter

45 just went down east of Grand River! Repeat: Copter 45 has just gone down and we are over the crash site!"

The City 10 crew watched helplessly. "We're going to stay on site until help arrives for Copter 45, which may have been shot down," Luis said in a rapid and excited voice. "Jesus, they just shot down a helicopter! Unbelievable!"

Various people headed for the downed helicopter as two people climbed out of the wreckage. A red pickup truck with men in the bed wielding rifles and shotguns came onto the scene. The Copter 45 crew climbed into the truck bed and waved an okay at the helicopter circling above.

The truck slowly pulled away. The City 10 helicopter circled above and filmed the truck's movement for nearly twenty minutes through residential streets. Luis remained silent throughout. Only when the truck pulled into Henry Ford Hospital did he breathe an audible sigh of relief, then commended the armed citizens below for aiding the crew of Copter Lake 45.

* * *

The Grand River Gs, or Gees—the G stood for "gangstas"—transected the neighborhoods of Northwest Goldberg to the south and Petosky-Otsego to the north of Grand River Boulevard.

With a rate of one hundred fifty-five violent crimes per one hundred thousand people, the neighborhoods were two of the most violent in the entire United States. The unemployment rate was nearly twenty-five percent, and as much as sixty-five percent of the population—which numbered just over ten thousand combined—weren't even counted as being in the labor force.

The area was once the territory of BMF, the Black Mafia Family, headed by the Flenory Brothers, Demetrius ("Big Meech") and Terry ("Southwest T"). They had built a drug empire that stretched all the way to California and to the Deep South. The brothers even relocated to Los Angeles and Atlanta respectively to oversee their network's operations and growth.

The whole thing came crashing down in 2007 with the brothers' arrest and conviction for multiple murders, racketeering, and a slew of drug trafficking charges. They were both sent to prison for life. Their entire organization, in Detroit and elsewhere, descended into civil war as different factions sought to inherit the kingdom, so to speak.

In Detroit, the Flenory Brothers' veteran lieutenants were divided. Each sought to consolidate his own power to the detriment of the others, and the civil war that ensued reduced their number in short order. The last of the lieutenants would be done in by the kids coming up.

It was kids, literally, that eventually took over the former territory of the BMF in Detroit. They were mostly teenagers, and some "enforcers" were as young as twelve. The kids were brutal and disorganized in their various efforts to seize control. They were quick to kill, and they totally disregarded any sense of tradition and norms such as existed among drug gangs. And they quickly descended into all-out war among themselves.

This was the opening that allowed an older and more disciplined organization like the Avery Organization—and the multiple military veterans they employed—to grow their territory at the expense of the old BMF areas.

The Avery Organization grew to encompass much of the West Side, west of Interstate 96. In turn, the Northwest Goldberg and Petosky-Otsego areas to the east of I-96 was consolidated by two murderous and depraved young men, Caleb Sessions and his drug-crazed boyhood friend Dmitri Johnson, who lorded over a vicious young gang that called themselves the Grand River Gees.

Caleb was the more studious of the two, if you could say that, and thought it a good idea to attack on all fronts while the police were not a factor. The "old guys," the Avery Organization that flanked their west on the other side of I-96, offered the best opportunity for expansion, Caleb and his gang surmised.

They went all out. What Caleb, being the more strategic actor amid the factions of the former BMF, didn't account for—and perhaps he should have—was the likelihood of his managing partner, the enforcer, getting swept up in the moment.

Dmitri and his crew attacked and annexed the first major intersection west of I-96, killing the Avery Organization's two dealers. In their euphoria, they followed the irate crowd, sliding down the grassy slope from the neighborhood and right onto I-96. Thus, a whole contingent of riled-up young men and women high on adrenaline (and, quite possibly, crystal meth), swarmed the road, unmindful to the dangers of walking out onto a high-speed interstate. When the cars stopped, there were mostly white suburbanites in them. They looked fearful, and some appeared indignantly angry, blowing their horns and snarling at the young protestors.

Snarling at Dmitri and his crew? You didn't get away with that.

Dmitri's crew pried open the door of a stopped Ford Fiesta, pushing and bending it beyond its frame until it nearly came off. Dmitri reached into the car.

"Get the fuck out, nigga!" Logan, one of Dmitri's gang, yelled as a panicked white man, soft and slick with sweat, desperately fended off Dmitri's punches and grabs.

The guy wasn't coming out of his seat as Dmitri and the others yanked and pummeled until someone had the sense to release the seatbelt. And then he came out with unexpected ease, trying to cover his head to protect it from the punches. But the gang's attention turned to the car itself, and three members of the crew got lodged in the open door frame as they all tried to scratch and claw their way at the same time into the now-vacated front seat.

Dmitri turned his attention to the white man, who tried pulling away, all the while whimpering and crying. It was the glasses and the button-down collared shirt. It was the khaki pants and paunchy belly. It was the slickness of the sweaty, milky-white fatty double chin, the parted hair, the boyish thirty something smugness. Most of all, perhaps, it was the fear in the young man's eyes that revolted Dmitri and fed an empowering sensation of pure rage. The frantic fervor of fighting and feeling and heavy breathing slinked into a droning din on both sides of his head like snug-fitting earphones as bloodlust coursed through him.

A silence of mind came over Dmitri; he was an automaton, a Dmitri bot, a warrior in battle, and he picked up a full brick among several that had rained down among the stopped cars. Most of them had broken into bits, but not this one; this one was fully intact and weighty in his grip. It fit his hand perfectly and, as he raised it up, the white man ducked, blindly waving his arms out to block what was coming.

Dmitri brought the brick down and, just before it struck home, the white man turned his head as if what was coming didn't come as expected, and that maybe it wouldn't, but it did, and his turned head was of the same length and width as the brick, which connected solidly with the side of his face.

Dmitri felt the brick in his hand make contact with something hard that quickly splintered into a million tiny cracks, then continued on into a mushy interior as his follow-through carried his weight forward and over the slumping mass of the white man.

"Whoa!" Dmitri bellowed in a high-pitched roar as he recovered his balance. The white man awkwardly tumbled onto the road and splayed out in the middle of the highway.

"Ye-eah, boyee!" Dmitri shouted again. He pumped his chest and raised the bloody remnants of the brick over his head. "Look at that!" he yelled as he walked menacingly around the white man's prone body, sliding through a pool of blood growing beneath the young man's head.

A helicopter circled above.

"Check that shit!" Dmitri shouted again, tossing the bloody brick pieces onto the motionless man's body. Then he jerked his arms over his head and held two middle fingers high in the air, taunting the helicopter.

Logan took a step back from the car and looked over at Dmitri. Despite the fervor of the crowd cursing and laughing and taunting drivers and passengers, amid the yelling, the breaking of glass, and the helicopters, the sickening sound of the brick striking home cut right through all of that. That sound, and what he saw—Dmitri prancing around the dead man, taunting anyone and everyone—Logan just couldn't get that out of his head.

* * *

It had been a long day for everyone. For the protestors, for everyday people, for victims caught up in the riots, for the police, for firefighters, for school teachers and administrators, for business owners, for the mayor and cabinet officials, and for news reporters.

Like Ernie Brown.

Ernie's normal daily shift began at 2:00 in the afternoon. Between that time, he and his crew had to prepare and film the usual nightly news coverage to be aired at 6:00, 10:00, and 11:00. So it was for most "normal" days. But the past two days were not that—not at all normal.

As the protests grew bigger by the hour as the day wore on, the station's three other younger reporters set up at different locations to record stock video, then live broadcasts, of masses of protestors marching or driving to downtown. Ernie took to the sky at 3:00 to provide more comprehensive coverage from above. SkyHawk 13 allowed the news channel to cover more ground and report from areas their on-the-ground correspondents could not get to, or where it wasn't safe for them.

It was the same for other local news channels.

The sun was setting, and Ernie checked his phone for the time. It was a few minutes after six p.m. He had been in the air for three hours straight, save for a brief refueling stop back at the station. *Only three hours*, Ernie thought. *Unbelievable.* It had seemed like an eternity.

And it was entirely surreal. From his mobile perch in the sky, Ernie watched as protestors fled from police lines and riot control vehicles in the downtown, massed on Jefferson Avenue between the Renaissance Center, the Coleman A. Young Municipal Building, and the Cobo Convention Center. A police fortress centered on the area around DPSH, the GLEE corporate headquarters, and the Grand Arnault Casino.

Police had cleared the four-block financial district between DPSH and the Renaissance Center, and now worked to clear protestors and rioters from the areas around Ford Field and Comerica Stadium. Interstate 75 separated the relatively new Pistons Arena from the two stadiums on the downtown side of the freeway, but the Woodward Avenue bridge linking Pistons Arena with the other two stadium complexes was a bridge too far. Police parked a riot control vehicle right on the bridge, and its wall-like extensions on either side encompassed the width of the bridge and prevented protestors from crossing back into downtown.

But the Pistons Arena was outside the consolidated police zone and was, from Ernie's perspective, geographically indefensible unless police were to give up ground elsewhere in the downtown.

The police apparently had the same idea. The arena was being systematically looted as police stood their ground on the other side of the freeway and watched.

And, while police seemed to be effectively dug into the roughly one square mile Central Business District between I-75 and the Detroit River, the rest of the 140-plus square miles—and beyond—of the sprawling metropolis appeared to have erupted in flames.

Plumes of black smoke rose in sporadic spots across the landscape, and their number seemed to have doubled, then doubled again, and then again, randomly appearing as thin grayish wisps before thickening and darkening. There were maybe fifty plumes, some more vigorous than others, and still they seemed to grow in numbers, with columns stretching nearly to the western horizon, itself alit with the fading blaze of the setting sun, which just moments before had settled beneath the horizon and disappeared.

Daylight was flickering out.

SkyHawk 13 headed back to the station nearly twenty miles to the west at Farmington Hills for another round of refueling. As the ground passed beneath them, Ernie noted countless glowing orange pyres—from his height, they appeared as the burning ends of cigarettes—flaring brighter than the dull hue of city street lights, pockmarking the darkening land below.

It was going to be a long night.

CHAPTER 11

A t the Channel 13 news studio in Southfield, Ernie's live report from Skyhawk 13 had given way to live feeds from reporters on the ground spliced with stock footage recorded throughout the day. An exhausted Josh Fink, the young Wayne State intern, stood just out of the news desk's camera shot.

Reporter Wally Mickiewicz, host of the daily morning news program *'Morning, Motown!*, was currently on duty. It was all hands on deck for the news station. "What do you have?" he asked Josh curtly. He kept an eye on the director, who indicated ten seconds before going live from the desk.

Josh handed his note to Wally, who quickly scanned it. "What is that? An 's'?"

Before Josh could answer, Wally was speaking to the camera. "Thank you for that report, Austin. Stay safe out there."

"Meanwhile," Wally continued, "our staff here at News 13 has been monitoring police scanners and reports all day long, and our young intern Josh Fink has counted more than five hundred separate reports of fires coming across the air. We cannot confirm that as yet, of course, but that number certainly falls in line with what we've been reporting all day long. The Detroit Fire Department is working extremely hard today. It's all hands on deck for the Fire Department, Josh reports—and for us, too, I might add," Wally said with a chuckle, "and it's shaping up to be a long night for everyone.

"While reports of looting have come in," Wally continued, "particularly along Grand River Avenue, many if not most of the fires appear to be abandoned homes and structures, as Ernie Banks in Skyhawk 13 has reported. Of course, there are no shortages of abandoned buildings in Detroit. The city has lost nearly two-thirds of its population since its peak of almost two million in the 1950s. With the loss of more than a million and a half people in the decades since, more than seventy-five thousand abandoned structures and thirty-five thousand abandoned homes remain around metro Detroit. And, well, that's a lot of kindling."

Turning slightly to face a different camera, Wally changed gears. "We are getting word that unrest has spread beyond metro Detroit and across Michigan. We have colleagues from WFLN in Flint and WAAM in Ann Arbor standing by. Helen in Ann Arbor, are you there? Very good. What can you tell us?"

The "on air" light dimmed as Helen in Ann Arbor gave her report, and Wally waved Josh over.

"Good stuff, Josh. Thanks for getting me those numbers," he said. Wally lowered his head and added, with a grim expression, "Now, I need for you to do something *really* important."

Josh stepped up expectantly, ready to be a soldier.

Wally pulled out his wallet, withdrew a ten-dollar bill, and held it out for Josh to take. "Coffee run," he said, his face softening into something of a smile.

* * *

Alex and his fellow young executives at Apex Superior Bank had made it to the 72nd floor of the RenCen and entered the Top Hat Bar & Grille. They found it overflowing and uproarious despite the relatively early hour. They ordered beers and chatted about the GLEE shutoffs, the possibility of riots, off-season trades by the Detroit

Tigers, a co-worker's new Harley sportster, and other banter. From their station atop the RenCen, they watched as the crowds below on Jefferson Avenue grew so thick that there were no open spaces among them; they abutted right up against lines of police decked out in riot gear with helmets, shields, and batons.

A roaring wall of sound, a constant din, wafted up to the Top Hat from the street below. Patrons of the restaurant erupted with a cheer each time the police were able to corral and arrest an animated or physical protester. For executives and revelers, it was like watching a football game.

But things got crazy.

A pitched battle raged beneath them, with tear gas canisters launched into the crowd, which surged forward and scattered in all directions. The din among the executives and partygoers in the Top Hat audibly dipped and a hushed murmur spread through the restaurant. They feared that protestors might break through the police lines and storm the lobby below.

Their fears eased as a sea of helmeted police pushed out from spaces below that were out of their line of sight and, to their relief, practically all of Jefferson Avenue was quickly abandoned by protestors. The police were on the offensive.

While fears of the RenCen being overrun by protestors proved to be unwarranted, a new concern soon emerged: how to get home. As night descended on Detroit, partygoers could see the orange glow of multiple fires at varying distances burn bright like flares against the growing darkness of the night.

And, on the multiple, high-definition flat-screen television sets adorning the walls of the Top Hat, local stations abandoned regularly scheduled programs to cover the unrest live. Helicopter footage—some live, some from earlier in the day—showed crowds swarming onto the freeways, where they attacked drivers and passengers. Vehicles stood at a standstill far into the distance as the helicopter cameras panned out to capture the impact of the protests on interstate traffic. Nearly all of the executives and partygoers at the Top Hat commuted in from the outer suburbs, affluent places like the Grosse Pointes, Orchard Lake, Bloomfield Hills, or communities like New Baltimore on Lake St. Claire, and now their way home appeared to have been closed off by the violence.

On one television, the news channel replayed the downing of Copter Lake 45. On another, a chaotic scene of young protestors with bandanas covering their faces battled with helmeted police, some smashing storefront windows. But this scene wasn't in Detroit; this was the university district in East Lansing, home of Michigan State University, and the protestors were presumably university students. Another cut-in showed riot police lined up in Benton Harbor, a small city in far western Michigan on the shores of Lake Michigan. A ticker below reported that protests, in solidarity with demonstrations in Detroit, had spread to cities throughout Michigan's Lower Peninsula, including Flint, Pontiac, Battle Creek, Grand Rapids, Saginaw, Buena Vista, Freeland, Ypsilanti, and Muskegon and that some of them—like in East Lansing, Ann Arbor, and Flint—had grown violent as the day gave way to night.

* * *

Just off of West Jefferson Avenue in Delray, abutting the industrial zone along the Detroit River immediately south of downtown Detroit, Maria Aznar—a 28-year-old, part-time nurse assistant at a downtown nursing home—lay wide awake in her bedroom. Her five-year-old son Miguel Joaquin, "MJ," and her seven-year-old daughter Isabella, lay beside her, also wide awake and snuggled tightly with Maria. All three stared wide-eyed at the ceiling; Maria hummed softly while stroking MJ's hair with her right hand, her left arm wrapped around Isabella. Antonio, a six-month-old infant, lay momentarily asleep in his crib next to the bed. Outside, it was like the Fourth of July, except it wasn't fireworks they were hearing. It was mostly gunfire, people shooting guns into the air or... Maria didn't want to contemplate what else they could be shooting at.

"I smell smoke," whispered MJ, his eyes as big as saucers.

"Me, too," added Isabella. Maria took a moment, sniffing, wondering if she, too, smelled smoke and, thinking that maybe she did, wondered if it could be from the hundreds of fires burning in the night as the news had reported.

Maria got out of bed and walked into the narrow hallway. She saw that the apartment was definitely smoky. She spotted a vent on the wall near the ceiling in the living room from which heavy smoke poured in.

"MJ, Maria, grab some clothes!" she commanded, and rushed back to her bedroom. "We've got to go!" she said as she scooped up Antonio, who now cried loudly.

Maria grabbed MJ with one hand as she carried Antonio in the other, and headed for the door. "Isabella, come! Let's go!"

Just then, someone started pounding on the front door and repeatedly shouting "Fire!"

"But my clothes, momma!" Isabella whined.

"Forget that! We have to go *now!"*

As they rushed out of the door, Maria saw that a small crowd had gathered outside, mostly residents dressed in night gowns like her and t-shirts despite the frigid temperatures. Heavy smoke poured from the two units at the east end of the row. An orange lick of flame momentarily appeared in the window of the farthest apartment.

Maria loaded her children into her battered 12-year-old Kia Soul. She heard the window of the farthest unit break and looked over. A whoosh of flames vigorously pirouetted out of the window, followed by swatches of burning curtain that drifted out of the apartment and listlessly wafted to the ground like snow. Maria climbed into the driver's seat and drove off down Jefferson Avenue, not looking back.

Maria didn't give any thought to where they were going. It was automatic. Her parents lived nearby on Vernor Highway, just across I-75, and she naturally headed there. She couldn't find her cell phone and decided she had left it at the apartment in her panicked exit. She couldn't call to tell them she was coming.

She followed Jefferson Avenue toward Grand River, but traffic was very heavy and backed up at Fort Street, despite the late hour. Semi-trucks and cars converged on Grand River, and Maria slowly maneuvered into the stop-and-go back up as a trucker allowed her some space and waved her in.

Two lanes of traffic converged into one. Maria's view was blocked by semi-trucks on her left, and she was forced to make a sharp right turn with the traffic. Just a little over thirty minutes had passed before she realized that she was on the entrance ramp to the Ambassador Bridge into Canada. There was no getting off; she couldn't turn around amid the heavy traffic. Eventually, when she reached the middle of the Ambassador Bridge, the stop-and-go traffic came to a complete halt.

Maria and her children sat in the unmoving traffic, with the car's heater blowing at full blast and the fuel gauge in the red.

Maria's gas ran out after more than an hour of sitting in the middle of the Ambassador Bridge over the Detroit River, despite her strategically turning the engine off for as long as her children could stand the cold before turning it on again. She did that repeatedly, but eventually the car would no longer start. She kept the ignition key turned on to keep the heater going, but it didn't take long for the Kia's battery to drain.

Traffic hadn't moved even an inch since they had stopped, and now the sun was setting. People got out of their cars and walked to find some vantage point to see what was going on. It was windy on the bridge, and the river below was frozen solid. With the sun setting, the already cold temperatures would soon plummet further.

Maria had no time to grab coats or blankets when she fled the apartment and, with the gas having run out, her situation was becoming desperate. She popped the trunk and got out of the car to look through it, hoping to find a blanket or towel. She found an extra baby blanket in the trunk in addition to the one already covering Antonio.

She got back into the car to warm up. She bundled up Antonio and MJ, and commanded Isabella to grab onto her night gown, and together they got out and walked briskly toward Canada with their heads bowed against the frigid wind.

* * *

Matthew Pitt sat in his Willoughby International Trucking rig about two-thirds of the way across the Ambassador Bridge toward Canada, working the radio with fellow truckers stuck on the bridge to learn what was happening.

After nearly a decade of driving his own rig, Matthew had seen it all: horrible car wrecks, police chases, tornadoes, wild fires, you name it. But being stuck in traffic at a border crossing—in limbo on an international border-spanning bridge in below freezing temperatures, no less—because of a riot, was definitely something new.

Movement in his side view mirror caught his eye and he did a double-take. He saw a young woman in nothing more than a night gown and two small children huddled together and struggling against the freezing wind that cut to the bone. *What the hell,* he thought. *What the hell is she thinking?*

Matthew opened his driver side door as they approached. "Get in!" he shouted against the wind. "Get in!" he shouted again as they got closer, and the woman led her small daughter to the truck cab. Matthew reached down and effortlessly lifted her into the cab, then did the same with a small boy. He got out and helped the young woman up as well. He was shocked to see that she was holding a baby wrapped in blankets snugly to her chest.

He shut the door behind her and ran around the front of the truck to the driver side and climbed in. The woman and the two children were shivering uncontrollably, and the baby was ominously silent. Without words, Matthew lifted both the boy and the girl into the sleeper behind the front seats and wrapped two blankets around them both.

He checked on the baby, who looked up at him with large and curious bright brown eyes. The baby smiled and looked away, its eyes diverting to a dangling cross hanging from the rearview mirror. The baby was actually warm and seemed just fine. "Let me," he said softly as he took the blanket-wrapped baby from the young woman and placed it softly on the bed next to the two children, who stared out from the blankets at him with large eyes as they shivered.

"Oh, my God, thank you so much," said the young woman, her teeth chattering as she furiously rubbed her hands together to produce warmth. Matthew placed his hands over hers to help them warm up faster, and he couldn't believe how cold to the touch her hands were.

"Are you okay?" he asked. "Is anyone else with you?"

She shook her head no.

CHAPTER 12
DAY 3

News and footage of the unrest in Detroit, including the downing of the news helicopter and some of the most harrowing incidents, spread rapidly across the country and the world. Much of it was broadcast live through CNN, Fox News, and other national and international television outlets, and online media as well. The magnitude of the unrest in Detroit and the speed with which it happened was quite shocking. The largest riots and civil unrest in the USA since the Rodney King verdict in 1992 were clearly underway and spreading.

Amid the reports of violence and increasing chaos, Mayor André Murray held another hastily organized press conference in the early evening, along with various community and neighborhood leaders to plead for calm among the city's residents. The mayor and other leaders offered assurances that investigations into the Bernadette Price fire and GLEE's shutoff policies would ensue.

The mayor announced a city-wide curfew from dusk to dawn, and requested activation of the Michigan National Guard. After the mayor concluded his press conference, Governor Clifford Krueger held a press conference of his own eighty-two miles to the northwest in Lansing and announced the activation and deployment of the National Guard to both Detroit and Flint.

On the *Motown Mirror* website, and from there spreading to multiple social media and alternative news sites, was a series of filmed on-the-ground reports by Bernice Hamandawana and her cameraman, Daniel Rush. Bernice and Daniel's reports (and others, representing various other alternative news sites) showcased a disproportional police response to a few belligerent demonstrators, with police launching a full-scale frontal attack on mostly peaceful demonstrators at the first hint of aggression.

The panicked stampede that ensued, the fear on people's faces, the utter chaos as police advanced—helmeted, shielded, and swinging batons with total abandon, striking flesh and producing cringe-worthy *thwacks* that sounded like breaking bones, and the horrors of pepper spray and tear gas—was riveting footage. No other footage, neither from helicopters nor drones, had captured the on-the-scene thrill of people from all walks of life protesting together in one moment, singing songs and standing peaceably for justice, and then sheer terror in the next. It was reportage from the perspective of the protestors—whole families, generations of former students of Mrs. Bernadette Price, young activists, and more—and not the perspective of removed officialdom; it was not the spin of the mayor, the police chief, or corporate media. The videos and reports were raw and potent. Each would go viral within minutes of *Motown Mirror* and others posting them on their websites.

Included among the filmed reports for *Motown Mirror* was Bernice and Daniel's brief encounter with the playfully charismatic artist, LeRon Gordon, "The People's Mayor." His catchy turns of a phrase would inspire multiple online video memes, turning his words and rhymes into songs replete with beats and instrumentation. "The People's Mayor" would, overnight (literally), become a minor celebrity. It wasn't just his rhymes that endeared him to his new fans. His words and delivery presented a witty intellect; he pulled no punches.

"Why are you called 'The People's Mayor'?" Bernice asked.

"Because I'm a gainsayer, a truth sayer," he answered with his toothy grin, then launched into an on-the-spot rhyme (on the dime, in real time, no less):

The mayor's a player
Rhapsodizes the rich
A betrayer
Me, I'm a slayer
No sales pitch
I'm a bricklayer, a taxpayer
I'm the Real Mayor, the People's Mayor

* * *

Major Bradley Davis, commander of Alpha Company, 1st Battalion, 125th Infantry Regiment, U.S. Army National Guard, and an executive at the Detroit-based payday loan company Cash-in-a-Flash (which charged annual interest rates of approximately 500%, on average), left his home in Grosse Pointe Shores early for the twenty-minute drive to the Detroit Olympia Armory. He had watched the governor's announcement that he was mobilizing the Michigan Army National Guard and, though he had yet to receive official notice, he had ordered his 150-man company to report by 6:00 a.m. As the commander of Alpha Company, he wanted to be there at least an hour earlier than his men, so it was 4:30 a.m. and still dark when he climbed into his Mercedes G550 SUV.

He *still* hadn't received official word that the National Guard was being mobilized, even though more than eight hours had passed since the governor's announcement (bureaucracy, he mused), but Bradley had taken the initiative and ordered his men to report first thing in the morning. Alpha Company, 1st Battalion, 125th Infantry Regiment, was the designated Michigan Rapid Reaction Force that was slated to deploy within seventy-two hours anywhere in the state once activated. Olympia Armory, west of downtown Detroit, was the regiment's home base and rally point.

Normally Bradley would take Interstate 94 right to the armory at the junction of I-94 and I-96. But the news from the night before reported that I-94 was closed because of the previous day's unrest, with many cars set on fire and abandoned. So Bradley took Lake Shore Drive that paralleled the shore of Lake St. Claire and became Jefferson Avenue at the Grosse Pointe line.

Before he even crossed into Detroit at Alter Road, it was like entering a war zone. Hundreds of police from the various Grosse Pointes' police departments, and also police from Warren, Troy, and other towns to the north, and sheriffs' deputies from Oakland and Macomb Counties, were lined up all along the city-county line and decked out in full riot gear. All traffic into Detroit was blocked.

Despite Brad being dressed in army fatigues, the police at first refused him entry into the city. After he presented his credentials, he was allowed to proceed, but only after sitting through a stern warning that he was completely on his own from that point forward.

He crossed the border at Alter Road that, on any given day—because of the many empty lots, abandoned and deteriorating homes, boarded-up, run-down, and burnt-out buildings—resembled a war zone. But now, several buildings were either smoldering or burning outright, with no fire trucks or police in sight. Amid dancing shadows projected by the glow of a burning storefront two blocks ahead, Brad saw the movement of people in the street.

He stopped his SUV at the intersection of Chalmers Avenue. He had obviously been spotted, and he could see shadowy figures running toward him down the middle of the street. He sat there and watched them come, somehow not afraid—the calm and comfortable interior of his Mercedes provided a false sense of impregnable security.

The first rain of rocks that bounced off his hood, windshield, and roof snapped him out of a relaxed lull. An angry, sneering crowd was suddenly upon him even as he had watched them come at him from a distance.

Bradley threw the SUV into reverse and gunned it. Other shadowy figures, half a dozen maybe, emerged from the side streets around him that he didn't see until now. He clipped one, then a second, then a third—nameless, faceless, even shapeless. He never actually saw them, just felt the impact on his vehicle as he backed into Marlborough Street. He threw the SUV into drive and floored it, leaving a trail of smoke behind, but not before a thrown rock shattered the rear window.

Brad's heart raced as he crossed back into Grosse Pointe Park and behind the lines of police. He wondered if he had just hurt somebody, or worse. Then he wondered how in the hell he was going to make it to the armory.

* * *

The previous day was hell for Jayson Avery and his family. He still couldn't believe that Darrell was gone. They had grown up together, and now he was dead.

Fave's house was now a fortress. Jayson, Darrell, and Elijah's crews were all camped out, with cots and sleeping bags laid out on nearly every uncovered surface on the first floor.

Even Pops himself came over. It was war.

Young men came and went all night. The attack on Fave's house was just one among several. They counted ten separate attacks in total as the Grand River Gees targeted multiple corners run by the Avery Organization, and even some of their lieutenants' homes. Jayson's house a few blocks over was shot up in a drive-by as well, though he and his family were at Fave's.

Two of their dealers were dead, along with a lookout—just kids. The dealers were teenagers, both sixteen. The lookout, attacked at a different corner, was just twelve.

This was total war, and it came out of the blue.

Pops, Fave, and Jayson took over the kitchen. Pops and Fave sat quietly at the small kitchen table as Jayson made coffee. The news played silently on the kitchen's small flat-screen TV on the counter.

It played the scene of the I-94 murder over and over again, freezing on the young man as he looked up at the helicopter and flipped it a two-handed bird.

More than ten minutes of silence passed as Jayson worked. The only sound in the house was of Jayson scraping mugs, opening the coffee bag, setting up the coffee maker, and others awakening throughout the house.

He poured Pops and Fave a cup of coffee, then one for himself. Taking a chair, he and the other two men silently blew on their coffees and took a sip.

Fave tilted his head, his eyes resting on the kitchen cabinets, but squinting. He was in thought mode.

"These Gees," said Fave, now leaning back and stroking his chin. "They're exploiting this situation expeditiously."

After another moment of silence, Pops added, "Without a fucking doubt."

"We gotta game this shit out," Fave stated after more silence.

Jayson remained silent. Clearly, Fave was going over some deep shit. This is what made Fave so effective, thought Jayson. He was *never* irrational. Even when he was the gold-toothed, crazy-eyed son of a bitch in his youth, he must have been calculating. He certainly was now, and that kind of thing didn't just happen. Jayson focused on Fave's right pointer finger, which lightly tapped on the kitchen table, keeping time to Fave's thoughts.

Fave's finger stopped tapping. His eyes drifted to the small TV, which again froze on the blurry image of the I-94 murderer.

A shadow of a smile crept up his face, his eyes lighting momentarily before growing hard again. "End times," Fave finally spoke.

Fave looked at Jayson and squinted.

"Get your army crew together," Fave ordered. It was the handful of military veterans in Jayson's employ that he referred to. Jayson himself had served in Iraq with the Marine Corps after high school.

"We've got a lot of work to do," Fave said. "In the meantime, you and me," he said to Pops, "got some phone calls to make."

* * *

For the Ayalas, their previous day was no better than the Averys. Not long after reuniting under an overhang at Comerica Park, Detroit Police wearing gas masks marched up Brush Street, tapping their riot shields with their batons.

Arturo, Jackie, and Frederick heard them before they saw them, and then came the tear gas canisters. The family was forced across I-75 to the Detroit Pistons' Arena.

Arturo twice tried to approach police as they advanced to seek their help in finding Martín, but there was no reasoning with police in full riot mode. They aimed shotguns and fired tear gas in his direction on both occasions.

They had stayed at the arena until after sunset, hoping against hope to either find or hear from Martín, or to find a police officer or another first responder to whom they could report that their 14-year-old son was missing. There were none and, after dark, the arena was set upon by rioters all around them. They were forced to continue their trek north along Brush Street and, in some kind of ominous omen, Brush Street ended at the Children's Hospital of Michigan.

Thankfully, their son was not admitted, but the family was stuck there. They spent the night in the family waiting room.

* * *

On the Ambassador Bridge linking the cities of Detroit, USA, and Windsor, Canada, the morning was marked by a beautiful dawning sky of purple, pink, and orange. The situation for Matt, Maria and her children, however, remained desperate. Matt had only a few bottles of water and some bags of chips, and they were mostly gone now. He sure didn't have any milk or baby food. Maria had only one bottle of milk for baby Antonio that she used sparingly, and that was it. Further, the truck's fuel gage was now on empty. Despite the warmth and cozy comfort of the truck cabin, it was clear they could no longer stay.

After discussing the situation, Matt and Maria agreed to brave the brutal cold outside and join the throngs of bundled-up, shivering people trekking across the nearly mile-and-a-half long bridge to the border post on the Windsor side. Matt collected his paperwork, including his international commercial driver's license, bill of lading, passport, and other documents. It was time to go.

When they stepped out of the cabin, the bitter wind cut to the bone. *Holy shit, this is crazy,* thought Matt. But they had no choice. Matt hoisted Isabella in one arm and MJ in the other as Maria carried Antonio, and they huddled together against the dreadfully cold wind and walked as swiftly as they could.

Crosswinds on the bridge were absolutely brutal, sending the wind chill factor plunging to as low as twenty degrees below zero. They didn't have far to go but, if they didn't get inside somewhere quickly, their very lives would be endangered, particularly the kids'.

As they passed vehicle after vehicle, Maria saw that most of them were empty; their occupants had already abandoned them and walked into Canada as Matt and Maria and her children were doing. Some of the empty cars were full of clothes and even furnishings in some cases, and several of these had broken windows and looked as though they had been looted.

It was just over a tenth of a mile before the bridge reached land and the crosswind subsided, but it was the longest tenth of a mile that Matt or Maria had ever walked. The Ambassador Bridge, however, remained elevated for more than another half-mile inland, and they trudged on.

CHAPTER 13

Twenty-year old Brian Worthington learned of the Michigan National Guard call-up through social media. Then he got a text on his smart phone from his company commander. He was excited; it was the first time he had been called to duty. He tried to temper his excitement because he wasn't sure that it was appropriate to be excited about such a thing as quelling a riot, but it shook things up and that was definitely something to be excited about. He called the day manager at the Southtown Crossing Shopping Center Walmart in Southgate to inform him that he wouldn't be able to come in to work the following morning.

He called nineteen-year-old Diego Alvarez, his best friend in Alpha Company. Diego lived about twenty minutes away in Dearborn where he worked with his dad and two brothers as a drywall contractor. The two guardsmen decided to ride together to the Olympia Armory.

After picking up Alvarez, Brian turned onto Michigan Avenue, the most direct route into Detroit from Dearborn, and a road that both were completely familiar with. But Diego had reservations.

"Uh, I don't know…" said Diego, his voice trailing off, "but I think Michigan Avenue might be one of the places hard hit by the riots."

"I heard Grand River," Brian stated, "but I think it was pretty much all over the place, right? Still, how else are we going to get there? And Grand River runs right by the armory."

They came across a Michigan State Police checkpoint blocking the road into Detroit, and traffic was being forced to turn around. As they approached the roadblock, Brian rolled down his window. "We're with the National Guard," he said to the state trooper. The young trooper peered in at them and saw that they were in their grayish combat uniforms. Brian and Diego both held up their military IDs as well. An older state trooper came over and peered in through the passenger's window.

"All right, be careful, guys," said the older trooper, waving them through. "Whatever you do, don't stop."

Brian drove on, and soon the scenery changed into something out of a horror movie. Trash and debris lay scattered all across the street and surrounding lots. They passed a couple of burned-out cars laying on their sides, and several burned buildings were still smoldering. Nearly every single building along Michigan Avenue—garages, convenience stores, barber shops, you name it—were burned or still burning. It was still mostly dark despite the breaking pinkish and dark fiery orange sky to the east, but several still-burning fires lit up the road for them in a dancing, harrowing orange glow. Brian drove slowly as the two took in all the damage. The scale of it was unexpected and truly unbelievable.

Out of nowhere, a rock smashed into the windshield, leaving a large spider-web pattern of cracks. Brian instinctively stomped on the brakes, stopping quickly.

"Drive, man, drive!" urged Diego, and Brian floored the gas pedal.

Another rock smashed through the driver side window and into Brian's left cheek.

"*Oh, fuck!*" yelled Diego as the truck lurched to the right and slammed into the brick façade of a half-burned, boarded-up storefront.

* * *

Matt and his little group finally neared the end of the bridge. The two-lane Ambassador Bridge fanned out into a broad, twenty-three lane-wide Canadian Border Services tollbooth plaza, and every single one of them was besieged by a line of vehicles that just sat there. Amid the sea of vehicles was a sea of humanity; hundreds of people, maybe upward of a thousand or two (Matt couldn't guess how many, but it was a lot), angrily and desperately pressed up against the tollbooth plaza in the front.

The crowd was raucous, hollering and hissing, begging to be let through. On the other side of the tollbooths were throngs of Canadian Border Services Agency officers sporting helmets, shields, batons, and other riot gear, physically blocking passage into Canada. And behind the border officers were City of Windsor Police and Ontario Provincial Police. Several Canadian police and news helicopters circled above.

One of the cars near the center of the fanned-out lanes was enveloped in a raging inferno. Matt looked closer at the burning car. It faced the wrong way and sat at an awkward angle, and it was clear that all the other cars had navigated around it. It was a Canadian Border Services Agency police car.

Matt stopped and gawked. A realization settled over him that left him sputtering. *These people are Americans. Like me. This is what we've been reduced to. When did this happen?* he thought.

He felt MJ go heavy in his right arm. He gently bounced the boy. MJ was falling asleep and snapped to. His eyes were listless.

"You all right, buddy?" Matt asked.

MJ was silent. Matt let MJ down gently to the ground. Maria and then Matt felt his forehead; the child was hot.

"Aww, how do you feel, honey?" asked Maria, deeply concerned.

MJ pouted and a watery tear ran solo down his face.

"Come on," said Matt, swooping MJ back into his arms. "We need to get him out of the cold."

Matt led Maria and her children through a more subdued section of the crowd and to the northeast corner of the lanes where an entrance ramp took drivers from Windsor onto the east-bound lane of the Ambassador Bridge to Detroit.

The on-ramp was also blocked with stuck traffic and several police, but Matt walked as though he knew where he was going. When a Windsor police officer started to approach them, he and Maria ran.

"Hey, hey, *hey!*" shouted the policeman, alerting other police and speaking into a radio to alert still more. But Matt and Maria were able to dart between the cars and, to their surprise, ran smack into another melee, this one of hundreds of local Canadian residents and Windsor University students. They were protesting the police and Border Agency's refusal to allow them to bring food and blankets to the desperate crowds of Americans seeking refuge.

Members of the crowd surged and surrounded the young couple with children and shielded them from police.

"My boy is sick!" begged Maria, and they were led by what Matt would describe as an old hippie couple a few blocks north to the couple's home on tree-lined Askin Avenue, located a block over from Windsor University in downtown Windsor.

* * *

In Washington, D.C., the president and members of her national security team met in the White House Situation Room at 9:00 a.m. Along with the president, others present included the vice president, the secretary of defense, each of the Joint Chiefs of Staff, the national security advisor, the attorney general, and an assortment of support advisors and staff. Also present via video conference were the governor of Michigan, the adjutant general of the Michigan National Guard, the mayor of Detroit, and the mayor of Flint.

Mayor André Murray briefed the president and his team with the latest updates on the situation in the city and was followed by the mayor of Flint. Governor Krueger gave a briefing of his own following the two mayors. He outlined his order to deploy the Michigan National Guard to both Detroit and Flint, and he had also ordered the Michigan State Police to reposition assets from around the state to Detroit and Flint.

Michigan National Guard's designated Rapid Reaction Force was currently being activated, and mustering of its several companies was ongoing, reported Major General John Veazey, the adjutant general of the Michigan National Guard. A full deployment of Alpha Company to Detroit was expected by late afternoon or early evening, and a deployment to Flint was expected during the overnight hours.

At the Pentagon in Washington, military planners ran through various contingencies in the event that the Michigan National Guard and state police proved unable to pacify the city. They determined that the 10th Mountain Division based in Fort Drum, New York, and commanded by Major General Lance McIntyre, was the active duty unit best suited to deploy to Detroit given its relative proximity to Detroit by flight.

With the president's blessing, the division was put on alert.

* * *

It was just after 5:00 p.m. and, while the days were getting longer, it was still early February. Twilight was approaching.

Ian shivered as he sat Indian-style on the floor along with at least one hundred others in a large conference room of the Cobo Convention Center, named after 1950s-era Mayor Albert Cobo. Like Ian, each of them had their hands cuffed behind their backs with plastic zip ties. Tina sat beside Ian, her head buried into his shoulder. His whole body throbbed with a dull pain that sharpened whenever he moved or shifted his weight.

The police were entirely indifferent. Another fifty or so police officers from a variety of law enforcement agencies (most, in fact, were corrections officers), and paramedics, stood watch over the detainees and spoke loudly and incessantly to each other and barked orders to the steady stream of arriving prisoners.

It was a circus.

With Ian and Tina sat 14-year old Martín Ayala. Tina had spotted the boy sitting alone, his back to a sturdy conference room divider. It looked like he had been crying. Only when she and Ian approached did she see the mucus on his jacket and recognize the effects of tear gas. But he had also been crying.

"I'm Tina," she said, sitting beside him, "and this is Ian."

The boy was quiet and apprehensive. Tina told him they were students at Wayne State, and how they had ended up in custody. She asked him how he got here and, after a moment, the boy opened up. He told her and Ian how he had gotten separated from his family and that he had lost his phone. He started crying.

"Nuh, Nuh, Nuh-guy-guy-yen," a fat corrections officer read from a list, his voice booming across the large room. Another officer spotted Ian and walked over, poked his baton into Ian's upper back to lean him forward. "Here he is," said the officer, reading a name tag taped onto Ian's back. He poked Ian a bit harsher. "Answer when your name is called," he ordered.

* * *

Two pickup trucks carrying men armed with semi-automatic rifles in each bed slowly pulled up to the fenced and chained junkyard compound on Southern Avenue. They were greeted by a rusted old sign that read "Jimmy's Garage & Auto Parts" and a phone number on it, and another that read "Jimmy's Towing Service" with the same phone number. The trucks rolled to a stop.

"Want me to blow the horn?" asked Elijah.

"Just wait," said Fave softly.

"You see what I see?" Elijah nodded toward the roof of a building that peeked over the other side of the fence and dead-looking shrubbery. Two men were on the roof, armed with rifles aimed straight at the trucks. Both had long-range sights.

A young man with an AR-15 semi-automatic rifle slung over his shoulder stepped out from behind aluminum siding along the fence and to the chained, wheeled gate.

"Can I help you?" he asked.

"Fave Avery to see Mr. Auletta," said Fave. All of his men remained silent and bored-looking.

The young man looked to somebody else who, apparently, was behind the aluminum siding, waiting. After a couple of minutes, he removed a ring of keys from his pocket, unlocked the gate, and wheeled it partially open, just enough to walk through.

"Just you," said the boy, pointing at Fave.

Fave got out of the truck cab, stepped through the gate, then waited for the kid to close it behind him and lock it.

Fave looked around and counted fifteen armed men, each of whom watched him stoically. One of them, a lit cigarette dangling from his lips, stepped up. "Follow me," he said.

Fave recognized the man as Freddie, Frank's slightly younger brother.

Freddie led Fave to an L-shaped building with four large garage bays and a maintenance office. Junked and smashed cars piled on top of each other filled up the junkyard compound wedged between railroad tracks and a sprawling empty lot that once housed a hubcap factory that had been razed long ago.

Fave was led into the maintenance office. Frank Auletta, a thick-nosed guy with slicked-back hair, 50-something-year-old Italian, sat behind a metal desk spilling over with papers and carbon copies of invoices.

"Hey, if it isn't Flava Fave," he said loudly as he stood up, his delivery reminding Fave of Rodney Dangerfield, but not funny. Come to think of it, Fave never thought Rodney Dangerfield was all that funny, either. Four other men sat at various places in the maintenance office; a couple of them snickered at the not-funny reference. Freddie took up a position against the wall behind Fave.

Frank looked to his brother at the back.

"He's clean," Freddie said.

Frank nodded. He ordered everyone to leave. Everyone stepped out except for Freddie, who stayed leaning against the wall, silently dragging on his cigarette.

Frank sat back down and eyed Fave. "What can we do you for?"

Fave laid out his proposal in detail, then sat with his head tilted and eyes squinted.

Frank looked to his brother standing in the back, lighting up a second cigarette. Freddie took a long drag on the cigarette, held it, then blew smoke in a long exhale as he thought. After a while, he simply nodded.

Rubbing his head, Frank shifted in his seat, now taking a moment himself to think. He leaned back in his chair and eyed Fave. "What's in it for us?" he asked.

"You get the guns…"

"We've got guns," Frank interrupted, but Fave continued, "and that heavy shit. You can move it. That's money in your pocket," Fave said.

Frank and Fave just stared across at each other, each thinking in silence.

"Your boy was a Marine," Frank said, breaking the silence, but still in thought. Fave nodded slowly.

* * *

After seeing to it that their guests were properly fed with a simple but what was to Maria and Matthew an incredible breakfast of eggs, bacon and toast, and Gerber's baby food for Antonio, Maxwell and

Linda Levine sat at the kitchen table sipping coffee with their guests. All three of Maria's children were fast asleep in one of Max and Linda's two extra bedrooms, rooms that had once been their own children's before they had moved out more than a decade before.

Max and Linda were 60-plus-year-old retirees of the University of Windsor. Max had taught Physics at Windsor for more than thirty years, and now he taught part-time, primarily for the enjoyment of it. His wife Linda was a Mathematics professor and college dean before she, too, recently retired.

The two had taken their usual early morning stroll down to Sculpture Park on the city's waterfront across from Detroit and astride the Ambassador Bridge. Multiple helicopters circled over both Detroit and Windsor, and they heard a lot of sirens from police and emergency vehicles as they walked. Detroit had erupted the day before and, from the look and sound of things, it was still ongoing.

It was all so surreal; Linda admitted there was an element of the forbidden to continuing with their daily trek to the riverfront. Amid the acrid smoke drifting across from Detroit and enveloping Windsor, and even with the distant sound of gunfire from across the river, Windsor remained idyllic. To be able to take a stroll to the park on the waterfront across from all that was going on, and to watch with removed fascination; it was morbid fascination is what it was, like looking at a car wreck, Linda mused.

But it wasn't just Maxwell and Linda. Scores of people gathered at the waterfront park at all hours since the unrest across the river had begun, eying in disbelief the heavy plumes of smoke and circling helicopters, and listening to gunfire, sirens, and the constant chop of helicopters above. It was an awful juxtaposition. Detroit burns, and there by the Grace of God goes Windsor.

Smoke could be seen in the distance, which wasn't all that far, given the smoky haze. Linda shielded her eyes, trying to pick out individual smoke columns, and tracing the farthest spirals of smoke to the closest, and her eyes followed them right up to, and then onto, the looming Ambassador Bridge, where the length of the bridge was punctuated by at least three vehicles either smoldering or burning outright.

"Oh, my, it's come right over the bridge, Max," Linda said, looking up at the steel structure. "Are those people?"

Maxwell followed her gaze and saw what looked like a parade of people nearly the entire length of the bridge, all of them bundled up in winter jackets and scarves, their heads bowed to shield against the cold wind, all trudging slowly across the bridge from Detroit, USA, to Windsor, Canada.

Max thought of zombies as he watched the long lines of people shuffling along, framed by the apocalyptic skyline of smoke and chaos behind them. *Like a zombie apocalypse,* he thought momentarily, with a jolt of real fear, before he gathered himself and saw it for what it was.

"Oh, my goodness, they are fleeing Detroit." After a pause, he spoke with incredulity in his voice. "They are *refugees,* Linda, honest-to-goodness refugees. *American* refugees. Whoever would have thought such a thing?"

All of the police activity and sirens on the Windsor side of the border now made sense.

The couple walked back up Askin Avenue right past their own house to Wyandotte Street. Just three blocks to the west on Wyandotte was a secondary Canadian entrance to the Ambassador Bridge northbound to Detroit.

When Max and Linda reached Wyandotte Street, what they saw astounded them. Multiple police officers—some on foot and horseback, even more in riot gear—were attempting to cordon off the Wyandotte Street entrance to the Ambassador Bridge. Even more astounding was that throngs of people were running at the police on both sides of the tenuous police line. People on the bridge side of the line were trying to break through, and several did; when police tried to subdue them, the crowd outside the line surged forth to shield them.

Max and Linda saw a young man with two young children in

his arms and a young woman with a baby in hers being subdued by the police. A minor tug-of-war between the crowd and the police ensued, and Max and Linda found themselves enveloped by the young and energetic crowd. They apparently won, and the young man and woman were right in front of them, being ushered away from the police line.

"My boy is sick!" sobbed the young woman. That's when Linda marched right up to her and the young man—leaving Max wondering what in God's name she was up to—and said, "Come with us." And from there, she and Max escorted the young couple and their children straight to their home.

* * *

At the intersection of Michigan and Livernois Avenues in Detroit, Aaron and Michelle walked among the crowds growing despite the early hour. Schools were closed, and the atmosphere was electric. Aaron bumped fists with friends and neighbors that he and Michelle came across.

"Yo, this is *craayzee,* man," said his friend Devin excitedly as the crowd spontaneously erupted into a chant of *"No power, no peace!"*

A huge fire burned vigorously a few blocks to the west, with a large crowd of protesters bustling around. Aaron and Michelle, with Devin and two other friends Xavier and Reggie, jogged to the fire. As they approached, they could feel the heat as flames leaped high into the sky from two whole rows of old brick storefronts on both sides of the street that were fully engulfed in flames. The thick black smoke darkened the morning sky. The four boys removed their coats, took off their t-shirts despite the cold, and wrapped them around their faces like bandanas to protect against the smoke for breathing before putting their coats back on. Michelle buried her face up to her nose into her coat.

Xavier had just tied his t-shirt in place and was still putting his coat back on when he tripped over something. He agilely caught his fall and looked down, then did a double-take. *What's a mannequin doing in the middle of the street?* But after his eyes momentarily lingered on it, he at once flinched and recoiled.

That ain't no mannequin, he thought. It was the body of a Latino kid. The body was shirtless and pale despite the frigid temperatures, and it was unnaturally still amid the chaos of the flames and people running about. The eyes were open, like a mannequin's, and flames danced in their reflection.

Xavier recoiled again and jumped back. Michelle, seeing the body, screamed and ran back in the direction they had come. She shook her hands and shuffled her feet in a wave of panic. Aaron came and wrapped his arms around her, and she screamed again before burying her face briefly into his chest. *"Oh, my God, Oh, my God,"* she wailed repeatedly.

"It's a soldier," said Reggie. "There's another one over there." He pointed further up the road.

"Soldiers?" asked Aaron. "Man, this shit's for real now," he said, shaking his head.

* * *

Matthew and Maria settled in with their hosts. Linda had made a run to the store for groceries and medicine for Miguel. She monitored the five-year-old deftly with the love of a grandmother, while Max doted on Isabella and Antonio like a grandfather.

As the day progressed, the sounds of police sirens and helicopters only grew louder and more shrill. They half-expected police to pound on the front door or smash through with a battering ram at any time.

While playing with the children, Max paid intermittent attention to the television, which he kept on in the living room. The

Ambassador Bridge Canadian Border Station had turned into a real international refugee crisis with hundreds of people arriving every hour after braving the subfreezing temperatures and crossing the Ambassador Bridge to Canada on foot. Police were out in force all over Windsor and cordoned off the border station from the surrounding neighborhoods. Even the University of Windsor campus was on American-style "lockdown," and the university's Community Police patrolled the neighborhoods abutting the university, situated astride the eastern flank of the elevated Ambassador Bridge before it landed into the border station.

Dozens of Americans were known to have broken through and out into the city, the news reported. Most were easily tracked down and arrested after trying to run through backyards or hiding in bushes.

By late afternoon, the mayor of Windsor had declared a state of emergency and appealed to Ontario's lieutenant governor to deploy the Canadian Forces Reserves to help police the growing crisis unfolding at the Ambassador Bridge. Police and city officials warned Windsor residents to stay indoors and to keep their doors locked; newscasters repeated the call shrilly and often.

The images and reports coming out of Detroit and Windsor were reported globally. The United Nations secretary general weighed in; she called the Canadian prime minister and the U.S. president and demanded that both countries restore order and care for refugees. Seeing the UN secretary general on TV admonishing the U.S. and Canada, and talking about Detroit and Windsor as though they were in some third world war zone, was crazy.

Well, in the case of Detroit, that wasn't far off the mark, was it? thought Max.

* * *

Approximately four miles—as the crow flies—from Maxwell and Linda Levine's house in Windsor, Canada, protesters gathered for a third day at the intersection of Grand River Avenue and West Grand Boulevard in Detroit, and along West Grand Boulevard to the M-10 freeway, including the intersection of West Grand Boulevard and 12th Street, which was ground zero of the 1967 riots. Multiple businesses and parked cars were set on fire, and traffic was pelted with rocks and bottles all along West Grand Boulevard.

Right in the thick of the violent unrest along West Grand Boulevard and Grand River Avenue was the site of the former Detroit Olympia Arena. Parochially known as the "Old Red Barn," the arena was the one-time home of the NBA's Detroit Pistons and the NHL's Detroit Red Wings before it was demolished in 1987. The site was now occupied by the Michigan National Guard's Olympia Armory.

As many as fifteen soldiers worked at the armory full time. They maintained the property and equipment, worked as recruiters, and performed administrative duties for the various commands housed there. Four of the full-time soldiers managed to make it into work when this third, more intense day of unrest began, and each of them had a cracked windshield or other vehicle damage to show for their effort. The armory itself was largely left alone by rioters; most of the crowds gathered at the intersection of Grand River Avenue and West Grand Boulevard, and all along West Grand Boulevard eastward away from the armory. The section of Grand River Avenue that ran alongside the armory abutted I-96 and was largely devoid of businesses and buildings, with the exception of a small used car lot and a long-abandoned industrial building.

Still, people hung around on Grand River Avenue. Mostly they stood around socializing. They were largely teenagers and young men and women, but there were men and women of all ages mixed in. There was very little car traffic at all, and cars that did venture out were usually full of young people hanging out of windows sporting pistols and even automatic rifles. This was territory of the Grand River Gees.

The four soldiers stuck inside the armory were anxious as they fidgeted about. They watched the news on a television set and kept an eye on the CCTV screens that monitored the complex's property. Each nervously kept an M-16 rifle at the ready.

"Something's up, Sarge," reported Corporal Tony "Flaco" Alvarez, his eyes glued to the security screen. On it, at least four cars full of young people hanging out of the windows with assorted weaponry pulled up right outside the eastside property fence on McGraw Street. And, on the exact opposite side of the property, on the west end, several more cars had pulled up, also chock full of armed young men.

CHAPTER 14

Of the four soldiers at the Olympia Armory, 28-year-old Sergeant Willie Jackson was the most senior. After being laid off during one of the multiple rounds of job cuts at GM's Hamtramck Assembly Plant, he counted his lucky stars for landing a Title 32 full-time job as a recruiter for the National Guard, with whom he had already put in six years as a cook.

He watched the CCTV screens intently along with his three fellow soldiers: 25-year-old newly minted Sergeant Barry Washington, who was also a recruiter; 22-year-old Corporal Tony Alvarez, a logistics specialist; and 20-year-old Private First Class Andrew Stevens, a mechanic and the only member of Alpha Company to have made it in after the supposed call-up.

The two groups of armed young men outside the property fence on opposite sides of the building seemed to be just hanging around, waiting for something. Several U-Haul trucks and vans pulled up to the group on McGraw Avenue, across from the garage bays, and stopped. Several more young men piled out and joined the group. They all seemed to be relaxed and socializing. So, it wasn't the U-Haul trucks they were waiting for. Or, not *only* the U-Haul trucks, at least.

What are you doing? wondered Jackson.

Maybe they weren't all that interested in the armory after all, thought Jackson. *Wishful thinking.* As if on cue, the soldiers watched as a truck with a trailer that appeared to be hauling some kind of construction equipment—a bulldozer of some sort (a Caterpillar 323F excavator, to be precise)—pulled alongside the cars, U-Haul trucks, and vans. After some exchanges among the young men, the trailer's tracks were extended to the street. A man hopped into the Caterpillar and started it up. He carefully backed it off the trailer. The Caterpillar turned to face the fence and raised its boom, then brought it down on the fence and tore that section of it away. Security alarms blared inside the complex.

The armed young men—Jackson estimated twenty or so—gleefully walked and jogged through the now fenceless section and swarmed onto the property.

"Shit, they're coming in, Sarge!" announced Flaco, his voice nervous and high-pitched, and stating the obvious.

On the west side of the building, the other group of armed young men clambered over the fence. One by one, each of the four CCTV screens covering the four sides of the building went dark as young men methodically walked around the perimeter of the building and targeted each of the cameras with a rifle.

When the last of the CCTV cameras was shot out, Jackson and his fellow soldiers took shelter in an office just inside and past the main lobby of the armory. Except for administrative offices lined up along the east-west hallway of the Grand River Avenue facing the front of the building, the building contained no windows and the soldiers were essentially blind. They took turns ducking into an office to steal glances out the window to see what was happening, at least in the front of the building.

It wasn't long at all, maybe two or three minutes, when the Caterpillar excavator swung around the corner, roared into view and came right up to the front of the building. The operator, a young bearded African-American, about thirty years old or so, methodically raised the excavator's boom high above the one-story building's roof, then brought it, claws down, straight onto the roof.

The entire building shook with a *boom*, and dust rained from the ceiling, followed by a very loud, metallic rattling sound. That was the Caterpillar itself shaking as the operator navigated the controls in a jerky fashion.

The boom raised again, and then another *BOOM!* (*so that's why they're called 'booms,'* thought Jackson) and this time a few tiles fell off the ceiling, followed by a fluorescent light fixture that exploded in a blue flash and dangled tenuously at one end from the ceiling.

Jackson and his men had no time to think as the Caterpillar raised and dropped its boom yet again, and this time tore away the entire front office and caved in part of the ceiling. The front of the building faced the south-southwest, and the setting sun was almost in a direct line of sight. Fiery yellow-orange sunlight flooded in, and Jackson found himself having to squint from the sudden brightness of the setting sun.

"Let's go!" ordered Jackson, and the four soldiers retreated into the interior of the building as the Caterpillar tore away a whole section at the front of the building. Armed young men poured into the building.

* * *

Jackson and his men ducked into a corridor office while Flaco Alvarez dropped to a knee and fired a volley down the hallway at the intruders before following suit.

"They're organized," whispered Washington. "They're working as a fire team," he said. The armed intruders took turns laying down covering fire as individual members advanced room to room.

The building grew silent. The soldiers tensed up and readied their weapons. Jackson took deep, slow, calming breaths. The silence grew.

A baritone voice called out to them. "G.I. Joe," said the soothing baritone voice. "We got no beef with you. We're here for what's in the vault. Just give us the keys and we'll be on our way."

Alvarez automatically touched the key chain draped across his neck. "You know we can't do that," answered Sergeant Jackson in an equally calm voice. "You're trespassing on a U.S. Army facility," he added.

"Sure you can, son," said the baritone voice. "You're outmanned and outgunned. Ain't nobody coming, either. Those boys with you—you're responsible for them, right?"

Jackson didn't answer.

"Nobody will blame you," continued the baritone voice, "for looking out for your men. We ain't gonna hurt you. What would be the point of that?"

"They will kill us for sure," whispered Washington, his eyes wide.

"What kind of assurance can you give us?" asked Jackson as he motioned to each of his fellow soldiers, ordering them into specific positions. If they were going down, they were going down with a fight.

There was a momentary pause as Jayson Avery considered the question. "I am coming up empty, Brother G.I.," said the voice. Then a "hmmm," as Jayson looked over at Bobby "Bones" (for 'Skin n' Bones') Bailey, the youngest member of the day's crew at twenty. He was a goofy, happy-go-lucky kid. But Jayson liked having him around. He kept things light. But another role just revealed itself to him.

"Tell you what," said the voice, "I'm going to send my boy Bones here unarmed in there to demonstrate my sincerity. If you shoot Brother Bones, then you will have made your bed and that of your mates. Are you hearing me, Brother G.I.?" said the voice.

A muffled argument ensued. 'Bones' apparently objected.

"Nigga, pleez! Get your ass down there!" boomed the baritone voice.

What is this, Amateur Hour? A ruse? Jackson was perplexed.

A skinny, dreadlocked kid ducked his head inside their office momentarily, his eyes wide and, just as quickly, he hid back behind the wall outside in the hallway.

"Show me your hands!" bellowed Jackson, sending shivers of

fear down Bones' spine. "Show me your hands or I swear to God I will shoot you dead right there!"

Bones stepped in hesitantly, his arms raised. "H-h-hello," he said nervously. With his arms raised, palms up at either side of his head, he waved first his left hand, then both hands, at the soldiers. "Helllooo," he said again, his voice soft and tinny and trailing off. "Helllooo ...."

* * *

Overnight, Jackson and his men (and Avery and his crew, for that matter) faced a conundrum: 1) stay and fight against twenty or more armed tangos, whose numbers actually seemed to be growing by the minute; 2) surrender; or 3) leave.

He didn't have a lot of time to think, but the one thing Jackson was certain of was that he and his men were not giving up their weapons nor were they going down without a fight.

For Jayson Avery's part, did he really want four dead U.S. soldiers on his hands? That would bring the Hammer of God (well, of the U.S. government, anyway, which pretty much meant the same thing) down on himself and the whole Avery Organization. Robbing a National Guard Armory wasn't a small crime, of course, but killing U.S. soldiers was a whole other thing. They had the keys to the vault, and having them would certainly make things easier, but he had an excavator, for crying out loud, and he was getting into the vault one way or the other, with or without the soldiers' keys.

They came to a mutual agreement: number 3. "In case you didn't know it, there's a riot going on," protested Jackson. But, really, what was the alternative? Jackson agreed to depart the building, but he wasn't giving up the keys. And, surprisingly, Avery didn't ask for them again.

That was six hours ago, and it was now the dead of night. Jackson and his men had decided to make their way down Grand River Avenue to downtown, which was reportedly fortified and locked down. That's where all of the Detroit P.D. was hunkered down, protecting much of the city's major landmarks and corporate headquarters.

Fortress Downtown was two-and-a-half miles down Grand River Avenue, and that was a lot of hostile territory in between. But they had nowhere else to go. And, worse, they had to go by foot. A vehicle drew too much attention. There was too much debris in the streets, including burning tires, dumpsters, and abandoned and burned vehicles pushed out into the middle of the roads.

They operated as a fire team, individually sprinting from whatever cover they could find to the next while their teammates scanned for threats with their rifles. The first mile was uneventful, though they had to stay low and often stay in one place as they navigated through pockets of protestors. They pointed their M-16 rifles directly at people multiple times as they moved; the civilians only stared back at them, the glow of flames reflected in their eyes. The soldiers moved on and no one threw anything at them. But, man, did those stares chill Jackson and his men.

They had crossed over the M-10 freeway and entered perhaps the most dangerous final stretch, less than a half-mile to the bridge over I-75 into downtown, when a massive explosion shook the entire city. Jackson and his men dropped to the ground and took cover, feeling the searing heat of a massive fireball on their backs and then on their faces as they looked up at a giant, fiery mushroom cloud rising up over the city almost directly over their heads.

"Stay down!" shouted Jackson, as multiple *zips* and *pings* and all sorts of metallic clattering clanged around them. Bullets and shrapnel ripped through the air, and debris fell from the sky.

It was the arms cache at the armory. The mushroom cloud just as quickly faded and blended into the night sky. The flaming air cooled as it rose, but flashes of small explosions below intermittently lit up the sky, each time momentarily casting light on the ugly mushroom cloud as it now drifted eastward over the Detroit River to tower above Windsor, Canada.

* * *

It had been a restless night for Maxwell and Linda Levine, and their guests. Police aggressively patrolled the streets of Windsor all night long. Patrol cars slowly passed Max and Linda's house at least ten times during the night and aimed bright search lights into the darkened interior each time they passed, flooding each room with bright light while they searched for fugitive American refugees.

And, if that wasn't enough to unsettle the residents of Windsor, the massive explosion at the Olympia Armory in Detroit punctuated the uneasy night with a low rumble, and caused what felt like a minor earthquake, rattling windows in their frames, starting at about 2:30 a.m., followed by another rumble every few minutes thereafter for several hours.

It's World War III over there, thought Max as he and many of the residents of both Detroit and Windsor laid awake for much of the night.

With barely any sleep between them, Maxwell and Matthew sat in the living room watching television while Linda and Maria, with the help of Isabella and Miguel, who were as lively and outgoing as ever, prepared coffee and breakfast.

Overnight, the Essex and Kent Scottish, a reserve regiment of the Royal Canadian Infantry Corps based in Chatham, Ontario, had been ordered to mobilize. Max and Matthew watched wordlessly as a miles-long convoy of Canadian Army trucks and vehicles headed down the Macdonald-Cartier Freeway in Ontario to Windsor, with every mile of their fifty-mile trek captured by news helicopters and broadcast live on television.

CHAPTER 15
DAY 4

All of the 250-man-strong Foxtrot Company, 1st Battalion, 125th Infantry Regiment, were mustered into formation at 7:00 a.m. at the National Guard Armory in Bay City, Michigan. While not part of Michigan's designated rapid reaction force, the geographical extent of unrest across Metropolitan Detroit and beyond made it clear that the entire 125th Infantry Regiment would be required to deploy. The adjutant general ordered all companies to deploy as soon as possible.

After three hours of assembling equipment, assessing intelligence reports (gleaned entirely from the news on television and the internet), and coordinating with other companies, the first convoy of five AM General M35 troop transport trucks—two carrying twenty-five soldiers each while the remaining three were purposefully empty—departed the Bay City Armory and entered Interstate 75, which the small base abutted. Twenty-five minutes later, the small convoy of trucks pulled into the armory in Saginaw, Michigan, where Bravo Company was assembled and ready to board the three empty trucks. More convoys were to follow throughout the day.

* * *

Colonel Floyd Barksdale, along with his 24-year-old nephew Rickey—an actual corporal in the Michigan National Guard, but a captain in the Superior Volunteers Militia—and other Superior Volunteers sat, stood, and otherwise hovered nearby and intently watched the small twenty-four-inch flat computer screen perched on Floyd's desk in the command trailer in the woods just off Port Inland Road between McDonald Lake and the Seul Choix Bay limestone quarry at the southeast corner of Schoolcraft County in the Upper Peninsula.

They watched live news with rapt alarm as reporters in helicopters and stationed throughout Metropolitan Detroit spoke rapidly and with astonishment, reporting that the National Guard had yet to deploy in force and was nowhere to be seen. And yet, in Canada, the Essex and Kent Scottish of the Royal Canadian Infantry Corps had deployed in the pre-dawn hours, secured the entire perimeter of the Ambassador Bridge border station and, by midday, had set up a mini-tent city, with sleeping tents, a mess tent, a medical tent, and a processing center to record all of the American refugees and provide food, water, medicine, and shelter.

Floyd's heart raced. He had talked about the need to prepare for a breakdown of society—an EMP attack from North Korea, perhaps, or an invasion by China, even an Islamic takeover of North America, like what had happened over there in Europe, according to the internet. But what he mostly anticipated was a breakdown engineered by the socialist elites on the coasts who controlled the federal government so that they could, once and for all, round up true patriots, confiscate their guns, and implement their globalist world order.

And. It. Was. Happening.

No matter that the president was a Republican. Nope, they were *all* implicated and, for goodness sake, where did the woman even stand on Trump? To top things off, the president was a hedge fund manager on Wall Street before taking office.

Colonel Charlie Pike, who ran his own forty-man unit in Iron River near the Wisconsin border, and was commander of the entire two-hundred-strong Superior Volunteers, all based in the Upper Peninsula, had put all units on alert two days earlier.

But, in the early morning, Colonel Pike ordered all units to duty and called all unit commanders for an emergency teleconference via the encrypted WhatsApp program. Volunteers streamed into camp throughout the day as they got word. There were other militia groups, too, some of them really out there, according to Floyd, who believed in all kinds of crazy conspiracies. Like aliens, or lizard people. They, too, were mobilizing.

Floyd's Volunteers unit numbered about thirty. They were just about at full contingent, and some members had brought their families, making the camp swell to nearly sixty people. Despite the cold, it was like a big family gathering and picnic. Many had brought sandwiches, and they gathered around in various cliques and talked in hushed excitement.

The news reported that unrest had spread to Ann Arbor, Flint, Pontiac, Battle Creek, Benton Harbor, Grand Rapids, Saginaw, Buena Vista, Freeland, Ypsilanti, and Muskegon. The entire Lower Peninsula appeared to be blowing up.

Rumor had it that all of Michigan's State Police had been ordered south to Detroit and other cities, and many town and county sheriffs across the state had also deployed to Detroit and other lower Michigan cities. Streams of refugees, rioters and anarchists, meanwhile, were said to be on the prowl, even heading north, and the Upper Peninsula was totally unprotected.

It was up to them, the Superior Volunteers, to defend and protect the Upper Peninsula. It had to be done.

As the 'soldiers' huddled about, some using the downtime to practice shooting on the range, Floyd and other commanders strategized via WhatsApp. *Operation Superior*, they would call it.

On television, pundits debated the failure of the Michigan National Guard to deploy while the Canadian Forces Reserves swiftly and professionally set up shop across the Detroit River in Windsor.

Then came searing images of what appeared to be the bodies of two young soldiers sprawled in the middle of the road on Michigan Avenue on the west side near Dearborn, lying astride a smoldering shell of a pickup truck and burning buildings on either side of the road.

It was time to act.

* * *

"…Let me be clear. The tragedy that has befallen the family of Mrs. Bernadette Price and so many others is felt by all of us. We are all deeply hurt by the tragic and senseless loss of citizens to fires that were wholly preventable…"

Floyd clicked the 'x' on his browser in the middle of the U.S. president's speech and was off the internet. Things were happening fast now, he thought, as he stepped out of his command trailer. He was dressed in full army combat uniform camouflage, with brown combat boots and the dark green oak leaf of the rank of major worn on the center of his chest. In the place of "U.S. Army" stitched above his left breast were the words "Superior Volunteers." In place of the U.S. flag on the right shoulder was a camouflaged version of the famed Gadsden flag of the American Revolution, depicting a coiled rattlesnake at the center and the words "DON'T TREAD ON ME" above.

A sea of pickup trucks and cars filled in the lot between the command trailer and multiple picnic tables. The bustle and din of men in similar uniform, in various sizes and shapes, standing amid their vehicles, subsided.

Floyd looked out at his men and their trucks. They looked back at him with eagerness and, he thought, fear. I should say something profound.

"Men," he said in a squeak, then cleared his throat with a phlegmy *ahem* followed by a rattling smoker's coughing fit. After a moment,

135

he cleared his throat again and straightened up.

"Men," he said again, this time with authority. "Tonight we take our country back. Godspeed!"

A "woot!" from someone in the crowd elicited some laughs. But they still stood there, waiting for an order, and Floyd looked back at them, a little befuddled.

"Go," he finally said, wondering why they hadn't started up their cars yet. "Go," he said louder. "The mission is a go," and he waved his hands forward from his hips, motioning them to…*go.*

"Yeah, boy!" someone shouted with a raised fist as the first truck roared to life. "Yee-ha!" another hooted.

The rest of the trucks were started with an answering rumble, and men climbed into their cabs and beds.

Operation Superior was underway.

* * *

In Sault Sainte Marie, a small idyllic city in Michigan's Upper Peninsula at the southern bank of St. Mary's River and across from the slightly larger city of Sault Sainte Marie in Ontario, Canada, Sergeant Eric Andrews of the Michigan Army National Guard left his home for the local armory just east of the downtown at 4:45 a.m. Eric was an active duty Personnel Services Specialist, and he needed to be in early to prepare to process soldiers who would be reporting to duty because of the official call-up. There was a lot of paperwork to do in advance.

He lived only five to ten minutes away depending on traffic. He turned onto the riverfront East Portage Road and came across soldiers in the road just before the armory. A soldier held up his hand as Eric approached and he came to a stop. *Looks like some guys made it in early,* he thought, but was confused about why they were stopping traffic. He wondered what was going on.

He rolled down his window as the soldier approached. "Road's closed," said the soldier. "Go back," he ordered. An M-16 was slung over his shoulder.

"I'm headed to the armory," Eric said, fumbling for his military ID card. He was wearing civilian clothes because he normally changed into uniform on site. "I'm Sergeant Andrews," he added as he pulled out his ID card.

"Armory's closed," said the soldier again.

Eric was confused. And there was something off about the soldier's uniform. "But…," protested Eric, and was cut off by the soldier.

"Road's closed, Armory's closed, go home," ordered the soldier. Four other soldiers now flanked the young soldier, two on each side of him, each pointing their M-16s at Eric. It was only then that Eric saw the words "Superior Volunteers" on their battle dress uniforms in place of "U.S. Army."

"Okay, okay," said Eric, showing his hands. "Thank you," he said, and put his truck in reverse. His adrenaline flowed.

What on earth is going on? he thought. What do I do now? And why did I just say "thank you" to those guys?

Eric held his breath as he made several short starts and stops to turn his Ford F-150 around. And, as he drove back the way he had come, he half-expected a barrage of bullets at his back. He went straight back home and parked his truck in his driveway. He just sat there for a moment, calming down and collecting his thoughts. He dug out his cell phone. He had some calls to make. First things first, though. He dialed 911.

* * *

Meanwhile, far to the south in Adrian, just a few miles from the Ohio border, Army Signal Corps Captain Adam Coffey was the first to arrive at the Adrian National Guard Armory. After letting himself into the building and making his way to his office, he paused in the hallway. Something didn't seem right. He looked around but didn't see anything out of the ordinary.

He walked down the hallway and turned on light switches. When he turned back to walk to his office, something caught the corner of his eye. He looked back down the hall and saw it. The hair on his arms stood up. The door to the vault was open.

Adam cautiously made his way to the vault. He quietly peeked in and turned on the lights. The vault—or 'the cage' as the soldiers called it, since it was, essentially, an open-air cage that took up most of the room—was wide open.

The cage was stripped of most of the M-16s; only four remained. Papers lay strewn about the office portion of the room, and the desk drawers were open.

Adam thought that perhaps the battalion had already assembled and deployed without him. But that couldn't be. The cage wouldn't be left open like this, nor the room left in the mess it was in. No, they had been robbed.

Adam's heart raced as the realization set in. The armory had been raided.

* * *

At the southern shores of the Straits of Mackinac separating Michigan's Upper Peninsula from 'mainland' Michigan (or Michigan's 'Lower Peninsula'), is Mackinaw City, the 'Village of Mackinaw City' to be more accurate. Quaint, with a population of eight hundred fifty residents, Mackinaw City is the southern terminus of the 5-mile-long, 552-foot-high Mackinac Bridge, a landmark steel suspension bridge that is the sole link between Michigan's Upper and Lower Peninsulas.

Early in the morning, still a couple of hours before sunrise, a convoy of ten vehicles, a mix of pickup trucks and work vans, crossed the Mackinac Bridge from the Upper to the Lower Peninsula and into Mackinaw City. They turned east onto Central Avenue, which promptly ended at a marina. But the short distance between Interstate 75, which traversed the Mackinac Bridge, and the marina was the small-town heart of downtown Mackinaw City. And, just before the marina, to the right, was the municipal building that housed the city's government, including its tiny police department.

Mackinaw City's Police Department was comprised of seven full-time officers. Three officers worked the day shift, three officers worked the night shift, and one lone officer worked the overnight shift.

That lone overnight officer, Barry Schneider, sat in the cramped office, his head buried in his arms on his desk. He had tried to stay awake, but it was always a losing battle. At twenty-one, Barry was the youngest of the police officers and most junior. And so, after a couple of months of daytime training and supervision, he was stuck on the midnight shift.

Barry heard the front office door open and was startled awake. Hardly anyone ever came in during the overnight hours. Actually, no one ever had. He sat up, a little embarrassed at being caught sleeping, but the scruffy-looking man didn't notice him right away. Barry was sheepishly relieved.

"May I help you?" Barry asked.

The man looked around at the office walls, and two other men entered as well.

The first man, bearded and wearing army camouflage—in fact, all of them wore camouflage—looked at Barry with steely eyes.

"Yes, you may," said the man. "You are relieved." The two other men raised their M-16s and pointed them at Barry. That was the first time Barry noticed the weapons.

Barry gulped. "Um, okay," he said hesitantly.

Once they were satisfied that Barry was unarmed—his service pistol, and those of his fellow officers, were locked in the department's safe—the soldiers escorted Barry outside and he was free to leave.

Unsure of where to go, Barry climbed into his Ford F-150 pickup truck and drove north on Langdale Street. He turned left onto Jamet Street where he would pick up Nicolet Street, which ran parallel to I-75. Chief Ralph Wendowski lived a few miles south of town, on Carp Lake. That's where Barry decided to go.

Before reaching Nicolet Street, Barry could see that soldiers (*not* soldiers, he reminded himself, not *real* soldiers, anyway) had the Nicolet Street entranceway onto I-75 blocked off and were manning what looked like a checkpoint.

Barry navigated to Mackinaw Highway heading south out of town. At the Mackinaw Highway entranceway to I-75 ahead, Barry saw five or six cars stopped, their taillights glowing. He pulled into the parking lot of the Southside Liquors Minimart and watched. He guessed that another checkpoint blocked off I-75. He decided to double back again and take the long way south and out of town along Stimpson Road, wondering if that route, too, was closed off. If so, all routes into town would be closed off.

It's like Red Dawn, he thought to himself. Except they weren't Chinese or Russian invaders; they were armed American militiamen.

* * *

Ralph Wendowski was an early riser. The older he got, the truer that was. He was typically wide awake by 4:30, and he lay staring at the ceiling for a few minutes as he thought about the day's tasks ahead, then slipped out of bed without waking Mary, his wife of forty years.

He was in the kitchen drinking coffee and surfing the morning news and sports scores on his laptop when his cell phone vibrated. That can't be good, he thought as he stole a quick glance at the clock before reaching for the phone.

It was Barry. Ralph was slightly relieved on the one hand and irritated on the other. The kid probably had something come up and needed some guidance, probably something he should be capable of handling himself.

"What's up, Barry?" he asked, answering the phone. "You're *where?*" Just then, headlights briefly filled the kitchen windows as a car pulled into the driveway.

"Who did you say they were?" asked Ralph after he let Barry in.

"Their unis said 'Superior Volunteers'," responded Barry.

Ralph pecked away on his computer, googling the group. "Here we go," muttered Ralph. The Superior Volunteers had their own website. Ralph clicked on it. Definitely a militia group. There were photos of men in army fatigues, pictures of men at target practice with rifles, pictures of family picnics and, in all of the pictures, the men and boys were always dressed in camouflage. The 'who we are' link led browsers to a manifesto of sorts, outlining the Second Amendment right to bear arms and to form "well-regulated" militias.

Ralph clicked on their Twitter link, and there it was, their latest tweets:

@SuperiorVolunteers: In this time of need, the Volunteers are stepping up. We are maintaining peace & stability in the UP. Protecting our communities!

@SuperiorVolunteers: The Superior Volunteers are mobilizing! Join the effort! Yoopers, defend the UP!

Ralph leaned back in his kitchen chair and sighed. "You did the right thing," he said, "coming here."

"Good morning, Barry" said Mary as she walked into the kitchen clad in an ankle-length robe. "What brings you over so early in the morning?"

Ralph let Barry tell his story as Mary put on coffee. Ralph, meanwhile, called his second most senior officer, 58-year-old Frank Carrol, and ordered him to come to Ralph's house as soon as possible. "Take the back roads, Frank," Ralph added, cryptically, "you hear? I mean it; take the back roads."

Ralph called the remaining officers and ordered them, without explanation—time was of the essence—not to report for work for the day and await further instructions. He called the village president, Mackinaw City's equivalent of a mayor.

"What do I do?" asked Barry as Ralph finished speaking with the village president.

"You're going to eat breakfast," said Mary as she opened the refrigerator and retrieved a carton of eggs. "And then you are going to stay in the guest room," she added.

Ralph nodded in agreement.

A new pair of headlights flooded the kitchen as Frank pulled into the lot, just as Mary was lifting the frying pan off the burner to serve scrambled eggs, bacon and toast.

"Frank ain't no dummy. He knows when to show up," said Ralph.

* * *

Fed into contentness and, more importantly, fueled by coffee, Ralph and Frank—both dressed in their police uniforms, armed with personal rifles, and riding in Ralph's F-150 truck—pulled into the public boat ramp parking lot astride Conkling Heritage Park across the street from the Mackinaw City Municipal Building. Village President Bob Mollen climbed out of his car and waved. He had been waiting for them.

"Are those necessary?" he asked, nodding to the rifles.

"I hope not," answered Frank.

Ralph, Frank, and Bob made sure to walk around to the front entrance on Main Street where two 'soldiers' stood guard outside the door. They saw the two police officers with rifles slung over their shoulders approaching in the morning darkness and straightened with alarm, with one soldier bringing up his rifle.

"Do you see me pointing my rifle at you, son?" barked Ralph.

The young 'soldier'—he looked to be a teenager, certainly no older than eighteen—eased up just a bit to let his AR-15 rifle dangle at his side, but not freely, keeping his finger on the trigger.

"I want to speak to the man in charge of..." Ralph said, his voice trailing off before finding the words, "...of whatever this is. Who would that be, young man?" He turned toward the second 'soldier,' who was even younger than the first.

"Colonel Jenkins," the second boy replied nervously.

"But you'll have to wait here," said the first kid. "Who are you?" he asked.

"Chief of police, son," answered Ralph, and nodding to Bob, "and this is the village president."

"The what?" asked the boy.

"The mayor, son, the mayor," sighed Bob.

"Oh," the boy said, then nodded to the second one, presumably his younger brother. The second boy went inside the municipal building while the first stood silently and kept his eyes glued on the mayor and the two policemen.

The second boy appeared in the doorway. "You can come in," he said, and held the door open.

Ralph, Frank, and Bob walked in and the boy led them down the hallway to the village president's office. Of course, thought Ralph, shaking his head.

Several armed men, five to be exact, occupied the small office, and they were all in uniform. With the arrival of the village officials, the office was crammed now with eight men.

"I'm Colonel Jenkins. I've been expecting you," said a hard-looking man in his forties, sitting in the president's chair. "Not this early," he said, nodding to the clock, "but expecting you, nonetheless."

"What are you doing here?" demanded Bob.

"You've all seen the news, I'm sure," answered the colonel. "The Lower Peninsula is going up in flames as we speak, and so we—the Superior Volunteers Militia—we're doing our duty.

"Gubmint's gone to shit, fellas," Jenkins continued. "Those liberals down there have finally taken the cake. We can't let those people and all of that bullshit come up this way. So we closed the bridge. *We're* the government now, in the U.P."

Ralph was about to speak when Bob held up his hand, stopping him.

"How about we coexist?" said Bob. "Let us continue to do our jobs, and we'll stay out of your way. You've closed the bridge. Fine. But life goes on. Old folks need their medications. People need to grocery shop. Cats get caught in trees. Children got to go to school. People got to go to work."

The perennial politician, thought Ralph.

"You need us," continued Bob, "to do our jobs and keep people from panicking. Shoot, ninety percent of 'em probably agree with you. But keep them from earning their keep, even for a day, and they'll turn on you."

"And these boys," Bob said, nodding to Ralph and Frank, "are familiar to the public here. They're part of the community. You are not. Let them do their work keeping the peace. You'll *want* them to. I mean, for goodness sake, what are you going to do when Miss Gulley complains to you about the Sinclairs' poodle pooping on her lawn? You going to shoot her? Or shoot the Sinclairs? Or what if that truant Sawyer kid steals a canteen or something. You going to shoot him, a teenager? Or send him to jail somewhere, a jail that you don't have? What about ..."

"Okay, already!" sighed Jenkins, standing abruptly.

"Also," added Frank, "the Northern Militia boys are going to be mightily displeased when they find one of our towns is occupied by Yoopers. If you stick to keeping the bridge closed, it should all work out."

Frank and Jenkins stared sharply at each other.

"We can handle those amateurs," spit Jenkins.

"Uh huh," nodded a dubious Frank.

"Gentlemen, gentlemen," interrupted Bob, "I believe we are in agreement." He turned to Ralph and Frank. "Call your deputies," he ordered, "and bring them up to speed. And I don't want that kid on the night shift alone. See if you can switch him with a couple of your more seasoned officers."

Then, turning to the colonel, he added, "One more thing, Mr. Jenkins. Can I have my office back? Chief Wendowski here can set you up in the Police offices. In fact, it would be good for people to see that you folks are working right alongside our police."

Jenkins tried to maintain a poker face as he absorbed the village president's reasoning. He looked at his men standing silently against the wall. They offered no clues to what they might have been thinking. After a moment, Colonel Jenkins took a deep breath and nodded his agreement.

Ralph was impressed. Well, I'll be damned, he thought. Bob Mollen, furniture store owner and village president, took charge.

CHAPTER 16

There was an air of excitement that was palpable as Zach rode in the back of an army transport truck with twenty-four other soldiers in his unit. News of the riots, the cancellation of classes, and the call-up by his unit—it was all kind of surreal, even now as they neared Detroit. And things were getting pretty exciting; they couldn't see anything from the back of the canvassed truck, but the police sirens were non-stop now as they barreled down the highway with a state police escort.

Zach, like his fellow soldiers, bounced his legs and tapped his rifle as his adrenaline flowed. It was only five months since he graduated high school and made the decision to join the Army. His mother and stepfather had called him into the living room where they usually sat watching television. When the TV was turned off, Zach knew this would be a "serious" conversation. What the fuck, when did they ever want a serious conversation? Now that he was graduating, now that he was eighteen, he knew it was about getting a job, about moving out or paying rent, or something like that. Sure enough, it was.

"Zach, have you thought about what comes next?" asked his stepdad.

"What do you mean?" Zach replied, trying not to sound defensive but failing.

"You're eighteen now," his stepdad said, "and it's time to think about getting a full-time job."

"I want to go to college," Zach said.

"That's great, honey," his mother said way too soon, obviously expecting him to say that, "but we just can't afford college tuition. All our money is tied up in the garage, and things haven't been good for a long time now."

Zach could feel his face turning red with anger, but he already knew that they wouldn't pony up and pay for his tuition. His older brother Aaron worked part-time at Kmart during the day and at Burger King at night, all while trying to go to community college and keep his heavy metal band going. Meanwhile, their stepdad watched soap operas on TV all day while his garage turned to shit, and their mom worked ten to twelve hours a day processing the paperwork of repossessed cars for the Ford Motor Credit Company in Dearborn.

"I thought about joining the Army," Zach said with a sigh, looking down at his feet. He really had thought about it over the past few months, but really he just wanted the conversation to end before he was overcome with spitefulness.

"Oh, honey, I think that's a great idea" his mom said.

"That's an excellent idea, Zach," his stepdad said.

Zach felt the mood in the room lighten as his parents beamed about how smart and courageous he was. His parents really were happy, elated even, and somehow that elation was contagious. Zach felt like a burden had just lifted off his shoulders. He promised to follow the advice of his stepfather, that was, to not sign anything right away and to think about getting a job as a supply specialist or a job that was indoors rather than as a grunt or a mechanic. Still…Guess I'm joining the fucking Army.

And here I am, he sighed.

The truck shuddered to a halt. Sergeant Harrison stood and walked hunched over to the back of the truck and leaped out. "Lewis and Arnold!" he barked, and Zach's stomach tightened with nervousness and excitement. He clambered out of his seat, jumped off the truck, and stumbled into the arms of Sergeant Harrison.

"Shit, sorry, Sarge," he muttered as he straightened up and tugged on his uniform and backpack. He slung his rifle over his shoulder and looked around.

* * *

In Lansing, Governor Krueger and Major General John Veazey, the adjutant general of the Michigan National Guard, held a press conference. The first questions pertained to what was widely perceived as the painfully slow deployment of the National Guard in light of the fact that Canada had already actively and visibly deployed the Kent and Essex Scottish, its primary reserve regiment of the Canadian Forces Reserves. The governor deferred to his adjutant general.

"The National Guard is being deployed as we speak," Veazey said. "First Battalion, 125th Infantry Regiment, is tasked with deploying within seventy-two hours of activation; it has been a little over sixteen hours. Alpha Company is the unit based in Detroit, out of the Olympia Armory, which has been compromised by the unrest. We have therefore redirected the deployment of Alpha Company to other bases.

"To that end, soldiers are mustering with Bravo Company in Saginaw, Charlie Company in Wyoming City, Delta Company in Big Rapids, and the supporting Foxtrot Company in Bay City. That's more than a thousand soldiers. We expect convoys to start entering the downtown within the next few hours," the general reported.

Even as Major General Veazey spoke, the first convoy of National Guard trucks closed in on downtown as it traveled down I-75. With just over three miles to go, however, the traffic came to a complete stop despite a state police escort with lights flashing and sirens blaring. More than two miles ahead, demonstrators from the adjacent North End neighborhood had entered the freeway and sat down, blocking traffic.

Lieutenant Marco Gordon requested Staff Sergeant Harris, with

Specialist Zach Arnold and Corporal Jamal Lewis, both Detroit-area locals, to accompany him in his Humvee to help scout an alternative route into downtown.

They slowly turned the Humvee around and exited the freeway by going the wrong way up an entrance lane to Clay Street. They turned left on Oakland Avenue, and two blocks later they stopped at the intersection of Oakland Avenue and East Grand Boulevard.

"Back that way is a big Ford plant," said Zach, pointing east to the left, "And…"

"That's a GM plant," Jamal corrected. "My dad worked there," he added.

"Whatever," said Zach. "Woodward Avenue is just up here," he said, pointing to his right. "It'll take us right into downtown."

"Great," said Lieutenant Gordon, "but how do we get from here to there?" he asked, more to himself than to anyone else. Huge crowds meandered all over East Grand River, actively looting storefronts and otherwise just hanging around like it was a big block party. The shells of burned-out cars lay scattered and overturned in the middle of the boulevard. To their left, a pile of burning tires blocked the overpass to the GM plant.

"There's a road over there that parallels the plant that takes you in close on the North Side," said Jamal, pointing in the direction of the GM plant. "But I don't know if we can get past *that*," he added, pointing in a general direction across the interstate where a massive complex burned out of control. The road that Jamal pointed out seemed to go right through the inferno.

"All right," said Lieutenant Gordon, his mind apparently made up. "Let's see what Woodward looks like."

Heads turned in their direction as they drove slowly up East Grand River Boulevard. People seemed dumbstruck by the sight of an Army Humvee appearing on the road in the middle of a riot. The lieutenant made eye contact with an older man, about thirty-five years old, wearing an old desert camouflage army jacket, who gazed stoically at the Humvee.

Thirty-seven-year-old Jackson Mills saw the desert-camouflaged Army Humvee turn onto Grand River, and he just stared at it with a strange sense of nostalgia. It was the same vehicle that he had worked on in the Army and in Iraq. He knew the Humvee like the back of his hand. He loved his job as an Army mechanic, and he was proud to have made it through basic training and to wear the uniform. The Army promised job skills and a way out of Motown, and he was appreciative. He served in Iraq, where the work was non-stop, hot, and dirty. It was in Iraq that he had come to know the Humvee so well since they took such a beating in that Godforsaken country. But then came the drawdown and he was out of the Army with no money saved and with nothing to show for his time in the service. Certainly no job waited for him, at least nothing as steady as the Army. And here was the Army again, right in his very own Godforsaken part of the world, but it wasn't his Army anymore. With no steady job and a battle every three months or so with GLEE to keep his power on or to get it back on, it was clear to him that he was the enemy.

He was an Iraqi now, an insurgent.

Jackson nonchalantly picked up a chunk of debris, a piece of a rock in a pothole, and hurled it at the Humvee. That one rock turned into a hailstorm of rocks and all sorts of detritus as others took their cue and threw whatever they could find at the Humvee.

But it wasn't the bricks and rocks the soldiers were concerned about. Zachary pointed to a sizeable group of people standing over a collection of glass bottles glistening in the sun and organized in neat rows in the parking lot of a gasoline station, each being stuffed with what looked to be oily rags.

"Uh, guys," is all Zach had to say when he pointed out the group and their collection of bottles for Sergeant Harris to use his trademark colorful language. "Get us the fuck out of here *now*, El Tee!" he commanded, and Lieutenant Gordon obeyed, ignoring the fact that it was an enlisted sergeant giving orders to *him*, and gunned it while swerving to avoid a protester.

But it was too late. Their movement caught the eyes of the young crowd and, thinking they were police, one of them lit a rolled-up newspaper on fire and lit the oily rags. Others picked up the lit cocktails, some with one in each hand, and threw them hard at the Humvee.

The lieutenant did his best to swerve and weave in between raining bottles of flaming Molotov cocktails, but at least four found their mark, engulfing the entire outer body of the Humvee in flames. He continued to drive on, but with flames on the hood blinding him and smoke filling the cabin through the air vents, he stopped the vehicle and ordered his men out.

Staff Sergeant Harris unlatched the safety of his M-16 as he scrambled out of the door and ran from the burning vehicle. He then dropped to his knee and opened fire on a group poised to launch yet more Molotov cocktails. The deafening jackhammer sputter of the M-16 echoed off the boulevard's buildings, and three teenagers fell where they stood. Flames erupted alongside their bodies where they dropped their flaming cocktails. Demonstrators up and down East Grand River ran for cover, clearing the entire length of the boulevard.

Zach stood wide-eyed in the middle of the road, staring at the three fallen teenagers, flames licking at their unmoving bodies.

"Move your ass!" commanded Sergeant Harris, but Zach only stood there. "Move it, Private!" barked Harris, pulling the kid harshly until his feet moved under his own volition while Harris scanned the abandoned and boarded-up storefronts with his rifle. The four soldiers moved as a fire team, spreading out to give each other cover, but with Harris keeping the young private close. They began to make the nearly half-mile trek back to the interstate, taking cover amid the burning and smoldering buildings as they pressed forward. Their abandoned Humvee was now an inferno.

Behind them, they heard wailing as family members discovered the three fallen teenagers. Several people opened fire with handguns, shooting wildly at the retreating soldiers, even stepping into the middle of the boulevard with abandon for better aim.

The soldiers ducked into the alleyway behind the storefronts and continued to beat their retreat through the neighborhood. They followed the alley north behind Oakland Avenue, then turned east on Custer Avenue.

Well, that's just great, thought Lieutenant Gordon after misreading the street sign as "Custard" Avenue.

When the men turned onto Custer, they were met with nearly half of their entire 125-person company; they had all climbed up from the freeway on foot after hearing the gunfire, and were taking up positions on Custer Avenue and all along the service road parallel to the interstate.

* * *

Araminta had previously worked at the airport where she cleaned aircraft, making about $10 an hour, before landing the job at the university. Not only did Wayne State pay more ($13 an hour), it also had a significant employee benefit: free tuition for her if she took classes but, more important, it would be free for Brandon when the time came. It was hard work, but it was the only way on earth that Brandon would be able to go to college. If she could just get him to the finish line—graduating high school—let alone *live* to see eighteen.

A sense of total dread overcame her when she heard the gunfire. She was in the middle of doing the dishes and just stopped, listening intently. She was no stranger to the sound of gunfire, but this was different. It sounded…industrial. That was the word that came to mind and, with it, came dread, and its echoes were as loud as the initial barrage.

Brandon…

Araminta dropped the partially washed plate into the sink and was through the living room and out the front door in an instant. She walked-ran around the block south to Grand River Boulevard; she was certain that was where the gunfire had come from.

She heard a scream, a primordial scream that made her shudder. When she came around the corner at Brush Street, she saw the Humvee in the middle of the boulevard, engulfed in flames.

People came out from buildings and from behind them, coming out from taking shelter and checking if it was safe to do so; heads were turned toward the east, and she looked, too. The next block over was that gas station and garage run by Darius, that old mute, and in its lot lay three young men sprawled on the pavement, not moving, and they were the center of everyone's attention.

Brandon…Oh God, don't let it be Brandon. As she approached the scene, she saw a lake of blood between the fallen boys.

Sheila, the mother of Brandon's friend Dominic, came bolting into view. Her legs turned wobbly and she fell to her knees. A large woman, just crumbling to the pavement in the middle of the road. "Dominic!" she screamed, then crawled toward the unnaturally still bodies.

It was Sheila's voice that Araminta realized had made that awful scream a moment before. "Oh, Gawd!" she screamed now, tears streaming down her face.

Araminta could see them now. Dominic, Brandon's friend, so sweet, lay sprawled on his back, his tall skinny body stretched out and draped backward over the outstretched leg of Shawn, another of Brandon's friends, arching his back. Dominic's jacket was splayed open and his t-shirt was crumpled up to mid-torso, his tender navel pointing skyward. The teenager's eyes were open, gazing without expression at the clear blue sky, his mouth gaping. But it was his bare stomach that burned in Araminta's mind as she pried her eyes away and looked to the third body.

Chad was the name the came to her. Chad. Not Brandon. Not Brandon.

She took a deep breath and exhaled haltingly. Her hands, at her chest, were shaking. And then she saw him. He emerged from the crowd, his eyes glued to Dominic's outstretched body, gawking. His face was passive, his eyes distant. Araminta continued her walk-run, walking straight up to Brandon, and she threw her arms around him. Tears streamed from her eyes as she buried her face into the nape of his neck.

Brandon still stared at the bodies of his friends. He said nothing. Nor did Araminta.

Araminta composed herself, grabbed Brandon's hand, and pulled him along. Tears streamed down her face as she walked briskly, her back to the bodies, Brandon being pulled along, his face still turned back.

* * *

Lieutenant Gordon and Sergeant Harris briefed Major Stanley Payne ("Major Pain," naturally) on what had just happened when one of the soldiers on the knoll opened fire with warning shots at a group of young people—gang members, most likely, given their menacing body language and the fact that they were armed.

"Goddammit," muttered Major Payne as a high-flying bullet zipped by, fired by one of the gang members taking a pot shot at the convoy. "Cease fire!" ordered the major.

"We've got armed tangos coming down from the hood up there, sir," protested an excited young corporal.

The major ignored him, snarling as he stroked his beardless chin and assessed the situation.

His trucks were wedged in with traffic that backed up from here south to downtown, which was about three miles, and who knew how far back it was jammed behind them. The northbound lanes were entirely empty, but a series of concrete Jersey barriers the length of the freeway separated the north and southbound lanes.

Perhaps with a chain they could pull apart two or three of the Jersey barriers to create a space wide enough to get the trucks through. "Harris, do we have a chain?" he barked.

"I'll check, sir," answered the sergeant.

Payne continued his assessment. Then they could head south down the northbound lanes. Or they could march as fire teams the three miles into downtown, leaving the trucks behind. If they moved some barriers, how far could they go toward downtown before they ran into more traffic jams and then have to march into the city anyway?

"Yes, sir," came the delayed answer from Sergeant Harris. They had at least two chains.

Another *pop, zing* and a metallic *tink* as a bullet bounced off a car in front of the convoy. Which made Major Payne think, and what if there were rioters in their path? What then? Engage them? Kill them? He hadn't received any orders that extreme, at least not yet.

Or they could retreat, move a couple of Jersey barriers, and head north back the way they had come, regroup with proper orders and equipment, and go from there.

What a fucking mess. He sighed as another *zing* punctuated the silence the soldiers had allotted him while he paced back and forth, stroking his chin, his back ramrod straight.

"Listen up, men!" he yelled, having come to a decision.

* * *

Much of the unrest that emanated from Detroit spread largely west-ward along Interstate 94 to Ann Arbor, Battle Creek, Kalamazoo, and Benton Harbor on the other side of the state astride Lake Michigan, and north of I-94 to Flint and Lansing, both cities firmly in the orbit of Detroit City. The reported unrest, meanwhile, was largely peaceful demonstrations—demonstrations held daily in solidarity with the people of Detroit and against the indifference of a multi-billion dollar corporation that had cost the lives of hundreds of people.

Outside of these cities, the state of Michigan was primarily rural and, it must be noted, mostly white. In each of the counties where militias were active, like those in the Upper Peninsula, or even in the southern counties bordering Indiana and Ohio, whites comprised more than ninety percent of the population. Some counties were nearly ninety-nine percent white. And, while the GLEE shutoffs impacted poor people regardless of their skin color, in Detroit and beyond, the demonstrations against the GLEE shutoffs were widely seen in the militia counties as an inevitable breakdown of urban society, and in which "those people" (non-whites and, by extension, urban liberals) were the instigators. Never mind that entire families had died in unnecessary fires due to their electricity being cut off.

Radio commentators like George M. Whyte, professionally known as George Bruttale (pronounced as "brutally"), scanned the headlines before his 7:00 a.m. nationally syndicated radio talk show, *The Brutal Truth.* George Bruttale boasted and railed about the unrest in Detroit, holding up the city ruled by the Democratic Party for generations as a harbinger of things to come for America if conservatives allowed it.

"The *entire* state is rotten!" he bellowed on the air, shaking his fist for his webcam viewers. "Where is the National Guard?" he railed. "Where are the State Police?"

In one breath, it was the city dwellers. Welfare recipients. Thieves. *Takers.* In the next, it was outside instigators, professional left-wing East Coast and West Coast-based activists flocking to Michigan with ski masks, baseball bats, and brass knuckles.

Bandits paid secretly by the George Soros Foundation.

Socialists.

"People are being *killed* on the streets of Detroit, my friends. On the streets of Flint and Ann Arbor!

"And what are you going to *do* about it?

"Rise up, Michigan, lest it be you lying dead in the streets!"

* * *

In Coldwater, in the far south of central Michigan, a stream of nearly thirty pickup trucks, cars, and SUVs, many sporting full flags of the United States standing on each side of truck beds or held aloft out of passenger windows—and some sporting full Confederate Battle flags and yellow "Don't Tread on Me" Gadsden flags—had converged in the early morning hours at an open field slotted for future housing development some three hundred yards from a creek that connected Cemetery Lake and South Lake on the west side of town.

At precisely 9:00 a.m., the convoy of vehicles departed the field and meandered onto West Chicago Boulevard and headed east along the main drag into town.

It was mid-morning, and the long convoy slowly and deliberately crawled east on Chicago. They slowly snaked around a group of cars stopped at a red light at Clay Street, forcing right-of-way traffic to halt as they passed with blowing horns and flashing headlights.

The convoy continued east through the center of town, traveling at a slow, parade-like pace. Indeed, the convoy was very much a parade, with its multiple large flags flying amid the vehicles, the truck beds full of camouflaged men, women, and boys sporting an assortment of automatic and semi-automatic rifles, including Army issue M-16s. People in other cars and the sidewalks gawked at the procession. Heads turned in the local Arby's and McDonald's.

A Coldwater Police cruiser sped from out of the McDonald's parking lot after the convoy had passed. It raced east and, as it caught up to the convoy, it turned on its emergency lights and raced out ahead of it.

The convoy continued to the eastern side of town, with several police cars stopping traffic ahead of the convoy to allow it to pass through intersections unmolested. Drivers of the trucks and cars in the convoy tooted their horns in appreciation as they slowly passed.

The convoy reached Interstate 69, the eastern terminus of Coldwater and, like a slow-moving funeral procession, turned left onto the northbound ramp. With no Michigan State troopers to worry about on the freeway—they had all been sent to Detroit and other cities facing unrest, like Battle Creek in neighboring Calhoun County—the convoy continued northward for nine miles to the county line. There, the convoy slowed to a halt at a small turnabout ("emergency vehicles only," a small sign read), where the convoy disembarked.

Within minutes, the festive group of men and women had stopped traffic in both directions. They set up orange cones and plastic Jersey barriers to funnel traffic into a single lane.

.Checkpoints on each side of the highway were quickly established. Armed men stood alongside the checkpoints. Each vehicle would be inspected, each driver and passenger questioned.

"Where are you coming from?"

"Where are you heading and why?"

The South Michigan Militia of Branch County had arrived.

If the state couldn't protect them from those diseased zombies in the cities—if the state couldn't prevent the violent anti-Trump globalists of the past from pouring into God's country—then the good people of the South Michigan Militia would.

In Branch County, Cass County, Hillsdale County, indeed, across all of southern Michigan, the South Michigan Militia spread out along each of the counties bordering Indiana and Ohio and set up checkpoints to police traffic into and out of the southern counties.

The bulk of their forces concentrated in far eastern Monroe County, situated along the shores of Lake Erie, sealing the three major roadways into Wayne County: I-75, I-275, and U.S. 24. SMM troops lay siege to Flat Rock and Rockwood, each just twenty miles from the city center of Detroit.

The South Michigan Militia numbered around two thousand prior to the GLEE-related unrest in Detroit. Following news coverage of the spreading unrest, and the rhetoric of national talk show syndicates like George Bruttale and others, SMM's number of volunteers more than doubled in just a few days.

Likewise for other militia groups throughout the remainder of the tenth largest state in the Lower 48: The Superior Volunteers, which effectively seized control of the Upper Peninsula and policed the Mackinac Bridge; the Northern Michigan Militia; the Michigan Rifle Club; the Great Lakes Patriots; and many more.

CHAPTER 17

Governor Krueger and the adjutant general were huddled together with staff at the Governor's Mansion—a sprawling rancher straddled along the scenic Grand River in Lansing—and watched the hard-to-take images on a large screen HDTV.

The contrast of the two armies—one seemingly competent and professional, the other unresponsive, ineffectual, and in retreat—set off alarms in Washington, D.C., and in capitals around the world.

"An unmitigated disaster," national pundits decried.

More bad news filtered in from beyond Detroit. Massive crowds had overrun police lines in Ann Arbor, setting parked cars ablaze, and smashing storefront windows in the downtown area. In Flint, the city hall was reportedly on fire.

The governor and the adjutant general ordered the entirety of the Michigan National Guard, all remaining units, to duty, but it would take three days at a minimum for the National Guard to be ready for deployment. And now it appeared that they would have to fight their way into Detroit and possibly Flint and Ann Arbor, a task for which the National Guard was not designed.

Meanwhile, reports filtered in from the Upper Peninsula in the north and the Indiana and Ohio borders in the south that various armed militia groups were mobilizing and setting up illegal checkpoints on federal interstates and state highways.

The whole damned state was in rebellion.

The governor, adjutant general, and their staffs were in agreement. Mobilizing the entirety of the Michigan National Guard wouldn't be nearly enough.

"Get the president on the phone," ordered Governor Krueger.

* * *

Brandon's mind was empty, but it raced at the same time. It was full of images, of Dominic lying sprawled out on the ground, surely dead, right? He just laid there, he and Shawn and Chad. Dead. That Humvee on fire. Soldiers, too. There were soldiers. A crowd.

Dominic was dead?

Araminta's mind raced, too. Everything, all at once. She had to protect Brandon. Brandon was quiet, too quiet, his eyes still distant. Shock. He must be in shock. Maybe I'm in shock, she thought. We're both in shock.

She didn't let go of Brandon's hand, and he didn't try to pull away. He was still back *there*, gawking at the bodies. They walked through the front door, into the living room. There they were, her car keys. On the lamp table next to the sofa. She grabbed them.

Clothes. Forget about them, just go. Shoes? No, just go. Just go.

They turned around and walked back out the front door to the Jetta. Araminta opened the passenger door.

"Get in," she said, no *ordered,* and Brandon climbed in, still distant, still utterly silent. Araminta closed the door and held her breath as she went around the front of the Volkswagon to the driver side, certain that Brandon would bolt. She was no longer holding his hand.

She climbed in and started the car. Brandon stayed put, staring out the windshield.

Araminta put the car in drive, and down to Grand River Boulevard she drove, and then onto the interstate.

Brandon turned his head and looked at her. "Where are we going, Momma?" he asked.

161

* * *

At the National Military Command Center in the Pentagon, known colloquially as the "War Room," a lively debate ensued among military commanders and analysts. And, as evening approached, it became increasingly apparent that a full deployment of the 10th Mountain Division would be necessary to quell the violence in Detroit and perhaps beyond.

Major General Lance McIntyre and staff had flown in from New York in the morning and briefed the men in the room on the preparations and readiness of the 10th Mountain Division. He presented a detailed battle plan, including timelines and logistical needs.

After a series of technical questions about the logistics of deploying U.S. troops to Detroit, discussion turned to political ramifications of the deployment. Stephen Wright, the bespectacled Under Secretary of Homeland Security for Intelligence and Analysis, and a graduate of Harvard's Department of Government, spoke up.

"Gentlemen," he said, "the images of bodies of National Guard troops lying in the streets, retreating National Guard vehicles, the Olympia Armory burned to the ground, American refugees fleeing to Canada, etc., have been pretty shocking and, to civilians, potentially destructive. The government's legitimacy is severely undermined when its army is seen as ineffectual. Think Iraq after the U.S. withdrawal."

That brought howls of protest; General Hank Scranton, U.S. Director of Intelligence, bristled. "Let's not over-estimate the situation," he scoffed dismissively. "America isn't Iraq."

"Hey," said Wright, throwing up his hands in mock defense. "Don't shoot the messenger. I'm just saying that we need to be prepared for any contingency, as remote as some may seem."

"Violence has spread to Flint and Ann Arbor," added Brigadier General Aaron Palmer, U.S. Marine Corps, "and now to Plymouth, apparently," he said, pointing to one of the TV monitors showing demonstrators throwing rocks at cars in that city. "And now there are protests in Washington, New York, Chicago, even Rust Belt cities like Cleveland, all in solidarity with Detroit. I agree with Secretary Wright; we must go in full force; no monkeying around. Set an example. Shock and awe." He paused, and then added "Show of force," and "Nip it in the bud," in a clipped delivery. The general was smiling, apparently pleased with himself at his use of various but similar idioms to drive home the point.

"Exactly," said Wright, both slightly amused and a bit horrified by the general. "I heard something about militia groups gearing up as well. What we need to do, if I may be so blunt, is to reestablish a monopoly of violence. And we need to restore confidence in our military."

"I am going to need the full might of the U.S. armed forces at my disposal," said Lt. Gen. McIntyre. He folded his arms across his chest and waited for questions.

"What do you require?" asked Admiral Erik Sorenson, chairman of the Joint Chiefs of Staff.

"The full package," replied McIntyre. "A tank company and close-in air support, for starters."

* * *

Araminta drove west on Grand Boulevard. Brandon's question, *Where we going, Momma?* still hung in the air, unanswered. Brandon went back to looking out the window.

Araminta kept looking to the eastern horizon, waiting for those familiar steel towers of the Ambassador Bridge, the bridge to Canada, to emerge.

Araminta grew up just west of downtown, across the street from Stanton Park. Looking north from her house stood the abandoned and hauntingly beautiful Michigan Central Station. In the opposite direction loomed the two steel towers of the bridge to Canada, as she'd always known it. Many times as a little girl, she would gaze at those towers and wonder. *Canada,* she would think. What was it like over there? It seemed to hold some kind of promise. *Canada.* Butterflies, tree-lined streets, chirping birds, and little black girls like her on swing sets in the summertime, always in the summertime.

The bridge to Canada. All her life those steel towers loomed in the distance, and she would catch herself staring off at them as if in a trance, just like when she was a little girl, and think, *the bridge to Canada.*

Alas, a bridge too far.

The car was hit with several glass bottles along the way, but mostly they drove unmolested. Araminta was fearful when they came upon crowds in the road, but they would part as she slowly approached and weaved through the crowds and avoided burning piles of debris. Some peered at her with deranged, angry eyes, but they only stared and didn't attack. *Maybe because we're black,* thought Araminta, but a sudden splintering of her windshield into large spider-web cracks dispelled that notion.

Araminta and Brandon made it through the two-and-a-half miles to Interstate 96, where she entered the southbound lane. Traffic was light but, after just over a mile, the traffic came to a standstill. It was a parking lot; there was no movement at all. After waiting for just about two minutes, two minutes that felt like at least ten, Araminta opened her car door.

"Let's go," she said, and climbed out.

Brandon got out, too, a quizzical look on his still, too-stoic face. Araminta grabbed his hand and began walking, steeling herself against the cold, straight down the middle of the freeway between lanes of idle cars. It was a brisk twenty-five minute walk when it became clear to Brandon that the large steel bridge towering not too far in the distance was the destination.

The bridge to Canada, he thought.

* * *

At 6:00 p.m., Cynthia Belle, multi-billionaire founder of the Los Angeles-based global property developer and venture capital conglomerate Business Geography International (BGI), and currently president of the United States, addressed the country via televised broadcast.

"Good evening," she said, solemnly. "Earlier tonight I spoke with Michigan Governor Clifford Krueger and Detroit Mayor André Murray. They told me that the already frightful situation in Detroit and elsewhere in Michigan has deteriorated further. Particularly in Detroit, incidents of random terror and lawlessness continue unabated: More than twenty thousand fires, untold damage to private property, attacks on interstate highways, hundreds of injuries, and the senseless deaths of more than fifty people, including two young National Guardsmen attempting to report for duty in order to protect American citizens.

"Following the first day of unrest this past Tuesday, I spoke with Michigan Governor Krueger and Detroit Mayor Murray. They reported then that there are two thousand police on duty in the city of Detroit, and up to two thousand more law enforcement officers from surrounding communities and from across the state stood ready to augment Detroit's police forces. One thousand National Guard troops also stood ready if needed.

"These forces were mobilized within the past twenty-four hours but, given the dispersed nature of unrest throughout the City of Detroit, their deployment has met with great difficulties.

"To supplement state and local efforts, as president I have taken several additional actions. First, this morning I ordered the Departments of Justice and Homeland Security to dispatch one thousand federal law enforcement officials to help restore order in Detroit beginning tonight. These officials include FBI SWAT teams, special riot control units of the U.S. Marshals Service, the Border Patrol, and other federal law enforcement agencies. Second, another one thousand federal law enforcement officials are on standby alert, should they be needed. Third, earlier today I directed five thousand members of the 10th Mountain Division to stand by at Fort Drum in Upstate New York.

"Tonight, at the request of the governor and the mayor, I have ordered the 10th Mountain Division to immediately deploy to Detroit and other cities in Michigan and to use whatever force deemed necessary to preserve life and liberty. I am also federalizing the Michigan National Guard, and I've instructed Major General Lance McIntyre, commander of the 10th Mountain Division, to assume authority of these forces under his command…"

As the president gave her televised address, the first C-17 Globemaster III transport aircraft carrying soldiers and equipment of the 10th Mountain Division lifted off from Fort Drum in Upstate New York. The president had personally secured passage earlier in the day for military flights across Canadian airspace since the most direct and shortest flight route from Fort Drum to the Detroit area takes aircraft over the length of southern Ontario where more than twenty million of Canada's thirty million population live. This shortest-route plan ensured that the first, and subsequent, C-17 aircraft arrived at the Selfridge Air National Guard base, the designated staging area located on Lake St. Claire's Anchor Bay twenty miles north of Detroit, in just a little over one hour after take-off.

At Selfridge, the just-federalized Michigan Air National Guard scrambled to accommodate the hordes of media personnel, trucks, and communications equipment that descended upon the base. Even though it was already nighttime, once it became known that Selfridge would be the primary staging area for arriving troops, media personnel rushed to the base and captured the arrival of the first C-17 aircraft, the disembarking of soldiers and equipment, and the frantic movement of material and supplies on national and global television.

Some pundits expressed amazement at the transformation of the Selfridge Air Base from a sleepy National Guard air strip to a bustling

Army and Air Force forward base of national import within just a few hours, with aircraft arriving every few minutes, and young military personnel diligently moving equipment, setting up operations for incoming commands, and even establishing living quarters for arriving personnel of all ranks. The efficiency of it all—particularly after the inability of the National Guard to deploy—was both gratifying and humbling to outside observers and was quite a contrast with what was happening just a few miles to the south in central Detroit and beyond.

Throughout the night, the pace of activities did not slow down. Aircraft and helicopters continued to arrive overnight, and the number of military personnel more than quadrupled before dawn the following morning.

CHAPTER 18
DAY 5

The following morning, Selfridge Air Base was buzzing with activity, and aircraft continued to arrive every few minutes, bringing more soldiers and equipment. News programs showed an impressive array of aircraft and helicopters parked on the overcrowded flight line, which included four C-5M Galaxy cargo aircraft, the largest aircraft in service in the United States, several C-17 Globemasters and C-130 Hercules cargo planes, four small business class C-21A transport aircraft, more than two dozen Black Hawk and Apache attack helicopters, and four Kiowa Warrior observation helicopters. A stealthy U.S. Air Force Avenger drone also sat parked on the tarmac.

Each of the Galaxies had ferried two M1A2 Abrams tanks of the 1st Armored Division based out of Fort Bliss, Texas, along with support personnel. The tanks, along with several Army bulldozers, cranes, and other heavy equipment, occupied their own row on the flight line.

* * *

Mohammed "Moe" Ibn Adil cut an imposing figure. He stood six feet three inches tall and weighed around two hundred twenty-five pounds. He was dark-skinned and gruff-looking, but professional in appearance. His experiences growing up as the elder son of Nigerian immigrants, combined with his twenty-five years in the U.S. Army, gave him intelligent but world-weary eyes. He was stylishly dressed in a charcoal overcoat, tie, dark plaid winter English cap that covered his ears, black leather gloves, and blue jeans, as he entered his office at the U.S. Army Criminal Investigation Command, or CID (the 'D' a holdout from the original Criminal Investigation Division, established after World War I), in the Russell-Knox Building on Quantico Marine Corps Air Base in Quantico, Virginia.

He was just taking off his coat when the commanding general of CID, Major General Theodore Rose, stepped in.

"Don't get comfortable," the general quipped. "Multiple National Guard armories, including the Olympia Armory in Detroit, were broken into and raided last night in Michigan, possibly by militia groups. Get your team ready; you're going to Motown."

* * *

At 10:00 a.m., four low-flying Marine Corps F-35B Lightning II joint strike fighters—having flown some 700 miles from the Marine Corps Air Station in Beaufort, South Carolina—roared over Metropolitan Detroit in tight formation. The fifth generation stealth fighter planes were sleek and breathtakingly graceful as they sliced through the air. The four jets first made their appearance by flying low and extremely fast, so fast, in fact, that they startled anyone who happened to catch a glimpse of them as they flew by—*silently*—causing many people to duck instinctively even before looking up and catching a fuller glimpse. Then came the sound—a heart-thumping, ground-rumbling *BOOM*—causing nearly everyone, including those who had seen them, to jump and flinch in alarm. Minutes later, the jets returned, flying much slower but still in tight formation, flying in a full circle over the sprawling city as their engines roared, causing windows to rattle in their frames. After the jets completed two full circles over the city, their engines lit up momentarily as they climbed in altitude and disappeared over the northern horizon.

As short-lived as the flyover was, it accomplished its primary mission: rioters, spectators, residents, pedestrians, and even automobile traffic throughout Metropolitan Detroit paused momentarily as people stopped and gawked at the awesome prowess of the fighter planes above. More importantly, the jets announced that the U.S. military was close at hand, and that the firepower and resources under their command was qualitatively different than anything they had seen by the Detroit police or Michigan National Guard.

* * *

In Windsor, the deployment of the Essex and Kent Scottish Infantry Corps the day before did not end the refugee crisis, but it did bring a semblance of order and security. They documented nearly nine thousand American refugees securely fenced in between the toll booths and the landing of the bridge by scores of troops and police. The refugees were forced to remain in the car lanes, where they all stood around or slept. It was clear that there wasn't enough room for them, nor were car lanes an appropriate space to house refugees, even temporarily.

The Canadian government was adamant, however, about maintaining the border and was certain the Americans would voluntarily return to Detroit as soon as order was restored. But that hadn't happened yet, and conditions among the Americans was still inadequate. The refugees were growing more restless by the hour. After securing the perimeter of the border station and shoring up the Windsor and Ontario police, the Essex and Kent Scottish had been busy setting up what amounted to a mini-tent city in the open fields between Ascension College and Alumni Field, the University of Windsor's stadium, both just south of the border station, to serve as a more traditional refugee camp. A double-wide chain linked fence with barbed wire atop surrounding the camp site was also rapidly constructed.

Once the camp site was inspected and deemed ready to house refugees, the Essex and Kent Scottish, along with police from various agencies, formed a militarized corridor from the border station to the new camp site to allow the Americans to walk the less than half-a-mile distance to their new digs.

The Americans cheered as the riot police and soldiers along the toll booths at the border station parted to allow them to pass.

* * *

At Selfridge Air Base, the tall, lean general with steely blue eyes stepped up to the podium. He had a demeanor about him that exuded confidence and a no-nonsense attitude. He also had an air of the mischievous, a blend that lent him a measure of charisma.

Once the sharp-looking general stepped up, he wasted no time in making a statement: "Ladies and gentlemen," he began, nodding to the press corps and the television cameras. "We are a combat force. We are destructive. We are the very best of the United States Army. We do not fool around. We have a mission, and we do it. We are here to put down lawlessness. Raise arms against us and we will cut you to pieces. Period. There is nothing romantic or glamorous about it. We are a professional combat force. We do what we do, and we do it effectively and efficiently."

Major General Lance McIntyre turned and walked away without taking any questions.

PART TWO: BATTLE OF DETROIT

CHAPTER 19
DAY 6

N ot announced as part of the emergency build-up of the 10th Mountain Division at Selfridge was the deployment of a platoon of the U.S. Navy's SEAL Team 2, based out of Norfolk, Virginia. In support of SEAL Team 2, several Blackhawk helicopters on the flight line were part of a detachment of the U.S. Army's 160th Special Operations Aviation Regiment (Airborne), known as the Night Stalkers, based out of Fort Campbell, Kentucky. The Night Stalkers typically transported and supplied Army and other special forces in support of their missions, and were instrumental in the U.S. Navy SEAL raid in Pakistan that killed Osama Bin Laden in 2011.

Though the SEALs and the Night Stalkers didn't expect to find the kind of resistance when going up against an enemy state, the deployment to Detroit at least offered real-life training against urban-based non-state actors. More importantly, the 10th Mountain Division wasn't particularly trained for pinprick assaults on airports or securing bridges, and General McIntyre wanted speed and precision.

In addition, and perhaps more to the point, McIntyre felt the country could use a feel-good story, and one in which the power and strength of the U.S. armed forces could be provided as a counter to the disaster unfolding in Detroit. And so, embedded with the Night Stalkers and SEALs, were a couple of U.S. Army Public Affairs Broadcast Specialists, or journalists in civilian-speak.

In the pre-dawn hours, the Night Stalkers lifted off from Selfridge Air Base in four MH-60 Blackhawk helicopters and ferried two squads of SEAL commandos and a broadcast specialist to the Ambassador Bridge, and two squads and a broadcast specialist to the Coleman A. Young International Airport.

At the Ambassador Bridge, the two Blackhawks swooped in and hovered above, and SEAL commandos fast-rappelled onto the suspended roadway. The SEALs swept across the bridge in both directions, startling refugees hunkered down in vehicles, some of which they had broken into to shelter for the night. There was no resistance, and nearly everyone welcomed the commandos, even if reservedly, because relief—at least in the form of security—had taken so long. Food and water would be delivered later in the morning, the commandos promised.

The Coleman A. Young International Airport was located nine miles to the northeast of downtown, right off of Gratiot Avenue. Once the major international airport that served Metropolitan Detroit before the Detroit Metropolitan Wayne County Airport was expanded and modernized in 1947, it no longer hosted passenger air service; rather, it primarily served as a cargo airport in recent decades.

The airport had been left abandoned and unmanned since the unrest began and workers stayed home.

SEAL commandos fast-rappelled onto the tarmac and stormed the airport's small terminal and main hangar where, in each case, they encountered not a single soul. After the airport was secured, multiple helicopters and other aircraft were cleared to relocate from the overcrowded Selfridge Air Base.

During the overnight hours, meanwhile, Humvees and army trucks, including flatbeds with D9 armored bulldozers secured atop, and several large M88 recovery vehicles, formed three long single-file convoy lines at the Selfridge Air Base. Five M1A2 Abrams tanks painted in desert tan comprised the middle of the lengthening convoys. Starting around 5:00 a.m., throngs of young soldiers in full combat gear mustered near the convoys. By 5:45, all of the Humvees, trucks, and tanks had their engines revved up and ready to roll, and soldiers climbed aboard.

At precisely 6:00 a.m., a little more than an hour before the sun broke over the horizon east of Lake St. Clair's Anchor Bay, the lead Humvee carrying General McIntyre, sporting two large U.S. flags perched atop each of its side-view mirrors, crept forward and then sped up. The line of Humvees, trucks, and tanks behind it followed suit and traveled close behind.

Two sporty souped-up blue Dodge Chargers with Michigan State Trooper markings sped ahead of the general's Humvee with their signature single red dome light perched on each of their roofs flashing and sirens blaring. The convoy progressed north along Jefferson Avenue, exited Selfridge through the main gate, and turned slowly onto William Rosso Highway. After just over one-and-a-quarter miles, the convoy merged southbound onto Interstate 94, which remained clear at least as far as Gratiot Avenue.

In the sky above, a Kiowa Warrior-class observation helicopter with its distinctive large ball-like camera system perched above its rotors closely monitored the convoy's path for any threats. The ball—known as a mass-mounted sight, or MMS—contained an array of sensors like a high-definition television camera with long-distance zooming capability, a thermal imaging sensor, a laser system for target acquisitioning, and navigational tools. The Kiowa was General McIntyre's "eye in the sky" and kept close watch over the convoy and surrounding areas. The Kiowa maintained constant contact with four Apache helicopter gunships that circled above the convoy and which would investigate anything the Kiowa picked up as suspicious or potentially threatening to the movement of the convoy.

The convoy moved rather slowly and cautiously at no more than forty-five miles per hour, and slowed down even further whenever the Kiowa helicopter spotted something it deemed threatening. News helicopters flew at a minimum distance of ten miles from the convoy and covered its movement from Selfridge to Detroit live on national television. Though not many people were glued to their TV sets at

6:00 a.m. Eastern Time, the video at least provided footage for re-porters covering the deployment of the Army throughout the day.

Nearly forty-five minutes after departing Selfridge, the convoy passed under the Alter Road overpass and entered Detroit proper. Despite the early hour and below freezing temperatures, a consider-able crowd stood atop the Alter Road bridge. They had tied a large U.S. flag to the pedestrian fence and they jumped up and down, cheering loudly as the convoy passed beneath them. To the delight of the crowd, General McIntyre's Humvee honked its horn as it went by.

The convoy turned off Interstate 94 at Exit 219 and merged south-bound onto Gratiot Avenue. Entering the heart of police-fortified downtown Detroit, it slowed to a crawl, turned right onto Broadway Street, and then left onto East Grand River Avenue and into a sea of parking lots across East Grand River Avenue from the GLEE head-quarters that was now designated as New Fort Detroit. The site was just five blocks north of the original Fort Pontchartrain du Détroit, the isolated French outpost built in 1701 as a defense against British incursions into the interior of North America. The original site was now occupied by office buildings and the Cobo Convention Center.

The second and third convoys, each comprised primarily of AM General M35 troop transport trucks, approximately fifty in total, with each truck carrying twenty-five soldiers (some twenty-five hundred soldiers in total), closely followed on the heels of the first one. However, rather than turning into the parking lots of New Fort Detroit, one convoy continued northwestward on Grand River Avenue in full force. Accompanying it were the five M1A2 Abrams tanks, a flatbed truck transporting four D9 armored bulldozers, and an M88 recovery vehicle.

The third convoy continued, snaking left on Washington Boulevard, and then right onto Michigan Avenue.

The Grand River Avenue convoy, which included the five Abrams tanks, separated into thirds. The tanks took the lead as the first sec-tion traveled straight up Grand River and smashed through or flat-tened the burned-out hulks of multiple cars and cleared the road of pyres of burning tires and other debris. The tanks spread out and took up positions on all sides of the Olympia Armory, training their turrets on the armory's still-smoldering ruins. Two tanks sat on the McGraw Street Bridge over Interstate 96 and covered the western flank of the armory.

With the tanks in position to cover all sides of the armory, the other two sections of the convoy disembarked more than one hundred soldiers north and south of the armory, who took up defensive positions. Several cameramen and war correspondents with national media were embedded with the assault teams to capture the troops as they secured the armory.

At least that was the plan.

Armor Crewman Specialist Christian Beck, a twenty-year old tank gunner from San Diego, California, felt a deep rumble through the periscope his face was pressed against, and the world outside the tank trembled. He pulled his face away from the periscope and was about to ask his crewmates if there was an earthquake when the world turned upside down and he had the sudden sensation of falling. Then everything went black.

* * *

Twenty-year-old Private First Class Adrian Gonzales jumped out of a transport truck and got his first glimpse of Detroit. He let out an audible gasp. The truck was covered with a canvas, so Adrian and the other soldiers couldn't see anything for the nearly one-hour trip from Selfridge until they disembarked from the truck. Adrian kept up with the news and saw footage on TV and the internet before being deployed but, even so, nothing could have prepared him for what he saw.

It wasn't just the smoldering remains of the Olympia Armory and the acrid smoke it produced. It was the lack of people and buildings; the city was desolate. To his right, straight down Grand River Avenue, the tall buildings of downtown Detroit loomed four miles in the distance. The five towers of the Renaissance Center with its Marriott Hotel at the center, still the tallest building in Michigan, was instantly recognizable.

Apart from downtown in the near distance, Adrian could see only a handful of small buildings scattered around here and there, all of which appeared to be long abandoned. Some were blackened by fire, but Adrian couldn't tell if that was recent or not. Overgrown empty lots crisscrossed by streets and sidewalks filled up the spaces in between the smattering of abandoned buildings. Interstate 96 ran parallel to Grand River, at least adjacent to Olympia Armory, and it was eerily empty of traffic in one direction, but full of abandoned cars filling out the eastbound lanes. Most sat with their doors open and windows open or smashed. Some were burned husks. It was a scene straight out of a movie about zombies, perhaps, or some epidemic that killed off the population.

Adrian grew up in suburban Phoenix, Arizona, whose worst neighborhoods—at least from what he could tell—looked downright posh compared to here. *This...this isn't even America,* thought Adrian. *How can this be the USA?*

Adrian and his squad had been dropped off next to an old and small abandoned strip mall that sat across the street from the smoldering armory, and they had gathered behind it as two tanks took their positions on the bridge over the interstate, their turrets trained on the smoking ruins of the armory.

Adrian looked at the tanks on the bridge. Everything about the whole deployment became totally surreal the moment they had taken off from Fort Drum in Upstate New York. He turned his attention back to the armory

"Move out!" his squad gunny barked.

Adrian felt a deep rumble followed by an earth-shaking *CRASH* directly to his left where the interstate paralleled the armory. A massive cloud of dust hid the interstate and rose high into the air, the roiling dust mixed with black smoke.

Adrian could no longer see the tanks. Soldiers dropped to the ground and trained their rifles on the dust cloud where the tanks should have been.

"What the fuck was *that?*" someone loudly exclaimed.

The dust cloud slowly spread out and faded in density. Adrian saw that the tanks were not there anymore. Nor was the bridge they were parked on. *Did the bridge collapse?* he thought, then repeated his thought aloud. "I think the bridge collapsed!" he shouted, then shouted it again.

The McGraw Street Bridge was an unremarkable urban bridge that crossed Interstate 96 and linked the east side of the Northwest Goldberg residential neighborhood with the west. It was also unremarkable in the sense that it was one of the more than two hundred thousand bridges across the United States deemed to be structurally deficient by the American Society of Civil Engineers, and in dire need of repair. But the U.S. Congress had consistently put off funding for infrastructural improvement and even maintenance for decades. Consequently, the costs for upgrading U.S. infrastructure nationwide had jumped to nearly two trillion dollars, a cost that was politically poisonous.

And so, when the two M1A2 Abrams tanks, with a combined weight of two hundred eighty-eight thousand pounds, took up their positions on the bridge to cover the Olympia Armory's western flank, it was too much weight for the bridge to handle, and it disintegrated beneath them in the blink of an eye.

* * *

Aaron Jones awoke to the deep *thump-thump-thump* of helicopters flying low and seemingly directly over his house. It was not the more normal sound of low-flying police helicopters in the middle of the night. This was military grade, and it was one after another.

The sun shone brightly through the bedroom window curtains.

Aaron rolled out of bed and sat for a moment. His mind was empty. He closed his eyes and rested his head on his palm, supported by his elbow on his thigh.

Another *thump-thump-thump* and the house really rattled this time. But Aaron remained frozen in that Zen-like momentary lull. He allowed it to drag into the next *thump-thump-thump* that passed over the house.

With a grunt, he got up and went about getting ready for the day, and quickly. He wanted to see what was going on.

"Something's going on outside, Ma," he said when he walked into the living room. A small television set was on, but his mother wasn't there. He walked into the kitchen, tore open a pop tart and munched on it. He looked outside and saw crowds of people standing around and peering at the sky. His mother was among them.

Aaron grabbed his coat and walked out the back door through the kitchen, texting Michelle, Xavier, and Devin.

Another *thump-thump-thump* passed over the house and Aaron looked up at a large low-flying, double-bladed Chinook helicopter.

Cool, he thought. It looked like the helicopter was landing just a few streets away, and he chased after it.

It was actually about a mile away when the Chinook finally landed, but before it did, another one lifted off. It, too, looked like it had taken off right from a few streets away, but the distance didn't seem to lessen as Aaron still chased after the first Chinook. Two Black Hawk helicopters, meanwhile, circled in the distance.

Unexpectedly, a third Black Hawk appeared—again, seeming just a few streets away—as it lifted off from the ground, near where the Chinook had landed.

"Yo, Aaron!" It was Devin, jogging to catch up. Aaron waited momentarily, and then the two tentatively approached the crumbling Kronk Gym as another helicopter passed overhead.

It was their first time back to the corner since Nathan and Dwayne were shot. Aaron and Devin kept an eye out for River Gees, but they didn't see any. Xavier and Michelle waited for them the next block over, amid a crowd on Warren Avenue.

"Check it out," said Xavier, nodding to the broad street. "Army's here."

Michelle snuggled up to Aaron when he and Devin stepped up on the curb. Army trucks, one after another, drove past them. They stopped about four blocks to their west near a Coca-Cola Bottling center and an auto parts factory. Dozens of heavily armed soldiers disembarked.

But Aaron maintained eye contact with Xavier, who nodded toward the other side of the street.

Aaron scanned the crowd across the street and the boarded-up lone building—a one-time office of some sort—and when he saw it, his heart jumped.

There, among the weeds alongside the little building, were two sets of bare feet sticking out from beneath cardboard boxes and other trash.

Tears welled up in Aaron's eyes and he wiped his face. Surely it was Nathan and Dwayne. It had been five full days since they were killed. Rumor had it that the River Gees let them lay where they fell for days on end. It appeared the rumor was true.

More Army trucks barreled toward them. The air brakes on the trucks hissed and they came to a stop right in front of the growing crowd. Dozens more soldiers began disembarking, and Aaron saw even more large Army trucks coming down the road.

The soldiers massed in front of the lone business still in operation here, a Citgo gas station. The five other buildings clumped along the intersection were burned-out hulks of long-ago failed and abandoned stores and garages.

"Go home!" a soldier barked over a bullhorn. "Disperse or you will be arrested."

"We *are* home, muthafuckas," muttered a middle-aged man.

"Stay off the streets!" another soldier with a bullhorn ordered.

"You will not be warned again!"

"Come on," Xavier said, pulling Aaron, and he and his friends made their way over to the more residential McGraw Street, which crossed diagonally over Warren, as did some of the others of the now-dispersing crowd.

But, in just a few blocks, McGraw, too, was crowded with soldiers and their trucks. Aaron could hear the engines of various helicopters. A Black Hawk lifted off practically right in front of them, from out of some sort of indentation in the ground. The helicopter had lifted off from the interstate, he realized.

Another crowd stood in the middle of McGraw Street as Aaron and his friends approached. They couldn't quite see what the Army was doing, but they were doing something big.

"What's going on?" asked Devin as the four kids stepped in among the crowd.

"Bridge collapsed," said an older man. "Took down a couple of tanks," he added. "It's a big-time rescue operation."

The older gentleman looked the kids over. "You boys best be careful. The Army isn't going to mess around after something like this. They'll be looking to round up young folks for just about nothing. Something to show they're *doing* something."

"Uh-huh," mumbled Aaron, not paying attention. The excitement of helicopters taking off and landing, and the troops deploying, was long gone. His mind was on the bodies a few blocks behind him.

CHAPTER 20

As the rescue operation unfolded at the McGraw Street Bridge, and soldiers fanned out along Grand River Avenue and Michigan Avenue in the west and south, another series of Army convoys headed up Woodward Avenue—Detroit's vibrant main thoroughfare—from downtown to New Center. A squad of soldiers disembarked at the Pistons Arena at the foot of downtown, but the thrust of the convoys proceeded through Midtown, passing the Hospital District and Wayne State University.

Wayne State University, which had its own police force, was able to keep destructive crowds from the campus itself. Students in on-campus dormitories and in off-campus apartments and houses surrounding the university and in Midtown had joined in the city-wide protests by taking to the streets all along Woodward Avenue and on the streets surrounding campus, but they were entirely peaceful and were far enough away from the police response in downtown and the ensuing panic and violence. And so, while Midtown was largely left unpoliced during the unrest with the Detroit police hunkered down in the downtown, Midtown was left largely unscathed with the exception of a few smashed storefronts and restaurants along with some looting, but affected businesses were randomly distributed along the thoroughfare and not clustered.

Army trucks nevertheless disembarked soldiers to patrol along Woodward Avenue.

The main convoys continued up Woodward Avenue to New Center, a commercial island across I-94 north of Midtown amid a sea of residential neighborhoods that sprawled out to Oakland and Warren Counties and beyond.

Unlike Midtown, New Center was hit hard. Nearly every single store and restaurant was looted and burned.

The army convoys turned west and east along Grand Boulevard and dispatched over two hundred soldiers to patrol the more than three-mile length of the boulevard between Grand River Avenue in the west and the massive, now empty General Motors Hamtramck Assembly Plant, to the east.

* * *

The sound of helicopters jolted Lamar Griffin out of bed. He didn't want to, but something was happening outside again, causing his heart to jump in his chest. A pang of fear shot through him. Not a fear for his own well-being. This was a daunting fear of what the day would bring, because the last two days were the worst two days of Lamar Griffin's young life.

He kept replaying it in his head. He couldn't stop. First, his little cousin, dead. He and his friends, just lying there with all of those people standing around. And the sound of his auntie and his own mother crying—no, *wailing*—it was like a knife in his back that he couldn't dislodge.

That Army Humvee in the middle of the road, burning.

No one knew what to do. Everyone just flailed about, screaming. Then Chad Greer, with his own mother right there, pulled out his gun and started shooting at Army guys running down the street. People scattered. Others got their guns out, too. It was bedlam.

And then it was just Lamar and a few others left to stand over the bodies of Dominic, Shawn, and Chad. Women hovered over Auntie

Sheila, Dominic's mother, as she lay in the middle of the street, sobbing. Lamar saw his own mother—it was like she was somebody else, unrelated—trying to console Auntie Sheila, her sister.

Shouldn't we help Dominic? Lamar wondered. But looking at him—and Shawn and Chad, too—clearly, they were dead. It was just…definitive. A cold fact. You knew.

Lamar squatted beside the body of his cousin, facing away from it. He couldn't look at him anymore.

"We have to take him home," said a quiet voice. Lamar looked up. It was Felix, from the neighborhood. Worked at a warehouse or something. Lamar never spoke to him before.

"Can you help me get him home?" Felix asked. Lamar wiped his eyes and nodded.

When they gathered him up—Lamar taking Dominic's feet, Felix struggling to carry him by the armpits—the finality of the boy's death hit Lamar like a ton of bricks. He reeled in a daze as they carried his cousin's body, shuffling their feet as they went, for a full three blocks to his Auntie Sheila's house.

There was nothing dignified about how they struggled to carry him, and Lamar quietly seethed.

The neighborhood seemed to follow Lamar and Felix. They walked alongside, talking in hushed tones, sharing the news with others who were coming out to see what the commotion was. That led to more screams, more wailing. There was Christina, and her friends—school mates of Dominic and his friends—now screaming and crying.

When they arrived at Auntie Sheila's house, others met them there, laying out sheets and blankets for the body. They wrapped up Dominic's body and laid him on the couch in the living room.

Auntie Sheila, helped by a group of women and men, followed them in, wailing nonstop. "Oh, *gawd,* my *baby!"* she cried over and over.

Lamar found a quiet corner and stayed as a procession of family, friends, and neighbors crowded the small house throughout the day. Someone squeezed his shoulder, and Lamar stood up. It was his mother, and she hugged him tightly. He had to gently push her away after a moment because she didn't want to let go. Angelica, his girlfriend, was next, and now *he* didn't want to let go.

Men talked in hushed tones in the small dining room, away from Auntie Sheila. "He can't stay here," said an older man with a whitish goatee. "Not overnight," he said.

"No one is going to come for him," said another. "Not with all that's going on."

"Hendrick's Funeral Home ain't answering the phone," said yet another. "Ain't no one working in the middle of a damned riot."

The men and family organized a sort of funeral procession for later that evening. A friend of the family drove a pickup truck, and they loaded Dominic's body in its bed. Lamar, Felix, and five others acted as pallbearers and rode in the back of the truck with Dominic's body. A couple of the others were part of some remnant of the BMF, Dominic surmised, and they sported what looked like military-grade automatic rifles slung across their shoulders.

They trekked slowly for the one mile straight down Grand Boulevard to Henry Ford Hospital, the whole neighborhood walking alongside the pickup truck that crawled at pedestrian speed. Another car followed from a distance, and a third even farther behind, bearing the bodies of Chad and Shawn.

The following day was full of rage. Lamar was consumed by it. It was nonstop, all day long. Lamar, friends, and neighbors poured up Grand Boulevard into New Center. The big, official-looking buildings and businesses up and down the boulevard in New Center were always so close, but so far away. He sometimes wondered what was in those buildings, what it was like to work in them. One multi-story office building of bland 1960s architecture with "Work Force" in big bold letters followed by "Solutions" in a smaller font, the words spelled out in red, single-letter signage along the top of the building, stood authoritatively at the intersection of Grand Boulevard and Woodward Avenue. Work Force Solutions, a temporary employment agency, was just the latest company to occupy the building.

It was the first large, uninviting building the crowds had come across. They smashed their way into the lobby and found the building empty. All day long people went in and went out, looting what they could, some just taking out their anger on another cold and indifferent corporation. WFS wasn't GLEE, and it wasn't the Army that shot Dominic, but it was surely cut from the same cloth.

As the day gave way to night, several fires big and small burned in the various floors of the eight-story WFS Building. Three blocks over stood the historic thirty-story art deco Fisher Building skyscraper on Grand Boulevard and, across the street from that, the historic four towers with fifteen stories each, comprising Cadillac Place. Once the headquarters for Cadillac, Cadillac Place now housed state agencies. The Fisher Building housed a restaurant and bar on the ground floor, a law firm on the second floor, and Detroit Public Schools occupied all of the floors above the second.

These buildings were warmer than the WFS building. They were embraced by a patina that told of Detroit's history as a one-time center of manufacturing, commerce and culture, which somehow took the edge off the raging crowds, leaving both complexes largely untouched, at least in terms of looting floor by floor. In the central tower of Cadillac Place, however, someone had set fire to the trash cans in the lobby bathrooms, which had set off the building's fire alarm and sprinkler system, destroying and damaging hundreds of computers and furniture throughout the building.

The large buildings in the heart of New Center were not the only ones to bear the brunt of the neighborhood's ire. Even dentists' and doctors' offices were sacked and looted—anything that reeked of authority or economic gouging.

And now Lamar was spent. After a long day of running with his friends and even family members—other cousins, uncles, and aunts—all through New Center and along Grand Boulevard, throwing rocks, lighting up Molotov cocktails, and looting whatever was left of already looted pharmacies and stores, he made his way back to his own street and sat on a curb with Angelica and listened to gunfire near and far, and helicopters crisscrossing the night sky.

They laughed when he emptied his pockets of random, pointless loot from a nearby pharmacy: a Snickers bar, a small bottle of antacids, and a small bottle of some kind of laxative. Lamar tossed the bottles aside but tore open the candy bar and shared it with Angelica.

When he returned home, the events of the day before came rushing, crushing, back. *Dominic...*

Eventually, impossibly, sleep enveloped him.

And now something was happening. Something more. And it was not even 9:00 a.m.

Lamar threw on a t-shirt and jeans and looked out his bedroom window. He could hear some distant shouting and commotion but couldn't see anything. Only when he stepped out into the frigid morning air did he see others looking tentatively around and walking toward the boulevard.

As Lamar approached Grand Boulevard, his routine for the week now, he saw crowds had already gathered at intersections all along Grand Boulevard. Army trucks streamed along the boulevard, stopping and disembarking soldiers dozens at a time. And the trucks kept coming.

* * *

Gino Napolitano was the first to hop out of his troop transport truck. A sergeant and squad leader, Gino quickly barked orders and organized his young men and women. He passed each member of his squad a small card outlining the rules of engagement, and went through various scenarios.

Other squad leaders did the same as more trucks and squads arrived.

Squared away and ready for patrol, Gino only now smelled the acrid smell of smoke in the air. Then his eyes took in the buildings scarred black. Points of orange light danced in random windows high up on various floors of the surrounding buildings.

At only twenty-four, he was the veteran of the group. He had been deployed to Iraq, a country endlessly under siege by various armed groups, a situation that began with the United States' invasion in 2003, but he didn't know anything about that because it had happened long before he was born. Nothing could have prepared him for what he would see in Iraq. The bombed-out cities, the stoic faces of Iraqi citizens, including children. The constant awareness for potential attack. Maybe a sniper. Sometimes a mortar barrage. Every car, truck, even camel, was a potential vehicle-based improvised explosive device (VIED); essentially, a car bomb. Or camel bomb. Seriously.

That same palpable sense of danger that enveloped him in Iraq came right back to the fore. This was a war zone. *But this is America,* his mind protested.

Despite the early hour, throngs of people gathered along Grand Boulevard and watched the soldiers as they went to work.

Their faces were stoic, brooding. And their eyes…their eyes had that blank stare of the Iraqis.

Trouble, his mind flashed. There was going to be trouble.

A glass beer bottle smashed to the ground off to his right.

Here we go, he thought.

* * *

Jayson Avery was back at his Uncle Fave's house. Fave sat watching the television intently. News helicopters filmed from above as the Army sprawled out across the city below—from downtown to Eight Mile in the north; from the initial unrest centered on Bernadette Price's house in Jackson/Mack in the east; to Redmond Charter in the northwest; to Dearborn in the southwest.

That was a lot of soldiers. The Army was everywhere. Their Black Hawk and Chinook helicopters filled the sky.

But the biggest story was the rescue operation occurring at the McGraw Street Bridge adjacent to the still-smoldering Olympia Armory. Fave could hear the commotion from his house, which was only blocks to the south of the whole episode.

What captured Fave's attention—indeed, he was intensely focused on the television—was what was happening two miles to the east of the rescue operation along Grand Boulevard. Protesters in New Center and the surrounding neighborhood were confronting the Army. News helicopters could only film from afar with zoomed-in cameras, but what they showed was a real melee. Rocks and bottles rained down on gathering soldiers wielding shields.

Fave leaned back and grunted, and stroked his chin. New Center was Grand River Gees territory.

CHAPTER 21
DAY 7

I t was a busy night for the Army. Despite their deployment, protesters still gathered at the major flash points across the city during the overnight hours. But the Army methodically descended
on crowds with shields and rifles—and, in New Center, with tear
gas. They pursued and arrested anyone they could get their hands
on. It was after dark and, if you were outside, you were breaking
curfew—and the law.

The Army arrested more than a thousand people during the night,
but the soldiers' presence had kept the city mostly peaceful.

In the morning, Governor Krueger and Mayor Murray encour-
aged businesses to reopen and for people to begin the clean-up following the worst urban riots since Los Angeles. The dusk-to-dawn
curfew would remain in effect, however, and so businesses had to
close early enough for their workers and customers to return home
before nightfall.

Army soldiers continued to patrol the streets of Detroit, particularly along the city's major roadways and boulevards. Kiowa Warrior
observation helicopters kept tabs on the city and, wherever protestors
tried to gather, they quickly found themselves outnumbered by armed
soldiers. They would be very quickly set upon, subdued, zip-tied, and
placed into the back of M35 troop transport trucks making hourly
rounds. The arrested would face charges of unlawful assembly.

* * *

Four whole nights the Ayalas—Arturo, Jacqueline, and Frederick—spent at the Children's Hospital of Michigan. It sounded like World War III in the city outside the hospital campus, and the massive explosion at the Olympia Armory that broke windows and shook the entire city on their very first night ensured that they were going nowhere until they found Martín.

The hospital staff, though very busy with walk-in injuries, gunshot victims, and the like, were very accommodating. They checked each day with other hospitals in the region, but there were no records of a Martín Ayala being admitted.

After their third night, with the Army was being deployed across the city, the family walked back down Brush Street but once again found the downtown closed off. The Army was everywhere—convoy after convoy passed them by, and soldiers patrolled the streets. They were stopped and questioned by young soldiers (Jackie was shocked at how young they were) nearly ten times on their trek down Brush Street and, when they reached the bridge over I-94 into downtown, it was manned by a police checkpoint.

The police remained on edge despite the presence of the Army, but at least they appeared to be more approachable this time. They wore helmets and sported riot shields, but they weren't wearing gas masks. So the Ayala family approached a group of police loitering on the bridge. "Go back," yelled an officer as they approached, while the others kept an eye on them.

"Our son is missing!" shouted Arturo.

"Please!" pleaded Jackie, "it's been four days!"

"Go back!" the same officer shouted, but an older officer approached them. He listened as Arturo and Jackie told their story and was sympathetic. Since the boy had not turned up at any of the hospitals, he advised them to return to the city the next day and head for DPSH, the police headquarters. The city should be reopened then, at least partially so, and it was possible that their son was among the more than five thousand people in police custody. If he was, he should be in the database.

And so they spent yet another night at the Children's Hospital, then returned to downtown at first light.

The sympathetic officer was right. A single police car remained parked to the side on the Brush Street Bridge into downtown, but the family wasn't stopped as they walked across, nor were they interrogated by patrolling soldiers on their way in.

They made it to DPSH and found a madhouse. Police came and went, and they were ushered from one big office to another. And it was loud. People were talking everywhere, all at the same time, a constant din of chatter, as people came to report all sorts of things, including missing persons as the Ayalas were doing.

They had given their story and Martín's name and age to several different police officers, anyone who would listen for a few minutes, but they were forced to wait.

It was almost four hours of waiting before a policewoman found them in the chaotic lobby of the main entrance. The boy was in their database and was being held at the Cobo Center. He was slated for release within the hour.

"Oh, my God," sobbed Jacqueline. "Thank you so much," she said to the policewoman.

"Good luck," said the officer as the family headed for the door.

The family left one madhouse and found another at the Cobo Center. When they left DPSH, they counted themselves lucky to have arrived so early. A line of people outside DPSH trying to get in snaked for more than two blocks. When they arrived at the Cobo Center, several thousand people stood cluttered around the main entrance. At least as many police and soldiers were lined up on either side with gas masks dangling from their belts.

Meanwhile, lines of people streamed out of the Cobo Center. Most individuals would stop momentarily to look for someone they recognized, or to get their bearings, before walking off into the crowd.

As the Ayalas worked their way through the crowd, people were crying and hugging all around them as loved ones reconnected. "There he is!" exclaimed Frederick excitedly, pointing.

Yes, there he was among a group of young people hugging.

"*Martín!*" Jackie happily squealed and stomped her feet before nearly tackling him where he stood. "My baby!" she squealed again, as tears streamed down her face.

Martín absorbed the hugs and kisses, his face alight with joy. Tears streamed down his face. Frederick lightly punched him in the arm before hugging him as well. Both pulled away after a moment, wiping their faces.

"These are my friends," Martín said, turning to the group of young people standing beside them. "This is Ian and Tina," he said, his hand introducing a slight Asian kid and a white girl with curly brown hair, both of whom were being hugged by three other young people.

"He did really good," said Tina, and ruffled Martín's hair.

* * *

For Matthew and Maria, and for their hosts Maxwell and Linda Levine, the war across the border in Detroit was relentless. It was a long four days since Maria and Matthew were taken in by the Levines. The constant din of small arms fire day and night, and helicopters flying overhead, made it seem much longer.

Maria felt safe with Maxwell and Linda, and she couldn't be more grateful for their refuge. Her children were safe. That was what mattered most. In fact, it was the *only* thing that mattered, and she wept with the providence that she had made a wrong turn and ended up in Canada. Any misgiving drained away with each day that the unrest in Detroit continued.

Maria was able to contact her parents in the Mexicantown neighborhood of Detroit after arriving at Maxwell and Linda's, and she checked in several times a day. Her parents were largely trapped in their home. There were no police or other services; it was a free for all until the Army arrived the day before. Thankfully, they hadn't experienced any trouble and were able to ride out the unrest.

Most frustrating, strange even, was that her parents were only just over a mile away as the crow flies. Maria and her parents were on either side of the Detroit River but they might as well have been a million miles apart.

And while the U.S. Army was just getting a hold on Detroit, Canada's Essex and Kent Scottish had Windsor under wraps for three days going. Matthew was able to phone in to his company and, luckily, they didn't think he was completely mental when he told them that their truck was still sitting on the Ambassador Bridge. He had learned through television news that, after they had arrived, the Essex and Kent Scottish had gone right to work to clear the Canadian side of the bridge of abandoned vehicles, and that the U.S. Army was in process of clearing the American side.

Matthew wasn't entirely sure which side of the border the truck was parked on, but he thought that maybe it was past the half-way point. After a few phone calls and long holds, he found his truck. The Canadians had it. It was impounded in the Police Services lot on the east side of town. He had learned that the truck was in good shape and that it wasn't looted. He still had a delivery to make and it was time to move on.

After a teary goodbye from Matthew for Maria, Maxwell drove Matthew to the impound and, after paying the fees and filling out the paperwork, Matthew was on his way to deliver his goods to a warehouse in Hamilton, Ontario.

* * *

The unrest in Detroit came to an end with the deployment of the

10th Mountain Division. Much of the unrest in cities beyond Detroit, like Ann Arbor and Pontiac, also came to an end for the most part. But unrest continued in Flint, and General McIntyre ordered a battalion of five hundred of his 10th Mountain Division soldiers into the city, augmented by an additional thousand National Guardsmen from armories at Flint, Bay City, Saginaw, Cadillac, and Grand Rapids.

The four Marine F-35 joint strike fighters temporarily on duty at Selfridge did another flyover, this time over Flint, as did several Army Apache gunship helicopters. The small National Guard Armory in Flint was located alongside Interstate 75 and away from the downtown and any commercial district, and so it didn't suffer the same fate as that of the Olympia Armory in Detroit. The Flint Armory and Dayton Park, an open field that abutted the small armory, became the staging area for the National Guard troops, but the 10th Mountain Division soldiers would shuttle back and forth between Flint and Selfridge Air Base.

The appearance of the combined force of fifteen hundred soldiers quickly put an end to the unrest in Flint as well.

CHAPTER 22

Moe stood in the smoking ruins of the Olympia Armory near what was the front of the building, even as the Army continued its clean-up following the McGraw Street Bridge collapse. Chinook helicopters continued to land and lift off on the freeway astride the wreckage of the bridge.

An Army Explosive Ordnance Disposal (EOD) team combed through the crater where the rear of the building had stood, looking for and marking unexploded HIMARS rockets and other ammunition. The EOD technicians were dressed in full bomb suits.

Moe was forbidden to be on site until the EOD guys gave the green light, but the officer in charge acquiesced somewhat and allowed him to explore parts of the premises after a withering glare that read "try and stop me."

Moe saw where it looked like a large hand had swiped part of the front of the building away and understood why the hulk of a burned-out Caterpillar excavator sat in the smoking ruins of the building. *So that's how they got in,* he thought. Surely he would find that the Caterpillar was stolen from a nearby construction or demolition site. His team was already tracking that lead.

Also sitting in the smoking carnage were the burned-out hulks of three HIMARS trucks, but the number of parking spaces suggested there should be more. Was it possible that local gangs drove off with multiple heavy-duty artillery-launching vehicles? What on earth would local goons want with a platform that launched artillery more than one hundred fifty miles?

Moe looked around at the surrounding neighborhoods and highways. This was professional, he thought, even if it was opportunistic. You don't just drive off with army-grade heavy weapons systems, nor do you steal them for your own use if you are a local drug gang. No, this was high-end stuff, professional.

It was organized crime. *Had to be.*

* * *

Ian and Tina were met by Trevor, Sarah, and Dakota after departing the Cobo Center. They were surprised and relieved to find their three cross country friends waiting for them. They were tearfully hugging each other when Martín's family stepped up and embraced their son. Ian and Tina were doubly relieved that Martín had reunited with his family.

Ian and Tina spoke with the Ayalas for a few minutes to exchange contact information and to see the family off.

"How's Roland?" asked Ian, turning to his friends as the family departed.

Trevor, Sarah, and Dakota all looked at each other. "We thought he was with you," said Trevor.

Tina broke down and sobbed. She and Ian told them what had happened.

"Oh, shit," whispered Trevor. "He must be in the hospital, then."

The Wayne State students walked back toward campus and stopped at the Detroit Receiving Hospital complex, part of which encompassed the Children's Hospital of Michigan. There was no record of a Roland Morris.

The following day, the students called other hospitals in the area, and again there was no record. Even the Detroit Police said they had no record. Ian called and asked again, to no avail. A tingle went down his spine. *What could it mean that the Detroit PD said they had no record of Roland when they had obviously taken him?*

Ian and his friends went back to the hospital and asked about bodies. They were desperate to find Roland, and eventually a concerned nurse accompanied them to the morgue, where more than twenty bodies remained unclaimed.

The nurse went into the morgue and examined the tags of multiple bodies before coming to one with an approximate age and description of their friend. When she unzipped the body bag, a shoulder-length shaggy-haired boy stared wildly back at her. He was listed as a John Doe, but generally fit the description they had given her. She sighed and took a moment before going to the door.

She let only the boys in. "I can't be sure, but…," she said, her face grim. "You have to brace yourself," she said before leading them to the table.

Ian looked in and immediately looked away, his face breaking. He nodded that it was Roland and sniffled. Trevor just stared, his face pale. The nurse closed the bag.

"We have to notify the next of kin," said the nurse. "Do you have contact information for his family?" Ian nodded again and wiped his face.

"I need to fill out some paperwork," said the nurse. "Please come with me." She led the distraught boys to an office. "I'm truly sorry," she added.

* * *

Michigan's governor had ordered that the state of emergency and dusk-to-dawn curfew for Detroit and Flint stay in place for at least another week following the deployment of the Army. But things appeared to be slowly returning to normal. With widespread unrest now effectively over, the 10th Mountain Division focused on clearing the freeways and major roadways of abandoned and burned vehicles, tires, and other debris.

Businesses, schools, and government offices reopened.

National and global media largely moved on, except for some stories focused on the clean-up and costs of the unrest. The damage in Detroit was thankfully estimated to be less than $1 billion. While many businesses were looted, and some burned, most of the estimated ten thousand-plus reported fires were abandoned and deteriorating homes, factories, and long boarded-up businesses.

There were seventy-eight reported fatalities that occurred during the unrest, making the "GLEE Uprising" second only to the 1863 New York City Draft Riots in terms of fatalities: seventy-two of the dead were civilians, two National Guardsmen, and four active duty soldiers killed in the McGraw Street bridge collapse. One hundred twenty people had been killed in the Draft Riots of New York.

It was not known how many of the seventy-two deceased civilians were rioters, three of which were known to have been killed by the National Guard in New Center, and several others by armed motorists and business owners. Some of the civilian fatalities were bystanders or motorists set upon by angry mobs. Other fatalities appeared to be gangland murders, with gang members apparently taking advantage of the breakdown of civil order to target rivals or settle scores.

Local media focused on police efforts to investigate the seventy-two fatalities and other major crimes, like the raid on the Olympia Armory and other National Guard armories around the state. Various federal law enforcement agencies—the FBI, DEA, ATF, and the U.S. Army's CID—had all deployed to Selfridge along with the 10th Mountain Division. Each agency conducted its own investigations and aided the Detroit Police Department as much as possible because, according to crime statistics, nearly ninety percent of murders had gone unsolved in Detroit each year for nearly a decade.

It wasn't long before federal law enforcement made its presence felt. Early in the pre-dawn morning after the initial deployment of the 10th Mountain Division, an all-black Lenco BEAR armored personnel carrier pulled out of Selfridge Air Base along with four black SUVs and three police vans. Selfridge was well beyond the city limits of Detroit, and thus outside the designated geography under a dusk-to-dawn curfew. Traffic on the I-94 Edsel Ford Freeway was light at 3:30 a.m., but the appearance of the Lenco BEAR in the midst of police vans and black SUVs winding down the highway at breakneck speed nevertheless garnered attention from motorists.

In the city, some people still ventured out in their neighborhoods despite the overnight curfew. Most hung around close to their homes to dip back inside if Army trucks or Detroit Police patrols—each police car paired with an Army squad for support—happened on their street, or when helicopters passed overhead. But the police and Army stayed mostly on the main roadways in the overnight hours.

Even with a few people breaking curfew across the city, there was practically no one out and about at nearly 4:00 a.m. when the small speeding convoy passed into Detroit city limits. Nevertheless, the convoy did not go unseen by lookouts and night owls.

Within minutes of passing into the city, the Lenco BEAR and convoy housing an FBI SWAT Team had merged onto I-96 and exited on Livernois Avenue.

To those who caught a glimpse of the BEAR and convoy, there was no doubt that they were law enforcement. The all-black Lenco BEAR looked particularly ominous, earning the hashtag #batmobile by observers. Even before the SWAT convoy pulled up in front of a nearly one-hundred-year-old, two-story SEARs catalogue home on American Street in what Neighborhood Scout deemed the most violent neighborhood in the country, hashtag #batmobile had become a thing.

The hashtags #batmobile, #SlavePatrol and #GIJoe came to life on Twitter, Whatsapp, SnapChat, Instagram, YikYak, and multiple other social media, producing a moment-by-moment, play-by-play update of the BEAR's direction and location.

A few selections of the #batmobile / #SlavePatrol / #GIJoe social media storm with users and accounts redacted are listed below:

I, Detroit @I_Detroit 4:05AM wakie wakie yall #SlavePatrol on da go #batmobile

I, Detroit @I_Detroit 4:10AM #SlavePatrol #batmobile gr2liver ('gr2liver' for on Grand River Avenue and turning onto passing Livernois Avenue)

I, Detroit @I_Detroit 4:11AM #SlavePatrol #batmobile stop@ american (for the convoy stopping at a location on American Street)

As quickly as the social media hashtags became a thing, it was too late for 19-year-old Cedric Hart, the unlucky winner whose name was randomly pulled from the Detroit Police Department's database of unserved arrest warrants. Young Cedric was wanted for aggravated assault and other charges for a strong-armed robbery weeks before the unrest. He had so far been able, rather easily, to avoid apprehension. The Detroit PD simply didn't have the resources to track down wanted suspects for anything less than murder, and even there they weren't having much success.

And suspects like Cedric Hart didn't have a permanent address. The house on American Street was the address of a girlfriend, information provided by the Detroit PD's Gang Intelligence Unit (GIU). Cedric's name had come up in other investigations by the GIU, who suspected that Cedric might be an enforcer for some crew that had gone independent after the fall of the Black Mafia Family.

The FBI SWAT Team and police gang unit scored. Cedric was found scrambling shirtless out the back door into the cold night seconds after the front door was smashed in with a battering ram.

Four more suspects were caught before sunrise. And, with each movement of the BEAR and convoy, the hashtags #SlavePatrol and #batmobile grew more established.

A system of observation and intelligence regarding law enforcement and Army convoy movements was organically born.

* * *

North of Baltimore, Maryland, nestled amid the rolling green hills of Baltimore County's Horse Country, was Coventry Estate, the grounds and mansion of the esteemed William Coventry, Esquire, president of the private Standard & King Investment House.

Standard & King dated back nearly one hundred fifty years. It kept a low profile and managed the portfolios of multiple billionaire executives, two former U.S. presidents, several U.S. congressmen and congresswomen, and a few presidential appointees and members of the Senior Executive Service—and all by invitation only.

August Coventry, William Coventry's great-great grandfather, was one of the founding partners of Standard & King, which included Frederick Calvert IV, a direct descendant of one of the original barons of Baltimore. The stories that circulated down through the generations were so outrageous that they were not to be believed but, when they were accompanied by a wink—and they were always told with a knowing wink—they left one wondering if maybe, just maybe, there was some nugget of truth tucked away inside the hyperbole.

Among the esteemed class of alumni clients were Rowland Hussey Macy, founder of the now defunct Macy's department store empire; John D. Rockefeller, Jr., founder of the once-dominant Standard Oil Company; Rear Admiral Sidney Souers, the first Director of the Central Intelligence Agency; and none other than President Franklin Delano Roosevelt. Joseph "Don Peppino" Bonanno, an early boss of the Bonanno crime family, one of the Five Families of the New York Mafia, was rumored to have also been a client, along with a few other unsavory types.

Throughout the decades, Standard & King consistently produced returns that outperformed larger and more recognized Wall Street-based investment firms like Goldman Sachs or Merrill Lynch. It took money to make money, and so S&K kept its client list limited to a particular threshold of wealth, somewhere in the range of ten billion U.S. dollars. But to stay ahead of the market, this was where particular government and ex-government clients with strong connections to particular levers of policy-making were important. They could help undergird investments by steering government spending into particular places, by being knowledgeable of regulatory loopholes, or by being privy to classified information.

On this very day, for example, Paul Rinnier, S&K partner and a former U.S. ambassador to the Netherlands, had lunch with a flag-ranked naval officer at the elegant Army and Navy Club on Farragut Square in Washington, D.C. The two had been teammates on the Swimming and Diving team at the U.S. Naval Academy some thirty years prior before serving as officers with the Navy SEALs, albeit in different Teams. Paul left the Teams when he completed his service time and entered the world of finance. Vice Admiral Baltzer Oberkirsch remained with the Teams and had carved out a distinguished career in the Navy. Now he was at the Pentagon and worked directly under the Chief of Naval Operations.

The two old friends met once a month at the club for a few rounds of racquetball and then lunch. They'd banter as they played, swapping sea stories and catching up on family happenings. And Paul always brought his tablet with the latest numbers in Oberkirsch's portfolio that he could share over lunch in case the admiral had any questions.

After an hour of racquetball, the two old friends freshened up and then met in the club's Eagle Grill room for light fare and beer. Oberkirsch was quiet today, clearly distracted.

"Trouble at the office?" asked Paul, taking a swig from his bottle of beer—a Burley Oak IPA, a regional staple from Maryland's Eastern Shore.

"Busy," the admiral said after popping a steamed shrimp into his mouth and taking a drink from his own beer, a 3 Stars IPA. 3 Stars was a local DC brewery. "Lots of chatter right now," he said in between sips. 'Chatter' referred to intercepted communications among known and suspected terrorists around the world.

"Yeah?" said Paul, probing.

The admiral put his beer down and looked at Paul. Paul held his gaze. The admiral looked down for a moment, then scanned the room and leaned forward.

"Something's afoot in the Middle East," Oberkirsch said, his voice lowered. "We're going to have to shift some assets around, maybe put a carrier in the Gulf." The admiral leaned back in his chair and started on his shrimp again. "A ton of logistical stuff to work out," he added.

"Sounds like business as usual to me," said Paul, stabbing at a portion of grilled salmon. He took a sip from his Burley Oak. "What's got you spooked?"

"They're buzzing about the unrest in Detroit," Oberkirsch said. "They think we're distracted. Whatever they've got planned, they want to move it up. Something is imminent."

"I hope they're wrong," Paul offered. "I have a meeting in Dubai next week with a prospective client. That could muck things up."

"The State Department will probably issue a travel alert," Oberkirsch warned.

"*Great*," said Paul. He took a final swig of his beer and set the bottle down with gusto. He let out a belch. In his head, he did a quick mental calculation. A travel alert would cause insurance rates to spike for oil tankers and other corporate assets in the Middle East. That, in turn, would translate into higher oil prices. Never mind an actual incident in the region, or news of a carrier's deployment to the Gulf.

Following lunch with Oberkirsch, Paul would head back to Baltimore and alert the partners. The admiral's tip would allow S&K to discreetly move a few billion dollars into the insurance and oil markets before the prices spiked, and to move money out of markets like airlines and other industries that might be affected by a rise in transportation costs.

Plying some discretionary funds into the defense industry would also be prudent in times like these.

* * *

As for the *other* clients of Standard and King—the Bonanno types—they, too, were important to the success of S&K. They were able to persuade—as a last resort, you see—other firms and businesses, and sometimes low-level government officials, to make decisions that weren't detrimental to the investments of S&K and its clients.

Giorgio Santacroce, of Naples, Italy, who divided his time between Italy and Philadelphia, was one such client. He was the patriarch of the Santacroces, who were rumored to be part of *la camorra,* the Naples-based organized crime syndicate linked, ostensibly via multiple shell companies, to the Blue Planet waste management and recycling conglomerate that operated in Philadelphia, New York City, New Jersey, and Boston. Other businesses, some big, some small, some linked to the Santacroces, some not, included Donato's Pesce e Pasta (Donato's Fish & Pasta), a tiny but quaint Italian restaurant in Baltimore's Little Italy.

It was a very rare occasion when William Coventry patronized Donato's at lunchtime. The news coming out of Detroit, and the projections of investment losses there, necessitated his visit. But he didn't really like dealing with the Italians. They were useful clients, to be sure, and he immensely enjoyed the air of mystery and the hint of menace they lent his business, but he didn't trust them for a minute. He considered them dirty and uncouth, and unworthy of the investment opportunities that he provided them. But he could use their services now and again.

Donato Picucci recognized the silver-haired blue blood when he walked in. He could tell that the man looked upon him with disdain, but he did business with his Zio (uncle) Giorgio, and Zio considered him important. And so Donato would humor him by talking about the O's, and the old devil played along even though it was clear that he knew not a thing about baseball.

He had ordered his favorite dish, glazed salmon with angel hair pasta and a touch of olive oil, and a glass of vino rosso. Donato never presented his bill, but Mr. Coventry always dropped a fifty-dollar bill on the table. As he did so, the blue blood spoke. "I would like to meet with Signore Santacroce. It is urgent."

That was a day ago. Now, he stood by the large double doors to the promenade in the back of the estate and watched as a navy blue-and-orange 'Go the Distance' Air Charter Service Sikorsky S-76 helicopter landed on the helicopter pad adjacent to the tennis court. Go the Distance, of course, was one of the various businesses owned by S&K.

Sixty years old and still with jet black hair flecked with gray, Giorgio Santacroce was tall and lanky, sharp in appearance, and stately in his manners. He stepped off the helicopter wearing a gray suit that was finely trimmed. At his side was a young man, surely under thirty, fit and trim, and impeccably dressed in a skinny black suit that accentuated his own jet black hair.

William stepped out onto the promenade and greeted Giorgio and his companion, who Giorgio introduced as Fausto Santacroce, his youngest son and head of the Santacroces' American operations. And he was quite sharp, too; William learned that he was a graduate of Harvard Business School.

Facades, thought William. *Lipstick on a pig.*

After some preliminary talk and a brief walk through the promenade to stretch out their legs, the three men retired to the Coventry Library with beers in hand, and William laid out the problem that his firm faced in the simplest terms he could manage.

In normal economic times, S&K invested the bulk of its funds in global blue chip companies and promising start-ups which, in turn, provided solid returns. A scattering of investments in commodities, currency trades, real estate, derivatives, and other more risky assets rounded out a diverse and solidly performing portfolio for each of its clients.

But these were not normal economic times, and hadn't been for nearly a decade now. Global financial crises had left the blue chip companies of the world facing a crippling lack of demand and weak sales, and they in turn left investors with anemic returns and even losses. Investors were forced to seek better returns elsewhere, like in the more riskier assets of currencies, derivatives, real estate, and venture loans.

Anything that produced even a semblance of decent returns resulted in a stampede of investors, inflating the costs of the asset and potentially producing a bubble that, when it burst, was financially ruinous to anyone without a seat when the music stopped.

These were dangerous times.

The voluminous wealth of its clients enabled S&K to scour the earth to look for investment opportunities, no matter how small. They found Pleasant Peninsula Bank, a small regional bank in the Detroit region that performed quite well by serving a market that few dared to enter. They offered very modest loans in a highly depressed housing and commercial real estate market that enabled them to charge higher interest rates for the higher risk that the property values would either remain stagnant or decline outright. The way they saw it, the market in Detroit was so depressed for so long that it could only go up.

And they were right. Pleasant Peninsula Bank saw its assets double, then triple, in size in just a few months, then triple again and then again. They snapped up thousands of foreclosed properties to rehab and flip them, further growing their assets. Other regional banks, like Apex Superior, got in on the act. Pleasant Peninsula and other similar investments were one of the reasons that S&K performed so well compared to other investment firms in tough times like these.

S&K purchased many of the higher-rate mortgages from Pleasant Peninsula and Apex Superior and packaged them together as securities in the form of Collateralized Debt Obligations that offered a higher rate of return to investors so long as homeowners and business owners paid their mortgages.

Detroit had a relative dearth of new housing stock, and market projections suggested that the region had much more room to grow.

But then the riots hit. All hope that Detroit's housing and commercial real estate market had nowhere to go but up came to an abrupt end. Real estate values in Detroit were poised to crash again, leaving most homeowners and businesses underwater. If history was any guide, and it was, there was little chance of a rebound anytime soon. Areas hit by unrest during the riots in Los Angeles in 1992 still hadn't fully recovered more than thirty years later. The collective value of the Pleasant Peninsula and Apex Superior CDOs held by S&K, estimated to be roughly five billion dollars just a week ago, was now essentially worthless.

"Pretty soon and we're talking real money," quipped the blue blood.

In order to avoid further losses, S&K had to deleverage and extricate itself from the Detroit market. The only way out was insurance. But out of the estimated ten thousand fires that raged in Detroit, barely a fraction included Pleasant Peninsula or Apex Superior mortgaged properties.

"The issue," said the esteemed Mr. Coventry, "is one of scale." He paused for a moment before he spoke again.

"We need the city to burn."

CHAPTER 23

Life in Detroit was slowly returning to normal, including its night-life. For the Grape Vine Bar & Grille on Monroe Street, smack in the middle of downtown and a block up from the Greektown Casino, "normal" was greeted with subdued enthusiasm. That's because the club didn't really skip a beat, save for a couple of nights, during the unrest. When the downtown became a police fortress, the Grape Vine became a favorite among the cops—and then Army soldiers—cloistered in the city. It became an unofficial "cop bar" to the amusement (and profit) of its true owner, via the shell company "Motown Entertainment Properties, Inc.," one William 'Pops' Jefferson Avery.

It was rare for the Avery brothers to actually patronize the Grape Vine, but the venue seemed somehow appropriate for the business at hand. The Italians wanted a meeting, and what place was safer than a cop bar?

"Bring the Marine," was the last thing Frank Auletta had said on the phone, and so Jayson was present.

Pops, Fave, and Jayson sat in a booth downing Motor City Ghettoblasters, with Elijah and crew members mixed throughout the venue nursing their own beers but keeping tabs on everyone else in the joint. Marquis McKinnon, formerly Darrell's lieutenant, spotted Frank and Freddie Auletta along with a 20-something-year-old as they came in the door, and he led them to the Averys' booth.

"This is Fausto, a cousin," Frank said, introducing the young man who, to Pops and Fave, looked like Damien, the devil child of the old Omen films. "He's from Philadelphia," continued Frank, enunciating 'Philadelphia' to convey importance. Pops nodded. Maybe it wasn't Frank's intention, but Pops understood Philadelphia to mean that the kid represented the powers behind Auletta.

He wasn't wrong.

"Thank you so kindly," the young man said, "for bringing some business our way."

"Hear, hear," said Frank, raising his beer. The six men clanged their beer bottles together and took a sip.

The devil child laid out the business before them. "We would like to further our partnership," said the boy, finishing his proposal. "It comes with a bit of urgency," he said, "and, I must say, isn't without risk."

"You don't say," cackled Pops.

* * *

Reggie kicked up his skateboard with one hand and tapped Aaron on the chest with the back of the other as his eyes gazed down the street. Aaron followed his gaze and went quiet and still with fear and very nearly slipped off his own board as adrenaline flooded his body. A black, raised Cadillac Escalade EXT with darkly tinted windows and spinning rims pulled up so fast, he didn't have time to react. He thought they were dead when all the doors opened and members of the Avery Gang stepped out, including Jayson Avery himself.

"The Scooby Doo Crew," said Jayson Avery in his baritone voice, as he stepped out of the driver's seat. The other men who clamored out of the car included Willie James, Elijah Freeman, and Marquis McKinnon, all well-known Avery Gang enforcers.

Xavier and Devin went swagger, squinting their eyes and raising their shoulders and looking sinister gangster, even while holding their skateboards. Reggie dropped his board, hopped on, and rolled a bit, seemingly oblivious to the presence of killers. But Aaron's heart pounded so loudly in his chest and ears that he was certain it drowned out the traffic.

"Want to make some cash?" Jayson asked Aaron. But the way he said it, with his enforcers hovering over him from behind, it wasn't a question. Aaron, tight with tension, nodded.

"Hop in," said Jayson. As if he had no will of his own, the teen did as he was told.

After a short ride, the Escalade stopped and, when Aaron and the gangsters got out, Aaron saw they had stopped at Small's Bar-B-Que right across the street from the once grand and now beautifully apocalyptic Michigan Grand Central Station, which stood largely abandoned for more than thirty years. It was still abandoned, although some renovations had been done recently.

Aaron's eyes lingered on the abandoned train station. Somehow it told of his precarious state of affairs.

"Damn, nigga, move," commanded Jayson, opening the wooden gate to the restaurant's outdoor patio, and Aaron was ushered in.

"Mr. Jones," said an older man with braided hair and a beard. He stood up, wiped his hands on a rag, and extended a hand. Aaron took it, hesitantly, and flinched at the man's solid grip. He didn't say anything.

Catty-cornered to the man who spoke was another older man, who sat with his head tilted slightly, his eyes squinted but locked squarely on Aaron.

With the wave of his hand, the first man led Aaron to sit down beside him, across from the squinting man. Jayson Avery and his crew stood at different ends of the patio, legs spread and arms crossed behind them, like Secret Service agents.

On the table was a mountain of barbequed pulled pork.

"Do you know who I am, Mr. Jones?" asked the man as he sat down.

"Yes, sir," said Aaron, barely audible. "You're Pops Avery."

The man leaned back in his chair and chuckled forcefully. It was a deep, genuine laugh.

"*Sir,*" Pops said, and laughed even more deeply. "Jayson *said* you had manners." He nodded at Fave. "And this is my brother, Forrest." Pops eyed Aaron, who was starting to feel like somebody's next favorite meal. "Oh," said Pops, looking back and forth from Fave to Aaron. "You know Fave as well, I take it," he said, and chuckled. "Listen, Aaron—mind if I call you Aaron?"

Aaron shook his head, a confused look on his face.

"Good," Pops said, "I need young men from across our community who can help us with a significant project. It's an unusual project, and we need juveniles to do it."

Pops wiped his face with a wet rag and pushed the dish of pulled pork away. "We need to burn some buildings down, my man. I mean that literally."

Pops slowly leaned forward and *his* eyes squinted, sending a chill through Aaron. "This," said Pops, his pointer finger tapping on the picnic table, "is a big responsibility."

Pops leaned back again and eyed Aaron. "I understand you have a crew of your own, little man," he said.

* * *

It had been nearly two weeks since Ian and Trevor identified Roland's body. Campus had reopened, and classes were once again underway.

It was surreal for Ian. Campus and his classes were abuzz about the unrest, but the professors still had a job to do, and so they carried on with their instruction. Ian tried to busy himself with studying, and lose himself running, but he couldn't get the sight of Roland in the morgue out of his mind. He looked...different. He looked small, like a scrawny little kid. His physical energy, his fearlessness, his mischievousness, were gone. It wasn't him. Just some fragile, broken shell that kind of resembled Roland, but it wasn't him.

Trevor, Tina, and Sarah were gone. Tina's parents had come and taken her home. She texted Ian that they were transferring her to another college after the summer, probably to the University of Akron in Ohio where she had also been offered a cross country scholarship before she chose Wayne State. She didn't mention Roland. Ian assumed that it was just too painful to talk about.

Trevor went back home to Lansing. He said he would probably transfer to Western Michigan University.

Sarah told Ian that her parents pleaded with her to come home to Findlay, Ohio. When she told him that, Ian broke into a silent sob. He apologized through his sniffles; it was an unexpected reaction. He didn't know where it came from.

When Sarah hugged him, he lost control and bawled on her shoulder. "You'll be okay," she said.

Would he? Ian wasn't so sure. They were breaking up. Meanwhile, his own parents seemed oblivious to the unrest in Detroit. Or at least they didn't realize, nor did they even investigate, that the university was geographically in the thick of the sprawling unrest. Their lives revolved entirely around the Viet Taste Restaurant that his father had started twenty-five years ago in Sterling Heights.

"I don't know anything about politics," was his mother's response when he told her about the unrest. He didn't tell them about Roland, how his friend was killed by the police. How could they understand such a thing?

It was a small, hot kitchen, and a small restaurant with only a few tables. Yet, his parents had always assumed that Ian would take over some day. It was suffocating and claustrophobic.

Ian decided that he would complete the semester but, after that, he had no idea. Home wasn't an option, not anymore. It probably never really was.

* * *

Federal and local law enforcement reviewed hundreds of hours of video captured by news helicopters, ground-level reporters, and security cameras during the unrest, just as Fave Avery had warned.

Local television replayed over and over the scene of the vicious young man brutally smashing a brick over the head of a young driver commuting to work on the I-94, killing him. The scene was filmed zoomed in from a distance, and the image wasn't entirely clear. The young man had looked straight up at the helicopter and held up his middle fingers for a brief moment, and the news would freeze the image each time. But it was blurry.

Fave was certain that it was Dmitri Johnson, the bloodthirsty young River Gee who, along with Caleb Sessions, was trying to consolidate their control on the Motown Mafia by savagely waging war on any faction that dared to be independent. It was Dmitri and Caleb who ordered the attack on his house and killed his guys, of that he had no doubt.

And true to his out-of-control nature, Dmitri was Public Enemy Number 1, or soon would be. No doubt he would be quickly identified by police and the feds. And no doubt he would already be in hiding after seeing his face all over TV and the internet.

Fave also had no doubt that the police would quickly locate the stupid piece of shit. But that would not be the end of the war. Dmitri was just one guy, and the River Gees were full of other reckless punks ready to take his place. He needed the whole lot of them neutralized, or enough of them. Then he could deal with Caleb.

For Fave and his family, there was no getting to either Dmitri or Caleb. They couldn't just drive into their territory without being seen. They'd never get close enough. And there was still the issue of the rest of the Gees.

He had to be bold. He had to go big. So, it was End Times.

It was risky but so far, so good. One of Jayson's crews was able to park a rusty old Ford Econoline van from the Italians' junk yard along the street right in front of an abandoned garage on East Grand Boulevard, right in the heart of the neighborhood where the National Guard had killed those poor kids.

The neighborhood still seethed, and that part of Grand Boulevard was thick with patrolling soldiers. It also just so happened to be in the heart of Grand River Gees territory.

They drove in from the east along I-75, parked the van, and drove off in a following car back to the interstate. The van carried a Lockheed Martin-built HIMARS MGM-140 missile taken from the Olympia Armory.

Downtown was still a fortress of police and Army, with too much scrutiny on people and vehicles. *A restless neighborhood, however…*

The explosion was massive. More than three-and-a-half miles away, Fave's entire house shook, and the windows rattled in their frames. Armed crew members rushed outside to see what had happened and spotted the massive mushroom cloud of dust rising above the city in the near distance.

Fave sat at the kitchen table and waited for an update. But he didn't need one. A once-familiar knot of fear that he had buried in his youth took hold in the pit of his stomach. There was no going back now. He *had* to see it through.

End Times…

* * *

After nearly a week of patrolling, Gino Napolitano's fears were not assuaged. Not at all. The hard stares continued. The hostility was palpable. The first day saw a barrage of glass bottles on Grand Boulevard, and he and his soldiers were ordered to suck wind and take it, despite General McIntyre's much-ballyhooed "we will cut you to pieces" speech.

Well, not exactly. Gino and his soldiers went after the hard-looking young men snickering amid the crowds gathered along the sidewalks and intersections, but the crowds wouldn't part for them and, when they forced their way in to try and apprehend the young punks, it became an out-and-out street brawl between soldiers and civilians.

Some major ordered Gino and his men to pull back, and it went downhill from there. The crowds threw anything they could hold in their hands at them, and piled tires and other debris into the middle of the boulevard and set them on fire.

It was a mini-riot, and it threatened to spread all over again. When word reached General McIntyre, he reassigned the major and ordered a whole brigade to flood into the "zone" and clear Grand Boulevard once and for all.

Grand Boulevard was the main commercial corridor through New Center and, since that first day, more than a thousand soldiers patrolled by foot, day and night, the entire nearly three-mile length of the boulevard between Interstates 75 and 96.

Crowds, in turn, gathered, too, but along parallel side streets and residential streets encompassing the neighborhoods north and south of the boulevard. They gathered each day and all day long. Gino didn't understand it. No one seemed to have a job or go to school. The Army refrained from entering the neighborhoods themselves; they stuck to the commercial districts. Young men and teenagers, meanwhile, would taunt the soldiers on occasion, then dash back into the neighborhood when soldiers reacted.

The only forays into the neighborhoods would come in the dead of night when the FBI, DEA, or some other law enforcement agency served warrants, arriving in armored vehicles with Army squads in tow for security.

Grand Boulevard itself, though, was almost entirely saturated with soldiers on foot patrol. Army vehicles traveled up and down the boulevard, dropping off supplies and running errands. Businesses were reopening, and so commercial traffic mixed in. Residents ventured out as well, to grocery and convenience stores, gas stations, doctors' appointments, and the like.

Gino and his squad neared the eastern end of Grand Boulevard, where they would turn around and patrol back to their starting point. On most days, Gino and his squad would cover the entire length of Grand Boulevard at least once. They often stopped and chatted with the dozens of other patrols they passed. They had come to know quite a few other soldiers. It was Gino's job to keep them moving; his squad had made all kinds of friends. A chatty bunch, he started calling them 'ladies.' "Let's go, ladies, chop chop," he ordered often, ending a bull session until the next passing patrol.

"Keep it moving, ladies," Gino ordered as another patrol passed along at their left. They each nodded. One soldier wordlessly offered a high-five for each of Gino's squad mates as they passed. Just as it was Gino's turn to high-five the passing soldier, the entire street in front of him disappeared in an angry orange-and-black ball of flame that then collapsed on itself as it rose over the boulevard as a fiery mushroom cloud.

It was like a slow-motion silent film. There was no sound.

Gino's eyes and mouth widened as he tried to order his men to *get down,* but he, his men, and the soldiers around him were slammed by the explosion's shockwave as though from an invisible truck, which arrived a millisecond before a concussive thunderclap seemed to split the air itself as though ripping into the earth from some parallel universe. The soldiers were tossed like ragdolls for more than twenty yards.

After a moment, Gino stood up, covered in dust from head to toe that gently trailed from his body in a soft breeze, giving him a ghostly, ethereal appearance. A young private, himself in shock, ran to him. When Gino turned and looked in the private's direction, the private stopped, his mouth agape. Looking into Gino's eyes was like looking into a black, bottomless pit, and then the young sergeant crumbled to the ground in a rattle of bones.

* * *

Moe Adil was at a desk on the fifth floor of the Patrick V. McNamara Federal Building in downtown Detroit. The FBI had lent him and his team an office and a desk. The desk was Moe's since, well, since he was the boss. His team of five CID agents had their laptops and could use the floor. God bless the FBI.

The building shook. The FBI offices stirred. "What was *that?*" more than one person asked. Moe watched as people moved with urgency.

Moe knew what it was. And, for just a moment, he thought he was back in Iraq. *This isn't Iraq,* he thought to himself. *I am not in Iraq, goddamn it.*

No, this was worse. This was home. This was America. Moe walked to the window and looked out on the downtown. Everything was fine. He craned his head and looked with his face pressed against the cold window in order to see uptown. He saw a large gray-and-silver dust cloud that hung in the air over New Center, slowly drifting over the neighborhoods east of downtown and toward the river. A wisp of black oily smoke, meanwhile, curled into the air in swift, patchy waves, blowing east as it clung closer to the surface. It was a familiar sight from his days in Iraq and Afghanistan. *Car bomb,* he thought with a sigh.

And he was pretty sure he knew where the bomb had come from.

CHAPTER 24

Nine miles to the west, the Channel 13 newsroom was abuzz within minutes of the explosion. So it was for all local television newsrooms and print media. All soon dispatched a helicopter if they had one and news vans to get as close as they could to the site of the explosion.

There was a lot of confusion. Cell phones buzzed, land lines rang incessantly, and editors and reporters shouted commands and scrambled for information.

Reporter Wally Mickiewicz was in the thick of it, and his own desk phone rang off the hook. He snatched the receiver. "Wally," he barked into the speaker end as he took notes from the director, who shouted orders from across the newsroom.

"Is this Wally Mickie-witz, the reporter?" asked a calm voice.

"*Yes, goddamnit,*" snapped Wally, impatiently.

"We are the People's Armed Resistance. The Army is killing our people and occupation of our streets is an act of war."

The voice was electronically distorted, Wally realized. He held up his hand and waved it up and down for everyone to quiet down. They did.

"We demand a full withdrawal of the U.S. Army and police," the partially distorted voice continued. "These streets are our streets. The people's streets." The phone line went dead.

"I got a claim of responsibility!" Wally yelled out as he scribbled the voice's words. "People's Armed Resistance," he exclaimed.

The newsroom burst into a higher level of frenzy. "Find out all you can on this People's Armed Resistance!" barked the news director.

* * *

Bobby 'Bones' Bailey disconnected the phone, removed the battery, and dropped both into the Detroit River. He had made five calls and said the same thing each time. The phone was a burner, so there was no tracing it back to him or the Avery Organization.

Bones, dressed in a track suit, made his way back to the Grand Arnault Casino and Hotel where, two hours earlier, he had booked a room.

Bones ensured that his room overlooked Michigan Avenue, just as Jayson Avery had instructed. Across the street was the sprawling DPSH—Detroit Public Safety Headquarters—complex. The complex had its back to the M-10 John C. Lodge Freeway. The short and narrow 5th Street ran between the DPSH complex and the M-10 and was off-limits to the public. Strategically placed Jersey barriers prevented cars from entering 5th Street, as did a manned security gate on both ends. This was where police vehicles entered and exited the complex, including the Lenco BEAR armored personnel carriers.

This was where the FBI and police SWAT convoys departed from.

Bones unpacked a telescopic camera from his suitcase and set it up on a tripod. The camera was equipped with night vision, an expensive high-tech piece of equipment courtesy of the 'Corleones,' according to Mr. Avery. *What the heck was a Corleone?* Bones wondered. He didn't understand how old people talked sometimes.

He also broke open a cell phone box, one of five in his suitcase, and worked through getting it activated. He did the same for the next four. Once all of the burner phones were activated, Bones was ready.

He ripped open a bag of crispy onion rings and began munching on them as he sat with his feet propped up on the room's desk and peered out of his window through the camera.

* * *

News media desperately sought to understand the meaning of the car bomb in New Center. Bernice Hamandawana and Wayne State's newspaper, *The South End,* were quite suddenly thrust into the limelight. She had published the first of what she deemed would be a three-part series of articles based on interviews with multiple witnesses about how the National Guard killed three teenagers on East Grand Boulevard on the fifth night of unrest. No other news outlet had covered the tragic event. Much of the city was considered too dangerous for reporters to drive into during the unrest, but rumors swirled in Midtown and New Center. Bernice explored the rumors; she and fellow journalism student Daniel Rush walked across I-94 and the fifteen blocks or so from Wayne State to New Center to identify and interview dozens of witnesses even as the unrest continued.

A shaggy-haired white kid, Daniel was scared to tag along, but Bernice was fearless, and she admonished him. "If you're scared, major in accounting," she had said.

She and Daniel were led to the spot where the three boys were killed. The concrete driveway of a gas station was still stained with blood. Bernice interviewed orderlies and nurses at the Henry Ford Hospital. Lastly, she saw the bodies herself, still in drawers in the hospital morgue. Her news story had been picked up by the Associated Press, and since the unrest had ended, the Detroit Free Press was in the process of independently verifying her story when the car bomb exploded.

Surely the killing of the three teenagers was the impetus for the car bomb. It happened on the very block where the boys were killed.

More than fifty people were killed in the explosion, including more than forty U.S. Army soldiers, and up to one hundred people were injured. Surely it was revenge.

General McIntyre surveyed the scene with an entourage of senior officers. Soldiers had swarmed in and cordoned off Grand Boulevard for the full three-mile length between I-75 and I-96. Army CID agents inspected a crater that swallowed the entire width of the westbound lanes of Grand Boulevard, plus its sidewalk and part of an adjacent parking lot. Tiny flags marked fragments within the crater.

"Welcome to the Occupation, General," said a large black man wearing a CID jacket. General McIntyre glared at the man, and the man held his gaze. "Moe Adil," the man said, "CID special agent in charge."

"The British Army was initially welcomed by the Catholics in Northern Ireland," Moe said. "It was supposed to be a brief operation, not unlike your deployment. That brief deployment lasted for thirty-eight years, from 1969 to 2007," Moe said.

"Tell me something I *don't* know, Mr. Adil," said the general, annoyed by the history lesson. Moe looked down into the crater and nodded to an axle in the center of the still-smoldering crater. "Looks like a Ford Econoline van, probably early 2000s model," Moe said. "Car bomb," he added. "The explosive appears to be a rigged MGM-140 missile taken from the Olympia Armory."

"You can ascertain all of that already?" the general asked.

"Not definitively, not yet, but we're pretty sure," said Moe. "I've picked through enough MGM-140 fragments in after-battle postmortems in Iraq and Afghanistan to make a good guess."

The general nodded to the west, in the direction of the Olympia Armory, which was just over two miles straight up the road. "From there?" he asked, already knowing the answer. Moe just nodded.

General McIntyre looked around at the landscape beyond the immediate scene. "You think this is the work of locals?"

"Right over there," Moe said, pointing a block to the east, "was where those three teenagers were killed after tossing Molotov cocktails at a National Guard Humvee."

The general continued to look about the landscape, his arms folded across his chest, his brow burrowed in thought. Moe remained silent. Without a word, the general walked away and left with his entourage of senior officers.

* * *

William "Pops" Avery was an extroverted man, perhaps an unusual characteristic for a gangster. It was a personality more suitable for a politician. But his loquaciousness and laidback demeanor—the complete opposite of Fave, his brooding younger brother—was disarming, which opened doors for Pops in meaningful ways.

He had met Lynn Edwards more than two decades earlier, when they were both in their early thirties, and more than a decade before she landed a job as a records keeper for the Detroit Police Department. It was a pittance, what she made, and Pops plied her with jewelry and sometimes just plain old cash.

Her bosses preached a good game. God and country, for example. Law and order. Us versus them. But "them" were people like her, struggling to make a living and getting their power turned off. Having little or no health insurance. No way to afford college for her children, or even being able to put them into decent public schools. You had to live in the suburbs for that. Driving While Black. The list went on. She feared for her boys when they were teenagers. She feared that the very police department she worked for would ultimately kill them.

And so she did her part. Goddamn right. Whenever Pops wanted information that didn't require some off-the-charts risk, then, well, why the hell not? It was rare that Pops asked for anything anyway.

But after a week of riots—some were calling it an uprising, which Lynn thought was more appropriate—and after those poor teenagers being shot by the National Guard, Pops called.

Lynn had worked in multiple capacities for the Detroit Police Department over the years. Her current position was as an overnight police quartermaster, and she managed the storage room for weapons, ammunition, bulletproof vests, batons, flashlights, and various other tactical equipment.

Pops wanted Lynn to text him on Whatsapp whenever the police were suiting up for a raid and whenever the Lenco BEARs were rolling out.

That was all. It wasn't like she was stealing anything.

* * *

Fave's phone buzzed on the kitchen table. The small flat screen television on the counter played the news. The video of the I-94 killing played again and again, and this time, in the upper left quadrant of the screen was a months-old mug shot of Dmitri Johnson with the word "WANTED" beneath the photo. A ticker at the bottom read: "I-94 suspect identified as Dmitri Johnson…Suspect is at large and considered to be armed and dangerous…if you see suspect, call 911…"

Fave picked up the phone, looked at the number and hit the answer button.

"I've got an address," said Freddie Auletta. Fave jotted it down and hung up.

He smiled.

* * *

"9-1-1, what is your emergency?" said the dispatcher.

"Hello, I think I've seen that awful man on TV, the man wanted for that terrible murder on the freeway," said the woman. "I was walking my dog when I passed a house with a man on the porch smoking a cigarette. He looked right at me and I knew right away it was him. Then he went inside the house," she said.

"I'm scared," she added. "He saw me. Please hurry," she said, and disconnected the call.

Fave took the burner from Greta, took out the battery and sim card, and broke the phone and sim card into pieces. He wrapped his arms around Greta from behind and gently kissed the back of her neck.

She turned to face him. Fave squinted his eyes and smiled.

The two kissed softly as the kitchen TV played the I-94 scene again along with Dmitri Johnson's mug shot.

* * *

Jackson Mills and Jayson Avery had climbed the stairs to the top floor of the fifteen-story Lee Plaza Building before sundown. The building had stood vacant since 1997 and was in a sad state of disrepair, despite being listed in the National Register of Historical Places.

Jackson had misgivings when Jayson found him on Grand Boulevard. But he was a fellow veteran, and what did he have to lose? They weren't aiming to shoot anyone. Just hold the Army at bay as part of some bigger plan.

Shooting target practice with Jayson in preparation brought back fond memories. He was a soldier again.

Jayson kept an eye on his smartphone as they settled in for the night. It was a really nice phone for a burner, Jackson thought.

The phone buzzed. It was a text message from Bones. "It's on," it read.

Finally, after all freaking night.

Jayson dialed a number and relayed the message. "Stay sharp," he added. "Could be any time now. Keep the line open," he said.

He and Jackson peered through their rifle night scopes.

Twenty more minutes passed. And then, there they were. An armored personnel carrier sped toward them on Grand Boulevard, followed by several vans and a convoy of Army Humvees.

They were more than a quarter of a mile away, but close enough to engage.

"Not yet," said Jayson. "Just wait."

A massive explosion followed by a deafening *KABOOM!* momentarily blinded them.

The whole building—already in poor condition—rattled and creaked in its frame, and dust fell from the ceiling. Jackson felt the air pressure change in his ear drums. He opened his mouth wide to try to equalize the pressure in his ears.

Jackson and Jayson peered through their rifle scopes again. After a moment, the dust cleared somewhat. The armored carrier wasn't there anymore, nor were the vans. Jackson scanned the road with his rifle. The mangled remains of a vehicle lay burning in a parking lot of an abandoned and now partially demolished apartment complex. An entire line of retail stores, mostly boarded up, was also demolished. Fire burned in a crater beside them, and Jackson could see a twisted wheel axle to the side of it—the remains of the car that had blown up. That fast, Jackson couldn't remember what kind of car it was.

The dust cleared further and the Army Humvees came into view. They had stopped about a half a mile down the road. Soldiers piled out of their Humvees as their commanders assessed the situation.

Several soldiers ran to the aid of the stricken law enforcement vans.

"Now," Jayson said, and Jackson fired four rounds into the lead Humvee's windshield.

It was bulletproof, as Jayson and Jackson knew it would be, but sudden large bullet-sized pockmarks and splinters on the thick windshield was what they wanted.

Soldiers dropped to the ground and scrambled for cover.

Jackson would fire a single round every minute or so, aimed at keeping the soldiers on their toes.

Jayson kept an eye on the time on his phone. After several more minutes, he spoke into his phone.

"Now," he said.

Two stories below Jayson and Jackson was Team C, comprised of six shooters. They faced the residential neighborhood to the north. They opened fire, not with sniper rifles, but with M-16s, shooting haphazardly at the houses and spaces in between over an area covering five to ten streets, but it was the seventh street over that they tried to focus on, with one particular house as their general target.

* * *

Dmitri's phone buzzed. His girlfriend, snuggled in his arms, moaned. He picked up his phone and looked to see who was calling, but it said Restricted. Agitated, Dmitri hit the answer button.

"Who the fuck is this?" he said, sitting up in bed.

"They're coming," a voice said.

"Who is it?" asked Jamaica, lying naked beside him.

Just then, the whole house felt like it was collapsing around him. The windows blew in, and he scrambled to the floor for protection. It was an explosion.

"They're here," said the voice on the phone.

Logan burst through the bedroom door, slinging an AK-47. "Dmitri! You okay?"

Jamaica, backed up to the bedrest with her knees and bed sheets drawn up to her chest, screamed incessantly.

"Yeah, muthafucka!" Dmitri said, ignoring Jamaica as he got up from the floor and pulled on a pair of jeans. He scrambled for the closet and pulled out his own AK-47.

"It's the *police!*" Dmitri said, catching his breath. "Let's *go!*"

Dmitri and his crew turned out the lights and cautiously looked outside. They didn't see anything.

Dmitri nodded to Logan. He cracked the door open and looked. Cold air filtered in. Logan went out, crept low, and darted for the line of cars parked out front. He waved the next man out.

The whole crew came out onto the street like an Army scout unit, their rifles at the aim.

They heard gunfire and dropped. They waited. It was four large cracks they heard, then nothing more.

A fire burned a few streets over. A single shot rang out every few seconds, but apparently aimed elsewhere.

What the hell is going on?

They saw movement and dropped to their knees and were ready to fire when they were seen. It was Jamal Parkins and his crew running from their homes blocks away.

"Don't shoot!" Jamal yelled, holding his hands and rifle aloft. "It's Jamal!"

There was more gunfire, a distant but rapid and nonstop *pop-pop-pop-pop*. Bullets seemed to rain haphazardly down on their street.

"Go, go, go!" ordered Dmitri, and their combined crews of fifteen gangsters worked as a large fire team toward Grand Boulevard, sharing turns at providing covering fire as they moved.

"There!" shouted one of Jamal's crew members. It was the Army, a line of Humvees sitting in the dark.

More gunfire sent the crews ducking for cover. Then they opened fire on the Humvees.

* * *

"I.E.D.," Major Jose Hernandez calmly spoke into the radio. "We have many casualties."

Major Hernandez was calm, but it was chaos all around him. "We're beginning rescue. We need medevac," he said, still in a calm voice. He turned and began issuing orders, again in a calm manner, to his soldiers as they unloaded out of the Humvees and ran to aid the guys in the demolished FBI vans and personnel carrier.

"Sniper fire!" yelled a sergeant, and everyone, including Major Hernandez, dropped to the ground. Looking back over his shoulder, Hernandez saw the tell-tale pockmarks of bullet strikes on his Humvee windshield.

"Take cover!" shouted Hernandez. He snatched the radio microphone from the radioman at his side. "We're under attack," he said, again in a calm voice, "sniper fire."

Hernandez barked more orders to his men. A tall brick building, maybe twenty stories high, and about a quarter of a mile straight ahead, was the best guess for the sniper's location. Several more shots sharpened their assumption.

Soldiers cautiously reached the smashed FBI vans and began treating the men. The vans had been smashed by the blast wave, and they were sent rolling nearly fifty feet. The injuries were all kinds of broken bones. Several of the men were dead.

The personnel carrier was a different story. It wasn't even recognizable. None of its occupants could have survived the blast.

* * *

At the New Fort Detroit command center in downtown, everyone felt the blast. The ground shook. Men came out of their tents and ran to their posts. Everyone looked to the north to see the gray mushroom cloud rise against the night sky and drift quickly past to the northeast as it dissipated.

Awakened by the blast, General McIntyre had hurried into the command post. He arrived as Major Hernandez radioed in. Men could be heard screaming in pain in the background of Major Hernandez's calm report over the radio. McIntyre's executive officer assured Hernandez that backup was on the way.

Men pored over a street map stretched out on a table after Hernandez reported sniper fire. The single shots registered at the command center from over two miles.

"We're taking fire," Hernandez reported, and a distant and over-lapping *pop-pop-pop* of multiple automatic rifle fire was heard at the command post.

McIntyre ordered a rapid reaction force into action, and their convoy sped out of New Fort Detroit and straight up Grand River Avenue to 14th Street, which took them straight to the gun fight while avoiding the likely source of sniper fire.

McIntyre called the Pentagon as the firefight raged a couple of miles away.

* * *

Other sniper teams were stationed on each of the three floors below Jayson and Jackson to cover all approaches to the building and the area. The Army quickly ascertained that the Lee Plaza Building was the likely source of sniper fire, given the angles of attack, even as the gun battle raged below. The question was whether the sniper was alone. Given the car bomb and now the gun fight, Jayson guessed that they wouldn't think so.

Through his scope, Jayson could see more soldiers arriving along-side the first convoy, and quickly they joined in the gun battle against the River Gees firing from the neighborhood north of the boulevard while taking cover from presumed snipers in the Lee Plaza Building.

Jayson and Jackson watched as multiple cars and trucks full of armed young men with pistols and AK-47s came tearing down Grand Boulevard from the opposite end. They stopped and scattered when Army troops saw them coming and opened fire.

Other armed young men arrived on foot, streaming in from Wildemere, Lawton, and Linwood Streets, and those were the streets most visible from the Lee Plaza Building. These were the homes and territories of the patched-together factions of which the Grand River Gees were but one, even if the leading one, of the umbrella group that called themselves the Motown Mafia. Many of the GLEE shut-offs and subsequent house fires had happened in these very neigh-borhoods—LaSalle Gardens, Petosky-Ostego, Northwest Goldberg, New Center, and Boston Edison.

The gunfight was growing larger. Other crews of the Motown Mafia had gotten word that Dmitri and others were putting up a fight as police tried to arrest them. They came to join the fight. They came by cars and by foot from all around the surrounding neighborhoods. The spontaneous anti-GLEE protests and riots were one thing. This was something else entirely. The *Army* was attacking them.

This was all-out *war.*

* * *

Fifteen minutes into the attack, the appearance of a lone Humvee inching slowly from the opposite end of Grand Boulevard suggested more troops were arriving and flanking the gunfight. Wary of snipers in the Lee Plaza Building, the Humvee probed by moving slowly.

Team B fired on the Humvee, halting its progress. It tore back-ward in reverse until it was blocked by a large church on the intersec-tion of Dexter Avenue. Team B reported that they could see Army trucks unloading soldiers in the distance beyond Dexter.

Seconds later, Team C opened fire on troops gathering at the still-smoldering remains of the Olympia Armory south from the Lee Plaza Building. They were becoming surrounded at a distance.

Jayson decided that they had done their part and that it was time to vacate the building. First, however, they set multiple fires to con-fuse any drones or helicopters armed with infrared cameras.

They changed their clothes as well and used hand sanitizers to wash away any residue of gunpowder. They used their discarded clothes as kindling, and placed their weapons in the various piles to allow the fires to cook off remaining ammunition. It was a long shot, but ammo being cooked off might make the Army and the River Gees think they were still being fired on even after Jayson and his crew had gone.

As they headed down the stairs, soldiers from beyond Dexter Avenue opened fire on the building from a distance of nearly half a mile. Jayson smiled as bullets tore through the upper floors while they bounded down the stairs. The Army fire from Dexter would likely draw the attention of arriving crews of the Motown Mafia and Grand River Gees.

He was right. When they exited the building, they were met with a thunderous cacophony of gunfire that echoed down Grand Boulevard and throughout the surrounding neighborhoods. It was a crossfire of bullets from beyond Dexter and into the LaSalle Gardens neighborhood, with return fire from the neighborhood.

Jayson and his crew scrambled away on foot. They had a van parked on Ferry Park Street, a residential street just a block south of Lee Plaza Building. With the Army on Dexter Avenue now engaged with Motown Mafia crews spilling in from the sprawling LaSalle Gardens neighborhood, Jayson and his crew melted away.

The plan had worked like a dream.

CHAPTER 25

General McIntyre stood in the double-wide command trailer, hands on his improvised desk, his steely eyes fixed on a large wall map as he listened to reports come in from the battle on Grand Boulevard and now all up and down Grand River Avenue and spreading to Livernois. No one said anything as the general quietly seethed.

The gunfire reverberated throughout the city. It was like Fallujah out there and McIntyre was angry and aghast.

He had visited dozens of soldiers and civilians in the hospital wounded from the previous day's car bomb. He saw the bodies of the dead. And here they were, not even twenty-four hours after that attack.

The general had wasted no time in ordering the city under lockdown. The sun was coming up and commuters would have already been leaving their homes in the suburbs for work throughout Metropolitan Detroit if he hadn't acted with haste. It was, in retrospect, an easy decision. He had called the Pentagon overnight and informed them.

He had to clamp down, and hard, or risk another "Blackhawk Down." He shook his head in disbelief. *A major freaking firefight in the middle of an American freaking city. Un-freaking-believable.* And to worry about a "Blackhawk Down" scenario *in an American city* was…*unconscionable.*

He had declared martial law. Local TV and radio announced that schools and businesses were closed and passed on news that the city was on lockdown. McIntyre ordered the remaining tanks at Selfridge into battle, and they were on their way, heading down I-94 at full speed along with more convoys of soldiers.

But what gnawed at him was the Lee Plaza Building. Snipers kept his soldiers at bay, even as terrorists were engaging the stricken convoy. They couldn't get medevac helicopters in for the wounded FBI team until the snipers were neutralized.

Major Hernandez—a cool customer, the general thought—had requested close-in air support. McIntyre shook his head again. *Air support! In an American city!* Yet another point of disbelief. They were coming fast and furious now.

But he had a job to do, and he had to protect his soldiers. He was prepared for it. He had requested the accompaniment of four Marine Corps F-35s as part of his deployment, mostly for show. He hadn't expected to actually have to *use* them.

His decision made, he straightened, nodding to a captain with a radio in his hand. "Authorized," he said, and stepped out into the early morning twilight.

Fifteen minutes later, one of the U.S. Marine Corps' four F-35B Lightning II stealth fighters on detachment to Selfridge Air Base, took off in the dawn's early light. It was one of the planes that had conducted a flyover above the sprawling city at the height of the riots just days before.

Armed with two five-hundred-pound bombs, the Lightning II banked left and its sensors honed in on the laser-designated target twenty-two miles to the south. The jet covered the distance in just about seven minutes, traveling at approximately four-hundred-forty miles per hour.

Major Luke Schmidt, the 33-year old pilot from Tampa, Florida, let the aircraft do most of the work. He simply released the trigger on his joystick when the target-acquiring system emitted a high-pitched screeching tone in his ears.

"Bombs away," he announced nonchalantly into his helmet microphone. He felt the aircraft shudder and lurch upward as two five-hundred-pound Guided Bomb Unit (GBU)-12 Paveway II aerial laser-guided bombs dropped free of the aircraft. He banked sharply to the right and accelerated to six hundred miles per hour to the west of the city and waited for the reports and further orders.

General McIntyre stood outside the command trailer facing the northwest, meanwhile, scanning the early morning sky. Multiple plumes of black smoke rose from nearby battles like ominous monsters, all merging to form a single large black cloud that drifted west to east across the north side of the city and into Canada. The general heard the unique sound of a lone fighter jet ripping across the sky. He didn't actually see the jet, but there was no mistaking the orange flash of light followed by a deafening *boom* that marked an enormous explosion whose echoing rumble swallowed the sound of the jet racing away. The ground shook beneath the general's feet. A second *boom* announced that the unseen jet had broken the sound barrier as it peeled away.

Then, just under three miles to the northwest, a whitish gray column of dust, smoke, and debris rose rapidly and angrily over the urban landscape. It rose high into the morning sky and drifted lazily to the east toward Windsor.

The general sighed. He himself gave the order, but still... *An airstrike on an American city.*

A taboo had been broken.

* * *

Private First Class Adrian Gonzales of Phoenix, Arizona lined up with his squad mates to await the morning brief before they boarded a troop transport truck and deployed to their assigned patrol route along Martin Luther King Boulevard to relieve the overnight squad.

MLK Boulevard split the Corktown neighborhood, which was one of the most violent in the nation, according to FBI crime statistics.

But it was Grand Boulevard and Grand River Boulevard that were at the center of violence during this epoch of unrest, now being referred to in the media as the GLEE Uprising. MLK Boulevard saw no unrest at all; no protestors had gathered there, no cars were attacked, and no stores still in operation were looted.

And so, for Private Gonzales and his squad mates, deployment to MLK Boulevard was pretty boring. They simply walked all day long, back and forth, back and forth, "protecting" stores. Local residents, meanwhile, plied them with water bottles, sandwiches, and baked goods like cookies, pies, and cakes. The night shift was jealous.

"Gather around, men," ordered his squad leader, Staff Sergeant Dan Culver. "We have new orders."

Culver laid out a new set of engagement orders and explained that they were deploying to a different location.

They were going into battle.

Their convoy sped down I-94 past downtown Detroit and took the Livernois Avenue exit in a more circuitous route to engage the "terrorists," as Sergeant Culver called them, from the rear.

As the convoy crossed northbound on Livernois over Grand River Boulevard—a gas station on the corner flew the U.S. flag upside down—blood splattered into Adrian's face. The young soldier sitting across from him fell forward, blood spurting from between his hands as he clasped them across his neck.

He thrashed on the floor of the truck as Adrian and others desperately tried to give first aid while also scrambling to get out of the stopping truck.

Adrian helped pull the gurgling kid from the truck, and he and two other soldiers struggled to half-carry, half-drag him across the wide boulevard of Livernois Avenue to the gas station with the upside-down flag, but it was so far away. When they got halfway across the street, the kid went totally limp and became dead weight, and so they dragged him by his arm pits.

When they reached the gas station's canopy—they still weren't sure if they had reached a place of adequate cover—they laid the kid down and saw that he was dead.

The convoy commander, Major Thomas Warren, reported back to base that the convoy was under fire, more than a mile and a half from the fighting on Grand Boulevard. Another sniper, it appeared.

The soldiers identified an eight-story abandoned building—a furniture company was the last to occupy the building, according to the faded words "Dynasty Furniture" painted God knows how long ago on the top of the building's exterior—as the likely source for sniper fire.

* * *

Major Schmidt circled the city aloft as he awaited new orders. He could see that the fifteen-story, all-brick building was now a ten-story pile of rubble.

A red light on his heads-up display in his helmet visor caught Major Schmidt's eye. It was an engine fire light, and he pressed the lighted red button on the cockpit panel. It flickered and went out, but came right back on again.

"Selfridge, I have an engine fire light, requesting emergency landing," Jason calmly spoke into his headgear microphone. He steered his plane northeast toward Selfridge.

Multiple alerts came on all at once—fuel, engine power, hydraulics, and others—along with a beeping alarm.

Jason could see Selfridge in the distance, but his plane shuddered and lost power. It started to descend. "Mayday," he announced, still calmly, "no power," as acrid smoke filled the cockpit. Jason reached for the ejection seat cord and pulled, but he was a hair too late.

The F-35B stealth joint strike fighter exploded in a massive fireball seventeen miles north of Detroit and fifteen miles to the west of

Selfridge. Debris rained down for two square miles over suburban Troy.

McIntyre hurried out of the trailer and looked to the north. He saw a single black cloud in the distant sky with multiple contrails tracing to the ground.

What the hell just happened, he thought. "Get me Selfridge," he ordered.

"Jesus Christ," fumed the general a moment later, "what else could go wrong?" He slammed the phone down.

"Mr. Murphy," as the rogue warrior and founder of the Navy's SEAL Team Six Richard Marcinko himself liked to say, was paying a visit. It was a reference to Murphy's Law, the idea that anything that can go wrong, will go wrong. And always at the most inopportune or unexpected time.

A radio operator stood and interrupted McIntyre's train of thought. "Sir," he said. "Charlie Squad is taking sniper fire on Livernois and Grand River. They've got casualties."

General McIntyre slammed his hand on the main table in the middle of command trailer and stood hunched over it, resting his palms on the table with maps and soldiers' laptops on it. The officers and soldiers remained silent as General McIntyre glared at the stretched-out street map, deep in thought.

After a tense moment of silence, General McIntyre took a deep breath. "Okay," he said to no one in particular. "Okay," he said again, nodding to himself.

"We're going to seal these neighborhoods off," said the general. "We go door to door, house to house. The president has already de-clared the city to be in insurrection, so it's time for the gloves to come off." He stood straight, chin jutted out. "I warned them," he sighed. "God knows I warned them."

* * *

The city may have been officially on lockdown, but it took a while for word to spread despite being announced on TV and radio. It was the neighborhoods of West-Central Detroit that the Army focused on. The rest of the city was fine.

Aaron Jones and his friends didn't watch the news or listen to the radio. Besides, they were busy. They had a lucrative job to do, and it took all of every night of the past week to perform. They were good at it now.

They had a list of twenty-five addresses programmed into their phones. They didn't know it, but there were at least twenty other crews like them—nearly all of them teenagers, too—fanned out across the city and its suburbs with lists of addresses programmed into each of their phones.

It seemed that half of the houses they hit were abandoned. Others appeared to be lived in, and some obviously so. Especially in the suburbs, like here in Sterling Heights and Utica. These houses were all lived in.

They had it down now. They needn't torch the entire place, just enough to do damage. They quickly learned to aim for the roof. Fires on the roof that burned long enough would mean that the whole house would be condemned. That was the key. And, if there was anyone inside, it gave them enough time to get out. At least that was the thought.

In their van, they had several filled-up gas cans, loads of oily rags, and hundreds of empty glass beer and soda bottles. There were so many glass bottles that the unlucky ones stuck in the back had barely any place to sit. Or breathe, for that matter. The fumes were overpowering. When they got to an address, they plowed out, filled up and lit up two Molotov cocktails each, and firebombed the roof and, if they had time and the house appeared vacant, bombed all sides of the house.

They climbed back in the van and calmly drove on to their next address. The whole thing took about thirty seconds to a minute. If they were seen, which was rare enough, no one could identify them anyway nor even get a license plate due to the speed with which they operated, and the shock of it, too. Most people questioned what they saw since it happened so fast. But the fires that burned confirmed that what they saw wasn't a dream.

They had started on the very first night that the curfew was lifted. They had hit three houses that night, and Xavier nearly set himself on fire on one of them. They were paid $1,000 per house, and so each night they tried to hit more. They got up to seven to ten a night. They were making money hand over fist.

The twenty crews in total averaged seven houses a night. In ten nights, they would have hit fourteen hundred homes. The Averys contributed only a few of those crews. The rest came from other groups throughout the city that, together, comprised the Motown Mafia: the Brightmoor Boyz, the Corktown Crew, the Barton McFarland Gang, and multiple others—even factions of the Grand River Gees. Fred and Frankie Auletta put ten of their own crews on the job as well, and enlisted various groups they had done business with in the past.

The twenty crews grew to fifty. The Santacroces had even flown in crews from Philadelphia and Brooklyn. What was ten fires the first night grew to an average of one hundred forty by end of the first week. It was two hundred fifty a night by end of the second week, and nearly five hundred a night by the end of the third week.

The Army, police, and federal law enforcement agencies were entirely focused on West-Central Detroit and restoring order following the unrest. While the number of fires surpassed ten thousand within two weeks, that was a far cry from the more than forty thousand fires that raged during the unrest— and they were spread out over time and geography.

By the time the fires had forced anyone to take notice, they had already reached forty thousand in aggregate.

* * *

Alex Cooley sat in his office and looked over the first of twelve new vanilla folders on his desk. Twelve new folders meant twelve new fires. All in the same week. It was crazy.

That meant twelve more—*twelve more!*—tedious multi-page insurance forms that he had to look up data for and fill out. It had been a busy week, and yet the work was piling up. *So many fires.*

Outside his window, Alex could see the Ambassador Bridge in the distance. It was too far to see anything out of the ordinary, but helicopters buzzed around the bridge and the two cities it connected. Thousands more people had converged on that bridge to get across the river into Canada since the U.S. Army had restored order in Detroit. It was strange. He had a job and it was business as usual for him, but many people were still fleeing the city.

Yeah, it was weird to see the Army everywhere but, except for that, everything was pretty much back to normal. The unrest had ended, and that somehow opened the floodgates. The riots in Detroit might have been the catalyst, but Americans were now fleeing to Canada in droves.

It was all over the news. The government of Canada was teetering. Conservatives railed in Parliament against "illegal" American immigration, a crisis on the border. And it wasn't just the Ambassador Bridge anymore. The Blue Water Bridge in Port Huron connecting with Sarnia in Ontario over the St. Clair River way to the north was also swamped with American refugees. Regular commercial and non-commercial traffic had completely ceased as refugees from Detroit—"false refugees," according to prominent conservatives in Canada—overwhelmed the Canadian border stations.

American conservative media were equally vitriolic about the refugees—and Canada. "What a laughable irony," taunted the bombastic George Bruttale on Alex's computer. "Even liberal Canada doesn't want American liberals!" he snorted. And, in the next breath, he applauded the refugees. "A brilliant idea," he thundered. "Yes, go to Canada! Take your Hollywood with you! Take your Starbucks, your lattes, your electric cars! Take it all with you! And don't let the door hit your liberal asses on your way out!"

Alex heard a commotion in the hallway. He got up from his desk to see what was going on.

A group of twenty men in suits, the leaders gray-haired and austere, stormed into the executive suite and some marched straight into Donnie Tillman's office. All of the executives came out to see what was going on.

After a few minutes, Donnie Tillman came out of his office with the men, himself looking grave.

"Everyone, these gentlemen are with the FDIC, the Federal Deposit Insurance Corporation," said Donnie. "I've been informed that…"

Alex's mind drifted. Just a week ago, PIG, or the Pontchartrain Insurance Group, collapsed and was seized by the federal government. He had read about it in the news. And the week before that it was the Motor City Insurance Group. The more than forty thousand fires during and after the unrest was too much. Motor City and Pontchartrain were the insurers of many if not most of those homes and buildings.

The collapse of the insurance companies left tens of thousands of home and business owners with no insurance to cover their losses. And, with their houses and businesses burned to the ground or damaged to the point of condemnation, they were no longer paying their mortgages. And that meant trouble for local banks like Apex Superior and Pleasant Peninsula. Even worse, the local housing market was collapsing. Housing prices across Metropolitan Detroit were in freefall since the unrest.

The FDIC was here to seize the bank. Alex and his fellow executives, with the exception of the bank president, vice president, and the executive administrative assistant, were escorted by the men in suits to the exit. They could only gather their coats. Everything else was left as is, even Alex's computer with George Bruttale streaming vitriol from its speakers.

Alex and his executive friends stood on the sidewalk outside the

Pleasant Peninsula Bank building. They were stunned. They were, quite abruptly, unemployed.

CHAPTER 26

The deployment of the 10th Mountain Division to Detroit provided the support the now-federalized Michigan National Guard needed to properly deploy. General McIntyre had no intention of marginalizing Michigan's National Guard. On the contrary, he saw the National Guard as important for augmenting the active duty Army's mission, and especially for transitioning responsibilities to the Guard when the 10th Mountain Division wound down its deployment.

To that end, Michigan National Guard soldiers were tasked with providing support to the Detroit Police. National Guard squads comprised of four soldiers each were assigned to "shadow" police units as they responded to calls and when they conducted patrols. The support mission extended throughout Metropolitan Detroit wherever other jurisdictions outside the city proper requested it, particularly since police resources from around the metropolitan area had been directed at supporting Detroit's police.

Throughout the metropolitan area, including in Center Line, a suburb of Detroit in neighboring Macomb County, foreclosures were at an all-time high following the latest financial crisis widely referred to as the Shanghai Contagion. It was labeled that because the ensuing economic depression that swept the world all started with the crash of the Shanghai Composite Stock Market just a few short years ago.

On this day, Macomb County requested National Guard support

for its Sheriff's Department as it enforced an eviction notice on a home in Center Line that was foreclosed on by Pleasant Peninsula Bank. Before the unrest broke out in Detroit and law enforcement resources were redistributed to tasks in support of the Detroit Police Department, a county sheriff's deputy delivered the eviction notice, giving the homeowner seven working days to vacate the property. That homeowner, according to the deputy, was hostile and threatened to defend his home. It had now been more almost fourteen days. With the National Guard available, the county sheriff thought that it was better to be safe than sorry. Maybe a small show of force for deterrence.

The occupant, one Daniel "Dusty" Mulligan, was a divorced 55-year-old Iraq War veteran who suffered from severe depression, quite possibly linked to Post-Traumatic Stress Disorder, or PTSD, a condition that the Veterans Administration had so far resisted to diagnose.

Dusty worked at GM's Hamtramck Assembly Plant but was laid off for a second time when it closed a few years ago. Being over fifty, he found it difficult to even land an interview, and so he did whatever work he could find—as a handyman, for example, or working part-time at Walmart.

It wasn't enough. He fell behind on his mortgage despite owing just under $25,000 on a house that was recently worth about $180,000. He had no clue what the current value actually was, but it apparently wasn't close to that anymore. The house would not sell in a depressed market flooded with homes for sale and homes foreclosed on. The housing market was crashing.

Nor could he take out equity loans to try to stay afloat, albeit by digging an even deeper hole.

Dusty dreaded the moment when the police would come back and force him out. The home where his kids were raised. The house that he had put in a lot of blood, sweat, and tears, let alone money. But he knew they would come back.

When the knock on the door came, he knew it was them. Police always rapped with authority. The moment had come.

Dusty had prepared for this. In the past week he had purchased two AR-15 rifles, a shotgun, and boxes of ammunition. It was *his* house, by God, and he wasn't going to let the government come and take it. They *used* him in Iraq. Said there were weapons of mass destruction. Said that Saddam Hussein was behind 9/11. Said that Iraq was a threat to the Homeland.

Lies. All lies.

And now they had come for his house. They would have to kill him for it.

* * *

Zach Arnold sat in the front passenger seat as Staff Sergeant Harris drove, following close behind the Humvee in front and the sheriff's car up ahead. In the back seats, Private First Class Giovanni D'Amato looked out the window and silently bounced his head while listening to an iPod. Terrance Hubbard, a corporal, kept a keen eye on the neighborhoods they drove through.

The sheriff's car pulled up to the curb in front of the home on Central Street. The National Guard vehicle stopped, double-parked behind the police cruiser. The soldiers remained in the Humvee as the sheriff's deputy sat in his car filling out paperwork before getting out of his vehicle and walking up to the front door of the residence.

Zach looked up at the modest Carpenter Gothic cottage home. A red U.S. Marine Corps flag perched on a small pole attached to the front porch railing swayed lazily amid a soft breeze.

"Oh, man," said Zach to no one in particular. "This guy's a veteran."

The sheriff's deputy pounded on the front door and waited, holding a court order for the owner to vacate the premise. He raised his hand to pound on the door again when part of it exploded outward in a spray of wooden shards, with a *boom!* The deputy flinched in unison with the partially exploding door, and turned and ran, stumbling down the short porch stairs and regaining his footing as he sprinted for his cruiser.

As he ran, dirt and grass jumped twice at his feet as bullets struck the ground. Just as he dove over the hood of his car and tumbled to the street on the other side of it, his passenger side windows exploded in a shower of glass, and bullets punctured the passenger side doors.

The deputy somehow escaped being shot, but his right arm—the arm he used to pound on the front door—was heavily scratched and bleeding from wood splinters.

The four soldiers in the Humvee scrambled out and dove for cover just as the shooter took aim on them.

"Oh, shit, they're shooting as us!" yelled Zachary.

"No shit, Private," said Sergeant Harris.

The sergeant reached into the Humvee for the radio microphone, careful to stay behind cover. "Base, base, this is Foxtrot Squad," Harris said into the mic. "Repeat, this is Foxtrot Squad. We are taking fire, over. We're pinned down. We need backup!"

Within fifteen minutes of the radio call, dozens of police cars and multiple troop-carrying trucks arrived on scene, unloading soldiers on both ends of Central Street. Residents had come out of their homes, hearing the commotion of the initial gunfire followed by scores of police sirens. Crowds gathered to watch as soldiers took up positions behind parked cars.

The war in Detroit had come to the suburbs.

* * *

Along with the Army, other sheriffs' deputies and local Center Line police had come on the scene. The shooting had stopped, but soldiers and police milled about behind their vehicles for safety while officers phoned the owner to negotiate a surrender.

Neighbors were forced to evacuate and stood down the street from Mulligan's house on both ends of Central Street.

Zachary grew nervous, increasingly so, as crowds of local residents grew in numbers. The stares they were getting from the neighbors, and the looks on their faces, were similar to the crowds that had thrown Molotov cocktails and set his Humvee on fire on that first day when they tried to deploy in the city. He and his comrades were nearly killed that day, and that was the first time he had ever been in a firefight.

Terrance studied the young private and could see that he was agitated. "What's going on, my man?" he asked.

"Something isn't right," said Zach, his head on a swivel.

"Oh, you think?" said Terrance.

"It's just, they're all white," said Zach.

Terrance looked at the angry crowd gathered behind the Army trucks. "What, you thought all of this was about *race*?" he asked.

"No, I guess not," said Zach, meekly.

An egg landed and splatted on the ground near them, thrown from someone in the crowd.

"This is America!" an angry man, probably in his sixties, shouted, his face red and contorted in anger. "Dusty is a veteran!"

"Shame!" yelled an elderly woman. The crowds immediately appropriated her word choice. "Shame! Shame! Shame!" they chanted in unison.

The soldiers and police were hemmed in between an armed Dusty Mulligan barricaded in his house, and growing and increasingly restive crowds at both ends of the narrow suburban street.

James Roberts, the recently elected Macomb County sheriff who ran on a law-and-order platform, worried that a prolonged standoff might attract more sympathetic protesters and, worse, set a precedent.

Dusty Mulligan refused to negotiate a surrender. Sheriff Roberts ordered the police to storm the house by force.

* * *

Just a bit to the north, in Warren (there was no daylight between the two towns), not two miles away, Aaron Jones and his friends drove slowly past a house on their list. These were modest, single-story ranchers, maybe one thousand square feet on average.

Aaron, Xavier, Devin, and Reggie rode in a rusted Ford Econoline van on loan from Freddie's Garage and Auto Parts, its vehicle identification number tags ground out. Its license plates were old and no longer valid, nor could they be traced to Freddie's.

It was still early morning and most of the suburban neighborhood was stirring. People were getting ready for work, despite the Army operation in central Detroit, and kids were readying for school. The house on their list also appeared to be empty. Xavier was the driver, and he stopped in front of the house. He backed up into the short driveway.

The friends piled out of the van and took up stations in four points around the house, lit their Molotov cocktails, and heaved them onto the roof. Four separate flames flared up with a *whoosh,* and black smoke rose into the air. The four young men returned to the van and each grabbed a second rag-stuffed bottle. They lit up the bottles and threw them into the windows, then scrambled back into the van.

Xavier was careful to pull out slowly, as they had been told to do by Mr. Avery, and to drive normally. They had no trouble thus far in their now three-week-long full-time lucrative project. They alone accounted for more than two hundred fires over those three weeks.

They had heard that some other crews had been busted, and so Aaron and his friends were extra careful. The money was rewarding, however, and they were paid by the house. For the first week, they strictly worked at night, but they got more daring with time, starting before sunset and ending after sunrise, like now.

They were growing bolder with each fire they successfully set.

Warren Police Sergeant Adam Davis, driving east on 13 Mile,

noticed a wisp of black smoke that rose barely above the rooftops amid the endless rows of suburban tract housing to his right. He almost dismissed it, thinking the smoke was birds because the curl of smoke dipped below the rooftops, but it re-emerged as a fuller and more sustained cloud of smoke began to rise.

There had been a number of fires, most definitely set by arson, in the Warren area, and many more throughout Metropolitan Detroit, so Adam turned into the neighborhood and tried to estimate the street from which the smoke rose. He turned onto a street and sped up, passing an old van driving in the opposite direction.

He made eye contact with the driver. It was a young black kid, probably not even twenty. He looked nervous somehow, and so did the other kid in the passenger seat. So, two young-looking black guys, riding in the front of the van, who appeared nervous the moment they saw him.

Adam could see that the smoke ahead was rapidly gaining form. It was a fire, after all.

* * *

Xavier giggled, nervously. "Oh, my God," he said in a high-pitched voice. "That was so close!" He repeatedly peered into the rearview and side view mirrors, making sure the police car hadn't turned around. "The dude looked right at me," he said, giggling some more.

"Maybe we should wait until tonight," offered Aaron in the back, "you know, to be safe."

"What's next?" asked Xavier as Devin scrolled to the next address. It was in Harper Woods, to the southeast, which they could hit on the way back home.

"Okay," said Xavier. "We'll go back and wait for tonight, but we can get one more on the way."

That was reasonable, thought Aaron.

Xavier turned southbound onto Schoenherr Road. A few minutes later, they were eastbound on 7 Mile, following the directions of the GPS on Xavier's phone to Harper Woods. A Detroit Police car sped up from behind and turned on its emergency lights and siren as it pulled directly behind the van.

"Oh, *shit*," exclaimed Xavier, "where did *he* come from?" Everyone scrambled to get a peek at the police car behind them.

"What do I do?" asked Xavier, his heart jumping in his chest.

"Go, man, *go!"* said Devin.

"No way, man, pull over!" shouted Aaron from the back.

Xavier gunned it.

The van leapt forward and quickly sped east on 7 Mile, which turned southeast and became Moross Road as they crossed into Harper Woods. No matter. Detroit police were officially in hot pursuit and followed the van into the struggling inner-ring suburban township.

More than one siren screamed in the near distance now. They were had. Xavier turned right onto a residential street. He took the turn too fast, and the van side-swiped a parked car, sending the van careening to the right and flipping it onto its side as Devin overcompensated. It slid across the road and slammed into another parked car.

Aaron Jones, soaking wet in gasoline and gagging on the fumes, scrambled out of the back of the van on his hands and knees amid the broken glass of the multiple bottles. Reggie, bloodied, scrambled out behind him, limping and coughing.

Several police cars, their sirens screaming and lights flashing, came around the corner and screeched to a halt.

Aaron reached back to help Reggie out of the van when, in a sudden *whoosh,* flames flared up in a flash, engulfing the van and knocking Aaron backward on his haunches.

Reggie, like Aaron, was covered in gasoline, and flames enveloped him. He screamed a blood-curdling scream. He waved his arms and staggered toward Aaron, totally engulfed in flames.

Aaron, horrified, sat and stared up at Reggie, his eyes wide and mouth agape.

Reggie lurched toward him, and Aaron scrambled away, frightfully aware that he too would erupt in fire if Reggie touched him or got too close.

Aaron turned his back on his burning, screaming friend and ran. He sprinted across the front lawn of the house and into the backyard as Reggie screamed behind him.

Aaron continued sprinting, trying to put as much distance between himself and his burning friend, the van, and the police as quickly as possible.

* * *

After the van flipped, Xavier wound up on top of Devin.

"You okay, man?" asked Xavier as he frantically untangled himself from Devin and kicked out what remained of the windshield.

Devin didn't respond, and when Xavier looked at him, the fact that he was dead didn't register despite the contortion of his body, the unnatural tilt of his head, the staring eyes, and the alarming amount of blood streaming out of his nose and mouth.

Adrenaline flowed through Xavier's veins and he didn't notice that Devin's body was snagged on various protrusions of the smashed van's remains. He just reached under Devin's armpits and pulled, nearly ripping the kid's clothes right off of him as he dragged him out of the wreckage.

Nor did he hear the half-dozen cops feverishly shouting commands and aiming their pistols.

As Devin's body came free of the wreckage, the van erupted in flames. Xavier dragged Devin away from the van and heard Reggie's unnatural screams. He looked to the back of the van and saw someone stagger into the street engulfed in flames and collapse in the middle of the road. He knew it had to be either Reggie or Aaron.

Movement from his right caught his attention for the first time.

It was the police, lined up in a semi-circle, all of them crouched and aiming guns at him. Their faces were contorted as they shouted commands, but Xavier just stood there, stupefied. He could not hear a single word, just his own heart that beat thick in his head.

Nor was Xavier aware that he had been gripping his handgun in his right hand the whole time, even as he had dragged Devin from the wreckage. He had seen it on the floor and picked it up without thought.

Xavier laid Devin's lifeless body on the pavement and stood up, still gripping his gun. He was met with a hail of bullets. Later, his autopsy would reveal that he had been shot as many as twenty-six times.

* * *

Aaron ran on adrenaline. He ran from front yards to back yards, again and again. He stumbled across a high school just over a mile away in about seven minutes. School was about to start and kids were everywhere. Aaron stopped running and tried to blend in, but he smelled strongly of gasoline.

He tried to act nonchalant, just a kid walking to school. He remembered his cell phone and pulled it out. It was intact.

He called Michelle. When she answered, he burst into tears. "Reggie's dead," he told her.

"Whaaat?" asked Michelle, thinking he was somehow joking. But he was crying. She had never seen or heard Aaron cry before.

He told her everything. About how Jayson Avery and his organization hired him and his friends. About the house fires. About Reggie catching on fire and how there was nothing he could do to save him. About Reggie's screams.

"What about Xavier and Devin?" asked Michelle.

"I don't know," sobbed Aaron. "I...I think I heard gunshots."

A helicopter made a wide circle above, but he didn't think it was circling *him*. It looked to be circling the site of the crash. Probably looking for him, though, for sure. "I'm *scared,"* Aaron said. "What am I going to do?"

"Call Mr. Avery!" Michelle offered. "I mean, it sounds like he had a plan in case something like this happened, in case you got busted."

"I…I don't know," said Aaron.

"How are you going to get home with the police looking for you? Do you even know where you are?" she asked.

"Uh, no," said Aaron, sniffling, looking around. A street sign said "Kelly" and he walked through a cluster of long-abandoned store-fronts, probably abandoned decades ago.

"Call him!" Michelle pleaded. "Be safe, Aaron, please! And call me right back."

"Okay," Aaron sighed, and disconnected his phone. He dropped back among the abandoned stores, momentarily seized by panic. A police car was coming down the street.

When it passed, Aaron exhaled a deep, trembling sigh of relief. It was a taxi cab. Then he dialed the number that Jayson Avery had given each of them.

"Yo," someone answered.

"This is Aaron Jones," Aaron said hesitantly. "Reggie is dead and I don't know what happened to Devin and Xavier," he said, bursting into tears all over again.

"Stop," said the voice, interrupting Aaron. Aaron didn't know who it was. "Stay where you are. Mr. Avery will call you." The man hung up.

Within a few minutes, his phone buzzed. The number was restricted. "Hello?" asked Aaron.

"Yo, Mr. Jones," said a familiar baritone voice. It was Jayson Avery.

"Mr. Avery, I don't know what to do," said Aaron. He told Jayson everything that had happened. "Reggie's dead."

"Listen, Aaron," said Jayson. "Take a deep breath. Tell me where you are."

"I'm on Kelly Street," said Aaron, "and...there's a church. I don't see a sign. I think it's abandoned."

"Okay, I'll find it," said Jayson. "Stay put, stay calm, and stay out of sight," he ordered in his baritone voice, and hung up.

Aaron wiped his nose and held his phone, staring at it. He felt better. Mr. Avery was going to make things right. He called Michelle back.

"He's coming," he said.

"Oh, thank God," said Michelle. "You sound better."

Aaron didn't answer. "I can't believe Reggie is gone," he said, after a moment. He started crying again.

"I'll stop by your house later," said Michelle. "Hang in there, okay, and stay out of sight until Mr. Avery gets there."

"Okay," said Aaron. "I love you," he added with a sniffle.

Michelle chuckled suspiciously.

"What?" he asked earnestly.

"Just, you've never said that before," Michelle said, smiling. Aaron could practically *hear* her smile through the phone, and it made him feel good. "I love you, too," Michelle said before hanging up.

Aaron stayed hidden behind overgrown brown shrubbery branches between two abandoned and collapsing storefronts. In the summer, the shrubbery would be green, lush, and wild. He peeked out whenever he heard a car coming, but he was careful to stay low and not reveal himself, fearing the police.

Nearly thirty minutes passed before he spotted a black SUV coming down the street, slow and hesitant. He stood up, but ducked quickly behind the shrubbery again. He thought with a spine-tingling chill that it could be a police SUV.

The SUV sped up and stopped in front of the shrubbery. They had seen him.

"Yo, Mr. Jones!" yelled the familiar, baritone voice. It was Mr. Avery, after all. Aaron stepped out from the shrubbery. Jayson Avery was in the back seat, waving Aaron over. Aaron recognized the driver as Elijah Freeman.

Aaron jogged to the Cadillac Escalade and returned Jayson's smile with his own—a shy smile of gratitude.

A single gunshot to the sternum sent the slender teenager reeling backward, tackled by an invisible force, and he ended sprawled on his back in the middle of the road. One violent spasm jolted his body.

Jayson got out of his car and briefly stood over the boy. The kid's eyes were open wide with surprise and then dulled into a smoky, empty stare. He was dead, his arms splayed out over his head. Dark blood pooled on the street beneath him. Jayson knelt beside him and fished out the boy's cell phone from his pocket. He stood up and shot him again to be sure that he was, in fact, dead, and climbed back into his car. Elijah drove off, morosely eyeing the body in his rearview mirror.

* * *

Adrian vomited after trying to feel for a pulse on the young private's neck. The kid was unnaturally pale, and his skin had kind of shriveled. The amount of blood that had poured out of him was unimaginable. There was no escaping the fact that he was dead, and his death was nothing like on TV or in the movies. It was ugly and unclean.

Adrian and two other soldiers stood vigil over the corpse as their unit continued to take fire from a sniper or snipers in the abandoned Dynasty Furniture Building a few blocks to the west. Every time someone moved, a singular gunshot echoed loudly amid the flashy but sad-looking fast food joints and dilapidated light industrial buildings strung out along the cold boulevard parallel to I-96.

The private's body lay on the gasoline station's grease- and oil-stained tarmac strewn with trash. Adrian watched as a pool of blood from the dead young private slowly but methodically stretched out across the parking lot and enveloped a discarded cigarette butt with lipstick on it.

They waited a long time. The silence and stillness among the soldiers, all hidden behind cover, left an eerie pall over the already dystopian and economically-ravaged landscape.

The screech of a jet followed by a *KA-BOOM,* as if in exclamation, broke the eerie silence and marked the destruction of the Dynasty Furniture building. Hidden soldiers hooted and applauded. One of the soldiers with Adrian peeked his head around the gas station's convenience store and saw nothing but smoke and dust where the building stood, then retreated behind cover again.

"I think it's gone," said the soldier.

"Target neutralized," said a voice over the radio, confirming the soldier's observation.

A Humvee with a bright red cross on its doors pulled into the gas station. Medics quickly went to work on the dead private, largely out of protocol, given the fact of his death. Soldiers, meanwhile, came out from behind cover and seemed to be everywhere all at once.

"Contact, contact!" someone shouted, and soldiers once again scrambled for cover.

Adrian and his squad took shelter snuggled between an outdoor Kentucky Fried Chicken Drive-thru menu and the restaurant's building, and lay prone on the ground. Adrian could see that crowds of people had gathered on the boulevard stretching north in front of them, probably drawn by the commotion of army troops hunkered down and taking sniper fire, and then the airstrike.

It was Livernois Avenue that stretched before Adrian and his squad, and the crowds gathering along its sidewalks and center island had that hard look on their faces. Young people darted onto the roadway as far as he could see, dragging tires and debris and lighting various pyres on fire.

Detroit was stirring again.

A Humvee sped out ahead of the troops taking shelter and stopped about a half-mile up the road. Adrian could hear a bullhorn barking orders to the crowds ahead of them, but he couldn't hear what it was saying.

The crowds appeared unmoved. They only continued to look on; no one seemed to be leaving.

Adrian looked back at a group of officers hunkered around a Humvee with a radio and a street map laid out on its hood. They seemed hesitant about what to do about the gathering crowds. And just over two miles to their right, they could hear that the gun battle they were ordered to flank raged on still.

Adrian and his squad mates remained prone on the ground. Waiting. The officers presumably were communicating with the head honcho, General McIntyre. After a while, the officers began disseminating their orders.

They were going into battle, it seemed, but they would have to wait a little bit longer.

Nearly an hour later, a large low-flying cargo plane, a gray Army C-130, loudly passed overhead from behind, startling Adrian. He watched as it banked hard to the right. A steady stream of *something* poured out of the back of the large airplane as it flew. Papers, Adrian realized, as they floated down en masse, spreading out all over neighborhoods indiscriminately. Papers now fluttered all about, intermittently settling on the ground only to be picked up by a breeze and drift high in the air anew.

* * *

Like much of the city, particularly in New Center and its surrounding neighborhoods, Lamar Griffith was awakened by the massive overnight car bomb, this one a little farther away than the first one. Within minutes of the explosion, he could hear the tell-tale *tat-tat-tat* of small arms fire. Just like that day when the Army had killed his little cousin Dominic and his two friends.

But this was his girlfriend's neighborhood a couple of miles to the north in the heart of Petosky-Ostego. Nearly a third of the neighborhood's homes were long gone, either razed or burned to the ground over the decades, leaving a slew of empty, overgrown lots. Of the homes that remained, many were boarded-up and crumbling.

The gunfire was loud and filled the open-spaced neighborhood, and it sounded like it was everywhere. Angelica, his girlfriend, slept beside him, unbothered. When the jackhammers of automatic gunfire began, he woke her up and they moved downstairs, taking care to stay low and away from the windows because the gunfire sounded very close. Nor did they turn on any lights.

They sat side by side on the floor in the dark, and in silence, with their backs against the living room couch. Lamar wondered how many people in the neighborhood were doing exactly the same thing.

At daybreak, Lamar peaked his head outside and looked around. The fighting seemed to be more or less contained in one area and not all over the neighborhood, thankfully. He got a better sense of where the gunfight was and it appeared to be at least several blocks away. Perhaps not as close as he had thought during the night.

Still, the gunfight raged on.

Other neighbors, too, were beginning to cautiously step outside. Some were armed with either handguns or military-grade assault rifles for self-protection.

Lamar flinched and ducked as a large, low-flying aircraft flew seemingly right over his girlfriend's house. He looked up at the Army C-130 banking hard, leaving a trail of papers behind that rained down like confetti, the wind taking them in all directions.

A paper fluttered down and Lamar snatched it out of the air. The flyer announced that a U.S. Army operation was underway and that all residents in the neighborhoods of Core City, Northwest Goldberg, LaSalle Gardens, Virginia Park, Petosky-Otsego, North End, Arden Park, and Dexter-Linwood should evacuate immediately. They had only until noon, and then the Army would start going door to door to flush out what it said were "terrorists."

EVACUATE and DO NOT RESIST were written in bold font and in all caps. Smaller print coached residents on how to respond to soldiers at their door if they stayed behind. It warned residents that soldiers were ordered to search the entire house and seize all unregistered weapons. On the back was a crude, hand-drawn map indicating that people evacuating should walk to several key locations where city buses would pick them up and take them to the domed Ford Field for shelter until the operation was over.

Lamar looked up from the flyer and watched as a sea of paper fluttered in the sky, some going high up into the air even as others spiraled down. He went back inside and handed the paper to Angelica.

"We need to go," he said, as she looked it over.

"This is *bullshit,*" she protested. "They can't do this," she said. "They want me to leave my *house,* Lamar," she nearly shouted. "How can they do that?"

Lamar didn't answer. His eyes grew hard as he thought about Dominic and how the Army had rolled into his neighborhood. And now they were here. They had followed him to Angelica's neighborhood. The flyer said they were here to clear out "terrorists." *But who were the terrorists?*

Lamar looked at Angelica with far-away eyes. "We're not going anywhere, baby," he said.

* * *

Bernice Hamandawana had awakened to the pre-dawn car bomb and had immediately known what it was. It sounded just like the first one the day before and, like that one, her apartment shook so hard that she thought the building might come down. Within minutes, there was a pounding on her door. It was her friend and fellow journalist student Daniel Rush. He brought his camera taken on loan from the Journalism Department at Wayne State.

Bernice threw her clothes on as fast as she could, grabbed her cellphone and book bag, and met Daniel outside. Her nostrils were assaulted by the acerbic smell, and the sky glowed orange to the west of her, across the junction of I-96 and the M-10 astride the Wayne State University campus.

"What's going, Daniel?" she asked, looking toward the orange glow against the western sky.

"Don't know," he said. "I think it was another car bomb. Probably a mile or two away," he added.

"Let's go," Bernice said, and the two began a brisk walk north to cross over I-94 toward Grand Boulevard. As they walked, the unmistakable sound of automatic gunfire in the distance punctuated a growing cacophony of sirens near and far. They both instinctively stopped and dropped down.

"Whoa," whispered Daniel, "*that's* new."

They picked themselves up and renewed their brisk pace. As they approached Grand Boulevard in the heart of New Center, several police cars whisked by at high speed with sirens blaring and emergency lights flashing. Two fire trucks, moving not much slower, followed behind. Daniel, his camera held up to eye level, captured the police and fire vehicles as they sped past from their right to left, or east to west.

Bernice and Daniel had to dart across the boulevard. More vehicles—these appeared to be Army Humvees and trucks, and more flashing lights behind them—were approaching fast. Still, as they crossed to the median, Daniel panned to the west and stopped momentarily to adjust his view. A sea of flashing lights and Army vehicles filled the boulevard about a mile or so away. Just a few blocks behind him was the scene of the first bomb. Incredibly, the second bomb appeared to also be on Grand Boulevard.

The Army trucks loudly passed by, and sirens of more police cars hurt their ears as they, too, sped by. Daniel had grabbed Bernice's arm and was saying something, but she couldn't hear him at first.

"What?" she shouted.

"That guy is calling you!" he yelled over the sirens and nodded to somewhere across the street. Bernice followed his gaze and scanned the sidewalk where several people stood watching the commotion, some of them dressed in night gowns and robes despite the cold air. Among them stood a smartly dressed man in jeans and a tweed sports coat, waving his arms.

It was Walter Clay. "Walter!" Bernice yelled and waved. Daniel stopped her from running to him as another police car sped past.

After the police car passed, Bernice and Daniel ran across the street to Walter, who briefly hugged each of them. "Daniel, good to see you again, my man," he said with a brief hug after greeting Bernice. "Should've known you'd be out here covering this mess," he said.

"What's going on?" asked Bernice as Daniel turned his attention to filming more passing emergency vehicles. "Another car bomb?"

"Looks like it, and now it sounds like a war is going on down there," Walter said, looking to the commotion down the boulevard.

The three of them determined they would not be able to get close enough to see what was going on. The police and fire department were closing off the boulevard and preventing anyone from getting closer. So they headed north to cross over to the other side of the M-10 freeway in the Virginia Parks neighborhood and double back for a different approach to whatever was going on.

It was a leisurely walk. The sky was a vibrant red and orange as the sun peeked over the southeastern horizon. The gunfire largely subsided, but there was a distinctive single shot that occurred every minute or so, echoing off the buildings as they walked. When they approached the Seward Street bridge over the M-10, they found it blocked by police, too, so they continued north to the next crossing at Euclid Street. It was also blocked, and so they trudged on. A pedestrian-only bridge at Pingree Street was clear, and so they crossed there. As they walked over the M-10, Daniel filmed the highway from the pedestrian bridge. An Army convoy was passing beneath them. Daniel could see two bridges to their north, each of which was occupied by an Army M-1 Abrams tank, their turrets pointing west into the Virginia Parks neighborhood.

Their cell phones buzzed with an official alert. The Army had declared a State of Emergency for Central Detroit, and the city was officially on lockdown. A U.S. Army operation was underway, the alert read, and warned residents to stay indoors.

As if on cue, a single F-35B Lightning II stealth fighter roared high in the sky. Daniel panned his camera up to try and follow the plane as it quickly accelerated with a trail of bluish flame. Daniel lost it behind rooftops and a billboard, but he could hear its roar like a scratch in his ear.

"Oh, shit!" Daniel exclaimed. A roiling gray mushroom cloud filled his lenses and lifted angrily some distance behind the rooftops. A massive *BANG* followed, shaking the bridge they stood on.

"Holy shit!" Daniel exclaimed again, "that was an airstrike!"

"Tell me you got that," said Bernice.

"Hell, yeah!" Daniel said, excitedly.

After Daniel uploaded his brief video to the free and independent newspaper *Motown Mirror,* Wayne State's *The South End* student newspaper, and various social networks, the three of them jogged across the bridge for a better view, but none was to be had. The airstrike was too far away to get any clear view straight away. So they did their best to follow the dissipating gray cloud. Another, more muffled *bang* reverberated through the air, but this one was much farther away, and the three friends couldn't determine its cause. Was it another airstrike? If it was, it was too far away for them to immediately investigate, so they turned their attention back to the first one.

After almost an hour of walking they were closer, but the gray dust cloud had drifted completely away, and a low-hanging shroud of dust had spread out over a wide area. They still couldn't pinpoint the location of the airstrike. Another loud aircraft—this one sounded different than the earlier fighter jet—made them turn their heads up to the sky, and Daniel captured the low-flying C-130 as it unloaded its cargo of thousands of flyers.

Only until they were about six blocks north of Grand Boulevard did Walter notice the unusually jagged top of the Lee Plaza Building as it emerged from the shroud of fog-like dust. In fact, the top several floors of the red brick building were practically gone, squished together in a pile of rubble sitting atop the building's middle floors. The building's height had been reduced by a third. Several small fires burned in the rubble, visible as isolated and flickering orange orbs.

Daniel zoomed in with his camera, filling his lenses with the building's destruction while Bernice recorded an impromptu on-location report.

After uploading her report, the three students turned their attention to the throngs of people walking south, many dragging suitcases on wheels. It was clear that they were evacuating as ordered.

* * *

The massive overnight car bomb was less than half a mile from the long abandoned St. Agnes Catholic Church on the corner of South La Salle Gardens and Rosa Parks Boulevard. St. Agnes had once hosted Mother Theresa during a visit to Detroit in 1979. Completed in 1924, the sturdy gothic church joined the ranks of Detroit's structural remnants of a ghostly past when it was closed, permanently, in 2006. A revolving door of up to fifteen young artists and musicians at a time had taken up residence in the church as squatters in recent years, using the wide open spaces as art studios and space for performance—the prevalence of recreational drugs, some of it pretty heavy, notwithstanding.

LeRon "The People's Mayor" Gordon was among the group that currently called the church home. He had met his current girlfriend Rachel Lamont there. She sketched and painted. LeRon wrote poetry and rapped out lyrics, with various other squatters often joining in, and also sketched out ideas for murals.

The explosion rattled the old church, and it creaked loudly as the explosion reverberated through its rickety structure.

The young artists—there were nine of them this night, including LeRon and Rachel—huddled together and kept near the front entranceway, keeping wary eyes on the ceiling and walls. They were unsure if the grand high ceiling of the nave could absorb the abuse.

And then the jackhammer gunfire began, amplified by the church's open space. The young artists joined in on an impromptu rap, led by LeRon, in an effort to drown out the gunfire.

The war outside
A shiver down my spine
This old rickety church
A black birch
A sanctuary, a Hail Mary

Enough for LeRon to scribble down what he could to keep up as they took turns sketching out verses on the fly. And so it went on through the night until sunlight filtered into the nave from the high cathedral windows that still remained.

The constant barrage of gunfire had largely died down, but it didn't go away completely. Fits of machine gun fire would flare up into sessions of various lengths even after the sun had risen.

The gunfire was close, that much was certain but, as dawn drew into the latter hours of morning, the young artists ventured out into the neighborhood.

For LeRon, it was like stepping out into a war zone after a bomb had gone off. A bomb *had* gone off, and it *was* a warzone, he had to remind himself. Papers fluttered around all over the streets and in the air. LeRon had seen that before, on the internet. In videos of the 9/11 terrorist attacks in New York City years before he was born, papers fluttered in the air and clogged the streets. It was one of the images that stuck with him.

Looking down at the papers gathering in the street gutters, he could see that there were at least two different flyers. One of the artists picked up one of each and the others gathered around to read over his shoulder. One flyer said that they had to evacuate the neighborhood. The other flyer had wanted photos of nine people on both sides. The largest photo was of Dmitri Johnson, the freeway killer.

No one spoke. The young artist that picked up the flyers let them go, and the wind took them away. The kid walked away without a word and seemingly without a care in the world.

"Are we in the evacuation zone?" asked Rachel, grabbing LeRon's arm with both hands and pulling herself into him.

"Guess so," said LeRon, "we black, ain't we?"

"What do we do?" asked Rachel.

LeRon's eyes went distant. He sat on the curb and pulled out his worn-ragged notebook from his shabby book bag. Rachel sat beside him and rested her chin on his shoulder as he wrote.

Exacerbate

Infuriate

Discriminate

Annihilate

Invalidate

Premeditate

EVACUATE

"Seriously, LeRon?" said Rachel, smiling.

LeRon heard sirens as the backdrop to the lyrics.

"An artist *documents,* baby," he said, and pecked a kiss on Rachel's lips. "Where are we going to go?" she asked. LeRon didn't answer.

LeRon and Rachel stood up and looked around. To their south, there appeared to be a large commotion. A plume of smoke rose high into the air and helicopters hovered in the distance. LeRon could make out Army trucks and soldiers gathering as though for battle.

A pickup truck with several young men armed with machine guns tore past LeRon and Rachel. One of the young men in the truck bed flashed a 'V' sign and a big smile.

LeRon and Rachel were too close to the specter of gathering troops and police forces to head south. So they walked north, in the direction of the pickup truck that then turned out of view, unsure of where they were going.

As they walked north along Rosa Parks Boulevard, they ran into friends and acquaintances. LeRon was a minor celebrity of sorts. Bernice Hamandawana's filmed brief interaction with him ("they're lining up against us") during the initial big GLEE protest that kicked off the whole unrest had gone viral. Various DJs added beats to his rhyme. The unkempt hair, toothy grin, and charisma of "The People's Mayor" generated more than ten millions views.

The boulevard, meanwhile, was crowded with people and car traffic heading in the opposite direction. The car traffic thickened into bumper-to-bumper, barely moving vehicle traffic. Some people on foot pulled suitcases on wheels, and some dragged little red children's wagons stuffed with belongings, with children in tow. The boulevard was strewn with the flyers dropped by the C-130, and many residents were taking heed.

Some of their friends were among those that were evacuating. Others were staying. In fact, most people seemed to be either standing around or wandering about as though it were a big block party. One of their friends—more like an acquaintance, really—was a brooding kid, seemingly older than his nineteen years. The neighborhood did that.

The kid was Lamar Griffin. He stood among an armed and tragically dangerous-looking group of kids. An assault rifle was slung over his shoulder. "The People's Mayor," he said, nodding to LeRon and Rachel. "How's it going, Mister Mayor?"

"Not bad, little nomad," LeRon answered. "What's up with the guns, shogun?"

"Do you want to die?" added Rachel in her child-like earnest way.

Lamar lit a cigarette and studied her and LeRon while he inhaled. Both of their faces were open and sincere, like always, and devoid of sarcasm or edge. After a moment, Lamar, his face impassive, exhaled a cloud of smoke and answered. "This ain't living."

After more walking, someone waved his arms and yelled, "LeRon!"

LeRon saw that it was Walter Clay and the two journalism students. LeRon flashed a grin and, when they approached, he hugged each of them. "A brotherhood, a sisterhood, in my neighborhood," LeRon rapped.

CHAPTER 27

Antonio Gonzales and his squad mates waited no longer. It was almost noon, and the crowds gathered all along Livernois had not dissipated. Instead, they only grew larger. Multiple pyres of tires and trash were gathered at different spots far into the distance, and all of them set aflame.

It was time.

An M-1 Abrams tank roared to life and drove to the intersection of Burlingame Street and stopped. Antonio and his squad were directed to the next street over, the residential Woodside Street that stretched for only three blocks. Squads ahead of them stormed homes on either side of the street, and Antonio and his squad followed up and stormed the third house on their left as other squads behind them continued on and stormed the next houses.

The first house Antonio's squad hit was abandoned and boarded-up. They smashed through with a battering ram and swept through the dark, spooky house as fast as they could, squad sections working together in close quarters combat groups as they swept room to room.

They had to be fast, but also careful. The floorboards creaked under their feet, and they weren't certain they wouldn't fall through, especially when they went upstairs. They found no one in the long-abandoned house, and they painted a bright orange 'X' on the board that stood in place of a front window indicating that the house was swept and cleared.

271

Antonio and his squad mates walked briskly on to their next assigned house as they leapfrogged other squads conducting sweeps.

* * *

·General McIntyre had ordered a full-on assault on the neighborhood adjoining the two firefights, the one on Grand River Avenue
marking its western border, and the one on Grand Boulevard marking
its south.

Soldiers cordoned off West-Central Detroit from I-96 in the west
to I-75 in the east, to the M-10 in the north, and to I-94 in the south,
pretty much all of Central Detroit, save for downtown.

The president had given McIntyre full authorization by telephone
to neutralize the so-called Motown Mafia by any means necessary.
She wanted Detroit out of the headlines *yesterday.*

That made things clearer for McIntyre and his army. It was now
a matter of cold and methodical execution.

Soldiers surged south of Grand Boulevard into the six blocks or
so in New Center between Grand Boulevard to I-94, and into the
troubled Northwest Goldberg neighborhood between West Grand
Boulevard and I-94. They faced mild resistance in New Center as
they went door to door and through every single home and building.
Soldiers encountered several young gang members who didn't seem
to understand the gravity of the situation they were in. They refused
orders as soldiers stormed their homes. In two separate occasions, a
young gangster flashed a mere pistol only to be cut down by soldiers
in CBQ assaults. A third had an AR-15 semi-assault rifle slung over
his shoulder, and he tried to bring it to bear on soldiers as they rushed
through the front door. He couldn't even get his trigger hand on the
grip before a precision shot to his forehead and sternum flipped him
backward in dramatic fashion, like an acrobat, and he was dead before he hit the floor. Soldiers stormed past the prone body with barely

a glance as they continued with their sweep.

As Northwest Goldberg was being cleared, protecting his southern flank, Major Hernandez led his men north into LaSalle Gardens. Here, Hernandez and his men faced immediate resistance. It was not unexpected. In addition to the Army's two Kiowa reconnaissance helicopters flying above the area of operation, an Air Force MQ-9 Reaper flew high above the city and monitored the ground operations. The air surveillance teams found two primary areas of concern. The first was the LaSalle Garden neighborhood bordering all along Grand Boulevard, where Major Hernandez was deployed. Hundreds of young men who appeared to be armed with rifles wandered into and out of homes and streets. There appeared to be a degree of coordination.

The second area of concern was along Livernois Avenue, but whether the hundreds—perhaps a thousand or more—of people gathered along the street were armed or not could not be determined. The units assigned to the north would find out soon enough.

Major Hernandez's forces advanced into the first block north of Grand Boulevard. An M-1 Abrams tank drove into LaSalle Gardens on Linwood Street, taking up station at the intersection of Linwood and LaSalle Gardens Avenue. They immediately began taking small arms fire. It was hard at first to determine where the shooting was coming from; it appeared to be coming from practically every house.

A second Abrams tank lurched along Linwood and stopped. Its machine gun opened fire on a house straddling Linwood where muzzle flashes were seen from its front bushes. At another house—this one looked abandoned—young men streamed from, taking various positions behind other homes and parked cars as they fired at the soldiers that they caught glimpses of advancing in teams and taking cover. The Abrams' turret lowered, took aim, and fired a round with an earth-shaking *bang*.

The entire ramshackle Sears catalog house disappeared in a cloud of dust and splinters.

The tanks and soldiers behind cover laid down relentless fire as other soldiers advanced. They would lay down fire as the soldiers behind them advanced. And so on.

Hernandez's company advanced in a methodical and professional fashion. Yet the young men—gangsters, Hernandez was sure—continued to lay down fire of their own, and they appeared to be coordinated. They, too, moved more or less as fire teams, from one house to another, mostly in retreat, but armed young men continued to stream from the interior of the evacuation zones toward what was clearly the front line of battle.

General McIntyre, meanwhile, watched on a large flat screen television in the command trailer live video from the Reaper as a convoy of tanks penetrated straight into the Dexter-Linwood neighborhood, located in the heart of the evacuation zone, and took up positions at major intersections. The tanks fired their machine guns sporadically as the Army opened what essentially was a third front in the center of the evacuation zone.

It won't be long now, General McIntyre thought as convoys of troop carriers joined up with the tanks and discharged soldiers into the fight. Two separate companies were advancing into the neighborhoods from the outside, closing in like a vice. Meanwhile, the new front at the center pushed outward in all directions.

* * *

Caleb Sessions lived six blocks north of the second car bomb attack in a colonial manor on a well-maintained and leafy portion of LaSalle Boulevard. Caleb bought the large home with cash two years prior, at just twenty-two years old. It was spacious but, following the explosion, it was anything but. It was crowded with multiple crews that had descended on Caleb's home after the car bomb shook the neighborhood.

In the morning, when one of his soldiers handed him a leaflet dropped by the C-130 with Dmitri and his picture on it—old mug shots—and those of others of their gang, Caleb was stoically quiet. Word came that Dmitri was holed up with one of his girlfriends a few blocks to the east.

Caleb and his crews walked over.

They found Dmitri's crews hunkered down. Several were bloodied from engaging with Army troops during the pre-dawn hours. Dmitri's soldiers alerted him that Caleb and his crew had joined them.

Dmitri finished a rock of meth and passed the small bag to a soldier and went outside to greet Caleb. When he saw him walking up to the house, Caleb's face was impassive and his demeanor somehow deceptively humble. Dmitri could see it. He instinctively knew.

Caleb held out his hand and projected his shoulder for a bro-hug.

Dmitri shot him in the face.

* * *

Caleb's crew was caught entirely by surprise. Nevertheless, they each raised their rifles at Dmitri and his crew before Caleb's body had even hit the ground, and Dmitri's crew, in turn, raised theirs. It was a Mexican standoff; if only one person pulled a trigger, a maelstrom of bullets would ensue and it would be the demise of them all.

"I'm the boss!" shouted Dmitri, shoving Logan aside and walking up to a young member of Caleb's crew. *"I'm* the boss," he shouted again, standing in front of the young gangster's gun barrel. *"I'm* the man," he shouted and then walked around, pounding his chest.

Logan, seventeen years old but going on forty, was numb. He could still hear the sound of that brick in Dmitri's hand as it hit the young white man's head, and now Dmitri pranced about again as he did then, pounding his chest, daring anyone to challenge him. He then pulled out a pistol and held it to the head of the youngest member of Caleb's crew.

"Hey, hey," a member of Caleb's crew pleaded. Everyone adjusted their grip on their rifles as fear and adrenaline spiked among each of them.

"I'm the boss," Dmitri yelled again. *"Me!"* he shouted again and pounded his chest. He looked around at Caleb's crew, his face snarling. "Now get your guns out of my *face,* muthafuckers!"

Slowly, one by one, Caleb's crew lowered their rifles. When the last one lowered his gun, Dmitri lowered his pistol but immediately raised it again and shot the boy in the head. His eyes had flared wide with madness and a deranged smile broke on his face as he pulled the trigger.

Before anyone could react—or, rather, as *everyone* reacted, raising their rifles and turning to run for cover at the same time, Logan had numbly raised his rifle behind Dmitri and shot him between his shoulder blades.

Everyone froze. Dmitri went ramrod straight and slowly turned around, blood drooling out of his mouth and down his chin. He faced Logan and peered at him, accusingly. *"You!"* he spit, his face contorted in anger and disbelief. He walked chest-first into the barrel of Logan's rifle, forcing Logan back a step. *"You!"* he sneered again and tried to bring his pistol up to aim into Logan's face.

Logan fired once, twice, three times, straight into Dmitri's chest, and Dmitri cartwheeled backward to the ground, his body rolling over limply to land face up. His back arched and a volcano of blood burst out of his mouth, painting his entire face red. The body kind of deflated, then sank into the ground. It quivered and went still, the eyes bulging.

Several gang members of both crews stood mesmerized, gawking at Dmitri's body as if not believing that the murderous maniac was really dead. But the spell was soon broken as more gunfire erupted.

The U.S. Army had begun its operation. Soldiers advanced west into the LaSalle Gardens neighborhood and fired on the armed River Gees gathered around the body of Dmitri Johnson. Several gang members fell dead or wounded in the initial barrage. Logan ran for cover between two houses, firing haphazardly over his shoulder at the advancing soldiers. It was kill or be killed.

He didn't make it. Before reaching cover between houses, a bullet tore through the middle of his back. He stumbled into a fellow retreating gangster, and both went sprawling to the ground. The kid looked over at Logan—he was stretched out, dead, his eyes locked on the young gang member with a look of surprise etched on his face. The kid tore his eyes away from Logan's body and scrambled to his feet. He was immediately cut down by another volley of gunfire.

Soldiers ran past the bodies of Logan and the young gang member and advanced deeper into LaSalle Gardens.

* * *

Bernice and Daniel interviewed dozens of evacuees as Walter, LeRon, and Rachel worked in support, taking turns holding the camera. The sound of gunfire in the distance had marked the start of the Army operation. Walter pointed to the end of the street where an Army tank had turned onto the road, its turret facing inward toward the group, and it lurched forward. An Army Apache gunship helicopter soared past at tree-top level from behind the tank, causing Rachel to jump.

Daniel took the camera from LeRon, and he and Bernice jogged a few yards in the direction of the oncoming tank to get a better view of the operation, careful to stick to the side of a crumbling, three-story brick apartment building with empty windows for cover, if necessary. Daniel had his camera automatically synced with DIYtv for live streaming.

A young man, meanwhile, casually walked out into the middle of the street with an AR-15 assault rifle, took aim, and opened fire on the tank and soldiers advancing behind it.

With the presence of the Army the last several weeks, and now people walking around the neighborhoods with guns and rifles, the sight of weapons was normalized and LeRon, Rachel and Walter—standing back and out in the open at the intersection as they watched Bernice and Daniel cling alongside the abandoned apartment building—didn't even notice that Lamar and the gang of armed young men had come down the street until the jackhammer gunfire nearly burst their ear drums.

Everyone, including the procession of evacuees and other pedestrians, dropped to the ground as the young men took turns firing on the Army soldiers. When there was a pause, LeRon scrambled to his feet and ran to Rachel, who stood with her hands over her ears trying to block out the sound.

"Take me home, LeRon!" Rachel pleaded as he reached her and put his arm around her.

"Let's go, baby," he said, just as another burst of gunfire drowned out his words, and they both stumbled and fell, LeRon falling on top of Rachel.

Daniel had trained his camera on one of the armed kids, and now he and others fell altogether at once at the new round of gunfire.

"Oh, my God, baby," Rachel screamed, and tried to get up, but LeRon, though skinny, lay heavy on her. "Oh, my God!" she screamed, getting her feet under her and pushing on him, but he didn't get up, causing her to stumble again, backward this time and with LeRon more firmly on top of her in an awkward position. His face was planted on her stomach.

"Oh, my *God,* LeRon!" she screamed, frustrated and scared, trying to pull out from beneath him, but he never moved. In fact, he was completely limp, and that's when she saw that his back was covered in blood.

Rachel screamed and frantically scrambled to get out from beneath LeRon, but fell again. She lifted his head like a ball off of her stomach while she screamed. His bright, friendly eyes were open but just stared, unblinking, as blood gushed out of his mouth and nose. It just *poured* out, non-stop.

Rachel screamed continuously and dropped his head onto her stomach and desperately scrambled to get out from beneath him. She squirmed as she screamed, even kicking at him as she tried to get up. Walter ran to her and grabbed her by the arm pits to drag her out from under him, but her shoe snagged under LeRon's t-shirt, ripping it open and causing Walter to stumble and fall, too.

"Get out of the road!" screamed Bernice, not yet understanding what she was seeing.

"They've killed the People's Mayor," Daniel said in a hushed voice. He could see through his lenses that LeRon was dead.

"Oh, *no!*" gasped Bernice, and she scrambled to her feet to run to LeRon and Rachel. "Bernice, no!" yelled Daniel, and he scrambled after her.

Bernice stumbled into the middle road, tripped from behind, and exploding gravel stung her all over as bullets and shell casings tinkled all about. She never heard the explosion of gunfire; she heard nothing now, just a roar, like a jet engine, in her ears.

Bernice lay in the middle of the road and slowly sat up, a long moaning sob blending with the roar in her ears. Daniel lay on the ground right beside her, his face turned up to her, his slender body stretched out away from her, partially on its side.

Daniel was looking up at her, but his eyes were fixed and held no recognition, and his face was blank amid the chaos. There was blood on his cheek. His jacket was open and his t-shirt rested above his bony ribcage. His mouth opened and closed like a fish out of water as his bare pale white diaphragm flexed and released every other second or so.

Soldiers swarmed around them, and now Bernice was face-down on the gravel, a knee in her back and her wrists tied behind her. The world turned bumpy as a truck pulled up alongside and she was lifted up.

"Daniel!" she finally managed as they carried her. "Daniel!" she screamed as they dumped her into the truck. "Daniel!" she cried again.

Daniel lay unattended in the middle of the street. Soldiers streamed past him and past the bodies of the armed young men, all scattered about and motionless. LeRon lay halfway on the street and halfway on the brown grass. He was shirtless somehow, and lay draped backward over the curb, his legs splayed out on the road, his upper body tossed back in the grass, his face turned up to the sky. Soldiers streamed by, stealing glances at the body as they passed.

Rachel and Walter and others were bundled into the truck with Bernice. Walter sat between them, silently, as Bernice and Rachel sobbed. Walter stared ahead as tears silently streamed down his bruised and bloodied face.

* * *

Soldiers surged into all areas south of Grand Boulevard. They went door to door through every single home and building. They confiscated all weapons, registered or not, and illicit drug paraphernalia, and made multiple arrests.

North of Grand Boulevard was a different story. Here soldiers progressed street by street, house by house, pinching from the east and west. They went door to door, and they didn't knock. They forcibly entered each and every house and building and worked their way northward: Horton Street, then Custer Street, then Bethune Avenue, then Smith Street, and so on.

The Army faced heavy resistance here. Armed men seem to occupy every standing structure, most of which were crumbling homes or ruins of old factories, all of which were abandoned decades ago.

Tanks were brought to bear on the homes and buildings—abandoned or not—that people fired from.

A second airstrike flattened the Dynasty Furniture building on Grand River Avenue where the other sniper had kept soldiers pinned down. And, since the taboo had already been broken with the first strike, several more followed. With the tanks occupied, the remaining F-35s took turns circling above the city, diving in attack when called upon. Multiple abandoned buildings and homes served as cover for armed young men fighting the army.

But General McIntyre was on the clock, and rather than allowing his soldiers to get bogged down by single fighters or snipers hidden amid the countless abandoned, crumbled, and empty buildings and homes, McIntyre ordered the tanks, Apache helicopter gunships, and F-35 Lightning IIs into action. Building after building was obliterated, and the soldiers advanced uninhibited.

The general leaned on the railing of the short stairway grate outside his command trailer. He heard the intermittent scratching of the F-35s ricocheting across the sky, and a constant *tat-tat-tat* of distant automatic rifle fire.

This was the sound of war. A massive *boom* drove home the point. The command trailer and the stairway grate shook and rattled.

McIntyre sighed. Another airstrike. He had long ago come to know what they sounded and felt like. A secondary boom and rattle marked the sonic boom as the aircraft pulled away, again rattling the trailer and stair grate.

McIntyre stepped inside for an update.

Battalions deployed to the north were working east and south from Livernois and the M-10. They had skipped right past the Russell Woods neighborhood where there was no resistance and were moving into Petosky-Otsego.

Major Hernandez and his company worked their way from the south, engaged in house-to-house fighting from the get-go. They had largely secured LaSalle Gardens and were moving into Virginia Park.

The major had sent cell phone photos of some of the dead, confirming they had killed more than ten of the most known—and most wanted—members of the so-called Motown Mafia, including Dmitri Johnson, the freeway killer, and Caleb Sessions, who was said to be the group's co-leader along with Dmitri.

It would all be over soon.

Streams of people, meanwhile, continued to flee the neighborhoods even as the Army moved in and the battle raged on. They were forced to walk out and leave their vehicles behind. People walked solemnly, carting suitcases and carrying whatever belongings they could manage, as gunfire echoed across Central Detroit. They pushed shopping carts full of belongings, and dragged toy wagons loaded with clothes and other valuables. They commandeered anything with wheels: dollies, handcarts, shopping carts, toy wagons.

These were families—elderly people, children, toddlers, mothers and fathers. They suffered the indignity of the Army searching every box, every bit of clothing, every personal belonging, and even being individually frisked by soldiers as they fled their neighborhoods. Still, many stood tall, claiming their dignity even as their neighborhood was being leveled by war in real time.

It was a sad procession nonetheless. It couldn't be anything but. People walked along Grand River Avenue all the way to East Adams Avenue in downtown with their belongings in tow, right past the tents and trailers of the Army's New Fort Detroit, to the domed Ford Field, home of the NFL's Detroit Lions, where they would be housed.

Red Cross volunteers set up stations along the way where they handed out water bottles, blankets, soup, and other aid.

Much of the procession detoured southward at 14th Street, however, following a few hand-drawn signs left by others on utility poles that read "Canada this way."

* * *

President Belle watched cable news in the White House residence. The airstrikes on the Lee Plaza and Dynasty Furniture buildings in Detroit were played over and over again. It was like watching old World War II footage, except this was now, and this was in America. *Her* America.

Cynthia was furious, though she tried not to be. She had autho-rized General McIntyre, after all, to use "whatever means necessary" to restore order. The unrest had been spreading to other cities in Michigan, and after the National Guard fiasco, what else could she do?

And then the Army itself came under attack. She could not let that stand. No way, no how. But *airstrikes?*

The footage—and the fact—was shocking. The whole world was watching, and there was no rewind for this. She could imagine how this was being interpreted in Beijing and Moscow. The world had just become a lot more dangerous.

As bad as the ramifications were for the global order, the domes-tic ones were even worse. She was being pilloried by the conspiracy-prone far right in her own party. Paranoid "Trumpians" accused her of unleashing the military on defenseless Americans and, to them, the military's deployment to Detroit was seen as a harbinger of things to come elsewhere and throughout the country. To Democrats, she was leaning on a long history of heavy-handed government responses to minority neighborhoods in economic and social distress despite being a person of color herself. Never mind the breakdown of law and order, the murders of civilians and soldiers, the bombings, the countless fires, and the spreading unrest. *Damned if you do; damned if you don't.*

The raging gun battle in central Detroit was reminiscent of the urban battles of the 1960s, but with the addition of modern firepow-er, including airstrikes. *Airstrikes!* She still couldn't wrap her head around that.

In addition to the airstrikes and battle raging in central Detroit, and the miles-long procession of pathetic-looking refugees—*refu-gees! Like something out of a goddam Life Magazine coverage of war in some remote corner of the world*—her generals were insistent that McIntyre had made the right call. The Army could not be seen as ineffective or slow to pacify a mere riot. Not in today's world. And so that was how things stood.

CHAPTER 28

For Ian and the students of Wayne State University, the surrealism had returned. Campus was on lockdown again, and, once again, classes were canceled. It was start and stop, and it was old already. So long ago it had all seemed kind of exciting—the first protests, the march on downtown, even the tear gas. Scary, yes, but exciting nonetheless.

For Ian, the luster had worn off long ago. Even before Roland. *Roland. That sound.* Ian fought a sudden wave of emotion as the scene played in his head one more time. The baton coming down across Roland's temple. *He never saw it coming.*

"This is just *nuts,*" exclaimed a student, "right?" He looked to Ian with his eyes wide with wonderment.

He looked so young; he had to be a freshman, thought Ian, forgetting that he himself was still a freshman. But Ian was thankful for the distraction.

"Yeah, man," replied Ian, "it's crazy."

Dakota looked at Ian and smiled. Ian, Dakota, the freshman, and some twenty other students stood on the roof of the Belcrest Apartments, the historic twelve-story building nestled in the northern part of the urban campus. Invited up by a more senior cross-country teammate who lived in the building, they had a clear view of the battle raging just a mile to their north across I-94 in North End, New Center, and LaSalle Gardens.

They had watched as Major Schmidt's F-35 bombed the Lee Plaza Building to their west, and looked on in horror as the aircraft exploded in the sky miles to their north.

Small arms fire echoed nonstop like jackhammers. Multiple Apache helicopter gunships circled the neighborhoods to the north like angry bees. Plumes of smoke dispersed across the northern horizon, rising high into the sky, each of them vigorous at their base. The air was pungently acerbic and stung the eyes.

It was all so weird; the war, of course, but even that had become old hat. The presence of so many soldiers and Army vehicles and helicopters constantly flying overhead had surprisingly become normalized so quickly. It was amazing what one could get used to.

What was truly weird was watching it all from the comfort of an apartment building roof as the war unfolded just blocks away. Like what was happening was not actually real, but some kind of intense virtual-reality video game.

But Ian and Dakota knew it was all too real, and they were leery that the Army could easily fire on *them*. They would be written off as some horrible accident—a stray rocket, a misidentification. Oops. *You know, war is war. Stupid kids thought it was a video game.*

Ian was glad that Sarah, Tina, and Trevor were not here anymore. They were safe.

Ian looked out on the city, sweeping all around in a circle away from the battle in front of him to the neighborhoods stretching out to the suburbs at his left and right, and the downtown behind him, and back to the battle raging in front of him just across the way. It all seemed so inevitable to him now. The Downtown and Renaissance Center, the University and Hospital District, and New Center—all little islands of glitz surrounded by a vast sea of decay.

Desolation and destitution were always around, manifest in the crumbling infrastructure, abandoned and burned homes, countless empty and unkempt lots, and the hundreds of long-abandoned and crumbling factories and retail centers, all remnants of a bygone era. Ian had grown up in the midst of economic and social artifacts. But he never actually *saw* it. It was all around him but kind of invisible, hidden in plain sight.

Perhaps it was Romanesque, the abandoned factories and stores and homes not unlike the ruins that dot the landscape throughout Rome and Italy. Maybe. But it was jarringly contemporary. The blight was more than the relics of a bygone era. People lived amid the crumble. It was slow-motion economic and social collapse. Modern ruins of a faded, and fading, American empire.

Ian looked east where, on the horizon, he could see a line of filled-in spaces of dense housing and trees that marked the end of Detroit and the beginning of the affluent burg of Grosse Pointe Park, and the other Grosse Pointes beyond. That line was Alter Road. Ian knew that because whenever he had crossed over Alter Road—or Eight Mile, for that matter, to the north—he felt a palpable sense of relief that he never stopped to acknowledge or think about. A sense of danger that lifted when he crossed over into the suburbs, or a pall that settled over him when he came back into the city. A nagging sense of foreboding.

The stark contrast between Detroit and the Grosse Pointes that Alter Road etched in the ground was startling. The America beyond Alter Road was the America of television and movies, the America of news and social media, the America of dreams. But there was another America this side of Alter Road. An Alter Nation of abandonment and have-nots. The America of reality.

A flash and debris tossed high into the air that Ian saw out of the corner of his eye caused him to flinch and duck, followed by a massive *bang* that shook the building. It was another airstrike.

* * *

William Coventry, Esquire, sat at his large oak desk in his oak furniture-filled office at the Standard & King Investment House in

Baltimore's historic Mt. Vernon district. S&K was in a modest brick building right on the corner of Charles and Madison Streets, with a direct view of the Washington Monument, built beginning in 1815.

"Come in," said William after a soft rap on his oak door. It was his nephew, Charles 'Carlo,' who quietly stepped into the room and closed the door behind him. He was young, trim, blond-haired and tanned, a Hollywood ideal of a sun-kissed All-American Californian.

And he was a Coventry. William liked his young nephew. He was a recent graduate of Harvard's Department of Economics. While he didn't necessarily excel there, he did the work that was necessary and graduated. A Coventry understands that a little bit of living, some youthful indiscretion—and youth was a state of mind, mind you—was more important than pure academic excellence. It seemed that Carlo had taken a liking to various junkets to Martha's Vineyard, Ogunquit, and the Hamptons in Long Island. He particularly liked the nightlife in Manhattan, and an assortment of recreational, if illicit, substances, William knew. But you still had to do the work, and Carlo did.

"May I?" asked the young scion, gesturing to the oak cabinetry that housed a large flat-screen television behind sliding doors. He carried a leather portfolio under his arm. "Some breaking news," Carlo said. Carlo was soft-spoken and respectful around his uncle, another thing that William liked about him. He knew from whence his charmed life emanated.

William nodded and Carlo fished out the remote control, opened the cabinet doors, and turned the TV on.

* * *

It was 5:00 p.m. and Khalid Husseini wasted no time calling it a day. He didn't have too far to go—about two-and-a-half miles as the crow flies—but getting from Point A to Point B quickly in a crowded and bustling city like Manama could be a very daunting task. He had to walk nearly half a mile to the parking lot of the U.S. Navy facility to pick up his car, then drive out on Avenue 22 heading east to the Moharraq Third Causeway, then up Al Fatih Highway into the heart of the northern quadrant of the main island of Bahrain. Once on Al Fatih, he'd make his way onto Exhibition and then Qudaibiya Avenues before turning onto Road Number 2108. All in all, the trip took about forty minutes in the heavy traffic.

It was Friday and Khalid had put any and all thoughts of work behind him just as soon as he stepped off base; the weekend had officially begun. He looked forward to going to BJ's with his friends Ali and Ghazi. BJ's was an upscale nightclub in the Al Asasiin Hotel (the Americans called it the 'Assassin' Hotel, but in Arabic, 'Asasiin' was more akin to 'Standard') in Adliya that was a little more than hard to get into. But a couple of the American Navy guys that Khalid had become friends with would meet them there. Americans didn't have any trouble getting into BJ's.

Khalid had just slipped the key to the front door of his flat into the lock when something caught his attention. He looked up and down the street. It was a muffled *boom;* he didn't so much hear it as he felt it. He felt it in his hand that pushed the key in, the door rattling slightly in its frame; he felt it through his feet as he stood in the doorway, the ground vibrating to a deep bass-tone muffle; and he felt it in his ears with a subtle change in air pressure mixed with the strange and harrowing rattling of multiple doors and windows. And, as he scanned the scene to the ends of his street—his view was limited by the apartments hemming in the street—movement above the buildings caught his eye and he looked up. What looked like a flare streaked across the dimming sky, leaving behind a dark contrail. It arched downward and disappeared from view as it descended behind the apartments far away. Khalid heard a delayed high-pitch whistling sound from the flare that had passed. And, as he gawked, he realized he had heard a faint second and third whistle now that the first one had faded.

Khalid stepped back from his apartment, still looking up. He saw two more contrails that arched in the sky; one stretched far away to the northwest, the other looked like it sank a mile or so away to the east behind his building. Then, like Godzilla rising, a large orange-and-black cloud of fire and smoke and dust billowed up high into the sky from behind his building, and it looked really *close.*

Khalid stood wide-eyed and open-mouthed as he watched the ugly, angry cloud continue to rise and expand. Something, however, tapped him on the top of his head, breaking the spell. He looked around, a little confused. He tilted his head and listened: a pitter-patter filled his ears. He quickly realized that it was falling dust and debris, and when nearby car alarms began sounding all at once, he scurried into the doorway and waited it out. Nothing hit his street, but he heard a few bangs and clangs that echoed throughout the now eerily quiet neighborhood. It was over just as quickly as it had begun.

Khalid walked briskly down the street then, his eyes glued to the rising cloud. People cautiously stuck their heads outside their doors and looked around. Others pointed to the sky and covered their faces in horror. It was a surreal sight and, as Khalid rounded the street corner and joined a growing crowd gathered at the intersection of Qudaibiya and Exhibition Avenues, it grew ever more surreal.

Looming on the southern horizon was the massive American aircraft carrier, the Ford-class USS *George W. Bush,* anchored just offshore from the Arab Shipbuilding and Repair Yard (ASRY). And the cloud of smoke and dust growing high in the sky, the top half beginning to drift toward the west toward Saudi Arabia, looked like it stood upon the back deck of the massive ship. Balls of flame glowed red-orange in the bowels of the ship, cutting through the shroud of thick black smoke that poured relentlessly from invisible openings in the ship's structure. Flares intermittently streamed out from the flames like bottle rockets, whistling into and across the darkening sky before petering out or falling to the ground or into the sea.

Muffled popping sounds reverberated from the ship. A large blinding flash lit up the sky for a couple of seconds. Khalid threw up his hands to protect his face as he felt the heat of the blast, and a massive *bang* reverberated so deeply that it seemed like the air itself vibrated.

We're too close! Khalid thought as he stumbled backward before turning and running. Others around him did the same. As he ran, he felt a searing hot blast of air against his back—a sudden gust that nearly pushed him down, but he was able to agilely stay on his feet even as others around him stumbled and fell. Windows of the apartment buildings and some windshields of cars in the backed-up traffic, meanwhile, twisted in their frames and shattered.

Only until Khalid could duck behind a wobbly apartment building for uncertain protection did he look back. And what he saw astounded him. The ship was now largely shrouded behind thick clouds of black smoke and dust; several buildings in and near the shipyard had apparently come down from the force of the blast.

A strange and blinding yellowish flash amid the dust forced Khalid to turn and run again as another, this time much larger, blast seemed to shake the entire earth beneath him. He stumbled and fell as the shockwave engulfed him, but he quickly gathered himself up and continued to sprint. A car smashed upside down to his right, then to his left, both literally falling out of the sky, and flaming debris rained down all around him.

Khalid dared not stop and look back anymore as he ran for his life.

* * *

William came out from behind his desk and sat on the leather couch while Carlo sat upright in an oak-framed Victorian chair with red upholstery. William watched the television intently. He couldn't help but smile as the massive *George W. Bush* burned and listed in the water. The loss of life would be horrendous, he knew, but the price of oil had, in a matter of an hour or so, increased more than tenfold and shattered the historic highs prior to the Great Recession of the late aughts.

And, in this instance, with an American supercarrier aflame in the Persian Gulf, the prices wouldn't be coming down anytime soon. This was at least as momentous as the terrorist attacks of September 11, 2001, and all that flowed from that.

"There is going to be war," William said, his voice more upbeat than he tried to mask.

"You knew," said Carlo with admiration in his voice. He opened his portfolio and slid it across the table to William.

The business in Detroit, which had kept him up late at night in recent weeks, was wiped completely from the books. It was no longer even a blip in comparison to the windfall that the oil and insurance markets were suddenly generating.

"Not really, no," said William as he studied the numbers. "But that's why we have the clients that we have," he said with a wink as he looked up from the numbers.

* * *

The president sat quietly in her seat, her eyes fixed on one of the several large monitors in the Situation Room. She cursed herself internally for the sense of relief that she felt at one level, relief that *finally* Detroit would no longer be in the headlines.

But this, an apparent attack on a U.S. aircraft carrier in the Persian Gulf—or not. It was too early to tell exactly what had happened, hence the chaos in the Situation Room all around her—this was pure dread.

She turned to the secretary of defense, who was engaged in a heated conversation with a general on the Joint Chiefs of Staff, and several senior staffers.

"Bernie," she said softly, "The Detroit situation—end it."

* * *

Some 280 miles southwest of Washington, D.C., more than twenty large U.S. Air Force four-engine C-17 Globemaster cargo planes ferrying one hundred 82nd Airborne paratroopers each, lifted off, one after the other, into the morning sky at Fort Bragg, North Carolina.

It took the aircraft just over an hour and a half to reach their varying destinations. As they flew over Michigan—ten in the southern part of the state, and twelve over the northern part of the state, including the Upper Peninsula—they each descended to under two thousand feet. Soldiers and their gear and parachutes streamed out of the large aircraft in long trailing lines. The lines faltered and lost their linearity with the blossoming of the soldiers' olive-green parachutes, and the soldiers floated silently and slowly to the earth.

The sight was both beautifully graceful and ominous at the same time as the more than one thousand soldiers landed in the bucolic fields and farmland.

In Mackinaw City, 20-year-old Clyde Dodson, a part-time server at the Kewadin Shores Casino just north of St. Ignace before the Superior Volunteers kicked into gear, nervously manned the Jamet Street checkpoint to the Mackinac Bridge. The job was boring and repetitive, but motorists had grown increasingly hostile. The burned-out hulks of an SUV and a pickup truck left behind in the median were testament to two separate attempts at breaking the checkpoint by angry motorists.

Four people were killed in the incidents, all of them gunned down by the Volunteers. The pickup truck driver was a Navy veteran who had got out of his truck armed with an AR-15 and threatened to kill the Volunteers if they didn't let him pass. They didn't, and an argument—and brief gun battle—ensued.

The second incident entailed the SUV speeding north along the shoulder against the turned-around southbound traffic. Volunteers had opened fire with hundreds of rounds when the SUV burst past the turnaround and sped toward the bridge.

The SUV swerved out of control and rolled several times before coming to a rest wheels down, with bodies dangling out of the windows.

In both cases, Clyde had seen the immediate aftermath. He and other fellow Volunteers were asleep in their sleeping bags and startled awake by the commotion. A huge argument broke out among the Volunteers, both "officer" and "enlisted" volunteer alike. Clyde was fearful that they would start shooting each other.

And there were the bodies. Clyde had never seen a dead body before, and he wished he would never see one again, ever. Thankfully, the Mackinac cops took them away. They were weirdly careful with their words, going out of their way to be nice. Clyde imagined that they had sensed the tension among the Volunteers and didn't want to spark anything. That struck Clyde as odd somehow, but even so, he was thankful. Most of the Volunteers didn't trust the Mackinac cops, even though there were only a handful of them, and Clyde was grateful that their offer to take the bodies away wasn't met with yet another standoff.

But the tension only grew. Several Volunteers had left across the bridge in their trucks overnight. Clyde was thinking about splitting, too, but he didn't know how he could get away without being seen. He didn't really know the guys who had left, and now he wished that he had been more outgoing. And he didn't come in his own car; he had come in Rickey Barksdale's truck. What could he do? Walk across the bridge? He'd be seen for sure if he didn't freeze to death first.

Another commotion heightened Clyde's awareness. He looked around and saw Volunteers shading their eyes and looking skyward. Clyde followed their gaze and both fear and relief washed over him. Several large military cargo planes flew low and slow on the horizon, and what unmistakably were paratroopers streamed out behind them, then floated down lazily like large poplar fluff carried by a spring breeze.

The U.S. Army had arrived.

The Volunteers fell into a state of panic. The Army paratroopers were a ways off, but no one doubted that they would be at the bridge in short order. And there was no doubt why they had come.

Someone named Bobby argued that the Volunteers should remain and greet the soldiers peaceably, that they were all on the same side. Another, thin but grizzled-looking 50-ish Volunteer called Dutch, was certain that the Army paratroopers weren't going to cheerily greet the Volunteers and thank them for their work. Dutch argued that they should leave, and leave *right now.*

Twenty-four-year-old Rickey Barksdale, tattooed and sporting a buzz cut—and normally discomfortingly quiet—spoke up unexpectedly and argued for guerilla warfare. He suggested the revolution would start right there. Multiple Volunteers snorted and began to undress and remove their camouflage uniforms, and anything that read "Superior Volunteers."

The company of Volunteers disassembled and scrambled for their vehicles. It was a traffic clusterfuck. Horns blared and Volunteers shouted curses at each other. Several minor fender-benders were followed by scorching invectives from inside the vehicles, but no one stopped to argue.

Amid the chaos, some vehicles refused to cooperate by failing to start, and so they were abandoned where they stalled, a couple right in the middle of the roadway, adding to the disarray. The vehicles soon disentangled themselves from multiple self-inflicted traffic jams and a disorganized and un-unified motley convoy of pickup trucks, cars, and vans sped north across the Mackinac Bridge with due haste.

* * *

"Colonel" Jenkins sat in Chief Wendowski's desk going through his Orders of the Day—including how he wanted his coffee—when the "corporal" on the other end of his cell phone grew frantic.

"The Army's here!" exclaimed the young corporal. "They're parachuting in!" said the boy, his voice high-pitched with excitement. "Everyone's taking off!"

Jenkins stood up. "Now hold on there, boy, what exactly is…" but the call was disconnected.

Jenkins rushed out of the police office where his two boys stood guard. "Let's go," he said. He scanned the sky as he walked briskly to his pickup truck with his two boys in tow. His two sons exchanged a look but didn't say anything.

Jenkin's truck was parked in a diagonal directly across the street from the Mackinaw City Municipal Building. Tucker was too busy scanning the sky to see Village President Bob Mollen, flanked by Chief Ralph Wendowski and Officer Frank Carroll, waiting by his truck. His eyes fell on the three and he stopped.

"Going somewhere, *Colonel?*" asked Bob. The two police officers held rifles at the ready.

"We'll take those," said another voice as officers stepped from behind and stripped the "colonel" and his two boys of their weapons.

The "colonel" looked up while officers handcuffed him. Two F-35 stealth fighters screamed across the sky toward the Upper Peninsula.

* * *

When her name was called, Araminta stepped up to the podium. Brandon stood beside her, his head hung low and his shoulders slouched, but he looked around, stealing glances left and right and shifting his feet. Araminta nudged him with her elbow and whispered, "Stand up straight," which the microphone picked up, eliciting quiet chuckles from around the packed courtroom.

The judge, Elizabeth Ault, peeked over the glasses at the tip of her nose. "What is the basis for your claim of asylum?" asked the judge as she returned to the paperwork before her.

"Ma'am," Araminta spoke, "uh, Judge, Brandon—Brandon is my son here—Brandon's best friend, um, three of his best friends, were killed by the Army a—a few days ago."

"The United States Army?" asked the judge.

"Yes, ma'am," replied Araminta.

"It's 'Your Honor' when you address a judge in Canada, Ms. Cole, just like you do in the United States," said Judge Ault, sternly.

"I'm sorry, ma'am—um, your Honor," said Araminta, repeating "your Honor" in a trailing voice.

"I'm sorry about your sons' friends, Ms. Cole, but I fail to see the merit of your claim for permanent status. The current unrest in Detroit notwithstanding, the United States is currently at peace and is not generally a refugee-producing country. You have resources at your disposal in your country, Ms. Cole. I suggest you use them."

A court bailiff stepped up and held his arm out to usher Araminta and Brandon out of the defendant's box and allow the next defendants in. The docket was full, and the judge clearly wanted to move on to the next case.

Araminta hesitated, then pleaded with the judge.

"Please, your Honor," she said. "If you reject our case, then please…"—she grabbed Brandon by the arm and yanked him close to her—"please, I beg the court to put a *bullet* right here," she said, jabbing her left pointer finger into Brandon's temple. A collective gasp emanated from the pubic seating area. Brandon looked up at his mother, alarmed.

"Because," Araminta continued, pausing to regain her composure as tears streamed down her face, "because that's what you would be doing if you send us back, your Honor."

Murmurs passed through the courtroom as Judge Ault looked out on Araminta and Brandon over the glasses perched on the end of her nose.

"I feel your desperation, Ms. Cole," the judge said. "As a mother, I truly understand your desire to protect your son."

The judge looked down at Araminta's file and paused. She jotted something down in the folder. "I am denying your claim but, at the same time, I am recommending a full review by the federal court. Case adjourned," she said, and struck her gravel.

The court bailiff ushered Araminta and Brandon out of the defendant's box and toward the courtroom exit as the courtroom broke into applause.

"What does that mean, Momma?" asked Brandon.

"I don't know," whispered Araminta, "but I think it's good."

* * *

"The militias have pretty much scattered, Boss," Moe said into his phone, "as expected."

On the other end of the line was Major General Teddy Rose, the commanding general of CID.

"The FBI and ATF picked up a couple of sheriff's deputies down in Lenawee County and a city councilman in Coldwater, all members of the South Michigan Militia that raided the Adrian armory," Moe reported. "Mackinaw City Police gave us custody of the so-called colonel who took over the town and blocked the Mackinac Bridge. The guy works at Walmart up in Sault Ste. Marie in his other life," Moe said with sympathy in his voice. "He pretty much fingered the whole lot of them, the leadership of the Superior Volunteers. They were kind enough to maintain a website and social media accounts with their names listed," Moe chuckled.

"Very good," said General Rose. "Wrap it up, Moe, and get back here as quick as you can. You're needed in Bahrain. It's all hands on deck out there," he added.

Moe disconnected the call and looked out over the cold blue waters of the Straits of Mackinac while they crossed over the Mackinac Bridge.

In the back seat, agent Maxim Yanayev hung up his own cell. "Guess who's nephew is in the National Guard, Boss," said Maxim. "And guess which armory he drills at," he added.

"Yeah?" said Moe. He laughed and shook his head, not entirely with disbelief.

"Well, let's go get him too, then," he said.

* * *

Floyd sat in his usual seat at the Bull Moose Restaurant on Route 2 in Brevort, sipping his coffee and flipping through *Field and Stream* magazine while waiting for his breakfast.

"Thank you, darling," said Floyd as a presence stood at his table. Not hearing Amanda, the waitress, respond or place his breakfast on the table, Floyd looked up from his magazine and slightly recoiled at the sight of a tall, distinguished-looking black man with partial black-and-gray stubble on a rugged face peering down at him with soulful eyes.

Floyd had never seen the man before in his life, but the man's eyes knew *him.*

"Floyd Barksdale," the man said, softly but firmly. It wasn't a question.

Floyd licked his lips and looked out the window. A navy-blue unmarked police car sat in the parking lot with its engine running, a cloud of water vapor exiting the tail pipe and slowly dissipating in the frigid air. Further up the road, just at the bend, two county police cars sat blocking both sides of the four-lane highway, their emergency lights flashing.

At the restaurant's front door, two state police troopers hovered just inside the doorway. Amanda stood wide-eyed behind the counter, her eyes darting back and forth from the two policemen to Floyd and the black man.

Floyd looked back to the black man. Floyd opened his mouth as if to say something when his lower lip started trembling.

He burst into tears.

"I meant no harm," Floyd pleaded between sobs. "I meant no harm, I swear. Oh, sweet Jesus, help me," he sobbed.

* * *

As they rounded a bend, two state police cars blocked the highway ahead, each parked perpendicular across the road and with several other state police cars sitting behind them, all of them with their emergency lights flashing. "What the…?" Rickey asked, his voice trailing off, as he took his foot off the gas pedal.

"Is it an accident or something?" asked Clyde as the pickup truck slowed.

"Don't think so," said Rickey, applying the brakes now, but only slowing and not stopping right away. He peered into his rearview mirror. His heart pounded in his chest as he tried to make sense of it. "Roadblock," he said, his voice sounding distant.

He brought his truck to a stop. Behind each of the police cars, state troopers were crouched for cover and aiming rifles and pistols in their direction.

"Is it for us?" asked Clyde, now genuinely scared. "It can't be for us, right?" he asked, his voice low. "What the hell, man?" continued Clyde, nervously. "What did you do, Rickey?"

"Nothing," said Rickey as he reached behind his seat for his hunting rifle. A black SUV with flashing emergency lights and several state police cars roared into view from behind and screeched to a halt.

A tall, intense-looking black man stepped out of the passenger side of the SUV and calmly but purposively stepped right up to Rickey's driver's side window and smashed it in with a single blow. He placed a large pistol at Rickey's head. "Let it go, Rickey," he said in an authoritative but empathetic voice.

"Get the fu…" protested Rickey, but he didn't finish his thought. He was yanked in one graceful motion right through his driver's window and was flat on his back in the middle of the road, then forced over and handcuffed as he gasped for air, the wind knocked out of him.

"Corporal Rickey Barksdale," the intense man said in a crisp voice that cut through Rickey's confused state as he was yanked to his feet. "You're under arrest," the man said.

Rickey staggered at first but was held up by the large man before gaining his feet, and he was ushered into the backseat of the black SUV.

Only then, as he was literally forced-marched to the SUV, did he become aware of the commotion all around him. Police swarmed all over his truck, taking out his and Clyde's rifles, their backpacks and hunting gear, even auto repair receipts and miscellaneous stuff in his glove box and fast food wrappers on the floor in the backseat, and putting them into clear plastic bags. A tow truck pulled up alongside his pickup truck, and a helicopter buzzed loudly overhead. From the backseat, Rickey watched as Clyde was handcuffed and put into the back of a state police cruiser.

* * *

Petty Officer Second Class Jaime Rodriguez looked up from the paperwork on his desk.

"Is that our boy?" asked Senior Chief Petty Officer Javier Salerno, not even looking up from a file he was writing in.

It was the telltale spitfire sound of a blue low-rider Volkswagen Golf R with its muffler modified to be, well, less modifying, that caught their attention. They could hear the tinny rumble of the low-rider amid the pouring rain and the intermittent baritone vibration of thunder. Jaime spotted the car pulling into a parking space facing the Navy Recruiting Station.

"Yep," said Jaime, "that's our boy."

It was the seventh or eighth time, and four working days in a row, that the distinctive VW Golf pulled into the parking lot where it would normally sit for up to twenty minutes before it would leave. "Our boy" referred to the driver, an Asian kid, maybe eighteen or so.

"Why don't you go fetch him," suggested Javier, again without looking up from his work, "and see if we can't help him make up his mind."

Jaime chuckled and stood up. A suggestion by the senior chief was no suggestion at all; it was a command. Jaime pulled on his ankle-length black Navy-issue raincoat and took his black Navy-issue umbrella off the coat rack.

A flash of lightning followed by a crack of thunder made Jaime momentarily pause before he stepped out into the storm.

* * *

Ian sat in his car looking over at the Navy Recruiting Station as it rained loudly on his car roof and heavy metal blared from his car speakers. But he never saw Jaime step out of the Navy Recruiting office. Instead, he was lost in thought. Where would he end up with the Navy? Would he be in Europe? The Middle East?

Ian tried to imagine life overseas, and life in the Navy. Would there be a war? And, if so, wouldn't the Navy be the safest branch? Maybe the Air Force? But it was the Navy that traveled the world, wasn't it?

How about the Marines? If he was going to go military, maybe he should go all in—and the Marines were definitely all in.

Ian dismissed the idea out of hand, as he had before. No, if he were to do it, join the military, it would have to be the Navy. It was the conclusion he kept coming to. *Travel.*

Ian jumped as someone knocked on his driver-side window. A young uniformed Navy man stood there in the pouring rain, holding an umbrella aloft. "Come inside," the Navy man shouted over the rain and the music. "Let's talk!"

Made in the USA
Columbia, SC
25 March 2020